Dirty Like Dylan

TITLES BY JAINE DIAMOND

CONTEMPORARY ROMANCE

Dirty Like Me (Dirty #1)
Dirty Like Brody (Dirty #2)
2 Dirty Wedding Nights (Dirty #2.5)
Dirty Like Seth (Dirty #3)
Dirty Like Dylan (Dirty #4)
Dirty Like Jude (Dirty #5)
Dirty Like Zane (Dirty #6)
Hot Mess (Players #1)
Filthy Beautiful (Players #2)
Sweet Temptation (Players #3)
Lovely Madness (Players #4)
Flames and Flowers (Players Novella)
Handsome Devil (Vancity Villains #1)
Rebel Heir (Vancity Villains #2)
Wicked Angel (Vancity Villains #3)
Irresistible Rogue (Vancity Villains #4)
Charming Deception (Bayshore Billionaires #1)

EROTIC ROMANCE

DEEP (DEEP #1)
DEEPER (DEEP #2)

Dirty Like Dylan

JAINE DIAMOND

Dirty Like Dylan
by Jaine Diamond

Copyright © 2018 Jaine Diamond

All rights reserved.

No part of this book may be reproduced, scanned, uploaded or distributed in any manner whatsoever without written permission from the publisher, except in the case of brief quotation embodied in book reviews.

This book is a work of fiction. Names, characters, places and incidents are the product of the author's imagination or are used fictitiously. Any resemblance to actual events, locales, organizations or persons is coincidental.

First Edition July 2018

ISBN 978-1-989273-79-1

Cover and interior design by Jaine Diamond / DreamWarp Publishing Ltd.

Published by DreamWarp Publishing Ltd.
www.jainediamond.com

For Brittany. FBGM.

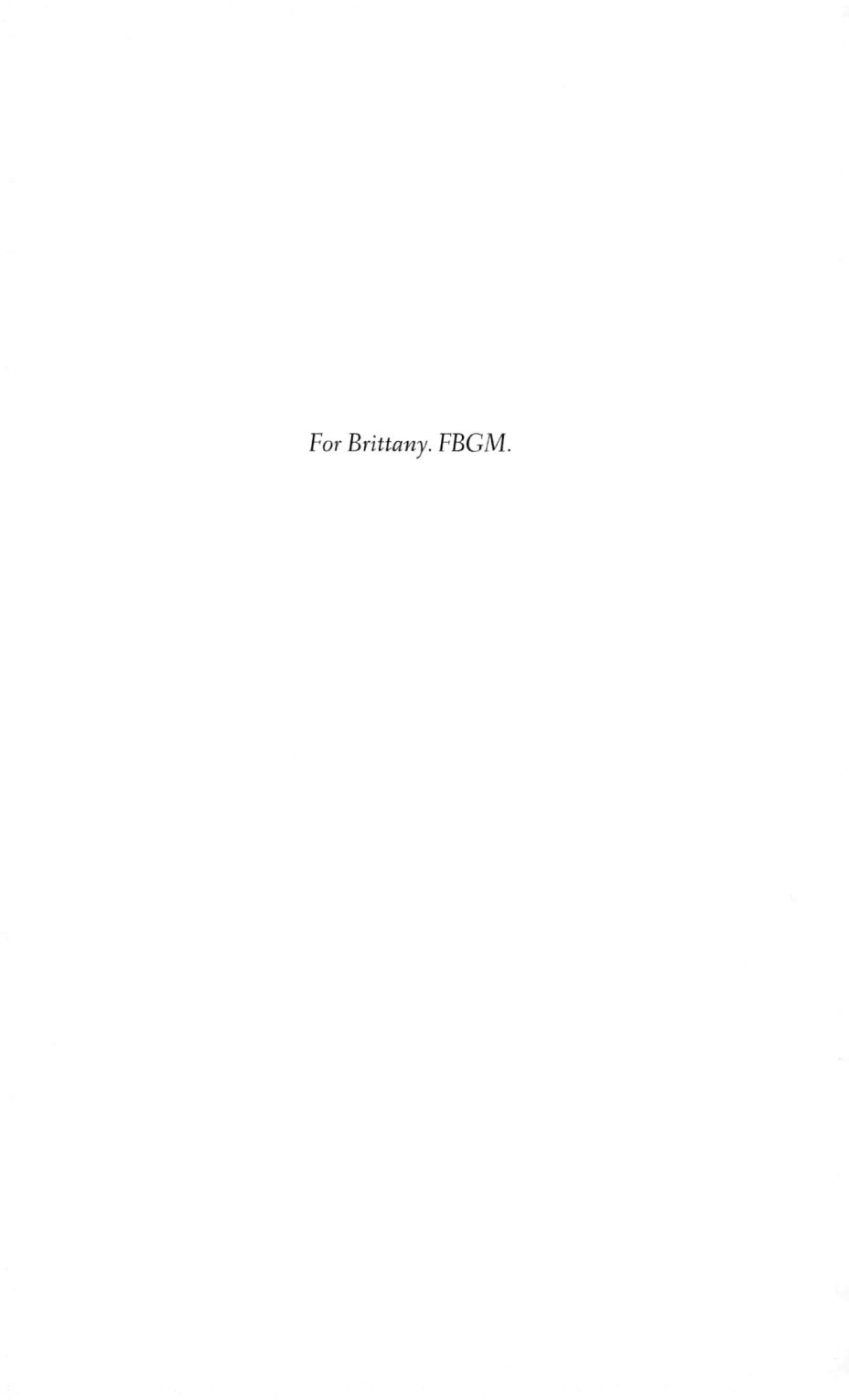

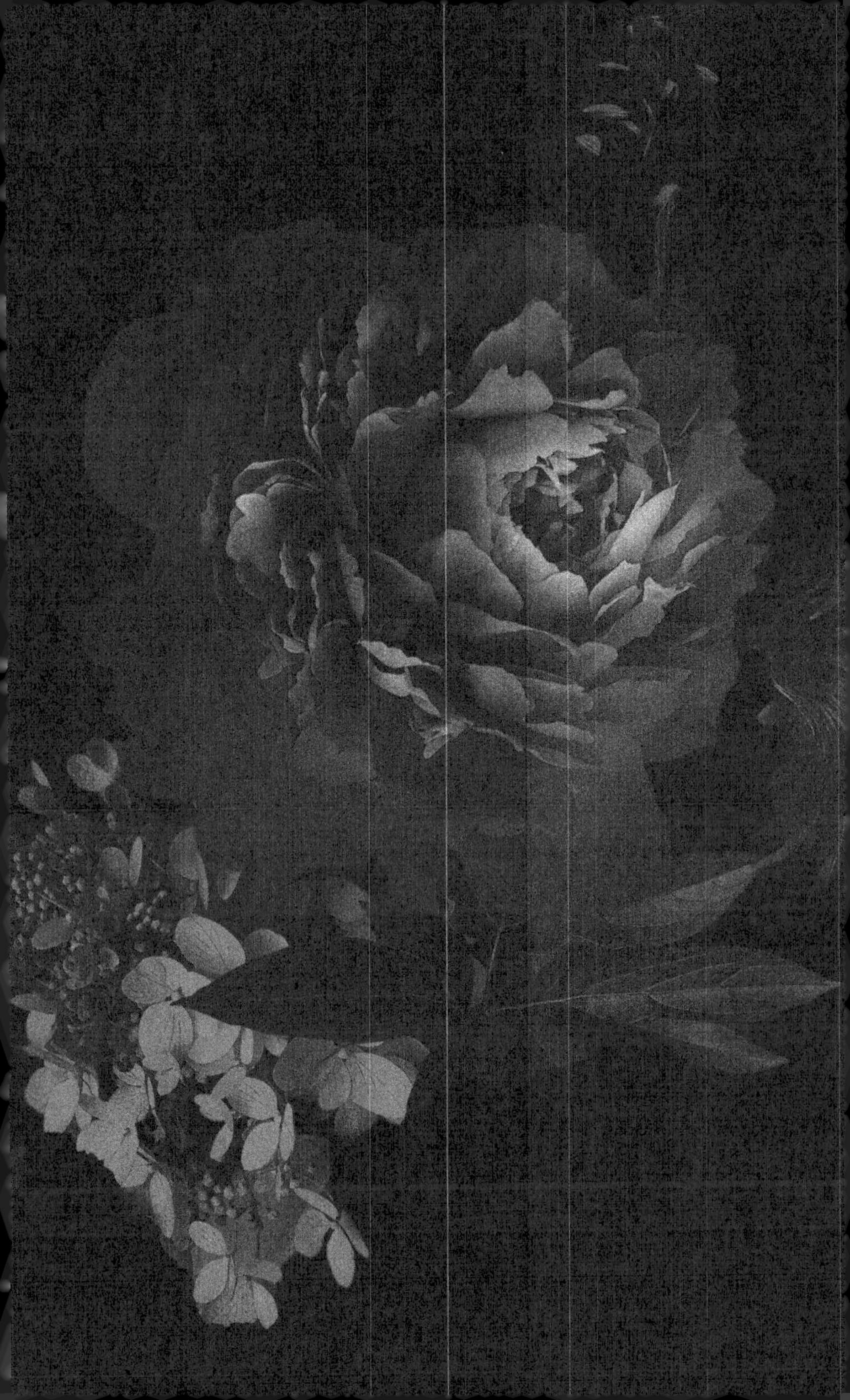

CHAPTER ONE

Amber

I STOOD on the curb with my travel backpack hoisted up on my back, my blouse all sweaty and stuck to me under the weight of the bag, even though it was October and pretty cool out. It was taking a ridiculously long time for the dude at the security gatehouse to let the Mercedes in front of me through. Not because there was a security issue. No, I had to stand here while the security guard and the driver of the car shot the shit like a couple of old ladies at a church bake sale. For seven minutes straight.

I could've put my backpack down. I could've sat my ass down on the curb and gotten at least a little more comfy. But it was the principle of it; I was standing right where the security guy could see me.

I might as well have been invisible.

Finally, he patted the roof of the Mercedes and waved the car into the gated lot. As his gaze fell to me, I walked right up to him like I belonged here. In the driving lane. I figured he didn't get many walk-ups; there was no sidewalk.

I glanced into the movie studio lot with all the big, windowless buildings and the expensive cars, and wondered if this guy was gonna give me a hard time. If I'd have to call my sister to come out here and collect me.

Worse, if I couldn't reach her, if I was gonna be a no-show at her shoot, miss out on this desperately needed paycheck and have to find somewhere to sleep tonight with approximately zero dollars to my name. Worst case scenario, I'd have to crash at my sister's place.

But that option would only ever be a dead-last resort.

Technically I was homeless, which was always weird to get my head around. But that was only until I caught my next plane out of here. Then, I was a world traveler.

It just depended how you looked at it.

"Yes?" The security guard looked me over, taking in my peasant blouse and my well-worn jeans with the patch of the Venezuelan flag on one thigh, which strategically covered a blood stain (long story). He had a pot belly in his uniform but, presumably, he also had a steady paycheck and a home, so who was I to judge?

When he actually looked at my face, I did my best to smile and remind myself why I was here: because this paycheck would be half the funds I needed for my next one-way ticket to the opposite hemisphere.

"Hi." I did my best to sound cheerful, even chipper, but it was incredibly forced. I probably came across as a caricature of myself: the happy, ditzy hippie. "I'm here for the Underlayer commercial. Amber Malone?"

As I spoke, the security guard reached through the window of the gatehouse and pulled out a clipboard. He flipped through several pages, scanning a couple of them. "No Amber Malone on my list."

Great.

"I'm the stills photographer," I informed him.

When he gave me a dubious look, I held up a finger to indicate *One sec* and hefted off my backpack. I laid it on the ground and dug in, unpacking all my shit to unearth my only credential: my most expensive professional camera. When I had the travel-battered Canon in hand, I hoisted it up to show him. "See?"

He didn't see. He kept half-heartedly scanning his papers. "Anna Malone?"

"Amber," I said, as politely as I could.

"Hang on," he said, heading into his booth. "And you'll need to clear that off the road."

"Thanks." Not even sure why I said that. But I started cramming everything back into my backpack, post-haste, before all my worldly belongings could get run over by a Hummer limo or something. I heard him mumbling to someone on his cell phone; always such a warm welcome at my sister's shoots.

It was a real wonder I didn't do more of them.

Admittedly, I wasn't in the best frame of mind to be showing up for a job. For one thing, I'd only touched down in this time zone less than twenty-four hours ago and I was severely jet-lagged. Also, I was more than a little irked that I'd been groped last night by an old ex who'd let me crash on his couch; that after a couple of beers, he'd cried on my shoulder about his recent breakup and decided it was okay to put his hand on my boob. I'd slept there anyway, since I was low on options, but skipped out this morning before he woke up.

I'd had a crappy coffee shop breakfast, accidentally caught the wrong bus, and arrived here late.

All-in-all, not a great start to the day. But truth be told, it was no worse than I'd expected.

I had very, very low expectations of this day.

Just as I finished cramming all my shit back into my backpack, Tetris-style, a tricked-out golf cart thing came buzzing through the parking lot toward me. When I saw it coming, my stomach roiled. Probably thanks to my crappy breakfast, but also: nerves.

So maybe I was more nervous about this shoot than I'd wanted to admit to myself.

Two men were riding in the cart; they parked across the lane in front of me. I took a deep breath and stood to meet them as they got out and strolled toward me. The driver, some film crew guy, was dressed no better than I was—worse, even—in his faded jeans and old sweatshirt, but he did have steel-toed boots on; there was a walkie on his belt, spewing snippets of barely-discernible conversation into the air. He looked me over, his gaze landing on my naked toes in my flimsy sandals.

The other guy was obviously security, though not the uniformed, pot-bellied kind. This one was tall and imposing and dressed like a biker—black boots, black jeans, black leather vest over a Harley-Davidson T-shirt. Cheesy skull tat on his muscular arm. Long blondish hair pulled back in a messy man-bun. He was cute, which just annoyed me.

Unfortunately, I had an incredibly long history of doing the stupidest shit where cute guys were concerned.

"Underlayer?" he asked me, no preamble, as if we were continuing a conversation we'd already been having.

"Yes. I'm the stills photographer. Amber Malone?" Why I kept saying my own name like it was a question, I'd never know.

He looked a little closer at me, squinting in the morning sun. The perusal went from head to foot, slowly and unnecessarily, like he'd just noticed I was cute. "Liv Malone—?"

"Is my sister."

He pulled out a cell phone and appeared to do some searching on it. Then he informed me, "You're not on the list."

Of course not.

I started to squelch a sigh, but then something occurred to me. "Can you try Amber Paige?"

He consulted his phone again. "Yeah. I've got that."

Well thank fuck.

"That's me. I go by my middle name, professionally. Amber Paige?" Damn it. *Quit saying your own name like you don't know who the hell you are.* "But they usually put my legal name on the crew list. Malone."

He kept looking me over, but made no move to welcome me into the fancy golf cart. "You have some ID, Amber Paige?"

Yeah, I had ID. Somewhere deep in the bowels of my backpack, probably under all the shit I'd just piled back in there.

The big dude arched his sexy eyebrow at me, waiting. (Truth be told, I kinda had a thing for eyebrows.) He hadn't even cracked a smile in my direction, but *shit*... was it my imagination, or had he just taken a flirtatious tone with me? Was there an opening here I was missing?

Briefly, my inner feminist turned a blind eye and the rest of me actually wondered if this guy would be amenable to a little eyelash batting and/or hair twirling.

Unfortunately, I just wasn't the girl who knew the answers to such questions. Nor was I the girl who could actually pull off flirting my way in here. No exaggeration, the last guy I'd consciously tried to flirt with had actually asked me if I was feeling ill. *Are you feeling ill?* Those were his exact words.

Apparently, when I tried to flirt with a cute guy, the ensuing blushing, fumbling, babbling and mild hyperventilating was concerning to some people.

So instead, I bit back another sigh, laid my bag on the ground again and started digging everything back out. Wondering all the while why I was doing this to myself.

Oh, right. *Paycheck.*

While I searched for my passport, I listened to the voices crackling on the walkie; the driver pulled it off his belt and chatted with someone in crew-guy shorthand. It sounded like they hadn't started filming yet?

So at least *maybe* Liv wouldn't be pissed at me for being late.

I found my passport, just as a vehicle rolled up behind me, music blaring. I glanced up; it was a pimped-out black pickup truck, Pink Floyd's "Young Lust" rattling the windows. I was almost blinded by the glint of sunlight off the driver's rings as he lifted his hand in greeting towards the security guys. The biker dude waved him through with a little salute. And as the truck rolled past, the guy behind the wheel looked right at me.

Black surfer-dude hair, black T-shirt, tattoos all down his arms... and hot as all hell. The kind of hot, once you've seen it, you don't forget it.

"I know that guy..." I said, getting to my feet. "Hey!" I called over to him. "I met you, at that party... you know... at that guy's place?" *Shit.* I'd definitely met him—at a party for one of the guys in

Dirty, about four years ago, when I was fresh back from Australia. The same party where I'd also met—

Never mind that.

I just couldn't remember much more than this guy's face, though. I just knew he was some rock star or another. Guitarist? Lead singer? Whatshisname?

Whatever his name was, he didn't seem to give one fuck that we'd met. Or maybe he couldn't even hear me over the bass vibrating through his truck. As he drove on into the lot, he actually flipped me the finger.

Admittedly, it wasn't the first time a man had ever given me the finger, but come on.

Fucking rock stars.

I shoved my passport at the biker guy. "See? Amber Paige Malone."

He inspected it, then closed it and handed it back to me. "Cool. You want a ride in?"

"Sure. Thanks."

"I'm Connor," he informed me. "You can call me Con."

"Nice to meet you." It wasn't, but whatever.

I stuffed everything back into my backpack—again—and hustled to follow him. When I reached the cart, he stood aside so I could climb into the narrow back seat, but not before I'd glimpsed the back of his leather vest. It had a big patch in the middle; a king of spades, like on a playing card, except the king was a wicked-looking skeleton. Across the top it said WEST COAST KINGS, and across the bottom, VANCOUVER.

So, he was a *real* biker.

Lovely.

I took a deep breath and just tried to relax; I was *in* now, and it didn't seem like filming had even started yet. Potential first couple of disasters averted.

"Sorry about the hassle." The cart dipped as Connor settled his big body into the front seat with the crew guy. "It *is* Dylan Cope," he added affably, as if that explained everything.

"Uh-huh," I said.

As if I cared who the star of this shoot was.

Apparently, it was a real stretch of the imagination to believe that a young woman such as myself was actually a professional photographer here to do a job, with no interest whatsoever in Dylan Cope. You know, like I might actually be some feral groupie hellbent on scamming my way into the studio to try to suck Dylan Cope's rock star cock, security be damned.

Because that's what all women probably looked like, at first glance, to Connor the security biker.

"I'm sure Liv will mention it," the crew guy told me as we reversed and turned around, "but you'll need proper footwear to work on set."

"I'm sure she will," I muttered, as we started motoring, slowly, through the parking lot. I hadn't brought steel-toed boots with me, but really, I wasn't about to keep a pair of steel-toes in storage somewhere just so that whenever I was—occasionally—back in Vancouver I could work on my sister's film sets. That would be far too much like admitting that *this* was something I actually did. That I, Amber Paige Malone, was a whore photographer.

Although today, I *was* a whore photographer.

And not because I was photographing whores.

Because I *felt* like a prostitute, whoring out my talent like this. *I'm just doing it for the money* seemed like a piss-poor attitude for a professional photographer to bring to any photo shoot. But the fact was, my heart wasn't and would never be in photographing celebrities. In my mind, this was the lowliest type of photography work.

Other than the paycheck. You really couldn't argue with the paycheck.

But you could argue with the work...

Sexist, misogynistic, abusive. I'd experienced all of it on Liv's sets. Most days I did not understand how my own sibling—my female, lesbian, smart-as-hell sibling—could work in this fucked-up, male-dominant world of celebrity bullshit.

As we picked up a modicum of speed, Connor turned to look at me, his mouth flipping up at the corners. "By the way, his name's Ash."

"What?"

"The guy in the truck," he said. "Ashley Player. He's the lead singer of the Penny Pushers."

"Good for him."

"He doesn't seem to like you," he noted, evidently amused.

Of course he doesn't, I wanted to say. *He's a rock star.*

"Yeah," I said instead. "It's a real travesty."

"Where the hell are your steel-toed boots?"

As soon as Connor the biker led me into the sound stage and deposited me in my sister's vicinity, Liv hit me up with an admonition and a tight hug. The hug was welcome, because as soon as I'd walked in, the nerves *really* hit me. My cranky veneer had cracked, and I realized how anxious I'd been about this day, however irrationally.

I was a professional. I had this.

But it wasn't the work I was nervous about.

I took another deep breath and collected myself. The studio was huge and somewhat dark, the overhead lights shut off, the production's lights shining onto a large stage where a massive rock 'n' roll drum kit gleamed, front and center. I was aware of the cameras and the lights, and the film crew milling about, tinkering with equipment as they waited for the shoot to begin. But all I really wanted to *feel* in this moment was my sister as I squeezed her to me and shut my eyes.

She felt so familiar in my arms, and so foreign. Smaller than I remembered, but stronger. We were about the same size; I was five-five, and Liv would never admit that she was an inch shorter. She was almost five years older, but we'd often shared clothes growing up. Now, we wouldn't be caught dead in one another's wardrobe.

I loved my big sister something fierce, and sometimes I couldn't stand her. I'd been out of the country for thirteen months straight and I'd missed her like my arm had been cut off. Yet I knew within days—if not hours—I'd be itching to get the hell gone again.

It had always been this way.

When we finally broke apart, there were tears sparking in Liv's hazel eyes. And I knew there were matching ones in my eyes as she held me out at arm's length, inspecting me.

"Hippie," she concluded with a shake of her head.

"Tyrant," I said. I took in the plaid shirt, buttoned up to her neck, and the ripped jeans, the laced-up boots; the same clothes she'd always worn, fashionable or not. Her short brown hair, very short on the sides, longer on top, looked cute on her, but like nothing I'd ever do with my own hair. I raised an eyebrow. "Hipster tyrant?"

"You're late," she said, very tyrant-like, and glanced aside at Connor, who'd taken up residence in the shadows. "You have trouble getting in?"

"Of course not. They really rolled out the red carpet for me."

Liv frowned at my sarcasm, glancing down. "You need steel-toed boots on set, Amber. Or at least boots."

I shrugged, trying to look apologetic. It was hard. "I forgot."

"Jesus," my sister muttered. "Every time." Then she got on her phone, presumably to sort out my footwear situation. Liv was directing this commercial; surely she could make a pair of boots appear if she really wanted to. Did I feel bad about making this her problem? Kind of. But I'd already warned her I probably wouldn't "remember" the boots.

Liv knew this wasn't my world, that I didn't really do this kind of work, yet she'd still chosen to hire me.

I turned away, glancing around the busy set, checking out who was here. But I didn't recognize anyone yet. The nerves were still with me, but I was gradually getting a grip. All I had to do was remind myself that it didn't really matter where I was. That as long as I had my camera, I was in my element.

Who cares about the rock stars.

When Liv got off her phone, she informed me, "You're lucky we haven't started rolling yet. I can take you around." Then she led me on a whirlwind tour of the facilities. The craft services table had better food than the cafe where I'd had breakfast, so I snagged a handful of grapes and ate them, despite my sister's disapproving look, as she walked me around.

She showed me the camera set-up—two HD video cameras, one that would glide in front of the stage on a dolly track, the other suspended above on a jib arm, to film Dylan Cope in all his rock star glory.

Then she introduced me around to some of the crew as well as the Underlayer execs and the creative director—the people she'd convinced to hire me for this shoot—and I did my best to project *grateful* and *professional*.

All the while, I kept one eye peeled, until I'd had a chance to scope out every last face in the room. And yes, I was looking for him. I couldn't exactly help it. It was kind of a nervous twitch.

Johnny O'Reilly.

Because running into my rock star ex was not exactly on my wish list for today.

All I really wished for, actually, was to get through this thing quickly, quietly, and with a little grace. Without falling on my face or, you know, falling in love.

It was Liv who'd introduced me to Johnny, and any time I rubbed shoulders with anyone in this particular sector of my sister's world—the rock star sector—I found myself looking for him. Not because I wanted to see him. Because I wanted the chance to vanish if I saw him, before he saw me.

"He's not here," Liv said, picking up on my wandering eyes. My sister never really did miss much. "Why would he be?"

Why, indeed. Johnny had no particular affiliation with Dylan Cope that I knew of. He wasn't in Dylan Cope's band.

But neither was that dude who'd just flipped me the finger.

"I have no idea who you're talking about," I said.

"Right."

When we'd returned to the area behind the cameras, where the "Video Village" was set up—viewing monitors for Liv and the execs to watch what was being filmed—I lay my backpack down out of the way and dug out my camera. Just as I'd switched out the lenses, Liv's assistant materialized to whisk my backpack away to one of the offices for me. I fiddled with my exposure settings, making adjustments to match the general light in the room. Photographing the star of the shoot under all those stage lights would be easy enough. But to photograph the crew at work in the shadows, I'd have to combine the available light with a high ISO and hope to capture enough detail without everything turning to mud.

Not the best conditions for photographing people, but I'd worked with worse.

I rejoined my sister after she'd had a few words with her camera crew. Everyone was beginning to look a little restless and put out. I'd checked the time on my phone; we were running over forty-five minutes late, yet there was still no rock star onstage. The drums sat, gleaming and untouched, waiting. And it was easy enough to figure out what was going on here.

The big rock star was making everyone wait for him.

Because he was that special, and really, there was nothing the rest of us could do about it. We were, after all, just regular mortals.

"So," I asked Liv, "any ridiculous rules I should know here?" I didn't even want to know, but I had to ask. I'd been on enough of my sister's film sets to know you always had to ask. Because no one ever told you the unspoken rules unless you asked. "You know, anyone I'm not supposed to photograph? Anyone to avoid eye contact with? Anyone I'm expected to address as *Your Highness*?"

My sister scoffed. "You can call me *Your Highness* if you really want to." Then her shrewd eyes narrowed at me from behind her glasses. "Just don't give anyone attitude, okay?"

"Me?" I balked, like I was shocked at the suggestion.

"Yes," she said dryly. "You, Amber."

"It's not always me, Liv," I informed her.

"Right..."

"Remember that made-for-TV movie I helped you out on?"

She frowned, which I took to be a yes.

"You know the one. I did that promo shoot with Mr. Action-Hero-of-Yesterday, and only 'attractive' women were allowed to be on his set, but we weren't allowed to speak to him?"

"The way I remember it," my sister said, "*you* weren't allowed to speak to him because you were rude the first time you met him. He was there to do a job and so were you."

"Uh-huh."

"You were lucky you weren't fired."

"Right. Lucky me."

"You know," she informed me, her eyes narrowing further, "you really bring it on yourself with that chip on your shoulder."

"Sure I do. How about that skincare campaign, starring Ms. Aging-Pop-Star, who *did* have me fired, for being 'too pretty'? I guess I brought that on myself by showing up with a face?"

"Amber..."

"You *know* the rules at these shoots are fucking ridiculous." I added in a grumble, "And the hot guys are the worst ones."

My sister arched an eyebrow at me. "Maybe *they* say the same thing about stuck-up hippie chicks."

"Whatever." I let her words roll off, however accurate—though mean—they might be. I wound my camera strap around my wrist. "I'm just doing it for the money, right?"

Why deny it? We both knew why I was here: to make money so I could go traveling again. I only ever came home when I ran out of money. Quickest way to make more money was to whore myself out to my sister. She knew as much.

But in the end, since getting paid was all that really mattered to me here, and she had hired me, I should be grateful to her. Plus, I did actually harbor a teeny, tiny desire to please her, in some minuscule little closet somewhere in the back of my heart that I'd never tell her about. So I forced out, "What I mean to say is, thank you for hiring me."

Liv just rolled her eyes. "The rules are fucking simple. Just do as you're told and keep your mouth shut. There won't be any drama."

"Gotcha."

My sister eyed me, but there was some sympathy in her gaze. Pity, actually. "You know, not every hot guy on the planet is a dick, Amber."

"Of course not."

"Not every rock star is an asshole."

"Uh-huh."

"And Dylan Cope is not Johnny O."

Right.

All I really knew about Dylan Cope was that he was the drummer for Dirty, the biggest rock band Liv had ever worked with; a band I'd met a couple of members of in passing, and really didn't give a shit about. Though, admittedly, most of the rest of the world did.

And now Dylan Cope was an underwear model. He'd been cast as the rock 'n' roll "god" in Underlayer's latest ad campaign—the *Underlayer of the Gods* campaign.

By that evidence alone, Dylan Cope should be an even *bigger* asshole than my ex. Nothing like the label of "god" to really humble a man. Especially a man who was already rich and famous.

According to Liv, Underlayer also had a hip-hop god, a couple of athlete gods, and a movie star god in the campaign, but they'd already shot commercials with them. For this final shoot, they'd worked around Dylan Cope's ever-changing schedule, bringing the entire production up to Vancouver to accommodate him. Because that's what people did when you were a rock god.

They came to you.

Though Liv had also told me that Dylan recommended her to direct this commercial, so maybe that was a point in his favor.

Or maybe he just wanted to fuck her? Wouldn't exactly be the first time a man had ever attempted to make my lesbian sister switch teams.

"So where is this rock god anyway?" I asked her. Everyone was still waiting on Dylan Cope to manifest; Liv kept glancing at her phone as the seconds ticked by.

"Dylan's always late, because he's always eating," she informed me. "It's a drummer thing." Like I was supposed to know what that meant?

"Right before you film him in his underwear? Isn't he worried about bloat or anything?"

She gave me a look I wasn't even sure how to interpret. "Clearly, you haven't met him."

True. I'd only met Elle, Dirty's bassist, and one of the guitarists, whose name I honestly couldn't remember. I only remembered Elle's because she was so famous—her face was everywhere these days, from magazine covers to makeup lines. Plus, she was a woman in an otherwise male rock band, which was pretty kick-ass. She was even nice to me, but I wouldn't let that skew my opinion of rock stars in general, since most of them were male. Elle, I figured, was an anomaly.

I raised my camera and snapped a photo of Liv's face, capturing her semi-scowl as she checked her phone again. The scowl deepened. My sister had never loved being on the other side of the camera.

"Just checking my exposure..." I said innocently.

"You really don't need to shoot me," she informed me. "But just make sure you don't *only* shoot Dylan."

"Why would I only shoot Dylan?"

She gave me another look I wasn't sure how to interpret. "Just shoot everyone and everything, but be discreet about it, okay? Candid. Use the longest lens you can and stay the hell out of the way."

"Intend to."

If I could get away with taking zero pictures of the star of this commercial, I'd be happy. I'd probably just take several of him right away to get it over with. After that, photographing the crew doing their thing could actually be interesting.

I was already mentally staking out the best vantage point, a clear shot of the drum kit through all the filming equipment, where no one would be in my way and the lights they'd set up should work in my favor. Stage left, just beyond the end of the dolly track...

"And Amber..." Liv caught my arm before I could wander off in that direction. "Don't talk to anyone."

Seriously? Did she seriously have so little faith in me?

I shook her hand off. "What if they talk to me first?"

"Then you answer as briefly and politely as you can, then fuck off."

I tried to keep the attitude out of my voice when I said, "Sure thing, boss."

Okay, so it wasn't like her lack of faith in me was totally unfounded. I knew that. I'd been known to put my foot in my mouth, and in front of the worst people to put my foot in my mouth in front of. It was kind of an unfortunate talent of mine.

But *still*.

I watched as she glanced at her phone again, checked her wristwatch, then frowned. "I swear," she grumbled, "he slows down every time I ask him to speed up." Then she looked at me and sighed heavily.

She reached out and smoothed a lock of my hair behind my ear. It was an almost-tender gesture—until she clucked under her breath as if my hair, which wasn't quite long enough to stay put in the ponytail I'd attempted, was a sad disappointment.

"Fuck it," she said, almost to herself. Then: "I need you to do something for me."

"Okay...?"

"Head down that hall over there..." She pointed toward a hallway that appeared to lead behind the stage. "And knock on Dylan's dressing room. His name's on the door."

"And why would I do that?"

"Because I told you to," she said, in a very *Do-not-question-my-orders-on-my-set* tone of voice. It was a tone I was, unfortunately, familiar with. Then she rolled her eyes. "I swear to God. He's like, the world's nicest rock star."

Riiight.

"He just has some punctuality issues—"

"I didn't notice."

"—but if anyone's gonna get him out of that dressing room..." She frowned at my blouse like she was disappointed in the lack of discernible cleavage, then frowned again at my naked toes. "Yeah... it's you."

"Um. *Wait*. You hired me to be rock star bait?" I looked down at myself; did I really look like some horny groupie today or something?

No. Definitely not. My jeans were tight, but not skintight. My loose blouse revealed virtually nothing about the size or shape of my boobs. This was not a *Come-hither-rock-star* outfit.

But then again... I wasn't wearing one of those when I met Johnny, either. And he'd definitely... come.

"Of course not," Liv said. "We hired you to take stills." Then she frowned at me. She was doing that a lot today. "But it wouldn't kill you to smile at him."

I scowled at her. What the fuck was this, 1958?

Liv scowled back.

Unfortunately, she won.

So I sighed, dredged up a fake-ass smile, and headed off in search of the world's nicest rock star.

CHAPTER TWO

Amber

AT THE ENTRANCE to the hallway, I told the 'roided-up security guy who was standing guard that Liv had sent me to get Dylan. Fortunately, he let me through without a fuss, so I didn't have to resort to any eyelash batting.

The shit I do for my sister...

I found the hallway empty—except for one person. As I approached, I could see that he was standing in front of a door with a handwritten sign on it that said *Dylan Cope*. But clearly, it wasn't Dylan Cope.

It was that other rock star—the one who'd flipped me the finger. The one with the ink-black hair, tats for days, piercings, the works.

Ashley Player.

This time, I'd made a point of remembering his name. It was easy enough to do. Ashley, because it wasn't such a common name for a man, and Player, because it was cheesy as fuck, a rock star's bullshit stage name. No big surprise, he wore the requisite Motörhead T-shirt, tight black jeans and rocker jewelry. He was looking down at the phone in his hand; a mermaid with perky boobs was tattooed down his right forearm, her white-blonde hair strategically covering her nipples.

Scripted lettering tattooed in a band around his right bicep said: *Fuck Bitches*. A matching band around the left said: *Get Money*.

Clearly, this guy was all class.

When he glanced up and saw me approaching, his posture didn't change. He didn't turn to face me. The only acknowledgment of my presence was the movement of his blue, blue eyes as they skimmed down my body.

There was no sign of recognition in his chilly expression.

Okay; so he definitely didn't remember me. Not like I really expected him to. We'd met for like five seconds four years ago. And I wasn't gonna kid myself that I was as memorable as he was.

Though he definitely hadn't seemed this cold the first time we'd crossed paths. As he looked me over now, his gaze was so frigid, my nipples actually pricked. I kind of shivered, and it wasn't a good shiver.

Or so I told myself.

When I stopped a couple of feet from him, camera gripped tightly in hand—kind of like a security blanket—I could feel the hostility rolling off of him before he even opened his gorgeous mouth.

"Who the fuck are you?"

I choked a little, torn between answering that and telling him to go fuck himself. The words rose up in my throat, but got stuck there. I swallowed the mild humiliation and managed, "Amber."

"Amber who?" He was examining my blouse with distaste, like the rosebud embroidery personally offended him.

"Amber Malone," I said, deciding to drop my sister's name again. It killed me a little every time I had to do it, but in this world, my sister's name carried far more weight than mine ever would. In this world, I was a nobody, as evidenced by Ashley Player's perusal of me: brief, critical and dismissive.

"Malone?" He returned his cold gaze to his iPhone. "You related to Liv?"

"I'm her sister."

"What's with the camera?"

"I'm the stills photographer. I've been asked to escort Dylan to set."

He flicked a glance at my camera, eying my beloved *1D X Mark II* like it was garbage. "Yeah? You just find that in the gutter?"

"*No*... I mean... I travel with it a lot..." I blathered defensively.

Shit. How fucking rude was he?

Was I actually going to stand here and explain to him where this camera had been with me, the things we'd been through together these last thirteen months, the things we'd seen and experienced... or the fact that making it look like garbage was kind of the point—meant to deter would-be thieves on my travels? Not to mention that this camera, brand new, cost me over six thousand American dollars—I'd bought it down in Portland to save the sales tax—which for me was a shit-ton of money. Several months' worth of travel money.

No. Why bother? Clearly, this guy was a professional asshole. Explaining myself wasn't gonna change that.

"Trust me," I said instead, "I could do more with your iPhone camera than you could do with a Hasselblad and a full support crew."

"Is that so?"

"Yep."

Finally, his cold blue eyes met mine again. "You don't know me, sweetheart."

"You don't know me."

"And neither does Dylan. So you can go back where you came from and wait just like everyone else."

"What are you, his bodyguard?" I looked him over, trying to appear as unimpressed and dismissive as he'd been of me. "The rock star gig didn't work out for you?"

Ouch. That hit a raw nerve.

His shoulders drew back as he turned toward me, the general air in his vicinity shifting from irritable to motherfucking pissed.

"Right," I said. "I'll just wait."

Screw Liv and her orders.

I headed back down the hall, trying not to think about how pissed she'd be—at me, probably—if she witnessed that exchange.

At least I fucked off at the end of it, so I got that part right.

Just as I was about to leave the hallway, though, I glanced back. Ashley the Asshole was staring at his phone again, his bent arm making his bicep pop, the ceiling lights that should have been harsh and unflattering skimming the curves of his muscles and casting his eyes in shadow. Unfortunately, he had gorgeous cheekbones and all sorts of sharp angles to his face that totally worked. He looked bitchy and ridiculously beautiful, and I snapped a photo of him.

When I walked back out into the sound stage, I found my sister. Or rather, she found me. "Where's Dylan?" she asked, throwing a glance toward the hallway behind me, like she seriously thought I'd be able to fetch him.

"No idea, but this guy was super nice." I showed her the photo I'd taken of Ashley Player, on the screen on the back of my camera.

"Great shot."

"Why's he such an asshole?"

Liv shrugged, thumbing her phone. "Why can't you show up in steel-toed boots like you know you're supposed to? Some people just like to be a thorn up other people's asses."

"Just yours," I grumbled in my defense.

"Looks like you made an impression on him." She held up her phone; a text message was open on the screen.

> **Ash:** Your little hippie sister is hot but she's got an attitude problem. Keep her away from Dylan.

My mouth dropped open.

Okay, so it wasn't the first time I'd ever been called a hippie. Liv did it regularly, but she was my sister; she was allowed, because she loved me. "Attitude problem?" I scoffed. "That's rich."

"Like I said," she told me, "you bring it on yourself with that chip on your shoulder."

I opened my mouth to respond, preparing to unleash a diatribe on discrimination and harassment in the workplace—not only had he called me a hippie and insulted my camera, he'd sworn at me and called me *sweetheart*—but just then, the rock god himself appeared onstage.

Dylan Cope had finally arrived.

I felt him before I saw him. It was the way the vibe completely shifted in the room, and everyone hustled up. And when I looked up, the words I'd been about to spew completely failed me.

Liv shooed me off to get to work, getting busy herself. So I made my way closer to the stage, carefully, just trying not to trip on anything or bump into anyone in my hypnotic state.

Because there he towered under the lights: Dirty's drummer.

Totally.

Fucking.

Gorgeous.

I stood to the side of the stage and stared, just trying to sort out what I was seeing. Apparently, my brain needed a moment to fully absorb and attempt to process the sheer majesty of such a sight—the way it might if I was standing at the base of Mount Everest gazing up, or maybe setting foot on the moon.

Because how did you adequately capture something like that with mere thoughts, or words, or a camera, anyway?

Awestruck didn't cover it.

First of all, the man had abs for weeks. A girl could definitely get her laundry sparkling-clean on that washboard. He also had the most beautiful auburn hair, a little casually mussed-up and wavy, about a zillion different autumn shades of red and gold and chestnut-brown. And his *face*... He was super-handsome, with a strong jawline, a straight nose and a little divot in his chin... but not in a nauseating way. He had kind eyes, actually, and an easy-going manner about him. He looked totally at ease on the stage, in front of the cameras, but not in a gross, cocky way.

I'd definitely seen gross and cocky in front of my camera. This was not that.

Liv and a few other people had rushed to meet him as he strolled out onstage, and I watched him smile good-naturedly as he chatted with some of the crew guys.

Not *at all* what I was expecting.

I was expecting attitude for miles.

I was expecting someone like Ashley Player, with hair too black or too blond. Piercings, too many tattoos, the usual cliches. But Dylan Cope was naked down to his white Underlayer briefs, and there wasn't a tattoo or piercing or blemish of any kind on all that perfect skin. His complexion was unusually golden for a redhead. And his entire body was so chiseled... he looked like a statue of a god, for real.

Well holy shit.

This was either gonna be super easy or crazy hard. Like if I couldn't manage to make *that* look good, I was the shittiest photographer who'd ever picked up a camera. I'd have to lay my equipment down and just walk away. Find some other profession where I didn't suck so much ass.

As more lights came on, lighting up the drum kit as if onstage at a rock concert, I shifted into the shadows, out of the way of the light stands and crew, and got to work doing my thing.

I quickly got lost behind the lens, shooting Dylan Cope as he chatted with the execs and Liv. He wasn't exactly a difficult subject. As it turned out, my camera fucking loved him. I checked a few images along the way, and thank God I seemed to be doing him justice. The photos were so good, I got that excited rush, that almost-high feeling; giddy, almost shaking with adrenaline. I was in The Zone, and I *knew* when I was making beautiful photographs.

I was making them right now.

I kept shooting as Dylan moved to stand behind the drums, casually spinning a pair of drumsticks in his hands. Music started playing, and I recognized the song that rocked through the room; it had been popular in a lot of the hostel bars on the travel circuit about five years back. So popular that I got totally sick of hearing it, even though I could admit I liked the song. It was a song by Dylan's band, Dirty: "Get Made."

Liv was giving him directions, showing him where the cameras would be as he played, while other people flocked around him, getting him ready. A makeup girl was checking his face—for what, I couldn't imagine; the man was perfect—and another girl started rubbing him down with oil. There seemed to be a debate about how much oil he should have on his arms, and some was wiped off in fear that the drumsticks would slip out of his hands if the oil ran down.

"You know I'm gonna sweat all this shit off," I heard him tell my sister.

"I'm counting on it," she said.

I watched how he smiled and laughed easily with her, like old friends, which I knew they kind of were. I got a couple of great shots of the two of them that I was pretty sure Liv was going to like, even if she was in them.

Then, as Dylan glanced around, he suddenly noticed me. He looked right down my lens and into my eyes.

His eyes were green in the light, a gorgeous green-gold, and I actually stopped shooting. I stopped breathing. My finger just kind of froze over the button as the unexpected jolt of eye contact hit me —like a lightning bolt, straight to the gut.

Actually, I could've sworn I felt my uterus contract.

Then Liv directed his attention elsewhere, and his gaze shifted away.

Holy. Shit.

I let out the breath I'd been holding and kept shooting. Kept doing my job, just trying to shake off that feeling. I definitely couldn't remember mere eye contact with a man ever making my uterus spasm before. But all I had to do was remind myself that it didn't matter if Dylan Cope looked at me or not. I was being paid to see him, and not the other way around.

With the camera to my face, it's not like he could really see *me* anyway.

Of course, even if he did see me and thought I was cute, it wouldn't matter. Even if he thought I was super cute. Even if he thought I was the girl of his dreams and it was love at first sight.

Wouldn't mean a thing.

Because I knew how moments like this played out.

It was pretty much a universal law: the men I was most attracted to never liked me back. Or at least, not for long.

It was kind of a curse.

The bane of my love life.

Somehow, it never stopped me from trying... and failing. From falling for the wrong men. Including the rock star who'd wined and dined me until I fell for him, then cheated on me. Repeatedly.

It was inevitable.

I, Amber Paige Malone, sucked at love.

Good thing I wasn't here to fall in love, then. Nope. I was here to do a job and nothing more. To see things as they were—through my camera. I definitely wasn't here to let my uterus get carried away with any notions of getting closer to Dylan Cope.

The truth was, after my last few romantic catastrophes, I'd actually become so averse to getting close to men, I wasn't sure I could even bear the idea of liking someone enough to actually date him—knowing he was just gonna dump me. Because that part was definitely inevitable.

They always dumped me.

Because I *totally* sucked at love.

Not that I was a loser or something. I wasn't stupid or naive or unlovable. I just made bad, bad decisions when it came to men.

I was romantically challenged.

But I was an intelligent woman (or so I kept telling myself). I could learn from my mistakes.

So I dismissed that ridiculous eye-contact-lightning-bolt thing and the whims of my over-eager womb and just kept doing my job. Because at my job, I definitely did not suck.

I rocked at it, actually.

I captured a few deliciously-suggestive shots of the oil girl, her brow creased in concentration, as she smoothed oil over Dylan's godlike chest and his rippling abs with her bare hand. All the while, he kept right on chatting with Liv, oblivious. The girl actually bit her lip, and I got an amazing shot of it. I giggled a little, actually, amusing myself.

"Bet you're thinking, 'Why didn't I get *that* job?'" a gruff voice muttered beside me, startling me out from behind the camera.

It was Ashley Player.

I didn't respond.

I definitely didn't feel lightning bolts to my uterus when he glared at me. But I did feel… something. The guy put me on edge. He had those piercing, penetrating blue eyes, and there was so much derision in them as he stared me down, it almost hurt.

Which was ridiculous, since I didn't even know him.

He didn't know me, either. But for some reason, he'd already made up his mind to despise me.

For some other reason that I could not fathom, he was standing too close to me. Like right beside me. And some stubborn, jaded part of me refused to give him the satisfaction of backing away or running scared.

So I stood my ground.

He crossed his toned arms over his chest and finally turned his attention away from me, toward Dylan. He steadfastly ignored me, actually, as we stood here, together, in the shadows beyond the lights. And he looked so irritatingly beautiful, with his edgy dark hair and his angsty, angry-at-the-world expression… It shouldn't have mattered to me, but honestly, it was annoying as hell that he was so hot.

Because it made me want to stare at him—like I was doing right now—even though I was pretty sure I already hated him.

So instead, I ignored him right back.

I kept right on photographing Dylan Cope.

The entire time, Ashley Player stayed right beside me. He never looked at me. Or at least, I never caught him looking at me.

But there was no doubt in my mind: he was keeping an eye on me.

CHAPTER THREE

Dylan

AS THE CAMERAS STARTED ROLLING, I played along to "Get Made." Obviously, it was fucking loud. But to her credit, the photographer at the side of the stage didn't flinch.

She also didn't seem to be aware that anyone in the room existed besides me.

After we'd run through several takes, I saw Liv's assistant hand her some work boots and a pair of socks. I watched her, amused, as she grudgingly put them on, while pointedly ignoring Ash, who was standing beside her. He'd been standing beside her the entire time.

Right beside her.

Interesting.

A while later, when Liv called for a quick break, the photographer had worked herself up onto the side of the stage, way back out of the way, without anyone seeming to notice or care. She'd seemed to be photographing some of the crew while I played, but only briefly.

Mostly, her camera had been locked on me.

She was still shooting me as I stood up and toweled off my sweaty face and chest.

"Liv said *cut*," I heard Ash growl at her. She almost jumped out of her skin; probably didn't realize he'd climbed up onto the stage with her. "That means you *cut*."

She lowered her camera. "I'm the *stills* photographer," she informed him. "Behind-the-scenes. Which means I don't 'cut.'"

"Yeah? Well, you can get behind *this* scene." Without another glance her way, Ash stepped in front of her, his back to her, completely blocking her view of me.

Total asshole move, but I chuckled anyway.

As Ash stalked past me, heading for the door at the back of the stage, I looked at the photographer. She wasn't taking photos anymore. She held her camera in front of herself, unsure, as her eyes met mine.

She was pretty. Impossible not to notice that.

Ash had clearly noticed, but he also seemed to have a problem with her.

I definitely had to find out who this girl was.

The crew was busy adjusting lights and discussing the next shot. So I raised a finger in her direction and crooked it, beckoning her to follow. Then I turned to follow Ash offstage.

As we made our way down the hall, he was already planning out our weekend. "Summer's having a party on Saturday," he informed me as we stepped into my dressing room. "We should go. And there's Zane's thing—" He stopped abruptly. He'd turned to me and noticed the photographer, stepping in the door right behind me. His mouth dropped open, then snapped shut, his jaw twitching. "The fuck is she doing in here?"

I just shrugged and grabbed a bottle of Gatorade from the fridge. I dropped into a chair, tussling my sweaty hair and took a swig.

The photographer took her cue from me, ignoring Ash completely. "Do you mind if I keep shooting?" she asked me.

"Nope," I said. So she started taking photos of me stretched out in my chair, all sweaty and half-naked. Well, mostly-naked.

I was watching her, closely, as she did it. In the brighter lighting of the dressing room, she was more than pretty. But it was a challenge to see her face when she kept covering it with the camera.

"Who are you?" I asked her.

"Amber," she said.

"How does it look out there, Amber?"

"You look great," she said neutrally.

"Yeah? How about the rest of it?"

"Can I ask you a favor?" she asked me as she kept taking photos. "Could you not look at the camera?"

I shot a look at Ash, amused. *Who is this girl?*

Ash stood behind her, glowering. His arms were crossed rigidly over his chest and the vein at his temple was popping out. His irritation was fucking palpable, and I smirked.

Very interesting.

Amber stopped shooting and checked the screen on the back of her camera. She seemed to be scrolling through some of the photos she'd taken. Now that the camera was out of her face, I took a good, long look at her.

Her sweet face, tensed in concentration. Narrowed, pretty eyes and full, pouty lips. Light freckles across her cheeks and small nose. She had a single piercing in the left side of her nose, a tiny, sparkly pink stone, barely larger than a freckle. She wore no other jewelry, and appeared to be wearing no makeup, just a simple blouse and jeans. Her thick, wavy, caramel-colored hair was pulled back in a short ponytail with chunks falling out.

Her cheeks were flushed, maybe with adrenaline—the thrill of photographing me?—but she seemed cool and composed, at ease behind the camera. Impressive, since Ash was tossing off angry sparks about two feet away.

She turned the camera to show me a photo on the screen and said, "Now *that's* an underwear ad."

The photo was fucking gorgeous.

Not to be an egotistical prick, since it was a photo of me, but it was totally fucking hot. I was all laid back in my chair, my muscles gleaming with oil and sweat. My sweat-dampened white underwear, almost transparent now, was clinging to my thighs—to the bulge of my cock and balls. My arm was tossed over my forehead, making me look totally at ease with my own sex appeal.

Which I was.

But when Ash leaned in to see the photo, he fucking scoffed, and Amber bristled.

She turned to glare at him. "You put *that* in a women's magazine," she said, "and what do you think the ladies are gonna buy for their man? The underwear they saw on *that*." She indicated my body. "No offense, but no one cares about the drums."

Ash raised his pierced eyebrow at her, sharply, and I kinda sighed.

Here we go.

I sat back and watched as he got his hackles all up at the perceived slight against me. Ash didn't handle anyone criticizing me —in any way—all that well.

"And how do you figure that?" he said, his tone flat. His eyelids lowered dismissively as he glared at her, like she wasn't worth the effort of his full attention.

"Because they're selling sex out there, right?" Amber replied. "Male virility? Not drums. But they're having him play to the camera. It's all just so... sterile. It looks like an ad for drums in a music magazine." She was getting worked up, and the more Ash stared her down like he didn't give a fuck, the more it seemed to irk her.

I noticed, though, that he'd somehow ended up standing a lot closer to her than was necessary as they argued over my body—the one on her camera screen, and the one laid out in front of them.

"He's a rock god, right?" she went on. "A wild animal? So take him, and his drums if you have to, outside. Shoot him, I don't know... on a mountaintop, on the edge of a cliff, like a conquering hero. Better yet, shoot him walking into a bedroom with three of the hottest girls you've ever seen on his arms. And not plastic-boobs-hot. I mean beautiful, natural, wholesome-as-apple-pie girls. The kind you want to believe a man like *that* would really want." Amber pointed at my body again for emphasis, and when her eyes met mine, her cheeks turned a deeper shade of pink.

She averted her eyes and dropped her hand.

Meanwhile, I just eyed them both, looking from him to her and back. Ash was still playing it cold; *too* cold.

But I knew him.

Usually when Ashley Player pulled this much attitude with a woman, he wanted in her pants.

I opened my mouth to speak, when a throat cleared behind me. I turned to look; Liv was standing in the doorway with one of the execs from Underlayer. The obnoxious one with the fugly golf shirts who was always asking me to "go for beers."

Clearly, they'd both heard what Amber said.

Damn.

I shot Ash a look; he was the only one of the three of us who was facing the door. He had to know they were standing there. When I caught his eye, he just shoved his hands in his pockets with a semi-shrug and tried to look innocent.

Unlikely.

In the pregnant, awkward-as-fuck pause, Amber finally turned around. She put two-and-two together fast, speared Ash with a quick, murderous look, then gushed, "Um, what I meant to say was—"

"You'll have to excuse my wayward sister," Liv said, cutting Amber off before she could say anything else they'd both regret. "She's been living in the jungle a little too long."

I glanced from Liv to Amber, searching for the family resemblance. Liv was cute, in her way, but Amber took pretty to a whole other level.

The Underlayer exec just smiled his smarmy smile. "I have to take a call," he said. Then he nodded at me, shot Liv a look that didn't match the smile—a look that said *Clean this up, fucking now*—and vanished.

"Liv..." I started, as soon as he was gone, but Amber cut me off.

"Sorry," she said, taking a step toward Liv. "I know this is your shoot—"

"Actually, it's not," Liv informed her, crossing her arms. "But there you go, as usual, opening your mouth and spouting off about things you know nothing about, in front of people you don't know—"

"Not *nothing*," Amber protested. "And I was just—"

"That man you just drove out of here?" Liv said. "He signs your paycheck for today. This shoot is his, and you just pissed all over it."

"But Dylan—um, Mr. Cope?—he asked my opinion—"

"I did," I said, amused at being called *Mr. Cope* by this girl.

Liv leveled me with a glare. "Don't encourage her." Then she added, "And you know I agree with pretty much everything she just said about the shoot."

"See?" Amber said. "So then—"

"BUT," Liv told her, fixing her with a look that said Amber was not long for this job, "sometimes it doesn't pay to be right, little sister."

"Shit." I attempted to intervene again. "Liv—"

"But I was just—"

"No. It's a lesson you're just gonna have to learn," Liv said, her mind clearly made up. "Right now."

Then she fired her sister from the shoot.

CHAPTER FOUR

Amber

SO THAT WAS A LOW MOMENT. Getting fired from a job I didn't even want. By my own sister.

As the ferry skimmed across the water, away from the mainland, it kinda felt like I was being banished. Clearly, it was as obvious to everyone else as it was to me that I didn't belong at that commercial shoot. I wasn't fooling anyone.

Least of all Ashley Player.

Yes, I knew photography, but I wasn't exactly an expert in advertising, much less men's underwear. Liv had told me not to talk to anyone, and that probably covered following Dylan Cope to his dressing room—even though he'd beckoned me to follow him—then letting Ashley the Asshole put me on the defensive and mouthing off about the shoot.

So yeah, I'd definitely overstepped. I could see that now.

But the way Ashley had *scoffed* at that gorgeous photo of Dylan on my camera? It abraded me. I just couldn't let it lie.

Maybe I really didn't know shit-all about selling underwear, but I knew a gorgeous man when I saw one, and I sure as shit knew how to make a heart-stopping beautiful photograph of him. I was never gonna apologize for that. The best photos I'd taken of Dylan Cope had been in that dressing room, and if no one else there could see that, or acknowledge it, just because their fancy set with all the expensive lighting wasn't involved... so be it.

It's not like I was looking for any kind of future in that ridiculous world anyway. Liv and her crew and her rock star clientele could go ahead and bite me. Including Connor the friendly biker, who'd escorted me off the property and put me in a cab with a white-toothed smile.

Damn, though. I did kind of feel like an asshole about the whole thing now. Why couldn't I just smile and keep my mouth shut?

Because you're not wired that way.

Neither was my sister, but Liv had just always been better with people.

We'd both been born with a love of cameras, been kind of artsy and nerdy growing up, but that was where the similarities had ended. Liv just had a knack for directing people, for issuing orders or kissing butt, for knowing who to tell off—and get away with it—and when to keep her mouth shut. She knew how to keep the whole machinery oiled and chugging along, without losing her soul in the process. She'd always been that way, maybe because she'd learned how to handle ridiculous people—our parents—at such a young age.

Somehow, I'd missed that lesson.

While Liv knew how to manage other people's crazy—including mine—without letting it get under her skin, I totally fucking floundered and drowned under social pressure.

Which was maybe why I'd never had a lasting relationship. Why every guy I'd ever been with had dumped me. Or totally screwed me over, then dumped me.

When Liv had her assistant literally ship me off to one of the little islands off the coast, it wasn't exactly a new feeling—being run out of town. I hadn't been fired as many times as I'd been dumped, but it had happened often enough.

I wanted to be offended, but I was secretly pretty grateful for the relocation, even if I wouldn't admit it to my sister. I really was kinda pissed about being fired, but mostly because it was embarrassing in front of Ashley Player and Dylan Cope—for different reasons.

Ashley because he was such an asshole, and he was probably gloating about it right now. He *knew* Liv and that exec were standing behind me when I said all that shit, and he didn't stop me. He just let me drown.

Dylan because he really did seem nice. He looked as surprised to find Liv and the exec standing there as I was, and he even looked a little sorry for me when Liv fired me. Plus, he was so totally beautiful. Like I-could-stare-at-him-all-day-and-night beautiful. Every time he'd looked at me, my uterus flipped out and I wondered stupid things like *Is my bra strap showing?* and *Do I have grape skins in my teeth?*

I knew Liv didn't exactly relish having to fire me, and she definitely didn't want to see me destitute. With the ferry gesture, she was just trying to make up for it a little. She knew I couldn't afford much in the way of rent, she knew I wouldn't be staying long, but she also knew I hated taking handouts. I was an independent woman. I worked for my money, I always paid my own way, and it hurt my pride to have to crash at her place. So, she'd offered up a friend's cabin, "very quiet," where I could chill, get over my jet-lag, and get caught up on my photo editing, until I figured something else out.

Don't worry, she'd told me. *He never uses it.*

As long as it doesn't belong to Dylan Cope, I'd said. I didn't particularly want to run into him again after making such an ass of myself—no matter how beautiful he was. Because I'd probably just want to stare at him and take more photos of him, and it would get weird, for us both.

Nope, Liv had assured me as she sent me on my way.

Once I'd gotten over the sting of the embarrassment, I'd decided that I preferred some quiet little island to the city anyway. There wouldn't exactly be high-paying photography jobs dropping in my lap, but after a little R&R, I'd work that out. Meanwhile, Liv had assured me I'd still be paid for today, even though she'd given me the boot before lunch.

I'd spent the afternoon bumming around the city, browsing some shops on Commercial Drive and walking the seawall before heading to the ferry terminal. Now, as I arrived at the small marina on the eastern side of Isabella Island, it was close to six o'clock. The sun was starting to sink below the horizon. The ferry was quick to unload, since there weren't many cars onboard.

The island was even smaller than I'd expected; it took me all of fifteen minutes to walk from the marina at the southeast end to the house at the northeast tip.

You can't miss it, Liv had said. *Just follow the road north until you get to the skull gate.*

Skull gate? I'd echoed, picturing some gnarly cemetery-like lot overgrown with weeds and an eerie mist rolling in.

Just what I said, Liv said. *You can't miss it.*

And she was right, though it was nothing like I'd pictured it in my head.

A narrow driveway veered off the road to the right, just before the road took a hard left. The drive was lined with trees, dense green, others rendered brilliant shades of autumn in the dusk—scarlet and crimson, copper and gold and burnt sienna—reminding me of Dylan Cope's hair. A couple of planter boxes hammered together out of driftwood were artfully arranged at the sides of the gate, and some hardy flowering plant was still blooming despite the lateness of the season.

The metal gate in the tidy wooden fence was about chest-height, ornamental black scrollwork, and in the middle of it was a Grim Reaper-like figure, a smiling skull peeking out from the cowl of its hood, with one skeletal hand raised. It was flipping me off with a bony middle finger.

Ashley Player.

That's who instantly came to mind.

Or Connor? Though this skeleton looked nothing like the picture on his biker vest.

I stood in front of the gate and stared at it, as birds twittered in the trees and insects chirped around me, and that oddly haunting feeling of being the only human in the vicinity crept in.

No. No fucking way. My sister would never do that to me. There was no way in hell she would send me to stay at a house owned by that rock star asshole, even if he wasn't here.

Wasn't possible.

I looked past the gate, up the short drive through the trees, where I could glimpse the house. Homey-looking, very west coast, all medium-dark stained wood with some green painted trim and pretty plants in the window boxes.

Definitely not some biker clubhouse.

I put the idea out of my mind and pushed through the gate. It was latched but not locked. I closed it behind me, breathing in the incredible, cool green air. There were more planter boxes bursting with foliage and flowers, all along the drive. There were no cars or motorcycles. Just some surf boards stacked up in the car port at the side of the house, and a mountain bike hung up on pegs on the wall.

And the house was... *Wow.*

As I stood in the driveway looking up at it, I was kind of weirded out. Considering that I was staying here for free and that Liv had used the word "cabin," I'd expected something a lot more rustic. More like the places I'd been staying these last thirteen months in South America.

This place, compared to those, was a palace.

Really, it was just a house. But a beautiful house that probably cost more than I'd made in—well, my entire career to date. By Liv's rich friends' standards, it was probably kinda basic. A cozy little home-away-from-home, with all the luxury fixings of moneyed west coast island life.

I pulled out my phone and wrote a text to my sister.

Me: Who owns this place...?

I sent the text, hoping for a quick response, but none came. So I found the spare key where Liv said it would be, and after knocking on the door, I let myself in.

"Hello?" I slipped out of my sandals and padded through the

silent house. The floors were hardwood, polished and shiny. Everything was polished and shiny and sparse. And there was definitely no one here.

I set my backpack down on the kitchen island in the middle of the open-concept house, and took a better look around.

Foremost, I examined the photos stuck to the front of the fridge with beer cap magnets. A very down-to-earth-looking middle-aged couple in matching blue parkas smiled back at me from one photo, white-capped mountains filling the landscape behind them. There was also a school photo of a little boy, maybe seven or eight years old. And a drawing of a dragon that appeared to have been made by the boy.

My hosts.

Not some biker or asshole rock star.

I relaxed a little. Or actually, a lot.

I wandered around. The place was as nice inside as it was out, with exposed wood everywhere and luxury finishes. It was smallish by a wealthy person's standards, only one level, with two bedrooms in back, but you definitely had to be wealthy to own a place like this that you didn't even live in most of the time.

As I tried to get comfy, I found it weirdly hard. Everything was so clean and modern and perfect. Screens on the windows. No bugs. Crystal-clear, scalding-hot tap water.

But there was also a giant soaker tub in the bathroom off the master bedroom, and when I saw it, my spirits lifted. One thing I could definitely get comfortable with was a luxury tub soak. I hadn't had one of those in months, and fantasies of soaking away the travel grime from under my toenails instantly wooed me.

I drew the water as hot as I could stand it, shed my clothes, pinned up my hair, and for the next half-hour I indulged gratefully in the soak of the year. Very gratefully. I even texted my sister from the bath, although she hadn't replied to my other text yet.

Me: I forgot to tell you I love you. XO

I even forgave her, officially, for firing me, though I didn't text that part.

As the bath gradually relaxed me, I lazily brainstormed what I might do for the family on the fridge; the nice people who were letting me stay here for free. The Johnsons. That's what I'd dubbed them in my head. The Johnsons seemed to like their plants; maybe I could check the planters on the driveway for weeds? There wasn't exactly much to clean. The place was spotless. Maybe I could whip up a batch of veggie chili or some muffins and leave it for them in the freezer?

I texted Liv again, to ask if she knew how soon the Johnsons would be back.

Then I texted a few friends in town, putting out the feeler for any jobs that might come up. Unfortunately, I really didn't know many people who could get me work in Vancouver anymore. Even though I was from here, originally, and I still had some friends here, I'd really built my photography career on my travels; my work contacts were all over the world.

And it wasn't as if high-paying clients were easy to come by, no matter where I was.

Damn. The more time passed, I was really regretting my fuck up at today's shoot. It didn't exactly bode well for Liv hiring me in the future. If she wasn't my sister, she'd probably never hire me again. I bitched about it, and I did kind of hate the work, but the fact was I *needed* her to hire me when I came to town.

Shit.

I'd really have to kiss butt on this to get her to forgive me.

Or, maybe I'd impressed Dylan Cope so much—in the three minutes he'd known me, before I was fired—that he'd hire me? Maybe he needed a personal photographer to follow him around and take photos of him looking gorgeous?

Dare to dream.

That thought got me pretty impatient to look through the images I'd shot today. Because ultimately, I'd mostly photographed Dylan. Of course, I'd figured I had the rest of the afternoon to photograph everything else. *Oops.* I knew I'd gotten carried away, experimenting with my shutter speed as the whole scene dazzled me—capturing ultra-crisp images with his hair and drops of sweat frozen in the air, and artfully blurred ones, his flailing arms and the gleaming cymbals colorful smears of motion. But I'd definitely gotten some gorgeous shots.

I was pretty damn sure I'd gotten some epic ones.

I knew I should go through them and send the best selects to Liv as soon as possible. They'd want them for social media and stuff. And I didn't need to give them any reason to decide I wasn't worth the paycheck after all.

I decided to get out of the bath and get to work before I turned into a prune, and started letting the water out. It was getting cold anyway. Over the sound of the water gurgling down the drain and the water splooshing off my body as I stood up, I thought I heard a noise. Like a door closing or something.

I froze. Naked.

The water gurgled down the drain, but there was no other sound from the house. The bathroom door was ajar, and I waited for a moment.

What I was gonna do if someone suddenly appeared, I didn't know. All I could really do was stand here, dripping.

Then I shook it off and stepped out of the bath. No one was here but me. I was just creeping myself out.

I toweled off, digging through my backpack with one hand to find some fresh panties and a T-shirt to throw on. Maybe there was fire wood? I could make a fire in the fireplace in the living room and look through the photos on my laptop there, figure out something for dinner...

I dropped the towel, panties in hand, and I didn't even hear him —but I full-on screamed when I saw him: a man in black suddenly filling the doorway.

"Holy *FUCK*," he growled. He stopped short—and some innate spidey-sense told me I'd scared the shit out of him. The hairs standing up all over my body quickly declassified him from rapist-murderer to hapless homeowner.

Holy fuck was right.

It was Ashley Player.

I'd already swiped the damp towel from the floor and was scrambling to cover myself with it.

"Oh. It's you," he said, sounding weirdly disappointed.

Fucking seriously?

Did he just see me naked?

Too shocked for my brain to function properly, I fired back, "Oh, it's *you*," with as much distaste as possible.

"Uh, yeah," he said as his gaze scraped over me. "This is my house."

"Where the hell are the Johnsons?"

"Huh?"

"Those nice people on the fridge!"

"That's my aunt Ginny and my uncle Joe. And my cousin." He was looking at me like I was a crazy person, but he was also staring at all my embarrassing nakedness like he didn't give one fuck that it was rude. My bare arms, my legs; everywhere there was skin, he was looking.

Like he didn't already see enough?

"They don't live here?"

"If they did, that would make it okay for you to break in and take a bubble bath?"

"I didn't break in," I said between clenched teeth. "I used the spare key." My face was heating up, and I knew I was turning red. There weren't any fucking bubbles in the bath, but it hardly warranted pointing out. "Liv sent me."

"Liv sent you?"

"Yes! There must've been some misunderstanding. She thought you—the homeowner—wasn't here right now."

"Well, I'm here right now."

"I see that." I was clutching the towel to myself, still feeling grossly naked even though all my private goods were covered. It was the way he just stood there, staring at me, like he could still see *everything*. "Um, if you can give me a minute, I'll just get my stuff and clear out."

"There's no ferry 'til tomorrow," he said gruffly, crossing his arms over his chest.

"What?!"

"Two ferries every day. Eight and six. You must've come on the six o'clock. Next ferry is at eight in the morning."

Holy fuck again.

I was gonna fucking murder Liv.

"Um, okay." No big deal. I could sleep anywhere, right? I'd slept outside, in way worse weather than this. "Well... do you mind if I just take the porch? If you have an extra blanket that would be great, but I can make do on the little wicker couch thing out there—"

"Just stay," he grunted, looking annoyed. "Use the guest room." He swiped a couple of things off the edge of the sink—razor, maybe, and some other guy-grooming stuff. "I'll sleep next door." He spared me another glance. Or rather, scowl. "Come over if you need food. I don't stock the kitchen." Then he stalked out. Seconds later, I heard a door slam.

Shit.

I peeked out into the bedroom; I didn't see him and I couldn't hear him in the house. Then I got dressed, quick, and took a look around.

He was definitely gone.

How the hell did he get here? He definitely wasn't on that ferry I was on. A private boat, then. One he clearly wasn't gonna offer to drive me back to the city on.

At least he wasn't kicking me out on my ass, so that was something. It was dark out now, and the temperature would be dropping fast.

I opened the fridge—sneering at the nice couple in the photo, who'd duped me—and discovered he wasn't lying. The fridge was entirely empty. Other than a bottle of ketchup, a bottle of mustard, an almost-empty jar of dill pickles, and a bunch of random beers that filled up the produce drawers.

What the hell? Liv had told me, quote, *Don't worry about food.* Which meant I hadn't brought any with me.

Maybe humiliating me and starving me was payback for my shitty performance at today's shoot?

I helped myself to a pickle and shut the fridge. I figured Ashley Player owed me at least as much for staring at me like that. The vivid memory made me full-on shiver.

Gross.

It also made me wonder if he liked what he saw when he saw me naked... which was all kinds of fucked up.

Because who the fuck cared if he liked—or didn't like—what he saw?

As I looked around the house now, evidence of him was everywhere. This was such a bachelor pad. Why hadn't I seen it? There were no little-boy toys in the second bedroom. The bathroom was stocked with dude magazines. Big, sparse leather furniture and plaid linens were abound. There wasn't a feminine item to be found.

I drew the line at opening his bedroom drawers, but I did open his closet. Nothing but dude clothes, and very little of it. A couple of black T-shirts and a hoodie hung up, and some jeans folded on the floor. Maybe Liv was right; he never really used this place.

At least he'd let me stay the night instead of evicting my ass. He wasn't exactly nice about it, though. More like I was a major imposition. Which I supposed I was. Unintentionally.

I tidied up his bathroom and cleaned out the tub, so there was no trace of my trespass left. I put my backpack in the second bedroom, stewing as I called my sister and she didn't answer her damn phone. Then I dug a half-eaten granola bar out of my bag, the only food I had with me. I ate it, and just felt more hungry.

I checked the time; it was almost seven-thirty. I hadn't eaten since noon.

I tried Liv's number again. She didn't answer. Very possibly she was working late. Or ignoring me?

This time, when the call went to voicemail, I said, "Is this because of that time I told Kelly Bannerman that you were straight, and she started dating that blonde girl, and you got all sad for like the whole summer? Because I was eleven years old when I did that. If this is payback, well played. When I catch the ferry back tomorrow, we will have words. Oh yes, we will have words."

As I hung up, my stomach rumbled and Ashley Player's words replayed in my head. *I'll sleep next door. Come over if you need food.*

Yeah. Fat fucking chance.

I had no idea what was "next door" other than Ashley Player himself, but that was plenty of a deterrent. I hardly felt like spending an evening with him and his asshole friends.

Better to starve.

On second thought, I took one of his beers out to the front porch and enjoyed it in the twilight as I sorted through the images from the Underlayer shoot on my laptop. I was hardly gonna ask Ashley if he had a Wi-Fi password I could use, so I snooped around the house until I found his modem and lifted the password from the sticker on the bottom, so I could get online.

As I uploaded the images to the cloud, I helped myself to another beer. I stared at a couple of the photos I'd taken of Dylan in his dressing room—by far the best ones. Other than converting a few of them to black-and-white and tweaking the contrast a bit, they needed zero retouching. I sent the very best of them along with the other ones to Liv.

I doubted Underlayer would be interested in those photos, since they didn't show off their ridiculous rock star set and lighting, but I wanted Liv to see what I was doing in Dylan's dressing room. To see that it wasn't all for nothing. That I had the talent, if not the other skills necessary for today's job.

Then I had another beer.

I flipped through some of Ashley Player's shitty guy magazines, checking out the photography. More photos of hot girls, cars and music equipment than I could ever want to peruse.

Then I went to bed, mildly drunk and hangry.

CHAPTER FIVE

Amber

I WOKE up the next day to noise from next door.

And I was still hangry.

I rolled over and sat up, peering out the window. I couldn't see any house over the giant fence, just trees. But I could hear the super-loud, cheesy music. It was that old Trooper song that I only ever heard on classic rock radio stations in Canada. "The Boys In the Bright White Sportscar." I actually didn't mind hearing it. I'd never admit it to anyone—especially my sister—but it felt kinda nice waking up in my own country. I did it so rarely, after all.

I could also hear a few men shouting, laughing, and the sound of a ball bouncing against the ground and banging against the wooden fence. It sounded like they were shooting hoops.

I rubbed my eyes. Was that Ashley over there? Didn't he have anything better to do than clown around on a Friday morning? Come to think of it, since when did rock stars get out of bed before noon anyway?

I checked my phone. Okay, maybe not before noon. It was already close to one in the afternoon.

Which was when I realized my alarm hadn't gone off, and my jet-lag had totally screwed me.

I quickly checked the settings. Yup, I'd definitely set my phone alarm last night—for six p.m., rather than a.m..

Fuck me.

I'd missed the fucking morning ferry.

There were almost five hours to kill until the next one.

I groaned at my idiocy, tossed the stupid plaid blanket and black sheet off, and got dressed. I picked out the most flowery thing in my bag, remembering Ashley's apparent distaste for the rosebuds on my blouse yesterday. It was a maxi dress, ankle-length and somewhat figure-hugging, with a pretty pattern of pink and red peonies, and spaghetti straps. I washed my face, brushed my teeth, finger-combed my wavy hair, and filled up my water bottle.

I made the bed and erased every trace of myself from the house, like I'd never even been here. Then I slipped on my sandals and my cardigan sweater, picked up my camera and my backpack, and headed out.

I spent the next three hours exploring the small island, very slowly, on foot, taking photos along the way. I found several trails snaking through the trees and followed them all. I glimpsed several houses tucked back in the trees off the winding road that looped around the island, and a couple of cars drove past me, but I didn't see another person.

The tiny shack of a general store by the marina was closed.

By the time I made it all the way around the loop, my empty stomach was totally pissed at me.

There was no noise coming from next door, but as I approached the fancy iron gate on the only driveway in the vicinity of Ashley's, just around the bend in the road, there was a car parked inside. A silver BMW with a license plate that read HONEY.

There was also a giant black-and-chrome Harley, parked off to the side, with an anatomically-impossible pinup girl painted on it.

My stomach rumbled.

I sighed.

Grudgingly, I tried the gate. It opened with a little push and I drifted inside. The driveway coiled around the yard and slightly uphill toward the house—and this one *was* a palace. It had the same darkish stain to the wood, the frames around the windows and doors painted green, but it was probably four times the size of Ashley's house next door.

I knocked on the door, and groaned inwardly when Ashley answered. I really tried to smile, but it didn't happen.

He looked me over, his blue eyes scanning my dress, then my face; he definitely looked at my chest before looking me in the eye, but he probably did that to every female. Actually, he looked damned disappointed to see me. Again.

I opened my mouth to speak, but he got there first.

"Starving, huh?" he said, correctly assuming that the threat of starvation was the only reason I'd shown up here. "Thought you were on the morning ferry."

"Missed it," I said, feeling like a royal idiot. How many times did I have to fuck up in front of this guy? "I tried the store by the docks, but it was closed."

"Shuts down in September for the season," he informed me.

"Right." Liv really might've mentioned that. She might've mentioned a lot of things.

However, she hadn't yet called me back, even though I'd sent her a series of increasingly irritated and bewildered texts.

Without another word, Ashley turned and walked back into the house. He left the door open, which I took to be his warm and fuzzy way of inviting me in.

I stepped inside and set my backpack down, but I kept my camera with me. The familiar weight of it in my hand and the strap wrapped around my wrist grounded me, gave me comfort; had gotten me through many an awkward social situation. Hopefully it would come through for me on this one.

"Kitchen's in the back," I heard Ashley mutter from somewhere up ahead of me. "Help yourself." When I looked up, he'd already vanished.

As I moved deeper into the house, the entryway with its sweeping staircase opened up into an expansive living room with a massive stone fireplace and a couple of leather couches. A sparkly blonde woman was perched on one of them.

Honey, no doubt.

She was chatting animatedly at Ashley, who was standing by the other couch, sipping on a bottle of beer and half-listening. Even though he wasn't looking at me, I could feel his rigid awareness of my presence from across the room. Kind of like he had a thorn in his ass he was trying to ignore.

Neither one of them acknowledged me.

Was this her house? I had no idea. But I didn't exactly feel oceans of welcome pouring over me.

I caught the scent of something roasting, both revolting and torturous. I really was hungry as hell, because it smelled like meat and I still wanted to eat it.

Maybe this was a mistake...

The ferry would board in about another hour, and there was a little cafe onboard. Surely I could get a muffin there or something. Meanwhile, I could starve for another hour...

I was just trying to decide if I should backpedal the hell out of here or stay and let myself go carnivore, just this once, when I heard footsteps.

I turned to find an unforgettable redhead strolling down the big staircase toward me. I actually felt my jaw drop in awe, but I was far too distracted to close it.

His faded jeans were zipped up but not buttoned. He was casually pulling a T-shirt over his ridiculously sculpted abs, in no particular hurry to cover his glorious nakedness. And his hair was slightly damp, like he'd just showered.

Somehow, out of the context of the commercial shoot, and without all the oil and makeup and hoopla... he was even sexier.

Was this his house?

The blonde bounced up off the couch and strode to meet him, but Dylan Cope greeted me first. Actually, his face kinda lit up when he saw me.

"Amber Paige Malone," he said, reaching for my elbow.

"Uh... hi." How did he know my full name?

Did he ask Liv about me?

He leaned in and I did the same... because when a man like that leaned in, you leaned in. He gave me a lingering cheek kiss that made the blood rush to my face. Oh... God... He smelled like spicy man-soap and oranges. I was so fucking hungry, I salivated.

"How'd you sleep?" He was still speaking to me as he greeted the blonde, his eyes on me as he kissed her cheek—and clearly, she didn't care for that, her smile kinda freezing on her face.

"Great," I said. "I love waking up to Trooper."

Dylan's answering grin was dazzling and sort of crooked, and up close, his green-gold irises were nothing short of mesmerizing; they actually sparkled when he chuckled.

I looked away. I could feel Ashley watching from across the room, his tense, unwelcoming vibe the polar opposite of Dylan's warm, laid-back manner.

"Whatever it takes," Dylan said, his voice a low rumble on the end of that chuckle. "I know how hard it is to drag a woman out of Ash's bed."

Ash's bed?

A full-body shiver of revolt rippled through me and my back straightened. I was in Ashley's *guest* bed. Alone.

Major fucking difference.

But when Dylan aimed his gorgeous grin at Ashley, I let it slide; he seemed to be ribbing him more than me anyway.

Ashley just scowled and drank his beer.

"Come on," Dylan said to me, "I'll show you around." And the blonde's pasted-on smile slipped a fraction. Unlike her, he seemed totally unfazed that I'd just turned up in his living room. "Oh, Amber. This is my realtor, Susanna. Susanna, Amber is a photographer."

As Susanna forced herself to acknowledge me, I was pretty sure we both felt Dylan Cope's gaze lingering on the curves of my body in my long dress.

"And she's talented as hell," he added.

"How nice." Susanna offered me a limp, cool handshake, as I wondered what he was basing that compliment on. The one photo I'd shown him in his dressing room? Or had Liv described me like that?

Had he looked me up?

"Speaking of photography," he went on, casually, "would be great to get some shots of the house, now that it's finished, don't you think?"

At that, Susanna lit right up. Probably thinking this meant more money for her when she used said photos to advertise the house and make a sale—and help Dylan Cope into yet another extravagant property. "I'll send you the portfolios of the top three real estate photographers in the Vancouver area," she told him, steering him away from me, clearly dismissing both me and my camera.

As they headed from the room, Ashley's gaze crashed into mine. He said nothing.

I followed Dylan and Susanna out.

Ashley didn't.

The house was three levels, if you included the walk-out basement—which was empty except for a gym area on one side and a massive drum kit on the other—with four bedrooms, three-and-a-half bathrooms, and three wood-burning fireplaces. As we strolled through, Susanna elucidated on the incredibleness of everything. "The vaulted ceilings!" "The maple hardwood floors!" "The granite countertops!" According to her, the house was designed by one the "premier" architects on the northwest coast. It was new, had only been built this year, and had been customized to Dylan's—"Brilliant!"—specifications.

Clearly, she'd sold him the property and was bent on kissing his ass for more of his business—and probably, a place in his bed.

But honestly, I was far more curious about her features than the house's. I'd always been mildly intrigued by women like Susanna/Honey, the same way I was intrigued by exotic creatures from faraway lands that I'd only glimpsed in magazines.

She wore immaculate designer clothes—I recognized the symbol on the gold buckle of her Gucci belt—with (very) high heels, diamond earrings that glittered when she laughed, and heavy but flawless makeup that could've been airbrushed on, not a pore in sight. She had extreme highlights in her perfectly round-brush-blow-dried hair (did she come straight from the salon?), blinding-white, perfect teeth, and an industrial-strength gel manicure. Her gym-toned body was overly tanned for October above the 49th parallel. Her lips were collagen-plumped, her forehead unnaturally smoothed in a way that suggested Botox.

And, rather predictably, she had breast implants.

Even the world's best pushup bra couldn't give you cleavage like that. Especially when you weren't wearing one.

By way of contrast—not that I was comparing, per se—everything on my body, other than my underwear, was second-hand, from the cardigan I'd picked up at a thrift store in Montreal to the dress I'd found at a clothing swap, and my sandals couldn't have been flatter if they were made of paper. I was fairly certain I owned a bottle of foundation purchased maybe seven years ago, before I went on my first overseas trip, which had dried up somewhere, maybe in Liv's guest bathroom? My hair was air-dried and finger-tussled. My teeth were, you know, teeth-colored, and my eyeteeth were sort of fangy when I smiled. (A couple of guys had told me, over the years, that they were sexy. I chose to believe it.) I hadn't worn nail polish since I was twelve. I had unsightly tan lines from my bikini. I was also pretty sure I was getting permanent squinty lines from always having one eye closed while looking through a camera, and I'd one day have very lopsided wrinkles.

As for my boobs, I was rocking a naturally conservative B-cup. My breasts were round but kinda flat, so the bra was actually optional depending on the top I was wearing. But no one was ever gonna accuse me of having implants.

In summary, Susanna/Honey belonged in Dylan Cope's expensive, custom-designed luxury home.

I did not.

I felt weirdly naked standing next to her in the enormous,

gleaming kitchen, even though she was showing much more skin than I was in her slit skirt and plunging camisole-that-barely-passed-as-an-actual-shirt.

As we came full-circle to the living room and stood before the huge wall of windows overlooking the back deck, she seemed perturbed by my lack of enthusiasm, as if I was being rude in my silence. There was an awkward pause when she finished babbling about the hardwood deck, as she seemed to be waiting for me to say something.

Finally, I looked at Dylan and managed, "Um... congratulations on all your money?"

It was kind of like saying to a beautiful person, *Congratulations on your face.* Like what was I supposed to do? Weep with admiration because he was grossly rich?

Dylan grinned.

Susanna looked revolted, like I'd said something vulgar. But I really wasn't dissing Dylan Cope or his house. I was pretty sure it would be awesome to be rich, just like it would be awesome to be as staggeringly beautiful as he was.

But here was the thing: I'd just spent the last year traveling around South America, where I'd become sensitized to an altogether different kind of richness, a different kind of beauty. As I looked around Dylan's home, all I saw was the kind of beauty I had no idea what to do with, other than, maybe, take photos of it.

Surface beauty.

I'd become much more accustomed to seeking out the deeper beauty in things with my camera. Subtler beauty. Meaningful beauty. Beauty that moved you. Beauty that, sometimes, you had to work for. When you looked at my best work, I hoped you'd *feel* what was going on inside the image, or just beyond the frame. Each photo told a larger story, or hinted at a story. It attempted to engage you.

What it didn't do was smack you in the face with its walk-through closets and floor-to-ceiling windows and exorbitant fireplaces... Or its washboard abs and dazzling chestnut-red-gold hair.

Well, unless it was a photo of Dylan Cope.

I followed them outside, onto the giant deck that wrapped around the back of the house. We were above the ground, maybe a dozen feet. One of those swimming pools that looked like a giant rectangular hot tub, used for swimming laps in place, was sunk right into the wooden deck. Cushy lounge furniture was arranged around the pool and the outdoor fireplace.

So make that *four* fireplaces.

Yeah. It would be pretty awesome to be rich.

Then I looked up... and for the first time, I actually *saw* the view.

As I attempted to start to process it, my jaw dropped, the same way it had at the sight of Dylan's naked abs.

It was like I'd just stepped into the middle of a photo spread in *National Geographic*.

The house looked out through an opening in the trees, over a rocky point that jetted out into the water. The water lapped at the rocks, birds chirped, a heron floated on the water. And then... nothing but water and the humps of islands, misty in the distance. And the mainland, erupting in hazy mountainous splendor, all blue-gray and majestic along the horizon.

It was a nature-lover's porn.

And I started to get it.

I leaned up against the deck railing, gazing out, breathing in the fresh coastal air. Right here... *this* was deep, profound, resonant beauty.

I glanced over at Dylan. He was standing a few feet away, watching me.

Behind him, Ashley had stepped out onto the deck, beer in hand, and stood half-listening as Susanna elucidated about the size of the property and the seventeen types of trees that could be found on it. If she'd just stop talking, it would really improve things. But even so...

This was why Dylan lived here? For this feeling...?

I looked out again, over the water, and I could feel it. Like you were standing on the edge of the world, and the rules no longer applied to you.

It was a sensation akin to total freedom.

I'd experienced this same feeling a few times in my life; always on my travels. I understood the pull and the power of it. And I understood, deeply, the lure to feel it again.

The need to pursue it, across the globe and back if you had to... again and again.

"You probably think I'm crazy," Dylan said. He spoke in a low voice that only I could hear, and when I looked at him, I found he'd shifted closer to me. His green-gold eyes locked on mine. "Just another crazy-rich rock star with too much money to burn while people go hungry elsewhere in the world?" He leaned on the rail and looked out over the water.

"People go hungry right here, where you live," I informed him.

"And believe me, I do what I can to change that." He glanced at me again. "And maybe I am crazy. But there's a method in my madness."

A method?

He was saying... there was a purpose in all of this? Beyond just living large?

"Hey boss, I'm heading out."

I turned at the sound of a man's voice, to find Connor stepping out onto the deck.

"Gonna catch the six o'clock..." he said. Then he saw me and lifted his chin in my direction with a cute, white-toothed grin. "Amber Paige Malone. How'd you slip past me?"

I shrugged, but I smiled, too. It was kinda nice to see a friendly face. In the brief time it had taken for him to let me into the Underlayer shoot and then escort me out of it, I'd come to like Connor the security biker, grudgingly. "What can I say? You let your guard down, Con."

He raised an eyebrow at Dylan. "Should I pat her down?" Then he looked me over, but he wasn't serious.

At least, I was pretty sure he wasn't.

"You could try," Dylan said, seemingly amused as they both stared at me.

I glanced at Ashley, suddenly feeling his eyes on me. Next to him, Susanna had stopped talking, and she was staring at me, too.

Ashley turned away, heading over to the farthest point of the V-shaped deck, where it overlooked the rocky promontory below. He leaned on the railing and drank his beer while Dylan and Connor gave each other a dude hug.

"Let Jude know when you need me, brother," Connor said.

"Yup."

Then, with a little salute to me, Connor took off.

"'Pat her down'?" I said, when Dylan turned back to me. "Do I look that dangerous?" I swirled my long, flowery dress around my legs for effect.

"You'd be surprised," he said, looking me over with a smirk. "I've been mobbed and molested by girls much more innocent-looking than you." Then he winked at me and my toes fucking curled. The guy was charming as hell, and effortlessly so.

And if I wasn't mistaken... he was flirting with me?

"Sounds rough," I said, doing my best to flirt back. It was kinda funny, actually, that such a big dude needed security. Dylan Cope was well over six feet, with muscles for miles. But then again, a mob was a mob...

"Tough job, but someone's gotta do it?" he said.

"Yo, Dylan." Ashley called over, and Dylan gave me another lingering look before heading over to join him at the railing.

In the distance, Connor's Harley rumbled to life. I heard it ease out of the driveway before roaring away, and unfortunately, it was so loud I couldn't overhear what Dylan and Ashley were talking about.

"So what's your story?"

I jumped a little; Susanna had popped up beside me. I didn't even hear her high heels coming.

"No story." I turned to look out over the water, keeping the guys in the corner of my eye. I wondered if Ashley was telling Dylan what a bitch I was. "I'm just a photographer."

"Mm-hmm. And I'm just his realtor."

I didn't even want to know what that meant. But she had my attention; I was curious what she might know about Dylan Cope. "You sold him this place? His dream home?"

"Oh, it's not *Dylan's* dream home," she said, as she touched up her lipstick in a mirrored compact she'd whipped out of somewhere.

I looked over at the guys. The motorcycle had faded away, but Ashley was speaking too low for me to hear. Dylan was grinning. Somehow, he didn't seem to find Ashley quite the asshole that I did. And even though I didn't know them, it was easy enough to interpret that look. They were close. Best bros, maybe.

"It's Ashley's dream home?" I ventured.

"Dylan bought it because he could afford the land on the point," Susanna said simply, snapping her compact shut.

Which implied... that Ashley couldn't?

"So." Susanna rolled her lips together, blending her lipstick as she looked me over—kind of the way I'd first looked at her. Like she couldn't quite fathom my fashion or grooming choices. But she seemed to conclude that I was no threat to her; I could practically hear her claws retracting as she sized me up. "You're probably wondering where you fit into all of this. The short answer is, you don't." She laid her hand on my arm. "That's free advice, hon," she added, like she'd done me a favor. "Though Con seems to like you. Maybe you have a chance there. You know, he's a little more..." She gave me and my camera another once-over. "... Working class."

Then she turned and strode over to Dylan and Ashley in her high heels—as both anger and embarrassment curdled in my stomach.

Because she was wrong about me... but also, kind of right.

I just watched as she laughed at whatever Ashley was saying, shaking her blonde hair down her back, and fused herself to Dylan's elbow again.

CHAPTER SIX

Ash

I KNEW she was trouble from the first fucking instant I laid eyes on her. Even when I thought she was just some fangirl, outside the studio gate, I knew.

You'd better believe I knew trouble in the form of a cute, stuck-up hippie chick when I saw it.

But this one was tenacious.

When I saw her up close, camera in hand, trying to get into Dylan's dressing room—I could see how right I'd been.

She was far too fucking cute.

She was also far too much Dylan's type, not nearly enough of mine, and she had an attitude problem to boot. I wasn't gonna claim that I didn't have attitude of my own, but I wasn't the one who was the problem here.

The fact that she was a photographer only made her more of a problem. And the more I'd seen her in action, the more of a problem she was becoming.

This girl had to *go*.

For some reason, though, everywhere I turned, there the fuck she was. In Dylan's dressing room. In Dylan's house. In my fucking bathtub.

I swiped another beer from Dylan's fridge and went to stand in his front doorway, looking out.

So what's your problem with her? he'd asked me, last night, when I came back to his place and told him I'd just found her in my bathroom.

Liv's fucking sister is in my house, I'd announced, after slamming the door behind me and heading downstairs to find him in the gym.

She's here already? he'd replied casually, from where he stood swinging a giant kettlebell.

Say what? I'd stopped dead in my tracks, staring at him.

I told Liv to send her over.

Why the fuck would you do that? I'd demanded, as if I didn't know.

He'd set the kettlebell down and took a slow drink of water, and looked at me like I had no reason to be irritated. *You never use your place anyway. You always just end up crashing here.*

I couldn't argue with that. But it was at that moment that I realized how bad this was shaping up to be.

And it was getting worse.

As I stood here, drinking my beer, I watched Dylan walk Susanna out to her car, stuff her inside, and send her on her way. Punctuality was suddenly important to him; he seemed pretty motherfucking bent on getting her onto that six o'clock ferry.

Amber, on the other hand, was parked in his living room.

Dylan had invited her to stay for dinner.

Though she'd tried, half-assedly, to turn down the invitation at first, she'd of course accepted, right in front of Susanna, which was at least part of the reason she'd accepted. Because when Dylan asked Amber to stay, he sure as shit didn't ask Susanna. Susanna didn't like that. Amber liked that Susanna didn't like that. She probably also liked that *I* didn't like it.

She probably also liked Dylan.

Why the fuck wouldn't she?

Then Dylan walked Susanna out, acting like he was oblivious to the whole dynamic. Either way, the message was clear to all.

Amber had snagged Dylan's interest. Susanna was on the next ferry.

At least, it was clear to all besides Amber. The girl didn't seem to have the first clue what she was really doing here, besides getting a free meal.

Dylan strolled back to the house as Susanna's car disappeared down the road, her HONEY license plate vanishing in an angry cloud of dust. He gave me a crooked, annoying smirk and patted my ribs as he strolled on past me to collect Amber from the living room.

I followed them, grudgingly, into the kitchen, barely able to resist rolling my eyes when he opened the fridge and asked her smoothly, "What can I get you to drink? I've got Prosecco." As if he ever drank anything besides beer and hard liquor.

"I don't know," Amber said lightly. "I don't think I've ever had it." I noticed her voice was a lot lighter when she spoke to him than it had been with me.

"Italian white wine," Dylan informed her, pulling a bottle from the fridge. "Bubbly. Kind of sweet. Perfect for you."

Now I did roll my eyes. At least my back was turned when I did it. I didn't wanna see it if he actually winked at her.

"Sounds good," Amber said softly, and I could just imagine the *Aw, shucks* blush blooming on her cheeks.

I started carving the roast I'd pulled out of the oven a few minutes ago, laying the meat out on a serving plate, as Dylan poured them two glasses of Prosecco. He knew better than to offer me that shit.

"Ash always stocks it in the fridge, for my mom and my sisters," Dylan explained. "They love this stuff."

"Well... that's thoughtful of him," Amber said, kind of fake-polite, like she was really forcing it.

"Yeah. That's Ash."

I couldn't even tell if he was being sarcastic or not.

I ignored them, scooping the roasted vegetables and sweet potatoes onto dinner plates for the three of us and laying the plates out on the island. If Dylan pulled a fancy tablecloth out of his ass and started clearing the dust off the dining room table, I was gonna have to say something. But he just pulled out a barstool at the island for Amber—right next to mine. She slipped off her sweater and sat down, and once she was seated, he slid onto a stool across from her.

I laid the platter of meat in the middle of the island, stabbed it with a serving fork, got myself another beer for backup, and sat down to unceremoniously start eating. I didn't wait for either of them, digging right in and tuning out their bullshit flirtatious small talk. Luckily, the roast was pretty good. I wasn't exactly a professional chef; Dylan couldn't cook to save his life, yet he ate like a Hoover, so I usually made sure he got fed. I didn't even mind being his fucking house bitch after everything the guy had done for me.

Least I could do was cook him a few meals and throw some pussy his way.

Good food. Hot chicks. Rock 'n' roll.

What the fuck else did we need?

All I really wanted in life was pretty fucking simple: me and Dylan Cope against the world. Touring. Partying. Casual hookups.

Mind-blowing sex.

And to never, ever fall for anyone again.

I was *not* fucking falling in love. I'd made that incredibly clear to him.

But there was no way in hell Dylan wasn't falling for this fucking girl with her flowery dress and her earnest eyes and the monumental chip on her hippie shoulder. She even smelled like flowers. Flowers and fucking gumdrops or something; I could smell it right over the roast and beer.

She smelled like fucking dessert.

I didn't even want to look at her pretty face. I'd managed to check out her ass, though. Unfortunately, it was as cute as the rest of her. I'd seen the rest, already, in my bathroom last night. Not for long, but long enough to get an eyeful of her firm tits, her hard pink nipples, and her toned legs. She was kinda bent over, so I didn't get a chance to see her pussy, but I definitely saw her legs.

I was just glad they weren't showing now; Dylan could get really fucking stupid at the sight of a nice pair of bare legs.

I glanced over at her.

She glanced back at me and narrowed her eyes.

Yup. I'd called it, from moment one.

Trouble.

Sure, Dylan attracted every sparkly Susanna wherever he went. They were dripping off him backstage, panting in heat whenever he strolled into a party, and he'd never exactly complained about it. We'd both enjoyed our share of Susannas, and we'd often enjoyed them together.

But I knew the kind of girl Dylan Cope *really* liked. The kind that made him lose his fucking shit.

The kind that rendered him blind-drunk infatuated, hallucinating rainbows and shooting stars and forgetting where he left his keys. And it wasn't the kind that just drove off in the silver BMW.

I knew what he wanted.

I knew what he *needed*.

And Amber Malone was it. It couldn't have been any clearer to me if she'd had *Property of Dylan Cope* tattooed on her forehead.

I watched her, eating her dinner, like the enemy had fucking landed in my backyard. Eating her roast veggies and potatoes as she listened with rapt attention to Dylan, who was telling her all about the workshop we'd just built in the garage—like she gave a shit.

There was no roast on her plate.

Christ, was she a vegetarian? If Dylan went veggie over this girl, I was gonna lose it.

I stared at her. Did he seriously think he was gonna hook her up with *me*?

I'd wondered, when he kept looking at her at the Underlayer shoot, at the side of the stage… and when he'd watched her in his dressing room while she photographed him, all sweaty and practically naked…

And I was pretty sure I knew what he was thinking.

That he wanted her—for both of us.

He thought the fact that she was rubbing me wrong meant that she was rubbing me *right*.

Knowing Dylan, he was probably even gonna be all altruistic about it, on account of my recent sexual drought, and let me have her first.

It'd really be no sweat off the back of his annoyingly patient self.

I'd seen Dylan Cope in action when he actually *wanted* a girl, and he could be crafty as fuck about it. All nonchalant, with his laid-back, couldn't-give-a-fuck attitude. Strolling around with his six-pack out, flashing easy smiles, all the while his brain was working overtime on every-which-fucking-way he was gonna get her into his bed.

The man could be patient as fuck.

And even though I knew all of this, I'd seriously underestimated the level of trouble this was gonna turn out to be.

The trouble *she* was gonna be.

"So Liv said you do travel photography?" he was saying, when I actually tuned back into their conversation. "Is that like landscapes and tourism stuff?"

"Um. When did Liv say that?"

"After you got fired," I cut in bluntly.

She glanced at me, but then her light-green eyes returned to Dylan and stayed there. "Well, most people think I'm a travel photographer, because I travel so much and work as I go. And my sister knows better, but she usually shorthands to 'travel photographer.' And that's okay. But actually, I specialize in environmental portraiture."

"What is that?" I asked flatly. "Like ducks covered in oil spill?"

"Um, no," she said, throwing me another cool glare. "It's photographing people in their environment. Like, if it's a farmer tilling the land in North Dakota," she explained to Dylan, pretty much ignoring me, "or a pottery maker in Peru, or a bunch of protestors at a march in Paris, I just try to keep as uninvolved as possible."

"So it's like journalistic stuff?" he asked.

"Sometimes. The end use really varies. It just depends where I can find a buyer for the images. But, you know, it's not like I'm photographing the Kardashians, so my images aren't always in demand..."

She took a sip of wine, then licked her lip. I tracked Dylan's eyes tracking her tongue as she did it, and my dick fucking swelled.

Christ.

"One editor I worked with called me 'paparazzi for the non-famous,'" she went on, "but I don't think that's fair. I don't shoot people without telling them, then make money selling their images. There's very little connection between me and the subject, but that's just so I have as little influence on what's happening in the photo as possible. I always introduce myself after I get the shot, if not before, and let them know what I'm planning to do with it. But I mostly sell to small online magazines."

"That pay well?" I asked, looking to curb her babbling. The girl getting all passionate about her work was hardly gonna kill Dylan's interest in her.

"No," she said, this time not even looking me in the eye. "Not really. But anyway. As I was saying, I'm far from paparazzi and it's not always journalism, either. I'm totally babbling, I know."

"No worries," Dylan said. "Babble all you want."

"It's my passion," she said, picking at her potatoes. "I have a hard time shutting up about it. And, um, you seemed interested."

"We are," Dylan answered for both of us.

Fucking annoying thing was, he really was.

"The thing is, as you kind of found out, what I don't love is people posing for me," she said. "Being hyperaware that I'm photographing them at the moment I make the photograph. Those are my least favorite types of shoots. Like the stuff Liv does. I really shouldn't have taken that job. It was just supposed to be behind-the-scenes, candid stuff, which is fine, but... I should've known. It wasn't the right job for me." She cocked her head a little, her green eyes locking with his, all passionate earnestness and dick-hardening charm. "Plus, I was in kind of a bad mood. I'm sorry I was so... rude. I didn't mean to be rude at your shoot."

Dylan just dismissed that with a shake of his head. "I get it. You would've done it differently, if it was your shoot."

"Yeah, well. I would've just filmed you in your environment. But I get that's not the vision they had for their underwear..." She trailed off.

"He's a drummer," I said. "The stage and the drum kit are his environment."

"I disagree," she said, sparing me another cool glare. Amazing, how her mood could shift temperature by several hundred degrees in the span of a nanosecond as she looked between us.

"How so?" Dylan asked.

"They didn't hire you because you're a drummer," she told him. "They hired you because you're a 'rock god.'" She shrugged, and one of the skinny straps of her dress fell off her shoulder. She didn't even seem to notice, and I stuffed down my groan with a forkful of roast as Dylan's gaze skimmed her tanned, slightly freckled shoulder... and her lacy pink bra strap. "I just would've tried to film you in an environment that expressed that. And preferably a real one, not some sound stage."

"Like a mountaintop cliff... or a bedroom?" he said, remembering what she'd said at the shoot.

"Right." Amber took a sip of her wine, and she was definitely fucking blushing. "I'd set you loose in one of those spaces and see what I could capture organically. And it would probably be the photos in-between the posed ones, when you weren't even aware I was still shooting, that would be the best ones."

Well, *fuck.*

Dylan was done. Hook, line, sinker. Fillet him and serve him up on a platter.

Not only was the girl hitting every hot button he had with her bright-eyed sincerity, but she was a fucking photographer, and talking about taking photos of him? Total dirty talk.

The guy had always been an exhibitionist.

Shit.

This was all happening way too fucking fast…

I watched them talking and flirting, and it all started to kinda blur together. I couldn't even hear what they were saying anymore. But I could see it all happening in front of me in weirdly slow yet too-fast motion…

Too. Fucking. *Fast.*

Yes, I'd expected him to go sniffing around. Checking in with Liv at the shoot, casually inquiring about her sister. And obviously, I knew he'd get Amber Malone on her back. The girl had an attitude, but I'd seen the way she looked at Dylan. She'd play the game, maybe she'd play it cool, but soon enough, she'd be giving it up to him. It really didn't take much. Dylan didn't even have to open his mouth to make a woman open her legs; I'd seen it too many times to count.

I'd never actually been jealous of another dude's skills with women until I met him.

But here was the other thing about Dylan Cope: when it came to women, he had some serious ADD. If this was any other girl, all I should've had to do was throw him off the scent. Whisk him off to the island and toss some flashy blonde pussy in his face.

But I'd underestimated that, too.

I did not expect him to blow Susanna off so easily after I'd invited her out here. After she'd dropped everything to come over on the morning ferry, and busied herself with her other clients on the island for most of the day, waiting on him, until I told her it was a good time to come over. Even when Amber had showed up in my bathroom, naked, I figured Susanna still had a fighting chance. Or at least, I managed to convince myself that her mile-long legs and juicy tits *might* have the power to eclipse Amber's natural appeal. Her sun-kissed hair and thrift store clothes. Her perky tits. The earnestness she wore as nakedly as the freckles on her face.

The girl had fucking *freckles*.

They were smattered faintly across the cutest nose in existence. And I wasn't even gonna get started on the tiny little pink nose piercing.

She also had a small tattoo inside her left wrist that I'd only just noticed; a few embellished letters or initials or something I couldn't quite read. Probably some stupid hippie thing. *Namaste* or some shit.

Made me wonder if she had any other tattoos on her body, though I kinda doubted it. Probably way too practical for that. Obviously, she took herself way too fucking seriously. She looked all clever and idealistic with her straight shoulders and short, bare fingernails. And when she was pissed, she twisted up her pretty lips and made an adorable little duck face. I'd seen it already, several times.

Add to that the thick, wavy hair just dusting her shoulders, the color of caramel melting at sunset, and the mesmerizing, light-green eyes, the little tan lines peeking out that made you want to undress her... She was a full foot shorter than Dylan, and as she gazed up at him now... *shit*. If she wanted Dylan's cock down her throat right now, she could have it. If he wasn't already, the guy was definitely gonna be hard for her in like five more seconds. All she had to do was—

Laugh.

I cringed as she fucking laughed at whatever clever shit Dylan had just said, tossing her head back, her light-green eyes sparkling, her canine teeth poking down a little longer than her other teeth... and Dylan fucking sprang wood. I knew he did. No way he couldn't. The girl had a sexy, infectious laugh and perfectly imperfect teeth, just like the rest of her.

Dylan's eyes caught mine as he sipped his wine. He raised one eyebrow a fraction, and I knew what he was thinking.

He was wondering if I was as hard as he was.

I totally was, but that was way the fuck beside the point.

Just because this was happening didn't mean I had to be involved.

No idea what I was gonna do to stop it either. I didn't exactly possess Susanna's assets, and if those weren't doing shit-all to diffuse the situation, I was fresh out of ideas. The blood rushing to my cock wasn't helping.

Wasn't exactly my fault, though, that Dylan getting turned on turned me on. I could no more help that than he was gonna be able to help falling for this girl, *if* she stuck around.

No way was I losing my wingman over some hippie chick with a perky little face and a bad attitude, though.

No way was he falling in love with this girl... and leaving me in the dust by the roadside.

Fuck that.

"Have you ever done any real estate photography?"

Wait.

What?

I shot him a look across the island, but he ignored me. I attempted to kick his foot, but he slid off his seat and reached to pour Amber another glass of wine. They were already hitting the bottom of the bottle.

"Um..." Amber looked stricken. Perhaps recalling Susanna and wondering if "real estate photography" included working "Honey" into the deal. She swallowed her mouthful of potato and washed it down with wine. "No."

"But you shoot people in their environment," Dylan said. "That must mean inside their homes sometimes."

"Sure..." she said.

"So you could take photos of my house."

What the fuck? What the hell did he need professional photos of his house for?

Short answer: he didn't. He just wanted to keep this girl around.

Badly.

"Well. Yes. I guess so. I mean..." She glanced around. "I have a tripod, and a wide lens. That's probably all I'd need..." She trailed off.

"Cool. It should take a few days, right? Then after that, we can see."

A few *days*?

And see *what*?

"You can stay at Ash's house. He's not using it anyway." He looked at me, deadpan. "Right?"

I drank my beer and said nothing. What could I say? The more I protested, the more he was gonna think I wanted her.

I made a noncommittal grunt and kept eating.

Amber looked from me to Dylan, clearly uncertain.

"Well. Um. How much does this gig pay?"

"I don't know. What's your day rate?"

"Well, I—"

"How much does that guy charge?" Dylan turned to me. "You know, that friend of Summer's. The photographer you guys hired on that Penny Pushers shoot last year."

"We hired him," I said, glaring at him a little, "because we had pro BMX guys doing tricks with us and he works with those guys a lot. I think he charges like three grand a day for his commercial stuff—"

"So three grand it is."

Amber's mouth, which was open, snapped shut. She pressed her lips together.

"Sound good?" Dylan was already heading to the fridge for another bottle of Prosecco.

Yeah. It sounded good. I was gonna go out on a limb and guess that a three-grand day rate was more than she'd expected.

"Okay," she said, still looking a little bewildered.

"Unless you think the rate should be higher," he said.

"Um. No. That rate is fair."

"Great. Then we can celebrate your new job." Dylan ripped off the foil and cracked open the bottle, topping up her glass with fresh bubbly.

"Well... okay then." She glanced at me, quickly, then lifted her glass, touching it to Dylan's. "Thank you. I look forward to working with you."

Jesus. Did she really think that's all this was? A job offer?

How fucking naive was this girl?

Dylan looked at me, his wine glass still out, but I turned away, swiping up some dishes and heading for the sink.

"Oh!" Amber exclaimed. "I wasn't finished with that—"

"Sorry," I said, dumping her half-eaten dinner in the sink along with mine. "Thought you were done." Then I stalked out like a prick, my skin practically crawling with irritation.

No doubt about it: I was allergic to the girl.

Dylan just chuckled in my wake. I rarely failed to entertain the guy. Usually the more surly I got, the more hilarious he found me.

The best friends were like that. Loved you, no matter what an asshole you were.

"I should probably stop drinking," I heard Amber say, just as she probably took another sip. I could already hear Dylan fixing her another plate. "You know, I'll want to get started early. Like sunrise-early, so I can get the early morning light."

"I'll be up," Dylan said, as if he'd *ever* been up at the ass-crack of dawn—unless he was still up from the night before.

I paused on my way out to the garage. I could see them through the cutout in the kitchen wall. Her, sitting up on her bar stool, back straight, cheeks flushed. And him, coy as a fucking rattlesnake, pretending not to notice how fucking pretty she was.

"I'll maybe start downstairs," she said, her keen green eyes gazing around. "Those big windows onto the backyard should let in gorgeous morning light..."

"I'll leave the door open," he said, casually. "You can let yourself in if I'm in the shower. I'll try to remember not to take a morning swim."

"Oh." Cute, batting eyelashes. "Why?"

"Because..." Killer, coy grin. "I like to swim naked."

"Oh!" She giggled, the Prosecco hitting her the way it was meant to, and Dylan sipped his wine. He tucked his hair behind his ear in that smooth way he did that made chicks cream.

I ground my fucking teeth and slammed out to the garage.

There was no possible way on Earth those two weren't fucking tonight.

Whatever.

Even if Dylan asked me—fucking *begged* me—to join in, I wasn't doing it. On motherfucking principle alone, that girl was not touching my dick.

I didn't care how long it'd been since I'd been laid—too long—or how cute she was, or how fucking amazing it might feel to sandwich her, naked, between Dylan's body and mine.

Dylan could just go ahead and fuck her himself.

Tomorrow, I'd just have to find some way to get her fired—again.

"I know you've been hurt…" Dylan said into the darkness.

It was late. Pitch-black outside, and all the lights were off.

Amber had stumbled back to my place a while ago, after polishing off that second bottle of Prosecco with Dylan and flirting with him like a horny schoolgirl on her first spring break, while he pretended not to notice. I still had no clue why he hadn't ended up balls-deep in her. But here he was, with me.

The two of us were laid out on the couches in his living room. We were watching *Shameless* on Netflix, but I could feel him looking at me.

I glanced over; he was shirtless, sprawled out on the leather, his reddish hair all lit up in the glow of the TV screen. He looked all motherfucking beautiful, and accessible to me in a way that he really wasn't. But if I let my mind wander a little, I could almost imagine…

That this was how life could be.

Dylan. Me.

Perfection.

Until he kept talking.

"Losing Elle..." he went on, and I fucking sighed. *Here the fuck we go again.* "Losing Summer. You've had other relationships that maybe didn't work out how you wanted them to. Your mom fucking left you. I get it." He counted off my relationship failures with annoying sympathy. "So this is what you do. You shut yourself down. You harden yourself. You make jokes, and when those don't work anymore, you get mean."

"Uh-huh," I grumbled and took a pull of my beer.

"You gonna tell me I'm wrong about that?"

"Nope. You're right. And I already know all this shit about myself, Oprah."

"So then you know that you're being an asshole to Amber because you feel threatened."

Yup.

"Because you're afraid you might actually like her," he went on, "and therefore she might actually hurt you."

Um, no. That would be where you're wrong.

"I told you," I said. "I'm not falling in love again. I was very clear about that shit."

"Right."

"I'm fucking serious. I start talking shit about going the distance with someone, picking out matching tattoos or whatever, you call Jude. You tell him to bring a gun. The two of you take me out back and you bury me in a fucking deep grave." Felt calming, actually, laying it out like that. I figured that Jude, Dirty's head of security, was the one person I knew who could be seriously counted on to bury a body if it came down to it.

Maybe I'd have to let Jude know the plan myself, though. Dylan was probably just gonna pussy out if he ever actually had to put a bullet in my head.

Even if it was a mercy kill.

"Uh-huh," he said. "Casual sex. No strings, right?"

"No strings."

"You think Susanna comes without strings?"

"I'm not fucking Susanna."

"Then you didn't invite her here for a three-way?"

"I invited her here for you." True. Whether or not it was gonna turn into a three-way was up for discussion.

"Hmmm." He took a swig of his beer and turned down the volume on the show so I couldn't even hear William H. Macy's drunken rant.

"Turn it the fuck up," I grumbled.

Instead, my best friend sat up, swung his legs off his couch and leaned forward on his knees, hitting me dead in the eyes with a rare ultra-serious expression. "Since Elle ditched your ass," he asked me, straight-up, "how many people have you had sex with?"

I rolled my eyes and drank some more beer. "A man can have a mourning period."

"She's not dead. She's alive and happy, and knocked up with Seth's baby."

"I'm aware."

He sighed and raised the volume back up. Barely.

But he just couldn't let it go.

"If sex is what you want, why aren't you having any?"

"Whip it out right now," I said, not looking at him. "I'm good to go."

Dylan ignored the invitation, like he always did. "Here's a better question. How come any woman who even gets close to feeling like a fit, you push her away?"

I grunted. "A fit for who?"

"I was flirting with her for *you*, you know."

"Fuck you."

I was watching the show, kind of, but I could still feel him watching me. "Just admit it. You like her."

"Who?" I looked at him, deadpan. "Susanna?"

He sighed and got up, stretching out his spectacular six-foot-five bod. "Christ, you're stubborn." He tossed the remote at me. "Get outta my house already. You go make an attempt to get laid, she might actually take you up on it. You know, if you stop scowling at her all the time."

I scowled and turned back to the show.

"C'mon, I'll let you have her." He strolled past me, scratching his ass, shoving down his sweats a bit as he did. "Assuming you remember how..."

"I remember." I watched him stroll on over to the stairs. His sweats now sat way-low on his sculpted, muscular butt, showing off a bit of crack. "You're such a fucking liar, you know that?"

He stopped at the bottom of the stairs. "Huh?"

"You're not gonna let me have her."

Dylan shrugged, then gave me one of his easy but sly-as-fuck smiles as he disappeared upstairs. I was pretty fucking sure I heard him say, "Probably not."

CHAPTER SEVEN

Dylan

JUST AFTER DAWN, I strolled down from my bedroom in my underwear, a little groggy, stretching. I was not used to getting up this early, but Ash was up, cooking breakfast; the house smelled of bacon and coffee. Lately, he'd made it his business to be up before me and cook for me, no matter what time it was.

As usual, the dude was probably drowning his sorrows in labor. Ever since his breakup with Elle, he'd been buried in one project or another.

First, it was some unnecessary modifications to his '68 Camaro. Then it was building the workshop in my garage.

Now he'd appointed himself my housewife.

Not that I was really complaining.

The morning light poured in through the east-facing windows as I wandered into the kitchen, seeking caffeine. Ash was wearing that ridiculous frilly apron Elle had given him as a joke. The fact that he was probably trying to keep the bacon grease off his clothes aside, I could've sworn he actually liked the thing.

"Morning."

"Yo."

"Amber here?"

"Downstairs," he muttered.

I glanced through the cutout in the kitchen wall, toward the steps that led downstairs. I couldn't hear anything, but the walk-out basement was pretty much one room. Probably wouldn't take her long to shoot it.

When I turned back to Ash, he was fussing over the sunny-side-up eggs in the skillet. Trying to look busy, avoid my questions. Like especially the one he knew for sure I was gonna ask.

I sighed, feeling exhausted already. All this bullshit of his was gonna start getting me down.

I poured us both a coffee. His black, mine with a splash of cream. I slid his mug over to him and he grunted a thanks.

I leaned against the counter and sipped my coffee, letting the caffeine do its thing, just trying to let Ash's bullshit slide.

It was getting harder to do by the day, though.

I didn't need or want any more bullshit. Any more complications. I was a simple dude. Really, there should be no problems in my life. No more fucking drama. No worries.

Dirty now had Seth Brothers, our original rhythm guitarist, back in the fold. Elle, our bassist, and Jesse, our lead guitarist, had both moved on, were happily in love—with Seth and Katie, respectively—since their own drama-inducing breakup last year. Which meant my band was finally *whole* again and we were moving forward, finally finishing up the songs for the new album. The documentary TV series we'd filmed about the process of searching for a rhythm guitarist, directed by Liv, would start airing before the end of the year, and the rough cuts that had been coming in, rapid-fire, for the band to view, were looking great.

Besides that, I'd just wrapped on the *Underlayer of the Gods* campaign for this year, and they'd contracted me for next season, again. I definitely didn't mind being a rock god. I'd keep that title as long as they'd let me. Gave me something to make Zane, my cocky-ass lead singer, jealous—even though he'd never admit to it.

To top it all off, I just got my best friend back. My wingman. Ash had finally gotten back in the saddle after losing Elle.

In theory.

At a glance, everything was as it should be.

But where was the fucking fun?

All I'd wanted this year was *this*. My life, back to normal. Me and Ash hanging out.

Partying.

Playing drums with my band.

And some fantastic sex wouldn't hurt.

Meeting someone who could hold my interest for longer than a few hot minutes; that would be the icing on the rock star cake. Someone who could also hold Ash's interest for longer than a few hot minutes, preferably. I wasn't looking for a girlfriend. More like the kind of girl I could share with Ash.

Someone to help me get him the fuck out of this epic slump he was in.

I watched him flip the eggs; he swore when the yolks broke. They always broke. My preferred style of eggs—over easy—were the bane of Ash's culinary existence. I watched him lose his shit and scramble them up in contempt, giving up.

Jesus, this was a bunch of bullshit.

Here we were, playing fucking house, with this super-cute chick downstairs, and all Ash could throw her way was attitude. I already knew from talking to her and talking to Liv—and from a little research of my own—that Amber Paige Malone was smart, talented, and single. After feeling her out over dinner and drinks last night, I was also pretty sure she was down to fuck—or would be, if Ash would just stop being such an asshole. But he was still playing it ice-cold.

Nothing new, right? Lately, we just couldn't seem to hit our groove with any woman we met.

At least, Ash couldn't hit his groove. And I was starting to feel bad hooking up without him. Like I was leaving him behind.

But what was I gonna do, hold his dick for him and help him put it in?

Something was off with him. Way the fuck off. He just wasn't happy, like he couldn't let himself be happy or something. And that was hard for me. Happy was my normal. All this angsty-broody-miserable bullshit was really gonna start fucking with my mojo.

For the first time in the six years that Ash and I had been best friends, there was tension, thick in the air between us. I couldn't remember a time, before this, that we'd ever been at odds. Usually the dude made me laugh my ass off.

But when was the last time we'd split a gut together?

Or had a woman in bed between us?

Too fucking long ago, on both counts.

I watched as he served up the scrambled eggs with a sneer, like they'd personally ruined his day—onto two plates.

"Sleep here last night?" I finally ventured, as if I didn't know the answer.

"Fell asleep on the couch."

Of course.

I watched him plate the bacon he'd already cooked up, along with the hash-browns and a handful of strawberries. The dude cooked better meals for me than any woman had ever tried to. "You gonna make up a plate for Amber?"

He shot me a pissy look. Then, without a word, he grabbed another plate from the cupboard and filled it. But I noticed he didn't put any bacon on it, which meant he'd been paying attention. *Busted.*

"So. Why didn't you go sleep at your place? You know, with the hot photographer chick?"

"She's too granola for me," he muttered, dropping the plates on the island.

"Too sweet?" I ventured.

"Too crunchy."

I chuckled under my breath. "Coulda fooled me, man."

"Please," he grumbled, shooting me a glance. "You gonna wear those tighty-whities all fucking day, or you gonna go put some pants on?"

I ignored that. This was my house. I'd put on pants—or not—

when I damn well wanted to. "So you're telling me that you're immune to her perky tits and her big green eyes?"

"She has eyes?" he said, sounding totally disinterested as he tossed cutlery and condiments on the island.

"Right. 'Cause you never noticed."

"I noticed. The freckles. The flowers." He shook his head a little. "Not my speed."

"Jesus," I muttered. "You doing this again?"

"Doing what?" He spared me another glance.

"I thought after Elle you'd sworn off this shit."

"What shit?"

I'd reached for the coffee pot, and when I turned back to him, I caught his gaze flickering down my body. He was checking me out, like he so often did, but as usual, he pretended like he wasn't.

Busted again.

"Pretending not to like what you like," I said.

"Huh?" he muttered, not looking up again.

I topped up my coffee, put the pot back, and dug deep for the kind of emotional-conversation stamina I'd really never had to find in myself until lately, with Ash. And the tolerance for drama I just didn't have at this time of the morning. If ever. "You pretended you weren't all over Elle until it was too late."

"I said I've sworn off falling in love," he corrected me, ignoring the comment about Elle. He never wanted to talk about her. Or any of the other people who'd ever rejected him, including his mom. "I'll still fuck whoever I want to."

"Uh-huh. So why'd you sleep here last night again?"

He flashed me an annoyed look. "I'm not into her, Cope."

"You can say that as many times as you want, but I won't believe you."

"Why the hell not?"

"Call it gut instinct."

He grunted, took a swig of his coffee, then set his mug on the island and finally looked me hard in the eye. "Don't worry, buddy. You'll always be my favorite."

He was using humor, sarcasm, to deflect, like he so often did. I knew that.

"Glad to hear it," I said, equally sarcastic.

I was just about to leave, to go put some pants on, when he blocked my way. I almost spilled my coffee on him. Then he took my neck in his hands, leaned in and kissed me.

If he wanted to catch me off guard and shut me up, it was effective.

I didn't say another word.

It wasn't exactly a mouth-to-mouth kiss; his lips had landed right next to the corner of my mouth, but it was soft and lingering. And as usual, I didn't know what to do with it.

I just stood here, letting him do it. It wasn't like he'd never done it before. I just waited for him to stop when he was done making his fucking point or whatever, because I knew he would.

But before he stopped, a flash of light caught my eye.

Amber.

She was standing in the stairwell to the basement. She was behind me, looking in through the cutout in the kitchen wall; I could only see her because she was reflected in the glass door of a cabinet across from me. Her camera was to her face and the morning sunlight had glinted off her lens. She looked like she was taking a photo—of Ash kissing me.

Great.

I was about to pull away when Ash withdrew. But he was still holding my neck, loosely, was still inches from my face, his eyes on mine. "You need anything from the city?" he asked me, eyelids lowered. "I'm gonna splash over today, get some food and stuff."

"Nope. Just whatever you think we need."

"Okay. Got it covered." He released me, and that's when Amber made herself known, knocking lightly on the wall.

When we both looked over at her, she'd dropped her camera to her side.

I exhaled; didn't realize I'd been holding my breath so tight.

"Um… is it okay if I come up? I'm finished shooting downstairs."

"Yeah. Come up." I watched as Ash retreated to the other side of the island and took off his apron. "Ash made breakfast, if you're hungry."

"Oh..." she said, cautiously, "that's really nice." She drifted in, setting her camera down on the island. "Thank you—"

By the time she looked up to thank Ash, he'd disappeared out to the back deck with his plate. We often ate out there, but still.

When Amber's eyes met mine, I smiled and tried not to stare at her legs. She was wearing short cut-offs, and her thighs were toned and tanned. Her recent months of backpacking through Brazil were showing. Not that she'd told me about Brazil; Liv had.

"He's not a morning person," I informed her.

She just smiled a little. Her thick hair was pulled back in a messy little pony tail again. She looked like the kind of girl you could make out with and she wouldn't give a fuck if you messed up her hair or smeared her makeup. Again, she wasn't wearing any makeup, as far as I could tell. She looked like the kind of girl who wouldn't taste like makeup either, but like sweet, clean skin.

She was wearing a flowing blouse with big, pink flowers and leaves on it that were the exact same color as her pale, minty-green eyes. It was the kind of shirt that gave up zero information about her tits, yet it looked sexy as fuck on her, kinda drifting off her right shoulder, showing the little freckles sprinkled there like pink-gold dust.

I couldn't take my eyes off her as she ate a strawberry off her plate, her lips sliding in a plump, round, very blowjob-like O around the berry for a moment before she bit down.

Jesus.

I shook my head, searching for something else to fixate on. Like *anything*. I offered her a coffee, but she declined. Apparently, she preferred tea. Unfortunately, I didn't have any. I made a mental note to tell Ash to get her some from that hippie tea place near Summer's house when he went into the city today. He wouldn't love it, but too bad.

"How's the picture-taking going?" I asked her.

I listened as she filled me in, all the while wondering where the fuck Ash was. And if he was coming back. It fucking irritated me that he'd taken off.

And why the fuck did he kiss me like that, when she was in the house? Kinda felt weirdly like he was marking his territory or something.

Very fucking weirdly.

Amber showed me a couple of images on the screen on the back of her camera, gorgeous shots of my drum kit all aglow in the sunrise. Girl had a serious eye. I noticed, too, that the only time she didn't seem unsure of herself or self-conscious or borderline prickly was when she was talking about her photography.

She didn't say a word about taking a photo of me and Ash. A photo of Ash kissing me, while he was wearing that frilly apron and I was in my underwear. I also didn't ask. I didn't particularly want a photo like that splashed all over the internet, mainly because everyone on Earth would then ask me about it, and I'd have to come up with some kind of response that didn't piss off Ash. Wasn't sure I was that clever.

But maybe she didn't even take a photo of us anyway.

If she did, I actually wasn't worried that she'd sell it to some online rag or whatever. I already knew that wasn't her style. She had too much integrity for that shit.

And besides that, she wanted me to like her.

That was made pretty clear to me last night.

If she took a photo of me and Ash this morning, she probably just did it because she was a photographer and that's what photographers do. I wasn't gonna make her squirm about it.

I really didn't mind if she took photos of me, half-naked or not.

And I *did* like her.

Any girl who could handle Ash's bullshit had my respect. The fact that she seemed so unsure of herself in my house, yet she wasn't letting Ash scare her off, was a major turn on. The fact that she wasn't impressed with the things that usually impressed the women I met—women like Susanna—was also a turn on. The fact that whenever she picked up her camera, she lost all that uncertainty and her green eyes blazed with passion, was also a turn on.

The fact that she'd spoken her mind at the Underlayer shoot, even though it had gotten her fired? Biggest turn on of all.

That, and the girl was the kind of ridiculously, naturally pretty that only got prettier the more you looked at her.

I hadn't found a thing about Amber Paige Malone, yet, that didn't turn me on.

And *that* was beyond interesting.

Plus, it was pretty fucking adorable that the entire time we spoke and looked at photos on the back of her camera, she very purposefully kept herself on the other side of the island, as far away as possible from me and my tighty-whities.

Mid-afternoon I hit the shower, briefly, to rinse off the sweat; I'd spent several hours playing drums and probably smelled like it. Then I threw on some sweats and headed downstairs, towel in hand, heading for the pool.

Amber was on her knees at the front entrance, photographing the staircase that swept up to the second floor and the sunroom off to the side of it.

And *shit*, the girl was sexy. I could really get used to finding her hanging out in my house like this. The fact that she was down on her knees didn't hurt. I really wasn't *trying* to get any dirty ideas about her kneeling there, but come the fuck on.

When she looked up at me, I peeled my eyes off her ass and smiled. She smiled back. When Ash wasn't around, she definitely smiled a lot easier.

"Check this out," she said.

Already am...

She had her camera set up on a tripod with a short, wide lens, and she clicked the shutter with a remote. The exposure lasted several seconds, then she showed me a series of identical images on the back of the camera, each one darker than the last.

"Multiple exposures," she explained, looking anywhere but at my bare chest. "I'm gonna do some HDR on some of them. It's popular with real estate photography, though it can get cheesy if it's overdone. The images start to look cartoonish and fake. But if you do it right, you get all this detail in the highlights and the shadows, with the various exposures, that you couldn't otherwise get with just one exposure, and if you merge them properly, it's gorgeous. Rich, saturated colors and tons of detail."

"Sounds like you know what you're doing," I said, impressed, trying not to stare at her legs again. It was just too tempting. She was still on her knees, right in front of me.

And I so had a thing for legs.

Shapely, slender calves.

Toned thighs.

All of which Amber Malone possessed.

"You, too," she said, blushing a little. "I heard you playing."

"Yeah. *Shit*. Remind me to give you some earplugs." Really should've thought of that before I beat the house down. "Sorry."

"It's okay. It really wasn't that loud, after I shut the door to the basement. You've got good soundproofing." Then her face fell, like she'd realized that might offend me. "I mean, not that I don't want to hear you play..."

I laughed. "Trust me, I know. No one wants to live with a drummer."

She smiled a bit, but didn't say anything.

"I'm going out for a swim," I told her, "so you might want to avoid the backyard for a while." I winked at her, but she didn't giggle like she did last night after all the wine.

"Um. Why?"

"Because I like to swim naked...?" Damn. Did she already forget our flirting last night? Or was she really that drunk on the Prosecco?

Her reaction was priceless as she seemed to strive for neutral professionalism, even as her cheeks flushed beneath her freckles.

"Oh. *Right*. No worries. I'll be here for a while..." She seemed to be trying, hard, not to appear wound-up by whatever mental image I'd just put in her head.

But I knew when a woman was wound-up over me, and Amber was definitely getting there.

Normally, that would've been great. Perfect. But with Ash being such a stubborn dick... I was gonna have to be careful here. Play this one slow. Like really fucking slow.

After all, the idea was to hook her up with *him*, right? That was what was important here.

I didn't mind baiting her a little, on his behalf, since he couldn't get his shit together to make a move. I also didn't mind if she decided she wanted us both. At all. The more time I spent with her, the more I liked that option best.

But what I wasn't gonna do was sweep on in and take her for myself.

Sometimes, I seriously regretted being such a generous guy.

"So, uh... catch you later," I said, and got the hell out of there.

Amber was maybe a little confused by my abrupt departure, but what could I do? If I stood there flirting with her any more, I was gonna poke out her eye with my dick. She was still down on her knees, and I was starting to throb in my sweats, with her pale green eyes gazing up at me like that. In about three more seconds I was gonna be rock hard, and it was gonna be obvious.

Fuck, Ash.

I went out back and stripped down, the way I would if no one was in the house. I took my time, letting the fresh chill of the October air cool me down. I didn't cover up. I didn't even worry about shrinkage; fact was, I had a lot to work with.

I checked the pool. It was warm, almost hot, the way I liked it. As I slipped into the water, I couldn't tell if Amber could see me; if she was just inside any of the windows. Really, she could've been anywhere in the house. She could've even left, gone back to Ash's place for a break. But for all I knew, she was in the living room or the kitchen, right now, watching me through the windows.

That thought sent the blood thundering to my groin. My dick grew heavy, stiff, even though I tried to tell it to cool its fucking jets. No matter how willing she might be, Amber wasn't for the taking.

Not yet.

So I tried to ignore my hard dick—though I could hardly fault it for being a little confused about the situation—and started swimming. As it turned out, doing the front crawl with a hard-on wasn't so comfortable.

A few minutes in, I'd managed to lose the hard-on, mostly. Probably because I was mostly thinking about Ash. Wondering, as I had many times lately, how and why he'd gotten himself to such a shitty, dark place—and what the hell I was gonna do to change it if the Amber thing didn't work.

If it were me... he'd try to change it. I knew that, without a doubt.

We were that close, and I knew he cared that much. He wouldn't want to see me in any kind of depressing funk.

We'd been best friends since pretty much hours after we met. We just had that connection. I'd always had a lot of friends, but since I'd never really had a best friend before, the position was open. Ash just clicked right into it.

We made each other piss laughing, we saw eye-to-eye on a ton of shit, and we were different enough in the right ways that we balanced each other out somehow.

We kept each other entertained.

Our relationship was the ideal ecosystem of fun, comfort and loyalty.

We even hooked up with the same women, sometimes.

But it wasn't until after Ash and Summer broke up a few years ago that he and I started *sharing* women.

Like everything else in our relationship, it just sorta happened. We didn't plan it. One night, we'd both made out with the same girl. It wasn't the first time that had ever happened, but it was the first time the girl in question had ended up in bed between us. And after that, we never really looked back.

Before Ash got together with my bandmate, Elle, who was also one of my best friends, I actually hadn't hooked up without him in a couple of years.

Weird, maybe. To some people. To me, though, it was the new normal.

Sex with a woman, with Ash in the room, was just hotter.

That was the simple truth.

I didn't examine it. I didn't overthink it, partly because it wasn't my style to overthink things, and partly because overthinking it might've ruined it. My other friends, by now, thought I was kinky as hell, or maybe they thought I was closet gay, or maybe they didn't quite know the extent of my extracurriculars with Ash.

I didn't care.

We didn't exactly broadcast our personal business, but we didn't lie about it either.

When Ash hooked up with Elle, I'd started having sex with women solo again, because no way Elle and I were hooking up. Elle was hot, but she'd been like another sister to me since we were teenagers. Sex would never be part of the picture in our relationship; we both knew that.

But Ash had had a thing for Elle for a long time. And when the two of them finally hooked up, he was more stoked about it than he'd let on.

And when Elle blew him off... he took it hard.

I waited it out, waited for him to bounce back to his old self—like he always did—so we could pick up where we'd left off.

But it just didn't happen.

The night Dirty officially announced that Seth was back in the band, at a bar show we played for the documentary series—and Ash found out Elle was pregnant with Seth's baby—Ash seemed to turn a huge-ass corner in the right direction. He seemed like he was back on the prowl. I even saw him making out with Summer's cousin for a while.

But he didn't leave with her.

He didn't leave with anyone that night.

Well, he left with me. Drunk. I'd dragged him home to his condo in the city and dumped him into bed. I'd taken the couch, even though it was too fucking small for me to get a good night's sleep on, and in the morning, I didn't even give him a hard time about it. Figured I should let it slide for a while.

Seeing Elle with Seth was maybe a harder blow than I'd realized.

And since that night, a few weeks ago, we still hadn't sealed the deal. With anyone.

I'd never known Ash to go without sex for more than a week, before Elle.

It was getting downright freaky.

Ash had always lauded "the breakup party" as the ultimate cure for a broken heart. You got dumped or you broke up with someone, no matter what the circumstances—whether you were happy about it or totally not—you had a party. An epic party, to celebrate your newfound freedom—and, of course, to get laid.

So I just kept waiting for the breakup party on this one. Surely Elle brushing him off was worthy of a sex bender.

Meanwhile, I'd attempted to instigate a three-way—several times. Dropping the names of a few women from our shared past. Suggesting we hit up some party. Dragging his ass out to parties.

But it just never happened.

I knew Ash wasn't hooking up with anyone on his own, either, because he was pretty much living at my place, sleeping on my couch or in one of the guest rooms every night.

A few mornings ago, I'd found him passed out on the floor next to my drum kit downstairs.

And I was starting to fucking worry about the guy.

I was definitely not gonna step in on the first chick to come along since Elle that I thought might actually have a chance at getting under his skin.

Not before he was ready.

Ash was broken, but even if he wouldn't admit it, for whatever fucked up reason—protecting himself, punishing himself, just being a dick—I could feel the sparks between him and Amber from moment one. I could feel the sexual tension between them. I'd been down and dirty in the same room with Ash while he got his groove on with a chick enough times to recognize it. It was an angry, irritable tension, but it was there.

And I saw how she looked at him. I'd definitely seen that look before.

Amber found Ash hot—in an aggravating, annoying way, the way a lot of girls did. Which, in my experience, meant that all the two of them really needed was a fuck. A good, long, hard fuck. An angry fuck, maybe. But whatever kind of fuck it turned out to be, one night with Amber, and my guess was he'd snap right out of his bullshit funk.

Melting that girl's misgivings and turning her to a molten puddle of *yes* would make his fucking month. Hell, maybe it would make his year.

Couldn't be any worse than his year was already going.

And I meant what I'd told him last night. I'd even let him have her, solo, if that's what it took.

For a while.

But then, of course, there was the way Amber looked at *me*. There was tension there, too. My dick was tuning into it like a fucking divining rod.

And fuck me, but as I finished swimming and stood up... I was hard again. The mere thought of that look in Amber's eyes when she gazed up at me? It had me stiff.

I climbed up out of the pool and stood in front of the living room windows as I picked up my towel from the chair where I'd left it. I didn't look to see if she was inside. But I did stand here longer than necessary with my cock up, the water dripping off of me, as I caught my breath. After the hot pool, the cold air felt good.

The idea that she might be watching felt even better.

Then I dried myself off—slowly. My dick was throbbing at the mere possibility that she'd seen me out here, naked; that maybe she could see me right now. I wasn't exactly some pervy flasher, but shit, this was my house. I'd warned her what I was doing out here. And maybe I was just too far gone with the raging boner and all my blood flowing south, but I'd never been shy about being naked. I'd never really been shy at all.

I liked attention. I liked being looked at. Craved it, even. I was at ease onstage, performing. In front of a camera. In front of a woman.

Not just at ease...

Turned on.

I did not mind one bit if Amber Malone wanted to look at me. *All* of me. If she did, she could go right ahead.

She could even take photos, if she wanted to.

I was hardly gonna be the one to stop her.

CHAPTER EIGHT

Amber

HOLY... *hell*.

How could I *not* look?

I glimpsed Dylan through the windows on my way into the kitchen, in search of a glass of water. I was suddenly dying of thirst. It was plausible. A girl could get thirsty, right?

And there he was in the pool, swimming in place, just like he said he'd be, his muscular arms slicing through the current generated by the pool. At that point, I'd decided I was finished shooting the front hall. How many images of a staircase did a man really need?

Better to set up in the living room and capture that beautiful stone fireplace, with all the light flooding in through those big windows to the back deck...

So I did that.

But then Dylan got out of the pool. And *Christ almighty*.

Male beauty personified.

The water sluiced off his naked body, *steamed* off him, and my very first impulse was to swing my camera around and photograph him.

My next impulse was to drop to my knees in front of those washboard abs and suck on every inch of his glistening wet skin. And his...

Very large...

Hard...

Holy shit.

I looked away. Sort of.

Because I wasn't gonna do any of those things.

Reason number one, I now worked for the man.

Reason number two, I wasn't a pervert. It would be unprofessional to stare at him, much less photograph him, naked, without him knowing—not to mention *wrong*. Especially when he'd politely warned me to stay away from the backyard. I wasn't about to go spying on him, camera in hand, like some creepy voyeur.

Well, other than that kiss this morning...

Which brought me to reason number three: he was gay.

Because, frankly, the universe always screwed me like that.

I should've known, from the first moment I laid eyes on him. It all made sense now. Because no man was that freakin' perfect.

Well, he *was* perfect, I supposed, if you were his boyfriend. Like Ashley Player seemed to be.

If you were me, he was just another near-miss in a very long line of near-misses.

A sudden noise behind me startled me from my staring—and my skin. I actually screamed a little, almost swallowing my tongue trying to squelch it as a door swung open. When I whirled around, Ashley was standing in the doorway from the garage, grocery bags in hand, staring at me.

I got busy fumbling with my camera lens, trying like hell to pop the lens cap on and failing repeatedly. I was pretty good at appearing absorbed in my work, oblivious to my surroundings. But we both knew what he'd just caught me doing... which was nothing much at all except standing here and staring out the giant windows to the back deck—where the evidence of my perversion stood in full view: Dylan Cope, buck-naked.

He strolled leisurely toward the stairs that led down to the lower deck and the walk-out basement, his naked body gleaming, big dick swinging. Or rather, stabbing. He was still half-hard. He was casually drying himself off, and sort of half-heartedly covered himself with the towel as he went, like it was a total afterthought. Because this was his home, right? He should be able to walk around naked without being gawked at. But gawking was exactly what I'd been doing.

I flushed about a thousand guilty shades of red.

"I'm just packing up for the day," I said, hastily doing just that, unscrewing my camera from the tripod and stuffing my things into my bag. "I should be able to finish up in the next two days, or maybe even one, and clear out of your house."

Ashley had walked through the kitchen and set the groceries on the island as I babbled.

"Good," was all he said. Then, just as I hustled my bag onto my shoulder and beelined for the front door, thinking I'd made a clean getaway, he added, "You can just leave the memory cards on the counter."

I froze in my tracks.

"Excuse me?" I asked, like I totally hadn't heard him.

Then I started to panic.

The first memory card I'd filled with images, this morning—the one with the photo of *the kiss* on it—was in my bag, not in the camera. No chance in hell I could quickly erase it without him seeing. Especially since, when I turned around, I found him leaning on the kitchen island, arms crossed, staring me down.

"We'll review the images," he said, "and as long as we approve of what we see, you'll continue to be employed."

Jesus. He really took Dylan's privacy seriously.

Although to be fair, he did just find me ogling the man. Naked.

My thoughts pinwheeled, trying to think my way out of this, but I really had no choice. I had to hand the cards over, if I wanted to keep this job. If I wanted to get paid three thousand dollars for my work today, and I really, really did.

If I tried to hold that first card back, they'd know a bunch of images were missing from this morning. All the images I'd taken of the basement.

If I handed the card over, I might get fired for my voyeurism. But maybe not. Maybe they wouldn't look that closely and would miss that one image.

And now I was just starting to look like a guilty freak, because Ashley was holding his hand out for the cards.

Seriously... why did this guy hate me so much?

I dug through my bag and gave him the three memory cards I'd filled with images today. I'd worked hard and taken hundreds of shots. My goal was to give Dylan about a half-dozen epic shots of each room of his house. But now, who knew if I'd even get that far.

Shit.

I handed over my backup camera, too, so they could use it to view the images. Then I got the hell out of there before Ashley could pop in the first card and discover the offending image.

The one where he was kissing Dylan.

The one they didn't even know I'd taken.

Oh, *God.*

Why the hell did I have to take that photo?

Because you're a photographer, I told myself, stubbornly. *It was a moment. It was beautiful. And you did what you do.*

I shouldn't have to apologize for that, right? They probably didn't apologize after playing a rock concert. *Hey guys, thanks for coming out, but I'm really sorry I rocked out like that. I'll never do it again, I promise.*

Right.

More likely, if anyone ever questioned what they did, they responded with a prompt—and in Dylan's case, probably very polite and charming—*Fuck you.*

Yet all I could think, as I hurried into Ashley's house stripped of my images from the day, was: *Thank God I didn't photograph him naked.* Then maybe I'd be fired *and* sued. I was on Dylan's property, after all, and he'd told me to stay away while he swam.

And as of this morning, I knew why. He wasn't flirting with me.

He was gay.

And he had no interest in me whatsoever.

Which explained literally everything.

Like how nice he'd been to me. Flirtatious, but not overly cocky about it. Gracious and welcoming, but never making a move on me last night, even when I was all giggly on Prosecco. He'd never asked me, *So what's your story?* Or, *So, do you have a boyfriend?* Or, *Hey, wanna go check out the view from my bed?* Or any of the other things horny straight guys said (sometimes it felt like I'd heard them all). He was far too polite for that. Respectful.

In other words: sexually disinterested in me.

I looked around Ashley's house, feeling stupid and helpless. It was such a man cave. It didn't feel like a gay man lived here—right down to the copies of *Maxim* and *Playboy* stashed in the bathroom—but that was probably an ignorant thing to think. Either way, my gaydar was definitely way off. I'd really thought Dylan was giving me sex eyes last night as we drank all that Prosecco.

But what straight dude drinks Prosecco, when beers are to be had?

One who's looking to get laid with the girl he's drinking it with—or so I'd thought.

Wrong.

I'd even wondered, as I lay in bed last night, drunk, thinking about the job he'd offered me and the ease with which he'd offered it —along with the generous day rate—if this gig was all a ruse just to keep me around because he thought I was cute. I was so unexpectedly thrilled with the idea, I definitely would've gotten off to it, if only I could stay awake long enough. But I'd been so boozy and tired, I hadn't been that lucky.

Damn, was I ever an idiot.

I dropped my backpack on the guest bed and fucking sighed.

No matter how it felt—between my legs—when Dylan hit me with those knowing green eyes of his, he wasn't actually into me. He knew I was hot for him; that was all. My ridiculous attempts to flirt with him, however cautiously, were probably just incredibly amusing to him.

Which meant this gig was *not* gonna be quite as fun as my Prosecco-muddled brain had started to think it might be—but fuck it. I still needed the money.

Had I blown it all with one simple photo?

Probably.

No matter how nice Dylan was, I could only assume that the photo of that kiss was going to go over very badly for me.

Though I *had* shot it through the cutout in his kitchen wall; maybe it could look like an accident? Like I didn't mean to catch them in the photo? Of course, other than the hot rock star kissing the other hot rock star, there was nothing in the photo but an out-of-focus wall.

Shiiit.

I went to grab myself a beer from Ashley's fridge and started drinking.

And pacing.

All I'd been thinking when I took that photo—other than the fact that they both looked so fucking gorgeous in the morning light streaming through the window behind them—was: *Really? Him??* I still couldn't believe Dylan was with that asshole, but clearly, he was.

I could only see them from the waist up, but Dylan was bare-chested. I didn't know he was only wearing underwear until I walked into the kitchen afterward. And the look on Ashley's face as he kissed him... I couldn't see Dylan's face as well, but Ashley's eyes were laser-locked on Dylan's mouth.

So yes, I'd definitely intruded on a private moment.

But the worse problem here was that I didn't *tell* them I'd taken the photo right after I took it—and I knew better than that. At least, I really *should've* known better.

This was such amateur crap. I was a professional. These guys were famous, and I'd just abused their privacy.

How could I fuck up like this?

My career as a photographer—albeit a modest one—was the single most important thing in the world to me. And my professional integrity had now completely shit the bed—Dylan Cope's bed, unfortunately—twice.

Fuck. Me.

And now I was starting to feel sorry for myself.

I was twenty-seven years old. Almost twenty-eight. I knew I'd passed that point, maybe around twenty-five, or twenty-four-and-three-quarters, where it was cute that I traveled the world staying in hostels and 2-star hotels, living out of a backpack. My sister would be first in line to remind me that it was time to get a real job—like her. Get a real life—like her.

Get a real relationship—like her.

But maybe I just wasn't wired that way.

If I was meant for any of those things, why did I always have such a hard time with them?

Why couldn't I stop fucking up?

And why was it bothering me so much that I'd fucked up?

Everyone was allowed to make mistakes.

Who cared about the gay rock stars next door anyway, right?

I didn't care what they thought about me. I only cared that they paid me. I'd done my job and done it well today. Even if they never wanted me to step foot in Dylan's house again or take another photo for them, they owed me my pay for today.

Except... we hadn't even written up a contract. I'd just taken this job on trust.

Why? Because they knew Liv?

Stupid.

Especially when my sister still hadn't even called or texted me back yet. For all I knew, she wasn't speaking to me.

I sent her another carefully-worded text, asking her when I was going to get paid. With the money from her shoot and the money from today, I'd have about half of what I needed to disappear in southeast Asia for eighteen months. If Dylan wouldn't keep me on, or if he screwed me out of today's pay, there really wasn't much I could do about it. I'd just have to make the money up somewhere else.

I might even have to swallow my pride and beg Liv for another shoot.

Christ.

My sister was right; I should've just kept my mouth shut.

I was much, much better at taking photos of people than bothering to even try to connect with them on any other level. At the end of the day, it was just easier that way. I connected with them just enough to get the photo I wanted, then I moved on.

Simple.

And my sex life was pretty much the same.

I could meet someone traveling and we'd hook up; maybe it was for a night or two while we were in the same hostel or hotel. Or maybe we'd travel together for a bit, through a certain city or a country, and then invariably we'd go our separate ways. And we always knew it was going to be like that.

Which meant there was no let-down at the end, no awkward breakup, no *It's not you, it's me...* I never even had to get to know them—or let them know me. For that slice of time, I could be anyone I wanted to be. Shy Amber. Sassy Amber. Serious Amber.

Kinky Amber.

Anything more than that, you started to get invested. Started to care about people. Started to care if they cared about you—or not.

Started to give something of yourself away.

Your freedom.

Your heart.

And before you knew it, you were plummeting, free-falling down that slippery slope known as a *relationship.*

Which led to all kinds of bullshit and pain.

Love.

Passion.

Finding the man you thought you loved in a hot tub with a bunch of naked women.

A shattered heart.

Maybe I should've just counted myself lucky that I was definitely *not* headed down that slope with Dylan Cope.

But it was a cold comfort.

I knew I shouldn't really care at all… but I totally cringed to imagine what he and Ashley might be thinking, what they might be saying about me, right now, if they found that photo of them kissing.

I tried to put it out of my mind.

I tried, all evening.

But the truth was, I really did care what they thought. Not about me, per se, but about me as a photographer. Because what I'd done was just plain shitty. Dylan had welcomed me and my camera into his home. He hadn't specifically told me not to take any photos of him, but for fuck's sake, the trust was implied.

I'd just shit all over his trust.

After wandering around Ashley's empty house about a hundred times, mentally spiraling, unable to sit still or focus on much else, I found myself in the kitchen. His friendly aunt and uncle smiled at me from the photo on the fridge, and I felt awful. Because I'd shit on Ashley's trust, too.

As much attitude as the guy had thrown at me, the fact was he was letting me stay here, in his house. For free. He'd even been feeding me.

And the other fact was, when he set his irritable, angsty blue eyes on me, it made me squirm with a feeling that was starting to drift south of irritation…

Okay. Who the fuck was I kidding?

The *real* truth was I was attracted to Ashley Player, in an annoyingly distracting sort of way.

I was attracted to them *both*.

Even before I'd found out they were *together*, I already knew getting the feels over either of these guys would only end in utter fucking chaos and tragedy. For me. But somehow, it didn't make me feel any better now that I knew I had zero chance with either of them.

Almost made me feel worse.

Because they weren't being generous with me to get in my pants. They were just being generous.

Unfortunately, I'd discovered that Ashley had stocked up his fridge—for me, presumably—on his grocery run, which made me feel even worse. He'd even left some organic loose-leaf teas on his kitchen counter with a tea pot and strainer and a mug; it all looked new.

And as the night wore on, my mood just kept plummeting.

Neither of them came over to invite me to join them for dinner while I ate my salad, alone. I kept wondering if they were furious with me. If they were calling their lawyers.

And I kept feeling like shit about that photo. And trying to figure out how I was gonna apologize appropriately.

But then, as I drank another beer in front of the fireplace, I also kept thinking about that kiss...

I stayed up as late as I could, just kinda waiting, in case either of them came over to talk.

They didn't.

On my way to bed, I stood at the door to the master bedroom and looked in. Ashley's room. The heart of his man cave, with the navy-blue, almost-black walls, all the dark wood and the giant bed... And I couldn't help wondering, as I gazed in at that bed, if Ashley and Dylan had ever slept in there.

Together.

I could easily picture them in there, rolling around... maybe Dylan on top?

Or Ashley...?

Were they rough together? Or tender, like that kiss?

Weird.

I'd never really thought about two guys together before. I'd definitely never *fantasized* about two guys together before. Because what the hell did two gay guys in bed have to do with me?

Nothing.

And yet... I couldn't quite get that kiss out of my head.

The details *made* a photograph. The emotions. And I'd caught them all.

Ashley's fingertips biting gently into Dylan's neck. His lowered eyelashes as he focused on Dylan's mouth.

The way Dylan's arms hung loose at his sides, trusting. He was holding his coffee mug in his hand. He didn't even touch Ashley, but there was something about that naked trust that was so intimate, so… sexual.

At least, my lady parts seemed to think so. Before I knew it, so much blood was thundering southward, I was helpless to resist my body's reactions.

It was the beer. And the emotions of the day. I was emotionally exhausted. Too fucking tired to fight with myself anymore.

I just wasn't thinking straight.

In the guest room, I stripped off my clothes and fell into bed. Then I started masturbating… wondering, as I did, if Ashley would be pissed if he found out the hippie girl had gotten herself off in his guest bed.

Probably.

But I was too far gone now to care, and my pussy quickly hijacked that fantasy, too: both of them finding me here, like this. Ashley, angry to discover I was naked on his manly guest sheets, touching myself. And Dylan, angry about that photo.

At first.

But then they slid onto the bed to join me, to punish me, to show me what a naughty girl I'd been… Pure fantasy stuff. I didn't even *like* Ashley, beyond his hot bod and his gorgeous face. And the two of them were clearly more into each other than they were into me.

Didn't seem to matter to my clit.

I thought of them *both* putting their hands on me—and I came, screaming and exploding, my body a one-woman fourth-of-July fireworks show.

The only thing I could conclude about that as I came down, panting, from the most explosive orgasm I'd had in months: it had been *way* too long since I'd been laid. That was the only explanation.

Temporary insanity, fueled by a hazardous buildup of guilt, tension, frustration… and horniness.

CHAPTER NINE

Ash

IT WAS GETTING LATE. The sun was long down and I'd finished working out, but I was still lingering in Dylan's basement, in the gym. Dylan had just finished practicing. He was covered with sweat and I was watching him at the drums. He was just sitting there, breathing hard, looking out the windows at the water as he came down, his head still somewhere in the music.

It was a slow come-down with him. The drums took him to some other place, and he was never in a hurry to get back from it.

I loved seeing him like that.

I'd stick around to enjoy it as long as I thought I could get away with, but I was overly-fucking-mindful of that kiss this morning. Of treading the line with Dylan. And he'd already busted my balls about not sleeping at my own place last night.

He'd also given me some silent warfare bullshit with his green eyes about the fact that I didn't go next door to invite Amber to have dinner with us tonight, like he'd suggested.

I also had the image of him naked, post-swim, in my head, looking like a fucking sex god with his cock all out, fucking messing with my brain.

Not like I hadn't seen it before.

But every time I saw him like that, it just gave me a fresh visual.

Made my head go to places I knew it wasn't supposed to—no matter how intimate shit had ever gotten between us.

Yes, we'd been naked in the same room. We'd had sex in the same bed, with the same woman—many fucking times. We'd gotten high together, drank our faces off together, thrown up with each other. We'd broken a hell of a lot of rules together. Broken laws. Broken bones. Broken hearts. When Dylan's dad died of cancer, we'd fucking cried together.

We'd been through just about every-fucking-thing two friends could be through together. I'd seen him bleed. I'd watched him fuck.

I'd watched him come.

He'd seen me come, too.

But there was a line. There was always a line with men like Dylan.

Straight men.

Of course, there was that one time…

And all it took was one time to really fuck with things.

"You wanna go pick up?" I threw it out there, even though he actually looked pretty exhausted. "You know, Summer's having that thing. Should be a good crowd…"

It had been a long while since the two of us had hooked up with anyone. While I was with—well, *kinda* with Elle—I wasn't with anyone else. Trying to prove something to her. To myself, probably.

But that meant I hadn't had a three-way with Dylan all fucking year. Not since before I first hooked up with Elle, almost nine months ago. Seemed like it was gonna happen after the Dirty show a few weeks ago, when Seth officially reunited with Dirty—and I found out he'd knocked up Elle. She'd brushed me off long before that, but that night, I knew it was fucking official: she was his. I'd been cut loose. For good.

I'd tried, at the afterparty that night, to hook up, but somehow it just didn't happen. I was more screwed up over Elle than I'd admit to anyone—even Dylan.

And since then, it still hadn't happened.

But tonight it could. It really *should*. Some sweet piece of pussy, taking my cock.

Taking Dylan's cock, while I watched.

As usual, I was getting hard just entertaining the fucking thought.

Dylan, though, looked disinterested. Bagged from playing drums all day. Practicing material for the new Dirty album; the guy was a fucking perfectionist.

Though maybe that was why Dirty outsold the Penny Pushers fucking ten-to-one.

Not that I was jealous or anything.

"Nah. I'm just gonna go get some sleep," he said. "Have fun, though. Crash over there if you're drinking. Don't drink and boat-drive." He punched me gently on the shoulder and headed upstairs to bed.

And there was no way he wanted me to follow him there without a woman between us.

I knew that.

I got up. Drank some water and toweled off. And headed, reluctantly, over to my house.

Dylan had had a stone path put in, connecting his yard with mine, and a gate built into the fence, so we could cut through from his back deck to my back door, without having to go all the way up to the road and around.

The guy really was the best fucking friend in existence.

I knew that was true even before he bought the property here—which he'd done mainly because I'd been bitching incessantly about the price tag on the land on the point, with its many acres and mountain bike trails and the killer view. The dude who'd owned it at the time, some rich prick plastic surgeon who'd given Susanna her double E's, refused to sell me a portion of it. And no way I could afford the entire lot. When Dylan then stepped up and bought it, I knew I'd never be able to match him in the amazing-shit-friends-do-for-you department. He'd officially knocked it out of the park.

At that point, I'd sworn a solemn oath to myself that if he ever needed a kidney, I'd hand mine over on a platter. That was pretty much the only way I'd ever get him back.

It wasn't like the fucker had even told me he bought the property because of me. But Susanna had alluded to it, and I wasn't fucking dense. Dylan had never mentioned an interest in owning property on the island, even after I bought my house here—until I started ranting and raving about how badly I wanted all that property on the point.

At least he'd really made it his own since buying it. He loved it now, had fallen in love with it just like I did. How could you not? But he also made room for me, just like he always did. Literally making room for me in his basement so we could jam. Building the workshop in the garage with me, where I could work on my Camaro, when he gave zero shits about cars.

I'd been sleeping at his house most nights, so it was kinda sorta like I even lived there. Kept my food there. I pretty much left some toiletries and clothes at my place just to prove it was still my home.

My condo in the city was even emptier these days.

But I didn't want to outwear my welcome. Crashing at my own house, or at the condo, a solid one percent of the time, at least made it official that we weren't actually shacked up together.

When I walked into my kitchen, first thing I noticed was the presence of a woman—some flowers she'd cut from the yard and put in a glass of water on the island. And it bugged me. Sure, I let that horny widow up the road tend the flower boxes in my yard; she had a green thumb and she just kept coming around. But I drew the line at letting her into the house. I didn't want her getting that comfortable here.

I definitely didn't want Amber getting comfortable here, the way I'd gotten comfortable at Dylan's.

Definitely didn't want her getting comfortable *there*.

I stalked through the house, headed for my bedroom, and I could smell the faint smell of her. That hippie-dippy flower-child smell. Like incense and flowers and candy, and natural fucking essence of sweet pussy. Amber's presence annoyed the fucking shit out of me, and yes, it was because I felt threatened.

Because I knew how much Dylan liked the girl.

He liked her a fucking lot.

Enough that he wanted her to be the filling in our next sex sandwich. Enough that he wouldn't go hook up tonight with some random because of it.

Enough that there was a very real fear building inside of me, fucking itching at the back of my mind, that I could lose him to her.

And any girl who'd ever made me feel like that, I'd gotten rid of —fast.

But I just couldn't seem to flush this one out.

Dylan could say he didn't feel like going out tonight because he was spent and tired all he wanted. But that was all bullshit. He just didn't want to admit to me that he was pussying out; waiting on Amber to fall into our shared bed.

And I knew why he was waiting.

Because Amber Malone was so clearly different from the other chicks we usually took to bed; the kind you fucked and forgot about. There was something about this girl, you got too close to it, it stayed with you. And good luck getting it out of your system after that.

Kinda like herpes.

I stopped in my tracks when I heard her. I heard her voice, soft and breathy. Breathing too hard, kinda whimpering in that way a woman only did when she was getting off.

She was fucking *getting herself off* in my house.

I crept forward, suddenly hyper-tuned to the fact that the floorboards in this place creaked like fuck. She didn't seem to hear me, though. As I reached the guest room door, I could still hear her, fucking loud.

Clearly, she didn't expect me to come back tonight, because she was masturbating like a horny fiend.

And she hadn't shut the door.

It was standing about half a foot open, and obviously, I looked.

I could see her there, flung on the bed in the faint moonlight coming through the window. Thank God for a full moon. But even then, I couldn't see much. Nipples. I was pretty sure I saw nipples poking into the air as she arched her back. I definitely saw naked flesh and a hand between her legs. The other one was fisting the sheet. Her head was tossed back; I could make out her open mouth, some hair strewn on her pillow, but that was about it.

I just stood here, staring.

And I was getting hard, my dick fucking throbbing as I watched her.

Then I heard her come. Those breathy, kinda half-choked-off screams... and my hand was sliding down the front of my pants. I was wearing sweats from my workout, and I had a handful of hard cock in seconds.

I backed off as she panted, coming down. Made myself scarce before she could gather her wits and saw me or heard me.

I went into my room and shut the door, quietly. Went straight into the bathroom and stood over the sink, shoving my sweats down. I leaned one forearm on the mirror in the dark, holding myself up as I jacked off. It was fast and fucking blinding-hot... Thinking about those sounds she made. Thinking about her coming.

Wondering what *she* was thinking about.

Dylan?

But it was all mixed up with that kiss this morning... With images of Dylan on his back deck. And when I blew... they were both in my head.

Amber, with her pouty lips and the perky mouthful of her tits, her soft cries as she came...

And Dylan, with the red-gold scruff on his jaw and his cock all out, standing naked in the sun.

I was up before dawn, scanning through the images on Amber's memory cards, unable to go back to sleep. I was still naked, still in bed, when I found something.

I managed to drag myself out of bed, shower and get dressed, before Amber emerged. She found me in my kitchen, perched at the small island, drinking a breakfast beer. It was the first time I didn't head over to make sure I could cook Dylan breakfast before he got up, in what, months?

Her camera, the one she'd given me to view the images on, sat on the island between us like Exhibit A.

"Good... morning?" She stopped abruptly on her way to the fridge when she saw the look on my face.

I turned the back of the camera toward her, so she could see the image on the display. The photo of me and Dylan that she'd taken yesterday morning. The photo of me *kissing* Dylan.

The one that was totally fucking with my head.

"What's this?"

Amber looked from the camera to me and back again, several times. Her mouth opened, but nothing came out.

"The other day, when Dylan asked you about your photography," I said evenly, "you said you always tell people when you photograph them. You tell them what you're gonna do with the photo. You didn't tell us about this."

"I know. I'm so sorry," she gushed. Her face was flushing pink. "It's just... instinct, you know? I didn't mean anything by it. I only took one..."

She only needed one. The photo was perfect. The way we were kinda backlit against the light coming in the windows, but you could still see all the detail you needed. Dylan with no shirt on, the light hitting the curves of his muscled body. Me in my Kiss T-shirt—*seriously*, I had to wear *that* T-shirt yesterday?—and fucking frilly apron.

And that fucking look on my face...

Girl had some serious talent with a camera.

But the photo said a lot more than I wanted it to say. The way our faces were so close together, the way I was holding Dylan's neck, my thumb on his jaw... It looked like two people in love.

Or at least, one person in love.

"What were you planning to do with it?"

"Nothing," she said.

I stood up to my full height, crossing my arms over my chest as I looked down at her. I wasn't above trying to intimidate her, if needed. Hell, I'd call Con over here, or Jude himself, if I thought Dylan needed the protection. "You weren't gonna post it online? Sell it?"

"No! I didn't even think about it. I just took it."

"Why?" I pressed.

"I don't know." Her cheeks beneath her dusting of freckles were growing crimson. "I was just... interested."

"In what?"

Her light-green eyes flashed to mine. "You."

I almost recoiled; I was that surprised. I actually put a hand on the island to steady myself.

Amber glanced away. "I mean... both of you," she said softly.

Je-sus.

Both of us?

I thought the chick couldn't fucking stand me.

What the fuck...?

I stared at her in her little jean cut-offs and peach-colored blouse. Then I looked down at myself, confused.

Weren't my Black Sabbath shirt with the devil on it and my non-organic beer and my *Fuck Bitches* tattoo against her flower-child religion or something?

When I looked at her again, she bit her naturally-pink bottom lip... and the imagery flashed in my head: her, getting herself off last night. And a wave of heat crashed through me at the familiar sensations: a woman's naked body smashed between Dylan's and mine.

Amber's body.

"I eat meat," were the first words that came out of me. The first words I could think of to repel her.

Her brow rippled a bit, but she didn't say anything.

"I eat every fucking kind of meat you can think of," I said. "If it had a face, I'll eat it. I smoke sometimes even though I say I quit years ago. I drink too much when I'm pissed off, and I'm pissed off a lot. I've lied to every person I've ever been involved with. I've cheated on most of them, too. I fuck guys even when I say I won't anymore." I told her every shitty thing about myself that I could think of; everything that would make her think I was a piece of shit. "And I don't always recycle. See that bin?" I pointed at the plastic blue box for recyclables sitting by the back door. "Haven't filled it in months. I threw a whole case of beer bottles into the trash just the other day."

She frowned a little, like that was a ridiculous thing to do. "Why?"

I leaned in close to her face and said, "Because I'm an asshole, Amber Malone."

She said nothing. She just held my gaze, undaunted, with her pretty green eyes. They were a pale, almost mint-green, unlike Dylan's, which were more of a hazel-gold green.

Then her gaze dropped—to my mouth. And I realized I was licking my bottom lip, like a man who was fucking starving. Which I was.

Why the fuck hadn't I gotten laid lately, again?

Her eyes widened when she glimpsed my tongue piercing.

I shut my mouth and turned away. "I don't think Dylan would like it if this photo got out," I said, not looking her in the eye. "Which means it's not getting out."

"Of course not. I can delete it. This is the only copy, Ashley," she assured me, gently. "I haven't had a chance to back it up yet."

Ashley. She fucking called me Ashley. It made my nipples fucking hard when cute chicks called me Ashley.

My dick was getting there, too.

"Not necessary," I managed to growl. My throat was getting tight and the words came out all rough and a little too quiet. I slid the camera toward her and met her gaze. "Enjoy it," I told her.

Then I walked out.

CHAPTER TEN

Amber

MY EYES FELL to the display on the back of the camera. To the photo of Ashley and Dylan.

To that private, almost tender moment between two people I hardly knew; a moment that now felt even *more* intimate.

I fuck guys even when I say I won't anymore.

Oh, *God*. I totally felt like a voyeur, as Ashley's words replayed in my head, again and again.

Enjoy it.

Yeah; he definitely thought I was a voyeur.

And what about Dylan? Ashley had been very specific, that *Dylan* wouldn't like the photo getting out.

Had I just been fired?

I didn't even know.

I blew out a breath and got to work uploading yesterday's images from the memory cards to the cloud, by way of my laptop. Ashley had laid them on the island, which had seemed like a good sign, at first.

Now, maybe not so much.

While I waited for the images to transfer, I thought about just getting the hell out of here. I had two more days on this shoot at best. I'd probably be finished mid-day tomorrow. I could maybe stretch it out to a full day, but I didn't want to abuse Dylan's kindness any more than I already had.

Shit. It was official; I was fucking terrible with people.

Especially hot men.

Because even when Ashley stood here and explained to me what an asshole he was, and that he liked to fuck men, I was still attracted to him.

Something was definitely wrong with me.

Or else my pussy had just been out of the game too long; long enough to get totally confused. Clearly, Ashley did not want me.

Dylan did not want me.

I told myself if I even let myself masturbate thinking about the two of them again, this was going to get messy. For me.

It was already getting messy.

As much as I would've loved to just disappear right now, though, I could not get around the fact that I owed them an apology, whether they fired me or not.

So I put on my big girl panties and headed over to Dylan's house.

When I arrived, the guys were gone. A woman let me in, but at least this one wasn't a living incarnation of a Barbie doll. She was middle-aged and friendly and said she was the part-time housekeeper. She seemed to have expected me.

She offered me a tea—more loose-leaf Ashley had obviously bought yesterday, for me—and told me she would keep out of my way. She even said if I needed her to tidy anything up for my photos, to just let her know.

So maybe I wasn't fired?

I wondered, had Ashley even told Dylan about my newly-discovered voyeur status?

I worked alone all morning. I was upstairs in Dylan's bedroom when I heard the drums thudding through the basement. I hadn't even heard him come home.

In the early afternoon, when I came downstairs, I saw him out by the pool, through the windows. He was on his phone, and he looked so fucking gorgeous laid out on his lounge chair. He wasn't naked this time, just shirtless, which was probably a good thing since the housekeeper was in the kitchen. But those fucking *abs*. A girl could suck some serious vodka off those abs.

Well, a guy could.

I was tempted, so fucking tempted to take his picture, but the last thing I was gonna do was pull another embarrassing mistake like I'd already made.

The house smelled like fabulous cooking, and the housekeeper lady fed me lunch as she cooked food to stock up Dylan's freezer.

In the late afternoon, Dylan came to check out what I was doing, just like he had yesterday. Like he was genuinely interested. He didn't say a thing about the photo of the kiss.

So I decided not to rock the boat by bringing it up.

Chicken shit move, I knew.

"So, hey," he said, leaning one shoulder against the doorframe as I shot his master bathroom with my wide angle. "I was wondering... if you want to come to a party tonight."

I looked up at him, my heart thudding. He was in my shot, but I wasn't about to ask him to leave. He hardly made the room look worse.

And as for my heart thudding? I knew he was gay. But somehow it just hadn't made him any less attractive to me.

Because apparently my lady parts were slow like that.

"It's just a small cocktail party," he added. There was a slight, crooked smile on his face, maybe because my eyes had gone wide. "No big deal."

"Oh. Okay," I said, despite the fact that I knew I should say no. I didn't actually *want* to say no. Historically, I hadn't always wanted what was best for me. Way too much like my mom that way.

"But you'll have to leave the camera behind."

I nodded, taking this in. "Right," I said, like it was no big deal, when in reality going anywhere without my camera was, for me, something like going naked.

If he didn't want me bringing the camera, I knew there was a reason.

Because his famous friends were going to be at this party?

Because he was planning to let Ashley kiss him some more?

"Um. How fancy is this party?" I ventured, in case it was the former.

Dylan's eyes dropped to my billowy blouse and ratty cutoffs, his gaze skimming down my bare legs as the smile curled his perfect mouth. "As fancy as you get."

As it turned out, Dylan Cope's idea of "no big deal" was a house party—at a multi-million-dollar house—where his entire band was in attendance, at least half the guests were famous and most of them were filthy rich.

When he'd picked me up at the front door of Ashley's house, I'd almost fainted from the sudden loss of blood in my head. He was wearing a natty black suit, very Don Draper, but sans necktie, and his hair was smoothed down, the cowlicky waves at the front doing their own adorable thing.

So. Fucking. *Cute*.

If a six-and-a-half-feet-tall underwear model with abs of steel and beard stubble could be called adorable or cute… Dylan Cope fit the bill.

He'd walked me down through the trees, to a private dock on the edge of his property where two boats were moored. The big one was white, an enclosed luxury speedboat, slick and pimped-out. The boat's name, *DIRTY DEED*, was emblazoned on the back.

The boat on the other side of the dock was a small, older speedboat with a sparkly silver finish and snap-on cover, and where its name, *FALCON*, was emblazoned on the back, someone had graffiti'd beneath it: *Silver Sparrow*.

I'd met Ashley's eyes after reading it; he was crouched down at the edge of the dock beside the silver boat, smoking a joint. He was dressed in a silky, charcoal-gray vest over a dark shirt, sleeves rolled up, and his trademark tight black jeans, his black hair slicked back, and I probably would've wanted to eat him with a spoon...

If I didn't know what a gay asshole he was.

"Is that your boat?" I'd asked him, feeling uncomfortable as he looked me over, kinda scowling at my dress. Dylan had hopped into the big boat to start getting it ready for us, leaving me there, all awkward. "The Falcon?"

Ashley had looked irritated, but what else was new? "Zane re-christened it."

I'd glanced at the graffiti again and asked no more questions. Zane, I knew, was Dylan's lead singer. Seemed like one of those inside jokes between guys that I wouldn't really get. Or didn't want to know.

Dylan had then collected me from the dock and helped me into his boat, and I'd caught Ashley giving his suit what I could only describe as an irritable once-over. I tried to ignore him, settling into a seat near the driver's seat, where Dylan placed me. He had the heat going and it was really comfy. There was a small bar, and I was kinda hoping he'd offer me a drink. With the attitude Ashley was putting off, I could've used one.

Ashley had followed us onto the boat, and he cranked up some music; surround-sound and loud. I recognized the song as it kicked in, one of those funny Andy Samberg songs, from *Saturday Night Live* or something. "I'm On a Boat."

I'd glanced at Dylan. He didn't look amused, and shot a look at Ashley.

Then I'd glanced at Ashley, who'd made himself comfy in the back, lounging on one of the cushioned bench seats. He returned Dylan's look, completely deadpan, eyes narrowing slightly as he took a drag of his joint.

There was definitely some kind of weird, silent, dude stand-off going on between them that I couldn't quite figure out...

It was almost as if Ashley thought Dylan was trying to impress me.

Then Dylan had shut off the song, turned on some AC/DC, and off we went.

Dylan had buzzed us across the water to the city, and by the time we hit dry land again his auburn waves were everywhere; the wind blew them all over the place while he tied up the boat. I felt giddy from the ride and the fresh night air. As I waited on the dock, I held my jacket over my head to try to salvage my hairdo; I'd done a side part and smoothed the thick waves down a bit in keeping with the retro feel of my dress. Dylan had seemed to appreciate my efforts.

Ashley, other than that first scowly perusal, had barely looked at me.

We'd moored in Coal Harbour—so quiet at night, with downtown all lit up above us, North Vancouver and the dark presence of the mountains across the water. We'd walked up a few blocks and climbed into an SUV Dylan owned, parked in the underground lot of a condo tower where Ashley, apparently, had a place. The cold steel-and-glass building on the edge of the financial district did not feel like Ashley, but I didn't mention it. I already felt conspicuous enough, just like I had in the boat, sitting there in the copilot seat—while Ashley sat in the back, drilling annoyed holes in the back of my skull.

Apparently, *I was wondering if you want to come to a party* actually meant *I was wondering if you want to come to a party with me and my angry boyfriend.*

If I'd needed any further evidence that this was not a date, there it was.

I felt even more awkward after we'd driven over the Lions Gate bridge to West Vancouver and up the mountainside, and I stepped into the beautiful house with the two of them. My heart was drumming in my chest. I wasn't even sure if I was more nervous about being with Dylan or *not* being with Dylan, but he seemed to sense my discomfort. He put his hand on the small of my back, introducing me to the homeowner the moment we walked in.

Zane Traynor, lead singer of Dirty.

The first thing I noticed: he was dead sexy.

The second thing I noticed: he was staring at me.

Like *staring*.

He had shocking light-blue eyes and a chiseled, gorgeous face, a nose that looked like it had been broken a time or two, and his blond hair was shaved super-short at the sides—blond velvet. The longer part on top had been slicked back, and he wore a black suede vest over a tight T-shirt, with a pocket chain dangling from it. He looked like a prohibition-era gangster—a ridiculously hot one. Fitted dark pants completed the look, but I didn't dare look down.

He laughed before Dylan could introduce me and said, "Who the hell is this?"

I felt my face turning pink. Luckily it was dark out and the lights inside the entrance were way low.

"This is Amber," Dylan said.

"She's Liv's sister," Ashley grumbled from somewhere behind me, as if to explain why I was here. Because God forbid I came with him.

"Amber..." Zane said, like my mere existence was somehow incredibly interesting, as he kept staring at me.

Then the guys did a round of back-slapping hugs. And as I soon found out, this wasn't just a cocktail party. This was Zane's *new* house, and this was a housewarming party.

It was also his thirtieth birthday.

No pressure.

We hadn't even brought a gift.

I immediately felt like an asshole, even though I'd never met the guy before.

"We didn't bring a gift?" I whispered at Dylan as we headed through to the back of the house, where the party seemed to be.

Dylan chuckled. "Trust me, he doesn't need anything."

"Okay, but—"

"I'll buy him dinner next time he forgets his wallet," he offered, amusement sparkling in his green-gold eyes. Then he winked at me.

For some reason, he was holding my hand, and it was kinda freaking me out. But I clung to it anyway.

The house was huge, modern and sparsely furnished, and all the lights inside were dimmed low. There was no one inside except us, Ashley and Zane and some giant security guy who'd come with Zane to the door, trailing behind us. It looked like Zane hadn't fully moved in yet, or maybe he just didn't own a lot of stuff.

But the backyard was where it was at, anyway.

The huge sitting room at the back of the house was an indoor-outdoor space, fully heated and covered, flowing out onto the patio and yard. Music was playing, lounge furniture was clustered all around, fires were burning in a couple of outdoor fireplaces, and in the center of it all was a swimming pool, all lit up from underwater.

The place reeked of money, but it was classy, too.

The actual party was small, maybe twenty-five people. But they all seemed to know one another. You know, just a bunch of super-hot rock stars, their super-hot dates and friends, and some big, intimidating, bodyguard-looking dudes.

And me.

Liv wasn't even here.

I made a mental note to take a photo with my phone later and text it to her. Maybe when I was nice and drunk, and I'd put my middle finger in it. It had been three days since the Underlayer shoot, and she still hadn't called me back.

So maybe I'd put my bare ass in it, too.

There was a DJ booth set up in one corner, and a gorgeous female DJ. She had a kind of Bettie Page look going on, with her sleek dark hair and violet corselette-like dress, and she was spinning a way-cool remix of Dinah Washington's "Is You Is Or Is You Ain't My Baby?" as we headed straight for the bar.

I was definitely glad Dylan had told me to fancy myself up.

The women here were all pretty, but at least they seemed… well, *real*. Surprisingly, I didn't glean a pair of obviously surgically-altered boobs in the place. But everyone, other than the security dudes, was definitely dressed to impress.

I didn't want to give a shit what people thought about how I dressed, but glancing around, I would've felt pretty fucking out of place if I hadn't put on my best dress—the only party dress I dragged around the globe with me in my travel backpack. It was a cute, off-white lace cocktail dress in a simple '60s style that I'd found in a thrift store in New York, fit me perfectly, and always made me feel fashionable, no matter what year it was.

Behind the bar, there were two women, about my age, chatting and making drinks. One of them was poured into a long red satin dress with side-swept dark hair, very Rita Hayworth. The other wore a short black cocktail dress, with her dark hair slicked back in a tight knot. Dylan introduced me to them right away: Katie and Maggie. And both of them were so welcoming—Katie hugging me and Maggie handing me a drink—that I made a mental note to remember their names.

A couple of sips into my melon-flavored martini-thing and I was already relaxing and starting to think this might actually be fun.

But then it got weird.

Like when Ashley brought Dylan—our designated driver—a coffee, beer in hand for himself, and absolutely nothing for me, even though my melontini was already getting low.

Or when Ashley kept interrupting and stealing Dylan away, just as he was about to introduce me to someone.

Christ. He wasn't just protective of Dylan. He was possessive, too.

Did he think I was hot for his man?

Well, I was.

Even more so when I noticed Dylan giving me sex eyes from across the room.

At least, he seemed to be... His green eyes locking on mine, kind of hooded and contemplative, as I stood by the bar, sucking back booze and trying to get drunk while I waited for Ashley to quit hogging him.

What. The. *Hell.*

I could not figure these guys out.

Maybe I just couldn't read gay guys?

Or maybe it was crazy-wishful thinking to hope that just because Dylan Cope seemed to be checking me out in my cute dress that he was actually flirting with me. Maybe he just appreciated my fashion sense. Ha. Maybe I was just drunk and should slow down on the melontinis.

I'm crushing on a gay guy...

Well, two gay guys.

If I'd ever had a more dumbass crush in my life, I couldn't remember it.

CHAPTER ELEVEN

Amber

AFTER A WHILE, since I was hanging out by the bar anyway, I tried to make myself useful by helping Katie make drinks. I was so totally uncomfortable without my camera as a buffer. That's all it was. I did not know how to relate to any of these people without a lens between us. I did not know what to say, what to do with my hands... or how not to stare at them all.

Usually, my camera gave me permission to stare. Now, I just felt exposed and gawky.

Weirdly, I'd never felt this way around the famous or the beautiful *before* I'd gotten my heart smashed by Johnny O'Reilly. But the number he'd done on my somewhat-innocent self had changed that. I now doubted myself, questioned myself, and occasionally just plain felt like a freak in the company of people such as these ones. People who appeared to have their shit all together.

Ridiculous. I knew that.

But I still hadn't been able to totally shake it off. The consequences of that breakup were, unfortunately, far-reaching.

So I just tried to focus on something other than my socially-awkward self.

I quickly discovered, from chatting a little with Katie and

Maggie, that Katie was married to Dirty's lead guitarist. Yet she seemed so... well, normal.

"Should I be here?" I asked her as she poured up a few bourbons for her husband and some other guys, and I popped open some beers for the biker-looking dudes in the corner. "Please, you can tell me. If it's weird, I can just leave."

She threw me a curious glance. "What do you mean? You're the new girl, right?" She gave me a smile and Maggie handed me another cocktail.

"Don't worry, we've got you," Maggie said. "Just have some fun."

I sipped gratefully. It was a paralyzer, and the Coke-and-cream mixture probably wasn't gonna sit too well with the melontinis, but oh well. It was fucking delicious. "Um. What new girl?"

"You know... Dylan's... and Ash's..." Katie blushed as she trailed off.

Dylan's and Ash's what? I wondered.

"Ashley is an asshole," I said bluntly. "Sorry if he's your friend, but he's definitely not mine." Oops. *Filter.*

Katie and Maggie exchanged a look. Amused, maybe?

"Oh." Katie didn't seem to know what else to say to that.

"I'm just gonna run these drinks out," Maggie announced, departing with a full tray.

Damn. Had I just put my giant foot in my mouth again?

I tried to change the subject, asking Katie what else we could make. It was an open bar with no real bartender; Katie and Maggie had said they were just making drinks because they felt like it. Anyone was welcome to come up and pour. But we kept passing the drinks out, at the ready. Katie seemed to know what everyone liked.

I helped her whip up a blender full of margaritas, garnishing them with strawberries and lime slices. I was pretty good at this assistant bartender gig. Especially when I kept sipping my own drink all along the way.

"I hate margaritas," Katie informed me as the smell hit her. "Tequila." She made a barfing gesture. "But Ash and Summer like them, so..."

"Summer?"

"Babe over there, on the music."

I looked where she pointed. The DJ. The one Ashley was now talking to. He was standing in her booth with her.

"Elle likes them too, so we'll make some virgin ones..."

"What?" I was distracted, watching as Summer put her hand on Ashley's bare forearm while they spoke.

He was smiling. It was the first time I'd seen a smile on his face. Ever.

It totally transformed him, taking him from gorgeous to blindingly-gorgeous.

Jesus.

"Virgin margaritas," Katie was saying. "Because Elle's pregnant."

"Oh." I helped her make the mocktails, and put out more bottled water in the tub of ice by the bar—apparently Zane didn't drink, and neither did the on-duty security guys—while I tried to sort out who was who. "I thought Elle was blonde," I said, looking from the platinum blonde I was pretty damn sure was Dirty's bassist to the visibly pregnant brunette on the other side of the room. I was really trying to keep up, but my booze buzz and the lingering nerves weren't helping.

"Elle is blonde. That's her, there." She gestured at the platinum blonde.

"Who's that, then?" I asked, pointing out the woman with the giant baby belly.

"Come on," Katie said with a smile, drawing me out from behind the bar. "Let me get you oriented. You really need the lay of the land."

"Okay." I grabbed my drink and followed her. "How well do you know Con?" I asked her, when I noticed him in the corner with the biker guys, looking over at me.

"Not well," Katie said, as Con grinned at me. I gave him a little salute.

A salute? Since when did I salute people?

Gawd, how did I get so awkward?

"How about Ashley?" I asked her.

"Hmm. Not well."

"Dylan?"

"Oh, he's a real sweetheart."

Great. Not gonna help my crush.

"How about Zane? Does he always stare like that?"

"Yes. He's just trying to figure you out," she explained, pulling me right past Zane and over to the far side of the pool. "My best advice? Ignore him. He's harmless enough." She turned to give me a meaningful look. "As long as you don't stare back."

"Um... and what if I do?" I asked, staring at him a little. I was fairly inebriated by now, and he was still watching me. He was smirking at me, actually.

"Don't," she said, turning me around so I couldn't see him. "You came with Dylan, so he's just feeling you out."

"Oh. Like to see if I'm worthy of hanging with his friend? Like a bro thing?"

"Right..." she said, twisting her lip in her teeth. "Let's just call it that."

Okay?

"I know," Katie said, "believe me. It's intense when you're the new girl. I've been there." She drew me over to a dark-haired dude in leather pants. "Hey, Jesse..." When he turned to her, he immediately threaded his fingers through hers and before she could go on, he yanked her to him and laid a thorough, very intimate, very deep kiss on her.

Wow.

When she recovered, Katie said, a little breathless, "Um... this is Amber. Amber, this is my husband, Jesse."

Katie's husband grinned at me and extended his hand. I fumbled to take it as his dark eyes and million-megawatt smile blanked out my brain. I hardly had time to shake his hand before Katie turned me toward the guy he was standing with, a big, muscular dude with almost-black hair, sleeve tattoos and the kind of unmistakable alpha presence that had probably made more than one girl swallow her tongue.

Holy shit.

"Amber. Jude," Katie introduced us. Jude shook my hand but said nothing. "My husband's best friend," she explained. "Also, head of security for Dirty." When we'd drifted past him and out of earshot, she added in a hushed voice, "He's also a biker. Don't ask."

"Ask what?"

"Anything. They don't like questions about the biker stuff."

"Oh."

"That's Piper," she said, pointing out another giant biker dude, with blond hair, sitting with Con. "Jude's brother. He's a biker, too. Don't ask."

"Okay..."

"You already met Maggie," she said, as Maggie rejoined us. "Dirty's amazing assistant manager." Maggie waved the compliment off, sipping her martini and dropping onto a couch by the pool. "That's Brody, Dirty's manager," Katie said, pointing out a hot brown-haired dude on the other side of the pool, as we settled in next to Maggie. "He's with Jessa." She pointed out the extremely pregnant, extremely gorgeous brunette next to him. Like if Victoria's Secret had a maternity line, she'd be modeling it. "My husband's sister."

"Oh. Wow." *Good genes.*

"Yeah. That's Seth." She pointed out yet another hot dude with brown hair and a short beard, who stood with his arm around Elle's waist. "He's the new rhythm guitarist, who's really the old rhythm guitarist... long story. He's with Elle, Dirty's bassist. She's my husband's ex-girlfriend... Also Ash's ex-girlfriend, more or less. They had a thing earlier this year. But it was kinda on the down-low."

"Oh. *Wait.*" I swallowed my mouthful of paralyzer, confused. "I thought Ashley was..."

Katie waited.

Shit, did I have to say it? What if he was in the closet or something?

"You know," I said, awkwardly, then whispered, "*gay.*"

Katie grinned a little. "Um... no."

"But. He has a boyfriend."

"He does?" Maggie smirked at me over her drink, seemingly amused.

"Dylan?" I ventured.

Katie laughed. "Mmm... Nope."

I looked from one girl to the other. They were both grinning. "Are you sure?"

"Pretty damn sure," Katie said.

Maggie waved her hand in the air. "Ash just, you know, dabbles. But Dylan doesn't dabble that way."

"Oh. Um. I guess I read that wrong..." How, exactly?

A kiss was a kiss... Wasn't it?

"No girlfriend, either," Katie added with a little smirk, eying me. "They're both single, actually."

"Oh."

"There's really nothing going on between you and them?"

Them?

"Um... no."

"Oh. Well, I wish there were more single guys here to introduce you to, then. But most of them are taken." Katie looked around, seeming to come up short. "I mean, there's Zane... but you really don't wanna go there." She looked at me. "Unless... maybe you do...?"

"No," I said. "Thanks."

"Smart girl," Maggie muttered, sipping her drink.

Katie looked over at the security guys. "Or Con...?" she suggested. "He's single, I think."

"No, thanks. I'm good."

"Or Flynn... but he doesn't talk much. He might be a little too..." Katie glanced at Maggie as if to confer. "Serious?"

"Boring," Maggie concluded.

"Or Jude," Katie said, raising an eyebrow and looking me over, speculatively. "But he's—"

"Oh, God," I said. "He'd break me in half."

Katie giggled.

"Really. I'm not in the market."

"You're seeing someone?" she asked.

"No. And I'm not really looking to. I'll be leaving town soon."

"Oh." Katie's shoulders dropped; she looked disappointed. She was still eying me, but it was a friendly perusal. "So... you can tell me to leave it alone if this is rude, but... Haven't you been staying at Ash's place?" I was about to ask how she knew that, when she added, "Thin walls," and rolled her eyes a bit. "No walls, actually. These guys gossip worse than housewives."

"True story," Maggie concurred.

"Con let it slip," Katie explained. "Oddly enough, the security guys have the biggest mouths sometimes. I think it's because they spend so much time standing around, just waiting for drama. Con is Dylan's bodyguard, sometimes. He's a biker, too, if you didn't notice. That's Flynn over there. He's Elle's bodyguard. He's not a biker, though he kinda looks like one... And that's Shady." She pointed out the beefy dude who'd answered the front door with Zane, the one who was more overweight than built but still looked like he could split my skull with his thumbs. "He's Zane's newest bodyguard."

"He goes through them like chewing gum," Maggie muttered.

"Wouldn't know it to look at him," Katie added, "but Shady's about the nicest guy you'll ever meet. He's a biker too, though, so—"

"Don't ask?" I finished for her.

"Right."

"Trust me, though," Maggie said, "you run into trouble at a party, you go straight to Jude or Shady. Flynn's solid, too. Con will flirt with you, but if the shit hits the fan, he'll have your back."

Katie nodded in agreement. "As for Piper, he doesn't work with the band and I'd just steer clear of him."

I glanced at Maggie for her take on this, but she just shrugged.

"You don't trust him?" I asked.

"I wouldn't say that," Katie mused. "He's kinda like my brother-in-law now. But let's be honest, the dude is scary."

Fair enough.

"Don't get me wrong. I now have Christmas dinner with him, and he'd probably take a bullet for me. Actually, I know he would. It's all about family loyalty with these guys."

"True," Maggie said. "The guys in the band grew up together. And now we're all a big family. Dysfunctional, sometimes, but there's a lot of love in this room."

"I'm one of the newest members, I guess," Katie said, "and some days I'm still figuring it all out. And you haven't even met any of the crew guys yet..."

"Jesus," I said.

"Yeah." Katie giggled. "This is just Zane's VIP list. Like the members of the band, and their closest people. But these are all good people, I promise you. Even the ones with the guns." She said it in a way that I could tell "the guns" made her nervous, but she'd made her peace with it. "At least, if you're on their good side."

Yeah. I definitely planned to be...

I glanced at Maggie, who sipped her cocktail and smirked at me, appearing unfazed. Then I looked around, wondering who, exactly, was carrying guns. Like right now, they were carrying guns? Was it legal to carry a concealed weapon here? I'd grown up in Vancouver and I didn't even know. I'd never really had to think about it before.

I was gonna assume not, though.

I looked at Katie and Maggie. Despite the fact that I maybe didn't need to know the thing about the guns, I was kinda moved by how nice they were being, telling me all this stuff to help me feel like I fit in. Even after I'd told them I wouldn't be sticking around long.

"Um, to answer your question," I offered, "I am staying at Ashley's place. For a few days. But just because my sister Liv set it up."

"Oh!" Katie perked up, which was saying a lot. She was already pretty perky. "You're Liv's sister?"

"Yeah. Dylan's hired me to photograph his house."

"You're a photographer? That's *amazing*. I'm a painter," she said, like it really was amazing.

I smiled. I really liked this girl. "Really? Can I see your work? What kind of stuff do you paint?"

"She's ridiculously talented," Maggie said. "It's kinda sickening. You should see the paintings she's done of the band..."

"I'd love to."

"I'm having an art show next weekend," Katie blurted, "and I'm *so* nervous. You have to come. Maybe you could even take photos...?"

"Oh. Sure..."

I didn't have the heart to tell her that there was a very real possibility I'd be on a plane to Thailand by next weekend. She'd already whipped out her phone to show me some of her work. She *was* ridiculously talented. And as we sat by the pool looking at her art and sipping cocktails, I got to know Katie a whole lot better.

I also got pretty drunk.

Then Dylan—finally—scooped me up, taking my hand and pulling me over to a few people he wanted me to meet. I got to chat with everyone in his band a bit, though if I hadn't had so much to drink, I honestly probably wouldn't have.

Con grinned at me a lot, and at one point, when I was sitting with the biker guys, he put his arm around my shoulders. I let him, for a moment or two, then drifted away. I was still confused about the Are-they-gay-or-are-they-not-gay thing, and if Dylan wasn't gay, I was also confused about the Is-this-a-date-or-is-it-not thing.

Last thing I wanted to do was kill any possible chance I might have with Dylan Cope because I let his bodyguard feel me up. Even if Con did smell all yummy, like leather and man-soap.

I also kept wondering if he was carrying a gun, and it was freaking me out a bit.

I lost both Dylan and Katie somehow, even though it wasn't that crowded.

The music got louder.

A few more people showed up.

The drinks seemed to get stronger, though maybe I was just drinking them faster.

At some point, someone shoved Zane, fully clothed, into the pool. Then a bunch of other people got pushed in, mainly by Zane himself.

I was one of them, though it was Ashley who picked me up and leapt in with me.

When I woke up in the morning with a man's heavy arm draped over me, my first thought was, *Oh, fuuuck, no.*

Because the arm had tattoos all over it. A mermaid with white-blonde hair on the muscular forearm, and scripted lettering in a band around the bicep that said: *Fuck Bitches.*

I must've stirred, because a rough, sleepy voice growled from behind me, "*Damn*... that was good."

I stiffened.

Ashley chuckled. "Relax, flower child. Nothing happened."

I knew that.

I remembered.

But all I could think as I lay here spooned against him with his arm over me was, *Now he knows I'm hot for him.*

I managed to slither, eel-like, out from under his arm while barely touching him. My brain slopped around in my head when I moved, the room spun angrily, and I collapsed back on the pillow with a groan.

Ashley rolled onto his back, away from me, but I could still feel the heat of his body inches from mine.

His *naked* body.

It was way too fucking bright, but I managed to peek under my half-lidded eyes at the naked expanse of his chest, his chiseled abs, his hips... the tattoos that ran down his side, right under the sheets... and the X-rated glimpse of dark, trimmed pubic hair at the base of his—

"I should get to work before Dylan comes looking for me," I blurted. The sheet was covering Ashley's cock, but there was no doubt in my mind he was naked under there. And it wasn't so much that I was worried Dylan would be upset that I was late to photograph his kitchen. More like I *needed* to get out of here, get to work and get lost behind my camera—where the world made sense to me.

"Where do you think he slept last night?" Ashley replied lazily.

Which was when it dawned on me, way too slowly, that we weren't in Ashley's bedroom. Ashley's bedroom was dark. Dylan's was bright. White walls with lots of windows and a skylight...

I looked up, and the sun streaming in through the skylight above the bed made me wince.

I felt the bed shift, but in a way that Ashley, on my right side, could not possibly have made it shift, and my head reeled with sudden vertigo. With some effort, I looked to my left.

Dylan was sprawled next to me on his stomach, naked—not a sheet in sight. All I could do was stare at the curves of his broad back and that perfect, muscular ass.

Holy fucking *hell*, I wanted to bite that ass.

But I did not remember ending up in bed with Dylan last night.

I slept with *both* of them? In one bed?

"Hey," Dylan said. When I glanced up, his green eyes were watching me, that crooked, sexy smile on his face. "How you feeling?"

"Fine," I said.

"Yeah? You drank a lot of bubbly last night."

Really?

"And beer," Ashley said.

Great. Cocktails *and* wine *and* beer. Awesome combo.

"I'm fine. I never get hangovers."

I didn't. Unless, of course, if you considered waking up with a splitting headache and two hot, naked, and possibly gay men in bed with you a hangover.

"I really didn't drink that much," I added, trying to save face, but they knew the truth.

Or at least, Ashley sure did.

The truth was, at some point, way late in the night, I'd tried to get some.

From him.

I couldn't even remember why, exactly, it happened. Just that I was alone in Zane's kitchen with Ashley and Zane, sometime after getting tossed in the pool. My wet dress was gone, and I was wearing a T-shirt and rolled-up sweats that belonged to Zane. The three of us were smoking a joint. We were laughing at some story Zane was telling about the time Ashley's boat broke down on them, and they had a bunch of raw meat for a barbecue that went bad in the heat and they got all sunburnt while they floated around waiting for Dylan to come rescue them, and Zane had "downgraded" the boat's Falcon status, dubbing it the Silver Sparrow instead because Ashley refused to "put it out of its misery" and sink it, as per Zane's suggestion—*He's overly sentimental, this one,* Zane had said—and I was laughing too hard, and the booze had started to make gravity disagree with me. I'd leaned into Ashley without even thinking about it. Because, well... all the booze. And then something strange happened.

Ashley put his arm around me.

He'd held me up and went right on talking with Zane as if it was no big deal that I was pressed up against him—just the way a boyfriend would. And I got a warm, fuzzy feeling.

Well, a horny feeling.

Then Zane had magically disappeared. And as soon as I'd registered that Ashley and I were alone, I put my hand on him. Flat against his stomach. I could feel his tight abs through his shirt. Or Zane's shirt, which he'd also changed into.

Then I'd looked up, and he was looking down at me, his blue eyes dark and intent. I slid my hand downward... and his hand caught mine. He'd stopped me, just before my fingers could venture south of his waistband.

He'd stopped me from groping him.

Even though I could've sworn the look in his eyes was pure sex... he'd rejected me.

After that, it was a blur. Mostly because I'd just wanted the whole night to be done with so I could forget about it. I'd drank some more. I'd avoided Dylan and Ashley, until Dylan collected us and drove us home in his boat. Dylan hadn't drank a drop.

Which meant he was stone-cold sober when he peeled Zane's clothes off me and tucked me into bed. I didn't remember him getting into the bed with me, but I definitely remembered the undressing part.

Which was all kinds of weird. At least, it was for me.

I couldn't remember a guy ever turning me down for sex before. Not when my hand was an inch from his dick. And not when I was standing right in front of him, drunk and naked.

In that type of scenario, I was much more accustomed to a guy just diving into bed with me, and me with him, because what did it matter when I intended to hit the road the next day and never see him again?

But now here I was. Stuck.

Right between the two of them.

And neither one of them had touched me.

Wow. I'd just achieved a new level of rejection.

"I'm gonna go for a shower," Dylan said, sitting up and stretching out his naked body. I looked away. "You want anything first? Juice? Coffee?"

"I'm fine," I repeated. Apparently I'd killed a few too many brain cells last night and could no longer speak in complex sentences.

"There's some water for you, on the table." He indicated the bedside table where a glass of water sat.

"Uh-huh. Thanks," I mumbled. Every time he spoke, my head throbbed.

I watched him smirk, then stand up, naked, right in front of me. I only saw his backside as he headed for the en suite bathroom. But that *ass*...

If he really was gay, I was gonna cry.

I glanced over at Ashley, wondering if he'd caught me staring. And instead, I caught *him* staring.

"You want eggs?" he asked me in his rough, sexy morning voice, and his blue eyes met mine. "Omelet or something? Toast?" He sat up, sliding his legs over the far side of the bed, turning his back to me.

"Toast," I croaked. "Please and thanks."

He yanked on his black briefs and a T-shirt so fast I barely saw anything, and headed down to the kitchen without another glance in my direction. But I'd definitely seen the way he'd just looked at Dylan, watching him disappear into the bathroom, bare-assed.

A straight dude did not check out his dude friend's naked ass, even given the opportunity, when a woman was in the room.

And I'd seen that kiss; my camera didn't lie.

Katie and Maggie were wrong. They had to be.

Maybe Ashley and Dylan were in the gay rock star closet? I wouldn't exactly be surprised. Coming out when you were famous couldn't be any easier than doing it when you weren't. I'd been through the whole coming out thing, vicariously, with my sister. She'd be the first person to tell you that it was liberating as fuck, in some ways, but it was far from fun.

There just *had* to be something going on here. My female pride insisted upon it.

They were either gay, or I'd become repulsive since the last time I looked in a mirror.

To be honest, I kind of felt repulsive.

I pounded back the glass of water. Then I dragged myself up, peeling my cocktail dress off the chair where someone had laid it last night, along with my lingerie. I headed down the hall to a bathroom, and examined my naked self in the mirror, critically.

Nope. Definitely hadn't become repulsive overnight.

Okay, so I was no supermodel. But I was definitely cute enough for two horny single guys—if they were straight, or even bi—to at least *try* to get up my skirt.

When I headed down to the kitchen a few minutes later, Ashley was there, alone, making scrambled eggs. He'd laid out tea and toast for me on the island, alongside jars of jam and honey.

"I'm heading into the city today," he said, not looking at me. "Have some things to do."

"Okay," I said. It hadn't escaped my notice that he'd been measurably nicer to me since sometime at the party last night. If I'd been more sober, I might've been able to pinpoint why. As it was, I was clueless.

Maybe his time of the month had passed?

I buttered my toast and carefully spread some jam on, not looking at him. He was standing at the stove, his back to me anyway.

"You'll be alone with Dylan," he said.

"Okay."

"He'll probably play his drums, work out, swim. Make some phone calls. You know the routine by now."

"Uh-huh." I knew the routine. The naked routine.

If Dylan was swimming, his clothes were coming off. And I was gonna get hand cramps masturbating to the afterburn—the image of him that was gonna get permanently imprinted on my eyeballs from all the staring.

Ashley turned around. I tried not to look down at his briefs, at the bulge of his dick. Which meant I looked into his eyes instead. They didn't look as cold as usual, or as filled with contempt.

But I really couldn't say what he was thinking when he said, "You should take some photos of him today. It should be gorgeous out."

CHAPTER TWELVE

Dylan

LATE IN THE AFTERNOON, I stepped out onto the back deck. Amber was there, photographing the deck and the view, by the stairs that led down to the ground level. I paused. She saw me and nodded, as if to say, *Go about your business*. So I did.

I did exactly what I would've done if she wasn't there. I ignored the camera. I stripped down. I didn't even look at her to see what she thought of that, if her jaw was on the floor. Then I slid into the pool and started swimming.

When I was done, I hauled myself out and stood for a minute, enjoying the feeling as the cool air chilled my skin. Then I wrapped a towel loosely around my hips. The heaters were on, chasing off the October chill, and I settled back onto a lounge chair.

All the while I could feel her there, taking photos. I could hear the familiar, barely-audible click of the shutter... and it was turning me on.

It was getting me hard.

Fuck.

I was so fucking predictable.

Or at least, my dick was.

Amber was off to my right side, and I tried to ignore her as I made a couple of calls. Brody. Jesse. We were meeting at the old church where Dirty rehearsed in a few days, to start rehearsing the newest songs for the album, massaging the material Seth and Elle had written into the mix. We were still trying to figure out which songs were making it onto the album before we hit the studio in a few weeks.

All the while, I kept hearing the soft click of Amber's shutter and wondering if she was taking photos of me.

Finally, I looked over at her. She was sitting at the top of the stairs next to her camera, which was on a tripod. The lens seemed to be looking off, toward the water, but I couldn't tell if I was in her shot.

Our eyes met.

My cock was way up. I shifted, trying to bunch the towel up a bit on my lap, to hide it. I really didn't mind if Amber saw my cock, hard or not. Just didn't want to be rude or anything. Wasn't sure if the towel did much good, though. Maybe just made it more obvious?

"It's really gorgeous today," she said, awkwardly. "I think it's supposed to rain..." She glanced up at the mottled sky. "Makes for amazing lighting though. The clouds, diffusing the sun like that..."

"What are you gonna do with the photos?" I asked her.

She looked at me. "I'll back them up, then I can put them all on a drive for you, if you like. I'll retouch the best ones for you, though. There should be a few dozen."

"Not the photos of the house," I said, holding her gaze. "The other ones."

I was taking a gamble, maybe, accusing her of taking other ones, but after catching her snapping a photo of Ash kissing me—or appearing to—and never saying a thing about it, I wouldn't doubt she'd taken more.

"I told you," she said, breaking eye contact. "I'm not a paparazzo."

"No?"

"No. And I'm not a groupie, either."

"I didn't think you were."

She looked at me again, and her eyebrows drew together. "Ashley thought I was, when he first met me."

I laughed. "Yeah. Well, Ash thinks that about any girl who gets anywhere near me until she proves otherwise."

"He has a hard time trusting people," she said, getting to her feet. "I get that. I can relate."

"Yeah? You have trouble with that?"

"Trusting people? Yes." She unscrewed the plate that fastened the camera to the tripod and carried the camera over, setting it on the low table between us. I liked the way she handled it, like it was precious to her, even though it was scuffed all to hell. "People in general…" she said. "Men." She glanced at me. "Maybe rock stars especially, if I'm being honest."

"Why?"

She sat down on the lounge chair across from me with a small sigh. She didn't lounge, though. She just sat there with her knees pressed together, looking at me. She was wearing jeans today and an oversized sweater, her wavy hair loose around her face. I noticed she kept her eyes carefully locked on my face, even though I was half-naked. She was really trying to keep this whole thing professional.

It was kinda cute.

"Let's just say you aren't the first I've ever met," she said.

"First what?" Ashley strolled out the door from the kitchen, plates in hand and a grocery bag full of supplies in the other. He had what looked like marinated steaks on the plates, with veggies on skewers. He never shared the menu with me ahead of time, and I never asked; I'd eat whatever he cooked.

"Nothing," Amber said, turning away a bit, pretending to be absorbed in the view.

"Rock stars," I said. "Amber was just about to tell me about the other rock stars she's met."

Ash raised an eyebrow as he fired up the barbecue, and I watched her squirm. Didn't intend to out her like this, but no point keeping secrets.

Of course, I already knew about one rock star she'd met. I'd had Jude do a little intel for me. Nothing too deep, just the basics.

I hadn't shared that intel with Ash yet, though. Wanted to ask her about it first.

"There've been a few," Amber admitted, brushing it off. "You know, I've worked with Liv before. Been to a few parties."

"That all?" I asked.

She looked at me. She held my gaze, and I could see that she was wondering...

I already know, I tried to tell her with my eyes.

But maybe she didn't want me to know.

Ash was watching her, too, even as he laid the food on the grill... and eventually she cracked under the pressure.

"Okay. I might've, you know... had a relationship with a rock star," she admitted. "In the past. It was brief. Who cares, right?"

But Ash cared. "Who?" He looked at me with a question in his eyes. *Someone we know?*

"It's not important," she said with a shrug, still trying to brush it off.

"If it was Zane—"

"It wasn't Zane," she said, cutting Ash off. "It wasn't anyone in your band," she assured me, then glanced at him, "or yours."

"Who was it?" he pressed.

Amber sighed, and I kinda felt sorry for her. "Johnny O'Reilly," she mumbled, so quietly I almost couldn't hear her.

Ash heard it. "Johnny O?! Fuck, no."

Amber's cheeks were turning pink.

"You serious?" As Ash stared at her, he seemed to be seeing her in a different light as he tried to digest this new information.

"Ash..." I warned him.

"Fuck. You're shitting me."

"Nope," Amber said. Then she frowned at him. "Why, though?"

"I just can't picture you with Johnny O," he said, still scrutinizing her.

Amber laughed a humorless laugh. "Neither could he, apparently."

"No doubt," Ash said. "Who'd you catch him in bed with?"

She gave him a sharp look. "That's presumptuous. How do you know I didn't cheat on him?"

He gave her the same look right back.

She sighed again. "And the answer is: Who didn't I catch him in bed with?"

"Right," Ash said, not surprised in the least. He looked over at me. "Johnny O," he mused under his breath. "You talk to that asshole lately?"

"Nope."

Ash poked at the food on the grill. It was starting to smell good. I figured I should go put on some clothes now that he was here, but I didn't want to miss this conversation. Ash actually talking to Amber. Other than at the party last night, when they were both drunk, I'd never seen them really have a conversation.

"So. How much damage did he do?" he asked her.

"Damage?"

"Like how long were you together, how many times did he screw you over, were you in love with him, et cetera?"

Amber cleared her throat. "Um. Seven months. Too many to want to remember. And yes, unfortunately."

"You still in love with him?" I asked her.

Amber laughed bitterly. "Uh, no. That was like four years ago. And I haven't even seen him since then. You could say I learned my lesson."

"What lesson was that?" Ash glanced at me. "Rock stars are untrustworthy assholes?"

"Can't say you haven't known a few of those," I challenged him.

"I dunno," Ash replied. "You're trustworthy. You're not an asshole. Most of the time."

Amber looked at me. I didn't even try to say the same about Ash. He was my best friend, yes. But that just meant I knew pretty much his entire sordid history with relationships.

"Um, since we're grilling me," Amber said, "how about you guys?" She looked from me to him, carefully. "Ever had a relationship with a rock star?"

"Nope," I said.

"No," Ash said.

I actually had to catch myself before I laughed out loud. "Elle?" I prodded.

"We didn't have a relationship," Ash said, then disappeared into the kitchen.

"Okay. I can amend that," Amber called after him. "Ever fuck a rock star?"

I grinned. "Nope."

Ash returned with a couple of beers, a bottle of Prosecco and two wine glasses. He cracked a beer for himself and put the rest on the table between Amber and me. "What?" he said, when we both stared at him. Then he got busy flipping the food on the grill. "I plead the fifth."

"We're in Canada," Amber said, smirking. "Don't think that works up here."

"Good luck getting details out of Ash," I told her. "He'll never admit he was actually dating Elle. Or that he screwed two of the members of a certain death metal band in the porta potty at a festival. But I'll tell you."

Ash glared at me.

"How do you even fit three people in a porta potty?" Amber asked, wide-eyed.

"Not *at the same time*," Ash clarified, giving me another death look.

"And *why* in a porta potty?" Amber asked. "Didn't you have, like, a rock star trailer or something?"

"There was some jealousy and smoke-in-mirrors involved," I explained. "It ended in an ugly brawl in the mud with a lot of toilet paper—"

"How do you want your steak?" Ash interrupted. "'Cause if you keep talking, you're gonna be fishing it out of the ocean."

Amber grinned and bit back a laugh. She met my eyes and I shrugged, grinning back. "You know how I like it," I answered Ash. Then I asked her, "You want wine or beer?"

"Oh, God." Amber looked a little green at the idea. "Neither."

"Anyway," Ash cut in, "so I've been with a few rock stars. It's not like I'm a groupie or something."

Amber shot him a look. "Neither am I," she said firmly. "For the record, other than Johnny O, who I *was* unfortunately in love with, I've never been with a rock star."

"Good to know," he said cooly.

"And how do I know you're not some photographer groupie?" she pushed back.

"I don't know," he said. "Maybe I am."

Amber blinked at him. Then she smiled a little, awkwardly, like she wasn't sure she should. "Why?" She glanced from him to me. "Have you ever dated, or screwed, a photographer?"

"Nope," I said.

"Roslyn Pike," Ash said.

Amber stared at him. Her mouth fell open in wordless question.

"She shoots for *Rolling Stone* and *GQ*—"

"I know who Roslyn Pike is," she said, clearly in awe. "And to hell with *Rolling Stone*. She shoots for *National Geographic*. How long were you with her?"

"Few months," he said, which would've been the same answer no matter what girlfriend from his past she'd asked him about, other than Summer.

"Did she ever photograph you?"

"Yup," he said.

Amber seemed to be processing that. If I had to put money on it, I'd say she was jealous.

"Ash dated Ros years ago," I put in, and winked at her. "Don't worry. He likes you for more than your talent with a camera."

"Next to Roslyn Pike, I'm not sure I have any," Amber said. But she was staring at Ash. Probably wondering why he hadn't made a move on her if he liked her so much.

Like last night, in bed.

If I were her, that's what I'd be wondering.

I was still wondering myself.

"So..." he said, as he carefully laid Amber's food out on a plate for her. Her eyes widened when she saw the spread: a giant grilled portobello mushroom cap that stood in for a steak, a veggie skewer and a roast potato. "Johnny O, huh?"

Amber cringed, blushed, and took the plate Ash handed her. She set it on the table between us, then sighed and cracked open the Prosecco. "Yeah."

"How did you two meet?" I asked. That, I hadn't bothered to dig into. Figured she'd tell me herself, if she wanted to.

"I met him at a party Liv invited me to. Actually, it was at Jesse's place. I just didn't really know who Jesse was at the time. Actually..." She took a generous gulp of the wine she'd just poured herself, shivered as it went down, then peered at Ash. "I met you there, too."

Ash stared at her, maybe trying to remember that party.

"Was I there?" I asked her.

"No. Think I would remember the auburn-haired giant."

"What was I doing?" Ash asked. "Who was I there with?"

"I don't know."

"Did I hit on you?"

"Um... no." Amber held the wine bottle up, offering me some, and when I nodded, she poured me a glass. "I was kinda busy." She handed the glass to me.

"With Johnny?" I ventured.

"He kinda sought me out and cornered me..."

"No doubt." We toasted silently, clinking our glasses together, and I watched as the blush crept over her cheeks.

"Funny how life goes," Ash mused. He stood looking down at Amber, arms crossed. "You meet me and Johnny O at a party... you end up dating Johnny instead of me."

"Well, what can I say." Amber took another sip of her wine and avoided his eyes. "He kissed me first."

When Ash looked at me, I smirked.

Amber looked at me, too, then finally glanced at Ash. "And, um, just to clarify. I didn't just date him. I married him."

CHAPTER THIRTEEN

Amber

ROSLYN PIKE.
Holy shit.
When I got back to Ashley's place that evening, I took a quick shower, then threw on my short cotton sundress; cute, comfy, and easily did double-duty as a nightie. I threw on my loose cardigan overtop and pulled out my laptop. The sun was already down, so I clicked on a couple of small lamps and lit a fire in the fireplace, keeping it cozy and cabin-dark.

By now, I was used to Ashley hanging out at Dylan's all evening, so I sat down at the dining room table and immediately did a Google search for *Ashley Player and Roslyn Pike*.

The search turned up a few photos of the two of them together. Mostly because Ashley was pretty famous. I was pretty sure no one, other than a photographer like me, would know or care who Roslyn Pike was, even though she was so successful in her field. I'd met her once at an exhibit of her work, and she looked pretty much how I remembered. She had wavy blonde hair and kind eyes, and she'd been really nice to me, down-to-Earth.

Which kind of made me wonder what she'd seen in Ashley Player.

Well, besides the gorgeous face and smoking-hot bod.

The search also turned up a couple of gorgeous, moody, gritty black-and-white photos of Ashley, closeups of his face, taken by Roslyn. I didn't want to feel jealous, but shit, I kind of was. She was so talented. And apparently Ashley had liked her. At least for a few months, according to him.

Which just made me wonder why he hadn't been nicer to *me*.

At least now I knew he didn't have something against photographers in general, so that was something?

I started uploading the images from today's shoot; I still had a lot of photos to go through from the previous days and I didn't want to get way behind. Especially if I was catching a plane out of here soon. The last thing I wanted to be doing while I was overseas was sitting at my computer trying to finish processing photos from this shoot when I could be out taking new photos where I was.

So I got to work, organizing the images into folders, highlighting and rating my selects to narrow down my favorites. I really wasn't thinking about Roslyn Pike holding Ashley's hand in those online photos. Or how hot he'd looked, or how cute he was with his hair a little longer. I definitely wasn't wondering if there were more photos of him out there, where he might look even hotter.

But then the curiosity really got to me...

I did an image search for *Ashley Player*, then another one for *Dylan Cope*. Until now, I hadn't even looked either of them up.

As it turned out, the photos of the two of them online were virtually endless. Official band photos. Red carpet photos. Concert photos.

Photos of Ashley sweating and singing into a mic.

Photos of Dylan playing his drums—in a kilt.

And it felt weird seeing them like this, by way of the internet.

I wasn't exactly in the habit of researching the men I met, no matter how famous they were. I'd learned, from my earliest brushes with the handsome and the famous, that it was often a bad idea. Put you in a weird place when you knew things about someone they hadn't even told you yet, simply because you'd cyber-stalked them.

And besides that, sometimes you saw shit you didn't really want to see—like the man you were crushing on on the arms of a whole lot of other women.

Which was a whole lot of what I found when I searched Ashley and Dylan.

There were no photos of either of them getting cozy with men, but that didn't mean much. Either way, I felt uncomfortable, looking at those photos. So I stopped.

Then I thought of something.

I wasn't famous, but...

I did a search for myself and my ex-husband. Because what if Dylan and/or Ashley did the same?

What would they find?

I actually had no idea. I'd seen a few photos of the two of us pop up when we were together, but since we'd split, I really hadn't looked. I didn't want to. I'd just hoped the whole thing would fade into obscurity in the back pages of the ever-expanding internet. Kind of the way Johnny O'Reilly had faded into obscurity in my heart and mind.

But once things were out there on the web... they just didn't die.

My search came up with several hits. Most of them repeats of the same five images of us. Just five.

Okay; I could live with five.

But *wow*. It was so weird looking at those photos. At how young I looked, only four-and-a-half years ago. More baby-faced and so starry-eyed I almost didn't recognize myself. And did I ever look fucking smitten. I was all aglow holding onto Johnny's hand as we walked into some party or club. Each of the photos was from a different event, and in every one of them I was smiling.

I'd almost forgotten how happy I'd been with him—for a while.

A very short while.

Fortunately, none of the images I found showed how I'd felt toward the end of our relationship, when I realized I wasn't quite as special to him as he was to me. It was kind of nicer this way. Who needed a visual reminder of that? I really didn't need to see my twenty-three-year-old self all crestfallen and heartbroken.

I'd just feel so sorry for that girl.

I allowed myself to really look at Johnny in each of the photos, once. Well, twice. And shit, he was handsome. With his bleached hair and overly-white teeth and deep tan, and those wide, mesmerizing blue eyes with all the lashes. No wonder he'd been able to play me. It wasn't his money or his burgeoning fame or the music that had gotten me, though I wasn't gonna lie to myself; those things were nice. It was just *him*.

He was so confident, so sure of himself, so sure of what he wanted.

And for the brief period of time that what he wanted was me, it was intoxicating. He'd swept me right off my feet. When I looked back, it literally seemed like I hadn't touched the ground in those memories, like I hadn't stopped to breathe for the first few months we were together.

But, man… when Johnny O'Reilly did a number on a girl? He went all in.

He'd smashed my heart to pieces.

The worst part was that he didn't even set out to do it intentionally. That would just make it easier to hate him for being an evil bastard. No, my ex just had other things he wanted out of life, things that were one-hundred-percent at odds with having a wife, and when he went after those things with the same certainty with which he'd gone after me… my heart was just the collateral damage.

If you asked him—if Dylan or Ashley asked him, God forbid—he'd probably just say something infuriating about what a great girl I was, and ask how I was doing. Yeah, he'd definitely do that.

Hell, he'd probably even try to get in my pants again, if he ever had the chance.

Yeah. I really knew how to pick them.

I couldn't decide whether it was a relief or totally depressing that Google couldn't even find a single thing about our marriage. It didn't even warrant a mention on Johnny's Wikipedia page. He wasn't as famous back then, so maybe that was it.

Or maybe when you're only married for sixteen days, no one really knows or cares.

Maybe Johnny preferred it that way. Maybe he'd rather just forget.

Personally, I preferred to remember. Because that seven-month relationship and sixteen-day marriage were the reasons I didn't do *impulsive* anymore when it came to relationships.

Sex was one thing.

Relationships were a whole other beast. One that tended to bite me in the ass—over and over again. Unfortunately, my ex-husband wasn't the only man who'd ever devastated me. Really, I'd been dumped, duped and dated more assholes than any girl should ever have to.

Couldn't fault me for trying though, right?

I closed the browser and went to find something to drink. I had no interest in more booze; I'd drank enough the last few days. So I poured myself a pineapple juice. I was feeling a little restless, so I threw together a salad for tomorrow. I didn't think I'd actually seen Ashley eat a vegetable himself, yet he'd filled his fridge with them since I'd arrived. For me.

I could probably thank him, though I didn't want to set off some kind of allergic reaction; me being nice to him would probably just give him hives.

I smirked at the thought.

When I was done making the salad, I brought my juice over to the dining room table and sat in front of my laptop, looking through the images from today. Wondering idly what the guys were doing next door.

I pulled up the photos I'd taken on Dylan's back deck, and started flipping through—until I got to the ones with Dylan in them. I paused on one particularly beautiful one. Dylan had just gotten out of the pool and stood looking down, wearing nothing but a towel. Well, he was kinda wearing the towel. He was in the middle of putting it on, maybe, and the fabric just barely covered the bulge of his—

"Nice photo." I jumped as Ashley appeared out of the goddamn ether behind me. *Jesus*, the man had a way of sneaking up on a girl.

"Fuck. What are you, a fucking ninja or something?"

He smirked, then glanced at the photo of Dylan and said, "Wow. You *are* freaky."

"I'm *not*—"

"I knew you were kinky. I knew it the moment I saw you." I watched him saunter over to the fridge and pull out the carton of pineapple juice.

"Um... Excuse me? You barely even noticed me when you first saw me."

"I knew he'd notice you."

Oh. *What?*

He poured himself a juice, then leaned back on the counter and looked from me to the photo of Dylan and back. "Do you want him?" he asked me bluntly.

"I wasn't stalking him or anything," I said, avoiding the question. "He knew I was there."

Ashley said nothing.

I got up, planning to clear out of his dining room, when he said, "Trust me, he wouldn't mind if you stalked him."

I stilled, my heart beating weirdly hard, and just tried to keep my voice normal when I asked, "What does that mean?"

"It means Dylan likes being looked at."

I turned to look at him.

"Why do you think he walks around with his shirt off in October?" he said. "Why do you think he plays drums in a kilt, and models those fucking see-through tighty-whities?" He took a long swig of his juice, his throat working. Then he walked over to me, joining me in the dining room.

"So... what are you trying to say? He's an exhibitionist or something?" I noticed that he hadn't actually said that Dylan liked being looked at by *women*, and in truth, pathetic or not, I was still waiting for some kind of proof that Dylan might actually be into females.

That he might be into *me*.

"I'm not much for putting labels on people, sweetheart." He was staring at the photo of Dylan, examining it, and I wondered what the hell he was thinking about it. The guy was a broody, bitchy mystery, impossible to figure out. "Dylan just likes being looked at. He likes being watched. People like what they like." He looked me over, slowly. "Take me, for example."

Okay. I'll bite.

"You?" I asked.

His blue eyes met mine, all serious and smoldering. "I like it all," he said. Then he took a sip of juice, very nonchalant, even as he totally eye-fucked me to hell and back with his blue, blue eyes.

I swallowed, hard.

"So," he said, setting his glass on the table. "How about you?"

"Me?" I swallowed again. I was suddenly salivating weirdly much.

"What do you like, Amber Malone?"

When I didn't answer right away, he glanced at the photo of Dylan again. "You like to be watched? Or... to watch?"

"I..."

He took a couple more steps toward me, getting all in my space. His eyes were kinda hooded and locked onto my mouth when he said, "Admit it... You're a photographer. You're probably more of a voyeur than I am."

"I thought... you don't like labels...?"

"Or maybe you're more of an exhibitionist?" He was looking me over, slowly, from head to toe. Then his eyes narrowed. "You and Johnny O got a sex tape floating around out there?"

"Uh, no. Definitely not—"

"Or are you inexperienced?" His hooded gaze lingered on my chest, where my sundress dipped a little between my breasts. I wasn't wearing a bra, but the cardigan was covering my nipples, which were rapidly hardening. Either way, I felt exposed by that look of his. "Is that what he liked about you...? That combination of sass and innocence..."

"I have no idea what he liked about me." I really didn't want to think about it, either. Because whatever Johnny had liked, it wasn't enough to make him treat me right, and that had just plain hurt my self-esteem. Sad, but true.

Ashley leaned in and whispered in my ear, "That's what Dylan likes about you."

Then his hand went up my dress.

He skimmed his fingertips up my thigh, just lightly, and fingered the edge of my panties.

Um…

I shifted, gripping the table behind me for support as all the strength seemed to leave my legs. Ashley's eyes finished their lazy journey back up my body, then met mine. And as they did, I felt that thrill you only feel when a really hot dude looks into your eyes up close… and you want him to kiss you. It didn't exactly help that his fingers were now drifting up over my panties. I was trying to remember which ones I'd put on after my shower. Were they sexy? The cute pink ones with the lace? Or the boring gray ones?

Was Ashley Player about to see them?

Shit. Why didn't I put on my sexy underpants? I was pretty sure I was wearing the boring gray cotton ones. The comfiest ones. Because I wasn't exactly expecting to have a rock star up my dress tonight.

"Breathe," he said softly, his gaze drifting to my lips again, and I realized I'd been holding my breath, hard, in my chest.

I exhaled… and he slid his hand down, between my legs.

My mouth dropped open. But I was hardly gonna stop him… It had been a while since a dude had been down there, and my clit was already pulsing with need. My pussy was swollen. All I wanted him to do was rub me, harder, faster, as his fingers whispered over the cotton of my panties, sliding deeper between my legs.

Holy hell…

What the fuck was happening?

I was so sure Ashley couldn't stand me. But considering he now had his hand on my pussy, I was really starting to rethink that. Then he leaned in, his body almost touching mine, and I could feel his heat. He smelled like soap and clean clothes and man. And pineapple juice.

I wanted to suck on his mouth... but he leaned closer, nuzzling into my hair and skimming his lips down the side of my neck. He breathed in, and a shiver of excitement ran down my spine. My pussy clenched.

Was he smelling me?

"Um... what happened last night, at the party?" I managed.

"Hmm?"

"You started being nice to me. Or at least... less hostile." I was gripping the table behind me so hard I thought my knuckles might burst. I didn't know what to do. I didn't know how to touch him.

Was this all some cruel joke? Was he just messing with me?

"Don't know what you're talking about," he said, his voice low and rough, and his blue eyes met mine. "I can't stand you."

Then he kissed me—on the mouth.

My head spun as his lips slid over mine and he thrust his pierced tongue into me... making my body melt, even as the meaning behind his words tore through me in a hot wave of confusion...

Holy fuck...

Did this guy like me or not?

Was this amping up to be some kind of hate fuck situation?

And if so, did I care?

He pressed against me and I felt the stiff bulge in his tight jeans, hard against me. So, okay. He liked me *that* way.

But he wasn't just trying to fuck me... Instead, he was caressing me between my legs, slowly, and he started licking and sucking his way down my neck.

"You stopped me when I tried to touch you," I reminded him, breathless, as some innate sense of self-protection tried to slow this down. Just a bit...

"You were wasted," he muttered against my skin. Then he suddenly turned me around, pushing me up against the table, his body pressing against my backside. He slipped my cardigan off my shoulders, and slowly down my arms... and dropped it aside on the floor. Somehow, his fingertips drifting down my arms as he undressed me was one of the most intensely arousing sensations I'd ever felt.

I swallowed as tingles raced all over my body.

Then he reached around in front of me, and I felt him pull my panties aside, exposing my pussy.

Oh, God...

I leaned on the table, my arms shaking, just trying not to collapse as the sensations overwhelmed me... as heat flooded me and my head got light. As I waited for him to touch me—my bare, needy flesh. "So... you didn't want to take advantage...?" My voice was getting all wobbly and needy as he finally touched me—slicking his middle finger down toward my opening.

I was wet already. *So* wet.

"Just wanted to be sure you really wanted it..."

"Oh. Um... and now you're sure?" I gasped as his finger slid into me.

He hissed in a breath between his teeth. "*Fuck*... you're wet..." he growled. "So fucking soft..."

And my eyes rolled back in my head. My mouth stretched open in wordless want. I spread my legs to give him access.

Even as I did it I knew, somewhere in the back of my mind, that I shouldn't be giving in to this. Not if I hoped to have any chance with Dylan.

So why was I giving in to this?

Why was Ashley Player kissing my neck?

Why was his finger up my—*oh, God. Two* fingers. And his thumb, rubbing circles around my—

"I—I really thought you... um... preferred men..." I managed, even as his fingers stroked in and out of my pussy in that way only a man could do it—rough, aggressive, hungry. And with skill. No hesitation. Even *I* didn't love putting my fingers up there all that much. And not like this. But his? ... Holy shit.

He's done this before.

Like, a lot.

"Doesn't everyone?" he murmured as he licked my neck.

"Ah... what?" I tried to turn to look at him, but he held me where I was, pinned to the table.

He snickered against my neck. "It's a joke. From *The Simpsons*."

"Oh." Huh? I was kinda lost, forgetting what the hell we were talking about, or not caring, as his fingers worked me into a hot panic. Shit, why was this so hot? *Ashley's fingers are up inside me.*

So. Hot.

He shoved me forward, bending me over the table, and pulled my dress up over my ass as he kept fucking me with his fingers. I heard him undoing his belt and my core clenched with need. My pussy squeezed on his invading fingers.

Oh fuck, yes.

Was I about to get fucked on Ashley Player's dining room table?

God, I hoped so.

But then he knelt down...

He licked me, his tongue circling lazily around his fingers, teasing me while he held my panties aside, his fingers working inside me, and I bit my lip. Hard. He was kissing my clit... Then he was sucking on me and kinda growling in the back of his throat, in a way that left no shred of doubt in my mind that the man liked pussy.

This man, apparently, fucking loved the pussy.

Maybe a gay man would flirt with you and even make out with you a bit, for shits and giggles... but he definitely wasn't gonna suck on your clit and lap up your juices, all the while growling like he was hungry for more... all the while he finger-fucked you, digging into your front wall in relentless pursuit of your inner happy spot...

Then suddenly, his fingers withdrew, and I mewled in protest like a starving kitten denied a saucer of milk. He laughed. But he pressed me down to the table, his hand warm on the small of my back, as if to say, *Stay right the fuck there.*

I stayed.

I heard him fumbling around below as he kept eating me out, his pierced tongue thrusting deep into me and undulating around. I writhed on the table, gasping. I would've purred if I knew how. I heard the rip of a condom packet, and a moment later Ashley rose to his feet, towering over me where I lay, melted onto the table, quivering.

After being tongue-screwed like that, I wasn't going anywhere—like even if the house caught fire. I was just gonna have to hope that if that happened, he'd be decent enough to carry me out; otherwise, I was going down in flames.

He rubbed his cock against me and it felt so so sooooo good. Warm and smooth, hard and slippery. Big. Enough to fill me up and then some.

Yes, please...

"You want this cock, Amber?" he asked, his voice rough with lust as I squirmed at his touch, trying to push myself onto him.

"*Yes...*" I breathed. I felt something hard but smooth nudge against me as he slicked his dick over me again. One of his rings? Or... *shit*.

Was his cock pierced??

In my lust haze, as I wriggled against him and tried to figure out the answer to that intriguing question, I dimly realized that I'd *almost* forgotten about Dylan.

And the fact that this was a bad move.

Because what if Dylan, like Ashley, also enjoyed the pussy?

What if they were both into women, and I was ruining my chance at ever—

Ashley thrust into me and my mind blanked out.

As he held me down with one hand on my back and the other gripping my hip, he said, "That's good... don't move," his voice tight and rough. Then he fucked me in a quick, forceful rhythm that had his definitely-pierced dick stimulating the amazing spot in the front wall of my pussy.

The spot that had me quivering from the inside-out... shuddering and shaking on the quickly-mounting verge of an all-over orgasm...

My panties hadn't even come off.

And I didn't move. I just took what he gave, moaning beneath him as he fucked me against the table. Clearly, the man knew what he was doing. He already had me on the edge, about to fall...

I didn't move... but I did look up. I looked at Dylan.

That beautiful photo I'd taken of him was still there on the laptop screen. I could hardly ignore it. It was inches from my face, lit up in the near-darkness.

His sculpted body slick and wet, his nipples pricked against the cold... and there was definitely a thick bulge in the front of the towel where his cock pressed against it.

Ashley rode me, ramming into me, his piercing doing some fucking crazy shit inside me as his balls slapped against my clit... until I suddenly couldn't take it anymore and I came with a gasping, shuddering scream.

The entire time, I was staring at that photo.

And when Ashley came with a grunt and a groan, ramming into me and shuddering against me, his dick jerking inside me... I couldn't help wondering: Was he looking at it, too?

"Let's do that again," I said, in the dark of Ashley's dining room, as we both righted our clothes, shakily. I already wanted him to fuck me again. The split second I came back to Earth from planet Orgasm, I wanted him inside me again.

When you hadn't been laid in as long as I hadn't been—like almost a year—one fuck was just a tease.

I needed more.

And Ashley didn't exactly object.

This time, though, I ended up on my knees in front of him. And while I was there, I was no longer thinking about Dylan.

But I only realized that afterward.

On my knees at Ashley's feet, all I wanted was his big, hard dick in my mouth. He was long and yes, he was pierced. I'd never been with a guy who was pierced there before, but how different could it be? I tongued the smooth steel balls of the barbell that ran through the underside of his glans and sucked on his head a lot, which made him crazy. He could barely stand still and he was breathing heavy, groaning.

And he was hard as rock.

All good signs...

I took my time, because I loved giving head. But I was hungry, too, and zealous as hell.

I deep-throated him a bit, which took him by surprise. He swore and stumbled, before widening his stance and digging his hands into my hair. The squeeze of my throat around his swollen head, his piercing rubbing the back of my tongue... it was crazy-erotic, but I was pretty good at not gagging. I'd just always loved sucking cock... experiencing a man's arousal and pleasure in that intimate way. The feel and the taste and the smell of him...

Since we'd already had sex, he tasted like his own come. The latex taste didn't even bother me, once I got going.

And once I got going... all I wanted was Ashley Player coming in my face. It wasn't even that *I* needed to come again. What I needed was to see *him* come, up close.

His hands squeezed in my hair and he growled, low in his throat, right before he let go. I gripped the base of his cock with my hand and sucked him deep as he came. I swallowed most of it. Then I pulled away and finished him off with my hands. He shuddered at my touch, gasping, his cock flexing in my grip as his orgasm finished.

I licked up the stray come and generally worshipped his dick, because shit, if I was having sex with a guy this hot, I was gonna milk it—literally—for all it was worth.

... Even if I was already starting to realize how much I might regret this tomorrow.

In the moment, all caught up in my horny bliss, I told myself I didn't even care if Ashley was looking at that sexy photo of Dylan the entire time.

And once, when I looked up at him... he definitely was.

CHAPTER FOURTEEN

Amber

THE NEXT MORNING WAS AWKWARD, to put it ultra-mildly.

I woke up—in Ashley's bed—to find him singing in the shower. After a few lines, I recognized the Red Hot Chili Peppers' "Suck My Kiss." He was really giving it his all with his sexy, slightly-raspy morning voice. *Damn.* The man had pipes. I giggled a little, sleepily.

Then I *really* woke up.

I leapt out of his bed like it was on fire.

The bathroom door was open a crack, but the shower was around the corner; he couldn't see me or hear me, I was sure. But giggling in Ashley Player's bed was so not happening.

I grabbed my clothes—or at least, my gray cotton panties, which had ended up on his floor—and scrambled the hell out of there.

I found my dress in the hallway, and his jeans in the dining room with my laptop. I didn't look for his underwear; his undies were his problem. Was he wearing any last night? I didn't even know. His clothes were off before I could really process such details.

I hurried into the bathroom in the hall, sped-showered, dressed, stuffed all my things into my backpack and got the hell out of there. Ashley's shower was still running, he was still singing his way through the Chili Peppers' catalog, and I felt like a grade-A asshole as I ran out the door; as I hurried down his driveway and out to the road, my hair still wet, the Grim Reaper in his gate giving me the finger.

It was the slowest getaway in history.

It wasn't even eleven in the morning; I had over seven hours to wait until the ferry departed.

I went for a walk, pulling out my camera and photographing the shit out of the island, again. By one o'clock I was running out of things to shoot, as I stealthily avoided the section of road where both Ashley's and Dylan's houses were. By two o'clock, it was getting ridiculous.

Around three, he found me at the marina.

"You know," he said, sitting down beside me at the end of one of the long wooden docks, "you really didn't have to jet. I could've given you a ride to the city."

"In Dylan's boat?" I said neutrally.

"Yeah." Ashley looked me in the eye, squinting a little in the midday sun. "His is better than mine. Story of my life." He didn't say it with an ounce of animosity. Envy, maybe.

Were we still talking about boats?

"Ashley—"

"You feel weird about what happened." It wasn't a question. "I get that."

"Don't you?"

A slight smirk pulled at the corner of his mouth and he looked out over the water. "Honestly, no. I know you're hot for Dylan. You're not the first girl who ever was."

"I didn't think so."

He looked at me again, his expression growing serious. "So. You like Dylan. It turns me on. Now you're gonna run away?"

"I'm not running," I said, kicking my legs in the air a little where they dangled off the dock. "Obviously."

So that was it, then? He'd gotten off on me getting off on Dylan?

Except I hadn't just been getting off on Dylan.

"I'm kind of stuck here," I admitted. "But, yes. I'm going to the city to see my sister." I ad-libbed that last part; until just now, I hadn't committed myself to where I was going. But Liv's place was the only place I really could go.

Ashley was staring at me and he wasn't smiling. He was searching my face. His blue eyes lingered on my lips, then skipped back up to my eyes. "So you want a ride or what? I've got a shitty, uncomfortable boat that might break down on us, or a comfortable-as-fuck boat. Take your pick."

"I'll take the ferry," I said.

"And she's stubborn to boot," he mused, half under his breath.

"Like a mule."

He sat there for an incredibly long minute, watching me as I pretended to be fascinated with the seagull nosing around on the deck of a nearby yacht. I felt him get to his feet while I was taking photos of it.

He stood there, maybe waiting for me to look up.

I didn't.

Then he walked away without another word.

📷

I wasn't sure what I was doing, exactly, except what I always did.

Looking forward.

Moving on.

There was always something else, somewhere else, *someone* else out there, just beyond the horizon, anyway, to distract you from whatever you'd left behind.

Admittedly, self-reflection was not my strongest suit.

I'd discovered that once, while trying to self-reflect.

📷

Kind of hard to move on when you still had over two hours to kill before a ferry pulled up to the dock to collect you, and in the meantime, a pimped-out speedboat with a couple of gorgeous rock stars motored up with a cold drink and a warm seat for you.

"You *didn't*," my sister said, as soon as Dylan and Ashley had dropped me off at her house—and I'd filled her in, briefly, on the sexual hurricane of last night. The one where my sex parts had unexpectedly collided with Ashley Player's.

Several times.

"Yup. I really did."

Liv was still holding the front door of her house open while I kicked off my shoes; I'd basically gotten the dirty details out before I crossed the threshold.

"*Son-of-a...*" Liv looked out the door and up the street, as if she could still see Dylan's SUV departing and will it to burst into flame, but the guys were long gone. She slammed the door. "So let me get this straight—"

"No pun intended," I muttered.

"You're telling me you fucked Ashley Player. Willingly." She headed into the house without waiting for my answer, and I followed.

"As opposed to what?" I could hear Lady Gaga's "Lovegame" thumping from downstairs, loud, which meant Laura was working out; Liv wouldn't be caught dead *willingly* blaring a dance song about cock.

"As opposed to you," Liv said, "making up some shit about being wasted-drunk and suffering a momentary lapse of, I don't know, eyesight? Sense of direction? Sanity? And me pretending to believe you." I followed her into the kitchen, letting her rant. "Just tell me you were totally fucking lost and/or blackout drunk, or something, when you ended up naked with him. I *want* to believe you, Amber."

"Nope," I said. "Not drunk. And I don't think I've ever been so lost that I accidentally ended up on top of a penis."

"Because otherwise," she went on, like I hadn't even spoken, "there is *no good reason* to have sex with Ashley Player."

"You mean other than feeling his dick in my pussy? Feeling his hands all over my body? Feeling—"

"Please. Don't *describe* it." She yanked her fridge open and frowned at the contents like they'd disappointed her, though they were probably just taking the brunt of her current feelings toward me. "Laura!" she bellowed. "Did you drink all the IPA?" She swiped a couple of beers from the depths of the fridge, scowled at them, and cracked them open, handing one to me. "Sorry."

"Cheers." We clinked bottles irritably and I took a deep swig of the honey ale.

My sister took a sip and grimaced. "Laura's beer," she complained.

"So can I stay here or what?" I flopped into a seat in her breakfast nook and kicked up my feet. "You know I hate to ask. You know I won't stay long. I just need to finish processing the images from the shoot at Dylan's, and then I'm off to Thailand."

"Uh-huh."

"What? You owe me, after sending me off to the Island of the Gorgeous Rock Stars without warning me, then ignoring my calls."

My sister sat on the edge of the table, looking down at me. "I've been busy." She had the gall to say it straight-faced while she was wearing sweatpants.

My sister sometimes worked on set, sometimes worked from home, and sometimes drank beers in her sweats on a Tuesday. As for Laura, she handled online sales for a local cosmetics company from home, part-time, which meant she did her abs-and-butt workout to Lady Gaga whenever she felt like it.

The two of them were living the dream.

"You *look* busy," I remarked.

"You want to take care of yourself, right?" Liv shot back. "How much money are you making shooting Dylan's house?"

I glared at her. "A lot." But that was hardly the point. Just because I'd ended up making a bunch of money and getting laid while I was there, I wasn't about to thank my sister for it.

She frowned. "And they kicked you out?"

"What? No. I'm just not staying there anymore."

"Hmm."

"Incidentally, why didn't you return my calls?"

She crossed her arms. "I needed a cooling period."

Right. Liv and her fucking cooling periods.

"You were pissed at me?"

"I was a little pissed. You made me look pretty bad at the Underlayer shoot, Amber. You were there on my recommendation. It took a little elbow grease to unruffle all those feathers."

"Sorry." I rolled my eyes a bit, embarrassed. "I really am sorry. And for what it's worth, I apologized to Dylan too. Sincerely."

She sat there, just kind of glowering down at me.

"And you would be thinking...?" I asked, glaring back up at her.

"I'm thinking, where the hell does Ash get off fucking my little sister."

"Um, hello? You shipped me off to an island to live in his house. You've seen his abs and that angsty thing he does with his eyebrows. You *knew* this would happen."

"Fuck that. I shipped you off to Dylan for a *job*. He said he'd throw you some *work*."

I groaned. "You did what?"

"I tell you, every time. You bring this shit on—"

"*Yourself*," I finished for her.

"You won't take help. You'll work for it, but you won't let me loan you money. You needed a place to stay and a paycheck. Dylan offered both. And I trust him."

I blinked at her. "What does that mean? You trust him not to fuck me?"

She gave me a sidelong glance as she sipped her beer. "At least he'd have the decency to provide a bed," she muttered, no doubt referring to the dining room table Ashley had provided.

Really glad now that I'd shared that particular detail.

"Right. Perfect." Dylan offered me a job as a *favor* to my sister? Could this get more humiliating? "And what did Ashley offer?"

"Nothing. Dylan said you could stay in Ash's house because no one was using it anyway. I didn't know he was gonna creep up your skirt."

"He didn't *creep*."

Liv made a disgusted sound and drank her beer.

I sighed. "There was nothing creepy about it. I wasn't lost or confused. And we were both stone-cold sober." *Though maybe a little drunk on the sight of half-naked Dylan Cope.* "We had, like, one drink with Dylan, hours before that, and that was it."

"*And* you have a crush on Dylan," my sister accused, her voice flat with disappointment. As if that was somehow *worse* than screwing Ashley.

"Says you."

"I surmised," she said, as the music downstairs shut off.

"Uh-huh."

"You keep angling your shoulders like you can't remember how to sit properly, and getting all twirly when his name comes up."

Liv's girlfriend, Laura, had walked in while she was talking, blonde ponytail bouncing, and now looked over at me for evidence of this angling and twirling.

"Hey, Amber. When did you get here?"

I raised my eyebrows at Liv. "Twirly?"

"You twirl your hair around your finger. Like this." Liv pantomimed me fluttering my eyelashes and twirling my finger in my hair, though she did it in thin air because her hair was too short to twirl.

"Good thing I don't really do that," I said firmly, as Laura swung a box of beer onto the table between us, "because it's really fucking pathetic."

"Oh, but you do."

"You do," Laura agreed. She swept in for a hug, squeezed, then released me. "IPA," she announced, patting the box of beer and giving my sister a loud kiss on the cheek before strutting over to the fridge.

"*Warm* IPA," Liv grumbled. "A couple of rock stars dropped her off a few minutes ago." She answered Laura's question distractedly, and Laura threw me a pretend-scandalized look, then winked at me. She was all perfect-Vancouver-blonde in her skintight Lululemon pants, her naturally exuberant boobs squishing out the top of her sports bra, an attractive sheen of sweat shimmering on her skin. Laura sometimes reminded me of a news anchor, but with less-stiff hair.

"Good for you, sweetie," she said.

I managed a brief, "Thanks," since the comment was genuine. "And I don't have a 'crush' on anyone," I informed my sister. Okay, so I was lying to her face, but was it really her business?

"Really."

"A crush?" Laura perked up. "On whom?"

"Dylan Cope," Liv said.

"*Oh*." Laura grabbed herself a honey ale and studied me, like she was looking for evidence that I'd somehow changed since she last saw me.

It had taken a long, long time for me to warm up to Laura. When I first met her, I didn't buy her whole "lesbian act"—my term. To my utter disdain, Liv was her first female lover and I was pretty fucking sure she was just some curious tourist in the gay "lifestyle." I figured within a month she'd move on, bounce right back to men and leave my sister a broken wreck. Or drag home some random dude for her and Liv to make out in front of.

It never happened. Not once in nine years.

So as it turned out, I was wrong about Laura. Liv wasn't some sexual experiment to her. She really did love my sister. Which meant I'd eventually come to love her—and find her about as annoying as my sister, though in different ways.

She dropped into the booth across from me and leaned toward me over the table, blue eyes sparkling; the look on her face said *deliciously intrigued*. "Do tell."

"There is absolutely not one thing to tell. Dylan is just, you know..." I caught my right shoulder dropping, and quickly straightened before Liv could open her mouth. "He's too... *perfect*," I finished, like that was the worst thing in the world for someone to be. "And Ashley is just... *pfft*."

"Right," my sister said, sliding into the booth next to Laura. "And when you talk about Ash, you chew on your hair."

"You do," Laura agreed.

I spit the lock of hair out of my mouth. "Gross." It felt kind of satisfying, crunching the ends lightly between my teeth, but I'd barely noticed I was doing it.

"Super fucking gross," Liv corrected me. "I haven't seen you chew on your hair since Robbie Masterson, by the way."

"You're an asshole," I informed her and drank my beer.

"Who's Robbie Masterson?" Laura inquired.

"Eighth grade," Liv said.

"He knocked my books out of my hands in the hallway when we changed classes. Every fucking day. I hated that guy."

"And you're full of shit," my sister said. "You're totally crushing on Dylan, just like you crushed on Robbie." To Laura, she said, "I can always tell when she's hot for a guy."

"You know nothing about being hot for a guy," I pointed out.

"I'd accuse you of crushing on Ash, too," Liv informed me, "but if that were true, you probably wouldn't have had sex with him already."

"Hmm. Suck it." I took another swig of my beer and looked to Laura for help.

"I know," Laura said. "Where does she get off knowing you so damn well, right?"

"Am I really that fucked up?"

"When it comes to men," Laura said, "yes."

I threw up my hands. "Who the fuck cares if I have a crush on Dylan Cope? I'm three-quarters sure he's into dick, ladies."

My sister frowned at me. "Since when?"

"How should I know? Since around the time he decided he wasn't into pussy?"

My sister glanced at her girlfriend, then threw me a look like I was the world's worst idiot. "Dylan Cope isn't gay."

"So everyone says," I said, unconvinced.

"He's not gay, Amber," Laura put in, glancing at Liv for backup. "He's just, you know..." She shrugged. "Laid-back."

I scoffed. "Gay men can't be laid-back?"

"What I mean is, he's used to women pursuing *him*."

"Yup," my sister said. "I've actually seen the man shrug when a woman approached him at a party, like five seconds before he started making out with her. He doesn't even have to lift a finger. The pussy just magically materializes in his presence."

Now there was a visual I didn't need.

"Don't be jealous," Laura teased my sister.

Liv narrowed her eyes at me as she studied me across the table. "But be warned. If he decides he actually wants you, *before* you've offered up the pussy, he'll be cunning about it."

"That's probably true," Laura concurred.

"Like a fucking leopard," my sister said. "I've seen the man in action when he's actually interested. It's gnarly, *National-Geographic*-level shit."

Laura nodded right along, making *Mm-hmm* noises.

I frowned, skeptical. "A leopard?"

"You ever see a leopard on the hunt?" Liv asked me.

"Maybe?"

"They stealth in, all camo'd up, just waiting for the perfect moment, then BAM!" She slammed her fist down on the table, making me and everything on the tabletop jump. "They *strike*."

Laura tipped her blonde head back, peals of laughter pouring from her mouth.

Right about now, I was really glad I'd come over. You know, so I could provide so much amusement for them.

"Well, he's *not* interested," I said, slamming back some more honey beer. "This is great beer, by the way," I told Laura, ignoring my sister's look. I wanted to believe them, desperately. I wanted to believe Dylan might be into me.

But...

"He hasn't even made a move, okay? Ashley came right up to me and licked my neck and stuck his hand between my legs and asked me if I wanted his cock."

"Oh, my," Laura said. "And I suppose the answer was yes?"

"And Dylan has done no such thing," I finished.

My sister studied me for a moment longer, her eyes narrowing to slits. "Oh, *shit*," she finally concluded. "You're serious."

"Um, yeah?"

"I figured you were shitting me. Like you'd already screwed them both in some dirty hetero three-way and didn't want to admit it to me."

"'Fraid not."

Liv glanced at Laura. Laura glanced back at Liv and shrugged, sympathy contorting her face, as they communicated telepathically.

Liv sighed. "They like you," she informed me, like she was breaking the news that I'd contracted some infectious yet benevolent disease.

"Sorry, Amber," Laura added.

"Huh?" I looked from one to the other. "You lost me there."

Liv leaned toward me over the table. "It's like this, Amber. Usually, Dylan and Ash just toss a girl into bed with the both of them, have at her, and move on. I've seen it, many times."

"True," Laura said.

Then my sister reached across the table and took my hand, giving it a little squeeze. And it was deeply disturbing. It was a kindly-mom gesture, and although Liv had often stepped in to parent me—for better or worse—after Dad left and Mom fell apart, she'd never done *that*.

"They're taking their time with you," she said.

"Okay. Why are you taking that gentle-mommy tone with me? I'm not sick."

"Because," Liv said, "I'm trying to be gentle here. I know how much you suck at it when boys you like actually like you back, Amber."

I made an exasperated sound, somewhere between a groan and an adolescent protest, complete with eye roll. "How old do you think I am, again?"

"She's right," Laura said, all sympathy. "Remember Robbie Whatshisname?"

"Masterson," I squeezed out.

"Right." Now it was Laura's turn to reach over and squeeze my hand. "I think those two rock stars just sent your books flying all over the hallway, sweetie."

"Yup," my sister said.

I resisted the urge to roll my eyes again. Just barely. But the fucked up thing was, they were right. At least, the part about the books and Robbie Masterson.

I did like Robbie. I liked him in ways that made me feel things that, until then, I didn't even know I could feel. And I had no fucking clue what to do about it.

Now, I liked both Dylan *and* Ashley, and I was just about as clueless.

CHAPTER FIFTEEN

Amber

AS IT TURNED OUT, I didn't have much time to get a clue. Because about an hour later, Dylan showed up at my sister's front door and asked if he could take me to dinner.

No sign of Ashley.

Laura, who'd answered the door, gave me an incredibly pointed and salacious look behind his back.

Liv conspicuously shut her mouth and narrowed her eyes at me.

For about an hour, they'd both been doing their best to dole out sound relationship advice. However, as shitty as I was, historically, with the whole relationship thing, I wasn't about to put a whole hell of a lot of stock in the heterosexual dating advice of two lesbians.

Kinda felt like the blind leading the blind.

"I'll... um... just get cleaned up," I told him, backing away as the three of them stood staring at me, Dylan looking me over, slowly, in that way of his, a crooked smile on his lips. Then I gathered up my ratty travel backpack and left him there. He looked perfectly at ease in my sister's foyer, chatting with her about the Underlayer shoot as I hightailed it upstairs.

Did Dylan Cope just ask me on a date? Again, I totally wasn't sure.

Liv and Laura kept insisting he was straight. They also seemed to think he was interested in me. If he really was straight, the fact that he'd A) hired me to photograph his house, B) taken me to an exclusive, swanky party at his lead singer's house, and now C) invited me out to dinner—alone—definitely suggested he might be interested.

But then, of course, there was that whole thing where I'd slept in his bed with him—oh, and his best friend—and he'd never even tried anything. And then I'd had hot sex with his best friend.

Because apparently I couldn't just keep things simple.

Mental note to future self: when you like a guy and you *don't* want to complicate things, don't have hot sex with his best friend.

Even if his best friend is insanely hot and has a pierced dick.

I stuck my tongue out at my reflection in the bathroom mirror and gave up a little growl of frustration.

Because only I could screw myself like this.

I really had nothing to get "cleaned up" with, but as I stared at myself in the mirror, I found myself frowning. I tussled my hair a little with my fingers and frowned again.

Then I headed down the hall to the master bedroom to plunder some of Laura's makeup, knowing she wouldn't mind. Actually, she'd insist on it. I wasn't planning to go nuts or anything. Maybe just a little blush?

Laura bounced in just as I was rooting through her makeup drawers in the bathroom, trying to decide if I should put on some lip gloss.

"Nervous?" she asked.

"Nope."

Of course I was.

She plucked a tube of gloss from the dozens on offer and tossed it at me. "Keep it. I haven't even opened it yet."

I cracked it open; a pale, rosy color with a slight sheen. I could handle that.

"And what are you planning to wear?" Laura was hovering as I carefully applied lip gloss; I hadn't exactly done it in recent memory. I could see her in the mirror, perusing my outfit. My long, peony-printed dress, with my comfy cream-colored cardigan layered overtop. The one Ashley had peeled off of me last night.

"I suppose *this* isn't the answer you're looking for," I said.

Laura started rummaging through her closet somewhere behind me. "How about this?" In the mirror I saw her over my shoulder, holding up a slutty-looking black minidress. "Or this?" She held up an even sluttier-looking pink minidress—with sequins.

"Um. Those aren't... me." *Logical*, I wanted to say. Those aren't *logical* things to put on one's body.

"If you're going to date a rock star," she said, "you might as well have some fun with it. Liv has taken me to parties, Amber. I've seen the girls these guys date, and sweetie—"

"And I'm sure those girls *would* have fun in those dresses. But I would feel like an idiot. As for dating a rock star, I don't even know if this is a date."

"Mm-hmm," she said, digging through her closet again. "So why are you putting on lip gloss? I mean, if not to give him a visual of what your wet lips would look like wrapped around his penis?"

I pressed my lips together, blending the gloss, my face heating at the thought—that that was what Dylan might think.

The thought was accompanied by the memory of *Ashley's* cock in my mouth, just last night... and again, in the middle of the night, in his bed. Just before he'd fucked me again.

Christ... I can still taste him.

And now I was going to dinner with his best friend.

"You think I want to look like a slob next to him at some restaurant?" I muttered. "He's famous. What if there's paparazzi?"

Laura laughed. "Then you can talk shop with them—camera lenses and shutter flashes or whatever."

"Right." I took a final perusal of my face in the mirror and turned to face her. Or at least, face the flurry of clothing she was tossing from the closet to the bed. There was a hell of a lot of shiny, ruffly stuff. "Do you have anything that looks like something I would actually wear, if I wasn't trying to be you?"

Laura popped out of the closet holding up a ruffled skirt and a pair of skinny jeans. "How about these, Miss Predictable?"

I frowned at the offerings.

Laura lowered the clothes with a sigh. "If you won't let me dress you, at least take this." She presented me with a small clutch that had been lying on the bed. It was cute, a blush-pink faux fur with a silver clasp. Then she held up a couple of condoms meaningfully and tucked them inside.

I raised an eyebrow. "And *why* do you have condoms?"

"They're yours," she said. "From the last time you stayed here."

"Oh."

"I checked. They haven't expired yet. And this should get you home from anywhere in the city, if you have to bail." She held up two twenty-dollar bills and a ten, then slipped those into the purse.

"Laura. I'm not destitute," I told her. Though really, my bank account was a little, well, empty. And I'd promised myself I'd only use my credit card for dire emergencies, until I was traveling again.

"That's your hard-earned *travel* money," she said, tucking the clutch into my hand. "This is sister-in-law money. Just take it. It makes me feel better to know you're safe."

"Fine." I hugged her, grateful for the love if not the condoms. Then I sighed. "I'll take the jeans. If you've got a cute sweater to go with them." Admittedly, I was a little tired of my limited wardrobe. Living out of a backpack could get wearisome, even for me.

That perked her right up. "You know I do." But as I reached for the jeans, she snatched them back and added, "And now that we know you're safe... I'll get the slutty ones."

Forty-five minutes later, I was ensconced in a giant wraparound booth in a posh restaurant downtown with Dylan Cope, wearing a cute pink sweater and Laura's sluttiest jeans. There was candlelight flickering and the clank of dishes and the din of dozens of other voices in conversation, and a piano where someone was playing Billy Joel's "She's Always a Woman." It was cozy and classy.

But I couldn't see any of the people or the piano. Our booth was tall and tucked back in a dark private corner under the curving staircase to the upper level. Which meant all I could see was Dylan Cope, with his crazy-handsome face and his wavy auburn hair.

He was wearing a fitted green sweater that he must've known made his eyes look fucking amazing, to say nothing of his biceps. And his forearms... His sleeves were casually pushed up and I could barely stand to look at the exposed skin there, the lines of the muscles and veins... or not look. I didn't know if it was the drumming or the weightlifting or just plain fantastic genetics, but something had given this man the sexiest forearms I'd ever seen.

There was wine in my glass, and Dylan had already ordered food for us. He seemed to know the restaurant's most delicious offerings, even taking into account my vegetarianism. I'd never eaten here before, so I didn't mind his recommendations. He also poured my wine instead of letting the waitress do it.

It sure as hell *felt* like a date, so far.

"So," he said, as soon as the waitress had departed with our order, "I wanted to pay you for your work." Then he produced a check from his pocket and slid it across the table toward me.

"Oh. Thank you." I glanced at it. It was a personal check, signed by him. And the amount had one more digit on it than I'd been expecting for three days' work. "This is too much," I told him.

"I threw some extra on there. Figured it might take you an extra day or two to go through all those images you took, do that retouching you mentioned."

Wow. Generous and thoughtful. "That's really covered by the generous day rate, Dylan."

He just shrugged that off.

"Thank you," I repeated, and tucked the check away.

"You're welcome." His gaze drifted over my face, and I sipped my wine, feeling conspicuous of the makeup I'd worn, however subtle. Was it occurring to him that I'd never worn makeup in his presence before? Did men notice things like that? "And now that we've gotten that out of the way... you're coming back with me tonight, right?"

"I'm..." I swallowed kind of hard, almost choking on my wine. "That's direct. Can I try the food first?"

Dylan laughed his easy laugh. "I just wondered if the fact that you took your travel backpack with you to Liv's meant we'd lost you."

We?

"I don't know. I'm finished photographing your house. I don't want to outstay my welcome." I could feel my cheeks heating up, thanks to the heady rush of my first couple of generous sips of wine *and* the embarrassment: the real reason I'd fled the island.

Because I'd screwed Ashley and couldn't deal with it.

Why did I think I needed to wear blush again?

"You *are* welcome," Dylan said, his green eyes looking extra-golden in the candlelight as they held mine, "at my place. And at Ash's."

"Dylan," I began, awkwardly, "that's really generous, but—"

"I can take you back on the boat tonight," he said casually, ignoring my protests. "We can pick up your things from Liv's."

I stared at him, just trying to process his words.

Okay. What the hell was going on here? The work was done. He could easily brush me off now.

Honestly, this was usually where they brushed me off. You know, like right when I started to really hope that they wouldn't.

Unless, of course... he actually did like me?

Fuck me.

Why was I so terrible at this? Like for fuck's sake, already. I seriously wanted to blurt out, *So do you like dick or pussy or what???*

But I managed to bite my tongue on that.

"Can I think about it?" I asked.

"Of course."

I stared at him. Everything about him said *relaxed*, from the casual way he leaned on his elbows on the table, to the lazy way he sipped his beer. But the look in his eyes was sharp, interested, and laser-locked on me. Actually, he was giving me sex eyes. Just like he did at Zane's party.

Only this time, as up-close and sober as I was... I was sure of it.

Dylan Cope was not gay.

No chance. Not the way he was looking at me right now.

Like he intended to drink his beer, eat his dinner... and then make me his dessert.

And my vagina was fucking thrilled about it. The eye-sex he was giving me sent warm tinglies racing below, and my womb did that same happy-freak-out thing it did the very first time he'd looked at me.

While the rest of me just got uncomfortable.

"Whatever you decide," he said, his gaze tracing my face, in no particular hurry, and landing on my lips. "Either way, you need to eat, right?"

"Right."

"Hope I'm not being too pushy."

"Um. No. I wouldn't describe you as a pushy man. It's actually... very leopard-like of you." Was that what was happening here?

Was Dylan Cope prowling on me?

That seemed to trip him up. "What?"

"Leopards. They're all, um..." I swallowed, struggling to remember what Liv had said about a leopard on the hunt, but it was hard with his green-gold eyes locked on mine. "They're all, you know, camouflaged. And then... they attack."

He put his beer down and sat back a fraction. "Do you feel attacked?"

"Well... no. I just meant—"

"I didn't mean to blindside you, Amber. If this is all news to you... I just thought you knew."

"Knew what?"

"That Ash and I are both into you."

"Oh."

Well, *shit*.

He smirked a bit. "I thought it was obvious."

"No. I mean… maybe?" Yeah. I was just plain bad at this. I was so confused I didn't even know which way was up.

Or which dick might be up. For me.

"You didn't know?"

"Well… I…" I drifted off. The waitress had reappeared, and laid out our appetizers. Some kind of goat cheese thing stuffed into little lettuce-leaf boats, with balsamic reduction drizzled over them. It looked delicious and I was hungry, but my stomach was all sparkling with nerves—even as my nipples throbbed and my pussy hummed with nervous excitement.

When she was gone, I tried again. "Even if I did, um, know…" I said, trying to find the right way to put it, to not make myself sound like an idiot, or a total slut. Was there a right way? "I probably wouldn't have thought your interest in me was… um… still valid. You know, after Ashley and I…"

"Valid?" He smirked again, so at least I was amusing him.

"Well, what I mean is…"

Shit. Was I about to send that gorgeous smile careening off his face when I said it out loud? *Oh God, am I really gonna ruin this?*

And did I have to say this out loud?

Yes, you totally do.

Put your big girl panties on.

"I had sex with Ashley last night."

Dylan didn't break eye contact. I knew this because I very purposefully made sure not to break it either. His smile faded a bit, but only because his eyes were darkening in that way a man's eyes darkened when you said something really sexy to him. "I know," he said.

I let out a breath. "It doesn't bother you?"

"Why would it bother me?"

"I mean… I don't know. Usually when a guy takes a girl out for dinner, he's probably hoping she hasn't had sex with someone else in the last twenty-four hours?"

"I don't mind if you have sex with Ash."

Oh.

Shit.

Wait.

"Do you...?"

Just ask.

"Do I...?" he said.

Yup. I'm totally gonna ask.

"Do you have sex with him?"

"No." A grin twitched at his mouth. "Unless by 'with' you mean in the same bed. With a woman in-between us."

"Oh. Um... no. I meant your cock, or his, in each other's—"

"No," he said. He leaned back in his seat and took a swig of his beer, his eyes sparkling with amusement. When he set the beer down, he added, "But I won't be having sex with you, either. Unless—"

"*Oh.*" I choked a little on my wine and dabbed at my mouth with a napkin, as ladylike as I could. My eyes were watering. "What?"

"Ash had you first," he said simply. "That means you're his. Unless he wants to share."

I blinked at him.

His?

Share?

I wanted to be offended by that. All of it. The entire idea that I now belonged to Ashley, like I was his territory or something, his property, just because he'd put his dick in me. That it was up to Ashley if I was allowed to have sex with Dylan. Or if Dylan was allowed to have sex with me?

It was pathetic. It was disgusting, chauvinistic, presumptuous bullshit, and I wanted nothing to do with it.

In theory.

But maybe *I* was pathetic?

Because in actuality, my body was responding to Dylan's words in ways that were far from disgusted.

Oh, God... Please *let him want to share.*

"So," Dylan went on, before I could recover, "supposing he is open to sharing, and you are, too..." He looked me over, slowly, like he wanted this to sink in.

So at least he *realized* I had a say in this.

"We'd ask you to stick around a while. Say a couple of months? And be exclusive. Exclusive with us. If you're into that." He sipped his beer. "Through the end of the year, anyway. Until we go on tour."

"Tour?"

"I'm going on tour with Dirty. Ash is coming, too."

"Oh..." A heavy feeling settled low in my stomach as I listened to him speak.

"The Penny Pushers are opening up for us on the first leg of the tour..."

"Cool."

"... so at that point, we'll be on the road. And you'll be off the hook." He smiled a little, studying me.

I smiled back, tentatively.

But what the actual fucking hell?

What if I didn't want to be "off the hook"? Didn't I get any say in *that* at all? Like: *But what if it turns out I really, really like you?*

What if you really, really like me?

What if I want you to stick around... and you don't?

I told myself it was natural to have these questions. To feel put off by what he'd said. It was weird shit to say.

Sure, I'd had a conversation something like this many times in the past, with men I'd met on my travels—other travelers. I'd never been invited into an "exclusive" threesome before, but I'd definitely negotiated the terms of a relationship up front. And it had never really fazed me. It had relieved me of the burden of worrying about getting rid of the guy after I'd had a little fun and wanted to move on.

Or, more specifically, him getting rid of me.

It rather tidily avoided the whole falling-in-love-and-ending-up-with-a-broken-heart thing.

So why did it irk me so much that *this* man was forecasting the end of our relationship before it had even begun? That he had it all planned out; that he'd laid it out for me, in his super-chill way, over cocktails?

Suddenly, it was like I saw all those other conversations for something other than what they'd felt like at the time. At the time, they'd seemed mature and honest and in the best interest of both parties. Now, they just seemed cheap and sad.

I felt cheap and sad.

Like the kind of girl a guy only got together with because he knew he was going to get to leave her afterward.

"Wow," I found myself saying, as I sucked back my wine. Neither of us had touched the food yet. "And how does one respond to such an offer?"

"I'd love to hear it," he said.

"Well. Let me take a stab at it." I finished the wine and set my glass on the table between us, gathering my thoughts. My pussy was still throbbing, but my heart had started pounding with a definite slam of angry adrenalin, and my head was fucking reeling in fifty different directions at once—not one of them good. "It sounds... interesting, Dylan. Like where do I sign up, right? But maybe you shouldn't be so quick to throw the offers around."

He raised an eyebrow at me as he reached for the bottle of wine to refill my glass.

"I mean, don't you need character references first?" I went on. "Because frankly, I don't know that Liv would give me a great one. I may have to dig pretty deep on that. Pretty sure I can find *someone* to vouch for me that I'm not a psycho, but I wouldn't put money on it. Oh, and speaking of money, I have none, so you may want to keep your gold-digger radar on high alert. Just in case. I mean, I would, if I were you. I once stole a stuffed kitten from a store. I was seven and I really, really wanted it, but I knew it was wrong. Still did it anyway." I picked up the glass he'd refilled for me and went on. "I also tend to make a lot of sarcastic or self-deprecating jokes when I'm nervous. I've been told it's cute at first, then it gets annoying. I have a fairly large chip on my shoulder, and I can be pretty dismissive of people. At least, my sister would say so, but who's listening to her, right?" I laughed at my own dumb joke, which didn't seem to land.

"Amber—"

"And anyway, unless you've been wasted the entire time I've known you so far, you must've noticed my prickly personality by now. I hold grudges like a motherfucker, and I don't really do relationships, exclusive or otherwise. Or maybe they just don't do me. I can't remember the last time I actually snuggled with someone. I don't snuggle. I don't spoon or cuddle. I only fork." I laughed. I wasn't drunk, exactly, and it wasn't a happy laugh. It was bitter and loaded with sarcasm. "Let's see. I also have this idea about myself that despite all my faults I'm a pretty good person who deserves good things. And this dream that I'm actually going to make something of myself one day, that what I do on this Earth actually matters. That the work I do is going to matter. That I'm going to make a good living doing what I love. You know, kind of like you do."

I slid out of the booth and stood, gulping my wine. That overly-generous check was festering in my pocket now, making me feel desperately uncomfortable in Laura's clothes.

"So, how did I do? Am I hired?" I set my empty wine glass on the table and looked straight in his green-gold eyes. "In case no one's told you this lately, you're a pig, Dylan Cope, and so is your best friend or your boyfriend or whatever the hell he is. Find another girl to scratch your kinky itch. I'm not 'his' and I'm not going to be yours."

With that, I stormed off, my body vibrating with anger and my eyes pricking with embarrassing tears.

And what made me most angry wasn't Dylan. It wasn't what he'd said about me being Ashley's, or about sharing me.

It was the thing about *leaving* me.

Like it would be so fucking easy to do, he just put it right up front, before anything else.

Before he'd even kissed me.

Before he'd even undressed me.

Before he'd gotten intimate with me at all, he'd already planned when, why and how he was going to leave me.

As I rushed through the restaurant, I passed Con, sitting up at the bar. His eyes followed me, but he didn't.

Near the front entrance, I passed the piano player. He was playing some Adele song I didn't know the words to. He was really good, and without even thinking about it, I pulled out one of the twenties Laura had put in my/her purse and stuffed it into his tip bowl. Because I'd meant everything I just said; I was going to make something of myself, my work was going to matter, and I believed in that, in following my life's passion. You didn't get to be as good as Dylan Cope on the drums or this guy on the piano if you didn't have a passion for it. And I believed in supporting other artists in the pursuit of their dreams.

Plus, I believed in good karma and good intentions.

And I *was* a good person.

I deserved more than a meaningless fling or some weird sex role in the lives of a couple of spoiled-ass rock stars who thought they could snap their fingers and make any woman they wanted just bend over.

Fuck that.

I pushed through the front door of the restaurant, shuddering as I sucked in a breath of cool night air, tainted with cigarette smoke and car exhaust and the faint stench of piss. Even right in front of a classy restaurant with a valet stand in downtown Vancouver, the sidewalk smelled of piss and people had to pollute the air by smoking.

I loved this city, and sometimes I hated it, too.

I strode past the valet who offered to get me a cab. I didn't know where I was going except that I was walking there. I'd walk through downtown and across the Cambie Bridge and all the way to my sister's house if I had to. By then, maybe I'd have cooled off.

Maybe I'd have stopped crying.

I was breathing shakily as I fought to hold the tears back, to keep them from cascading down my face. I *wasn't* crying. I was just angry. I was just gonna be angry and walk until I wasn't angry anymore.

Shitty plan, since I'd forgotten to grab my jacket on the way out of the restaurant and it was pretty cold out.

Why the *fuck* did this bother me so much?

I was leaving for Thailand soon anyway. With the money in my back pocket, I could leave tomorrow if I wanted to.

Dylan caught up with me at the street corner. I was waiting for the light to change, feeling cold and directionless and ridiculous, when I felt him towering over me.

"Hey," he said, gently draping my jacket over my shoulders. "You forgot this."

I looked up at him, carefully blinking back the tears.

"Sorry," I said, trying my best to chill the fuck out. "I guess I was trying to make a point."

"I think you made it." He hooked his strong hand around my upper arm. "Come here." He drew me off the sidewalk into a half-empty parking lot, then released me. No one was around, but I saw Con leaning on the wall across the alley. At least he was out of earshot.

Dylan stood in front of me, his hands shoved in the pockets of his jeans as he watched me slip on my jacket. He hadn't even grabbed his own jacket before he'd chased me out of the restaurant.

"So... you want me to fuck off?"

I said nothing. I just concentrated on breathing like a normal, non-crazy person, while I hugged myself and looked somewhere over his shoulder.

"You wouldn't be the first woman to tell me to fuck off, Amber. So don't feel too bad if you need to let it out."

"Okay," I said. "Fuck off." Then I glanced at him. When I met his bright eyes, I actually had to try really hard not to crack a smile. But I forced myself to frown instead. "I think you've got the wrong idea about me."

"Do I?"

"Yes." *At least, I think so.*

But now Ashley's words to me replayed in the back of my mind...

I knew you were kinky.

I knew it the moment I saw you.

And then those four other words...

Do you want him?

I was looking at him now. And yes, I wanted him.

I'd had sex with Ashley just last night, and I still wanted Dylan. *But.*

"I'm just not used to this," I told him. I could feel the tears coming, quivering, tickling my eyelashes and threatening to betray me, to streak down my face. I couldn't blink for fear that they'd fall, so I turned away and dabbed at my eyes.

Dylan moved in behind me. I felt him there, so crazy-tall and imposing, but so cool about everything when I was so freaked out; it made me want to reach out and close the gap between us. Yank him to me. Hug him. Actually, right now, it kinda made me want to throttle him.

He's used to women pursuing him.

The pussy just magically materializes in his presence...

Right. Well, maybe I just wasn't that kind of pussy.

"I'm not... that kinky," I confessed, and he laughed.

I turned to face him, too pissed to care that he could now tell I was crying.

"What's so damn funny?" I demanded.

His smile fell, and he shook his head a little. "You."

"Why?"

"I don't care how kinky you are or aren't, Amber. All I care about is you, wanting to be here right now, with me."

Shit. How much I would've loved to hear those words... like yesterday.

I took a breath and looked up at the sky. At the sparkle of stars that could barely be seen beyond the glow of the skyscrapers towering around us. And I felt weirdly trapped, the way I always felt when I was in a city too long. *Did* I want to be here? "Yeah. I love having emotional conversations in random parking lots with the smell of piss in the air."

He said nothing, and when I looked at him again, he was smiling.

And for some reason, I wanted to make him stop smiling.

"I took some photos of you yesterday. On the deck, by the pool," I said. "Ashley wanted me to take them. It was his idea."

Not that the thought hadn't occurred to me, but I never would've done it if Ashley hadn't suggested it.

Probably.

"So...?" I prompted when he offered nothing. No look of surprise. No request for an explanation, and none given.

"So." He just shrugged a little, his hands never leaving his pockets. "Ash likes to look at me." He said this like it was perfectly natural and no big deal at all.

"Yeah. So he told me. And he told me you like being looked at."

"I do."

A silence stretched between us as that statement clung in the air.

And I wondered, what the hell was I really getting into here?

You like Dylan, Ashley had said. *It turns me on.*

And Dylan knew it turned Ashley on?

But he wanted *me*.

With both of them.

"Would you want him to look?" he asked me. "If we had sex?"

I shook my head, but said, "I don't know."

The thought of it, though? It was already turning me on. I could feel the responses in my body. Excitement. Desire. Curiosity. The blood rushing between my legs, making me throb all over again.

The whole idea was getting me hot.

I had no idea, though, how the reality of it might feel.

But something told me, as Dylan took a step closer and reached for me, that I was about to find out. If I wanted to.

"This isn't a job offer," he said as his hands landed, lightly, on my waist. "There's no contract to sign, Amber. I'm not the boss of you. You're free to leave anytime you want. You could leave me here right now and never see me again, and there's not much I could do about it. I didn't mean for it to come across like that."

"Right," I said. "You're not the boss of me and neither is he. But he's just called first dibs."

He grinned a little. "You make it sound so childish."

"Because it is."

"It's also reality." His smile faded as he drew even closer to me. "You think I'd do my best friend like that? Move in on a girl he wanted, behind his back?"

"I don't know," I admitted. "I don't know you very well."

"I'll admit," he said, "I was trying to flirt with you. Test the waters a bit. But I guess I'm kind of off my game tonight."

"Maybe you're just out of practice. Word is you don't usually have to work so hard."

He raised an eyebrow a little, but didn't touch that. *"Truth* is," he said, "you make me a little nervous."

"Nervous?"

"Yeah," he said, his fingers tightening on my waist a bit and that crooked smile pulling at his full lips. "Nervous." His gaze drifted down over my face. "You make me nervous, Amber Malone."

Oh, *Jesus*. Was I buying this? That I made *him* nervous?

A man who'd played concerts for tens of thousands of people? Who'd been on countless magazine covers, some in little more than his underwear? Who'd been famous for pretty much his entire adult life?

I turned away, and his hands fell away. I just needed a moment to absorb all of this. Without him touching me. Without his gorgeous face and his sparkling eyes so close to mine.

And as I did, his fame slapped me right in the face—right along with his flaming hair and his washboard abs.

Unbelievable...

There was a giant billboard on top of a nearby building, all lit up in the night—a photo of Dylan, his muscular bod leisurely stretched out in a pair of skin-tight Underlayer briefs.

I turned back to him, shutting my eyes. I didn't want his beautiful face or his adorable crooked smile confusing me. I jabbed a thumb at the billboard over my shoulder. "Did you bring me to that restaurant because you knew that was there?"

I heard him sigh softly. "No, Amber. I brought you to that restaurant because I thought you'd like the food. And I was hoping to show you that I have some class." I peered at him and he smiled again. "Guess that's blown, huh?"

As I forced myself to meet his eyes, I felt the smile pulling at my own lips. This time, I couldn't even hold it back.

Maybe because, womb-fluttering aside, the truth was that I felt something for Dylan Cope. I felt how much I liked him, already. How drawn to him I was. How intrigued I was by him; by everything about him, and not just because he was so damn sexy.

How much I'd been trying to convince myself I *shouldn't* be attracted to him, because I thought he was gay.

Or maybe... I'd just wanted to believe he was gay because it made it easier to leave.

Yeah. Unfortunately, that sounded about right.

Which meant... *shit*.

Ugly truth time...

I'd liked Dylan first... but I'd had sex with Ashley. Because deep down, just maybe, I wanted to ruin this before it had any possible chance of getting started.

Well, that fucking backfired.

Because it didn't even bother Dylan. At all.

And now, if I was really being honest with myself, I not only liked both of them... I wanted to have sex with both of them.

And they were best friends.

And they possibly wanted to *share* me.

This was definitely outside of my wheelhouse. Maybe that was why I was so freaked out, so scared to take a chance on this? To try?

Because I really had no idea what I was doing. Or *who* I was doing it with.

This tall, gorgeous and seemingly-uncomplicated man in front of me was a complete mystery to me. I'd thought he was uncomplicated. You know, just your run-of-the-mill gorgeous, rich, gay rock star. But I was wrong. Way wrong. Like *he's-actually-straight-but-willing-to-share-me-with-his-BFF* wrong. Now, his washboard abs and green-gold eyes and kinky mind seemed like incredibly uncharted territory.

But his kindness was, too.

And that made me more than nervous. The reality was, it was easier to handle Ashley with all his thorns than it was to look into the compassion in Dylan's eyes right now and not squirm.

God, I had so many layers of fucked up.

I knew I'd been scared Dylan wouldn't like me. But I was more scared, maybe, that he would—and I'd screw it up.

I took a deep, deep breath. "I'm sorry I called you a pig. You're not a pig."

"Apology accepted," he said. "And I'll try to live up to that pronouncement."

"Just tell me one thing. Why do I make you nervous?"

"Because, Amber," he said, his voice low and gentle as he shifted closer to me. So close, his heat poured over me and his body brushed mine. "You act like you don't need me. And that puts me in a weird place. If I have nothing you need, why would you stick around?"

"Sorry," I replied softly, not sorry at all. "That's just how it is." My hands went up, landing on his biceps, and squeezed. Kind of holding him off, when I really wanted to pull him closer. "I don't need a man, Dylan Cope."

I didn't. I didn't need one at all.

"No?" He tipped his face down close to mine, drifting his lips over the corner of my mouth. He hesitated there as I sucked in a breath, then whispered in my ear, "How about two?"

CHAPTER SIXTEEN

Amber

ASHLEY WAS ALREADY WAITING for us when we walked into the Back Door, a little dive bar on the edge of Gastown, which we entered by way of a dark, sketchy alley. And by dive bar, I meant dive bar. The crowd was half bikers and bangers (I didn't even know any headbangers had actually survived the eighties, but here they all were, a little older, with slightly better haircuts, their old band T-shirts dredged up from the depths of their closets) and, like any bar in Vancouver, half hipsters. It was a rock bar with black walls, dingy lighting, and the stench of beer and sweat in the air—and an incredibly enthusiastic crowd smashed up against the small stage, rocking out to the live band.

I gave Dylan's hand a squeeze as he led me through the crowd, or rather, Con led us both through. When Dylan looked down at me over his shoulder, I cocked an eyebrow at him as if to say, *Nice place to bring a girl*, and he smirked back as if to say, *You're welcome*.

We'd returned to the restaurant to eat our dinner before heading over to the bar, which was a good thing. The food was fantastic, and the company was even better. And the drive to Liv's place to get my stuff, then to drop off Dylan's truck at Ashley's condo building before catching a cab to the bar, gave me a little time to adjust to this whole idea.

Time to digest the fact that not only was I definitely on a date, but that the date I was on was about to include *two* men. One of whom I'd already had sex with, and one of whom I wanted to have sex with... and who wanted to have sex with me—*with* the other guy.

Nothing unusual about that, right?

As we approached Ashley's table at the back of the bar, he rose to his feet. If I wasn't mistaken, he looked relieved to see me. He pulled me in close, gave me a kiss on the cheek and a hug. Then he gave Dylan a quick hug and we all sat down. Dylan stashed my backpack under the table. Con stood back against the nearby wall, leaving the three of us alone.

We were all on one side of the table, facing the stage. Dylan had already told me that some young up-and-coming band that Jesse had produced an album for was playing tonight, and he'd promised Jesse he'd make an appearance. The band was playing their asses off, but I really couldn't say if they were good. They were loud, for sure, but I really couldn't hear the music at all. My heart was hammering too hard and my head was too preoccupied with the men on either side of me, my senses overrun by their nearness, their warmth.

I'd never sat so close to either of them, but now both of them were right up against me; so close that our thighs pressed together under the table and Ashley's arm kept brushing me whenever he lifted his beer to drink. After a few minutes, Dylan slung his arm around the back of my chair and left it there.

Meanwhile, I was just trying not to hyperventilate. I would've ordered a glass of wine, or maybe a bottle, to take the edge off, but this didn't seem like that kind of place, so I had a beer with the guys instead.

Ashley's eyes met mine, once; his teeth dragged over his lower lip, briefly, before his attention returned to the band. Surely he saw Dylan's arm around me, and now knew that I was open to this.

When did I become open to this?

By now, I was pretty fucking sure that I wanted this to happen. Honestly, my pussy was sure from approximately the first nanosecond Dylan proposed the idea.

The rest of me had just taken a wee bit longer to catch up.

As the band rocked out, it was too loud to chat, which was a relief, at first. I was too nervous to say anything intelligible anyway.

But toward the end of their set, I was getting antsy.

Then Katie's hot husband, Jesse, appeared with Jude, the giant alpha security dude, and Brody, Dirty's handsome manager. They didn't sit down, but Dylan stood to greet them, while Ashley draped his arm around my shoulders. The musky-manly, clean-laundry smell of him shot straight to my clit, as vivid flashbacks of last night assailed my mind and body.

Apparently, I was now hardwired to get wet at the smell of Ashley Player. Instantaneously.

I wasn't sure if that was a good thing.

After Dylan sat back down, the other guys all stood back with Con to watch the band play their final song. But I could've sworn everyone had an eye on me, sitting here wedged between Dylan and Ashley.

Then Jesse, Jude and Brody headed backstage to talk to the band, leaving the three of us alone again, Con standing watch by the wall.

I was relieved as hell that no one else had come by. At least, no one I knew. Because the less people I knew who saw me on a date with two men, maybe the less weird it would feel.

It did feel weird, though not exactly uncomfortable. More like exciting weird.

And totally fucking hot.

As I sat here between them, my pussy throbbed incessantly. My nipples had gone perpetually hard. I couldn't get over the thrill of knowing I might have them both. *At the same time.*

That maybe they were both thinking about it, right now.

Two incredibly hot men want to get me into bed...

I just tried to focus on that, and not on the rest of it. Like the thing about them going on tour, and whatever happened between the three of us having an expiry date on it.

In reality, that was probably all negotiable. Logically, I knew that.

My jaded heart just had a bit of trouble letting it go.

But I did manage to let it go. For now.

The DJ cranked up some old-school Guns N' Roses, though the sex-fueled grind of "Anything Goes" wasn't quite as loud as the live band's music. I was just about to ask Dylan what he thought of the band—you know, to distract from the fact that I was dying of nerves and excitement and the anticipation of whatever was about to go down between the three of us. But just as I turned to him, Ashley reached behind me and tapped him on the shoulder. The two of them leaned in behind me and started talking. I couldn't hear what they were saying, and it was definitely fucking killing me.

Were they talking about me??

I'd already told myself I was just gonna sit here and drink my beer, try not to sweat right through Laura's pink sweater, and wait for them to take the lead. I'd be careful not to get plastered in the meantime, but I'd wait. No matter how long it took.

But I was curious as hell about how this was gonna work. Like did they need to negotiate who was going to have me in what position?

Or who was going to fuck me first?

The more I thought about it, the hotter I got, until my pussy was pretty much screaming at me over Axl Rose's vocals, begging for attention. Shit, were we still on the same song? Felt like a half-hour had passed since the band had finished playing. And the heat of Dylan's long, steely drummer's thigh pressed against mine wasn't helping my growing arousal. Neither was the warm, strong hand that Ashley placed on my other thigh.

They were *still* talking.

Maybe they were just talking about the band. Or the weather.

They didn't necessarily have to be talking about me, right? Just because they had a woman between them whom they were probably planning to fuck before the night was through, they could have other things to talk about, right?

Shit. I was starting to lose it.

My clit was pulsing and my nipples were diamond-hard and I could feel my whole body getting flushed. Why did I wear this stupid sweater? It was so fucking hot in here.

I took a swig of my cool beer and struggled to pace myself in every way. If I got too worked up here, I was probably gonna come the second I saw them both naked.

Oh. My. *God.*

My brain fucking melted at that thought.

Dylan. Ashley. *Naked.* Right in front of me. So close, I could touch them both...

Okay. *Deep breath.*

I really needed to calm the fuck down. This was no big deal. No. Big. Deal.

I'd already had sex with Ashley, right?

Hot, hawt sex.

Fuck.

It's just sex, I kept telling myself. *You've had sex with a man, plenty of times. You can have sex with two.*

What's the difference?

But there was a difference.

There was a big, huge, giant difference.

Starting with the fact that *both* of them had now put a hand on my leg under the table. Ashley's on my left thigh, and now Dylan's on my right.

I was going to die. Of a heart attack.

Right now.

Apparently, they were finally done talking. As they settled into their seats and drank their beer, I pretended to be absorbed in people-watching. But of course, the only two people I was interested in were right here. With their hands on me.

I was just gonna go ahead and assume, from the way his hand started traveling up my thigh, that Ashley knew exactly what Dylan and I talked about at the restaurant. That after my initial freak out and storm out, we'd discussed the very real possibility of them *both* putting their dicks in me.

Tonight.

In the end, I'd told Dylan I'd think about it.

But I was more than thinking about it.

I wanted it.

Right fucking now.

Like could we move this along, please? How could I let them know I wanted to find the nearest bed and go nuts, without actually standing up and yanking them both toward the nearest exit?

Sexual telepathy?

I glanced at Ashley, and his blue eyes locked on mine. He didn't smirk. He didn't say a thing. He didn't show any sign of what was going on under the table, other than the way his gaze dropped—and stripped off my pink sweater.

Then I felt Dylan's hand sliding up my other thigh...

Brain melt.

My pussy clenched in response. My nipples sang. I squeezed my beer bottle so tight in my hands I thought it might break.

There was a moment, as they *both* reached between my legs, that I knew their hands brushed. That they had to know they were both touching me.

And neither one of them stopped.

Ashley's fingers delved down, down between my legs, caressing the crotch of my tight jeans.

Dylan's fingertips brushed over my clit.

Amazing, what you could feel through denim...

I felt their heat. The gentle rhythm of Ashley's fingers stroking up and down. The slow, lazy circles Dylan started drawing over my clit.

I shifted in my seat, hanging onto my composure by a slippery thread. I wanted to spread my legs, but I couldn't; I just pressed my thighs against theirs, trapped between them.

I wanted them to tear off my pants and shove their faces where their hands were right now and lick me into next Tuesday.

Holy. *Shit.*

How was a woman supposed to handle this?

I didn't think my heart had ever beaten so hard. Was it safe for your heart to beat this hard? So hard, it felt like it was hammering against my rib cage. My whole body was thudding with the force of it.

Ashley was still watching me as he sipped his beer. He set it down, never taking his eyes off of mine.

I looked at Dylan. His eyes were hooded. His face was so close to mine, his gaze focused on me, like I was all he could see in the room.

Then his gaze dropped to my lips. And I really couldn't take it anymore.

Screw letting them take the lead…

I leaned in and kissed him.

Dylan

I wasn't expecting that first kiss.

I wasn't expecting Amber to instigate it. But more than that, I wasn't expecting to want it this much. To want *her* this much…

But as her sweet mouth pressed against mine, then she hesitated, her lips parting on a fragile intake of breath… I wanted Ash to share her with me. *Now.*

I wanted him to see what I was gonna do to her.

I wanted him to watch.

I wanted into her. Fucking *badly.*

My dick was already painfully hard in my jeans.

She was thinking about pulling away from me, though. I knew she was. Chickening out...

But fuck that.

I slipped my hand around the back of her neck, pulling her to me, and slid my tongue inside her mouth.

Ash

She kissed him first.

That's all I could process, all I could see as I worked my hand between Amber's legs, as I watched Dylan kiss her back.

And yes, I'd fucked her first. But she'd never kissed me while I did it.

I'd kissed her, once. That first kiss, before I went down on her. Before we fucked. But while we fucked, she'd never kissed me again.

As I watched them kiss, it was all I could think about:

She kissed him first.

CHAPTER SEVENTEEN

Amber

AFTER WE LEFT THE BAR, it was all a bit of a blur.

Not that I was drunk. At least, not on booze. Despite the three glasses of wine at the restaurant and the two beers at the bar, I was remarkably, sensationally sober. Hyperaware of everything that was going on, to the point that I could hardly keep track of it all. The hands on my body. The mouths on my skin.

The three of us took a cab back to Ashley's place. It was a small, modern one-bedroom condo on the eleventh floor of a tower, overlooking downtown, and I barely registered how we got there other than the fact that I was pressed in-between Ashley and Dylan in the back of the taxi while I made out with both of them.

Dylan paid the cab driver while Ashley led me into the building, and then the three of us were in the elevator, making out again. I was sucking face with Dylan and Ashley had his hands on my ass, his hard body pressed up against mine. My heart was racing and my body was on fire. I wanted them to tear off every shred of my clothes so they could touch me *more*... to hell with the fact that we were in an elevator. But even once we'd all piled through the door into Ashley's condo, they didn't do that. Not right away.

Ashley took a step back, drawing away from me. He looked like he wanted to eat me alive, but instead he clicked on a couple of lamps and tossed his keys on a table and looked at Dylan. Dylan dropped my backpack, and we all lost our jackets and shoes. Then Dylan hooked one of his long, strong arms around me and pulled me up against him. I could feel his hard-on pressing into my stomach as he kissed me until my head spun... as his warm tongue invaded my mouth and swept against mine in an increasingly-hungry rhythm that left us both breathless.

Then they undressed me, together.

Wrapped up in Dylan's kisses, I was very suddenly naked, standing between the two of them in Ashley's living room. I didn't even have the wherewithal to feel self-conscious, even though both of them were still fully clothed—because Dylan just kept kissing me and Ashley kept running his hands all over my body... squeezing my ass... lightly pinching my nipples... sending shivers of lust through me.

Then Dylan pulled me with him down the short hallway and into Ashley's bedroom. Ashley followed, turning on the lamp by the bed. When I looked over at him, he was stripping off his shirt, exposing his tight abs and the tattoos that ran across his sculpted chest and down his side, right into his jeans.

His eyes were on me as he undid his jeans and started sliding them off.

And I wanted them both naked. *Now.*

I helped Dylan peel off his sweater and the T-shirt beneath. I drifted my hands over his sculpted chest, his washboard abs, feeling him for the first time, as he slid his hands up over my hips and waist. His thick pecs tensed beneath my touch. His skin was smooth and silky, hot beneath my fingertips.

I leaned in, flicking my tongue lightly over his taut nipple.

He groaned in response and buried his hands in my hair, as my heart beat erratically in my chest.

Then I glanced down and drifted my fingers over his jeans. I felt the stiff package of his cock pressing against the denim, flexing under my touch.

Ashley pressed up behind me, his chest brushing against the

backs of my shoulders. I felt the soft fabric of his briefs, his stiff erection jabbing against the base of my spine. A shiver tore through me as he put his hands on my hips, holding me still, and pressed himself against me. He started kissing my neck just as Dylan cupped my breasts, and I moaned.

Dylan's eyes were on my mouth as Ashley feasted on my neck. Dylan ran this thumbs over my hard nipples, and I bit my lip at the rush of pleasure. I was trying to unbutton his jeans with shaking fingers; I was so aroused, I was shaking all over, my breathing rough and uneven. I managed to peel his jeans open and shoved them down his thighs.

He stepped out of them, but before I could wrap my hand around his cock like I wanted to, Ashley turned me around to face him. He tipped my chin up with his knuckle and kissed me.

And his mouth felt new to me. Even with all the sex we'd had last night, we'd barely kissed on the mouth. Just that one time, before all the sex. It wasn't intentional, more of a consequence of the positions we'd been doing it in. I didn't even realize it until now, as I tasted his mouth, his soft lips... as the kiss deepened and I felt the piercing in his tongue. I was so lost in his kiss, as the smooth steel ball, warm from his mouth, sent tingles running all through me, I almost didn't register that Dylan had dropped to his knees behind me... Until he grabbed my hips and tilted them, lifting my ass toward his face.

I felt his warm breath on my skin...

He laid his big, warm hands on my cheeks and spread me open. Then his tongue stroked deep between my legs as he started eating me out. His incredibly long, skillful tongue.

Oh... my... God.

Someone made a desperate little moaning sound. Pretty sure it was me.

"*Yeah*, Amber... *Fuck*, she tastes good..." Dylan mumbled, in a lust-hazed, blissed-out voice, as he made out with my pussy. Passionately.

Was there, indeed, a God?

And had I done something to make Him or Her spectacularly happy?

Because that was the only explanation I could think of for what was happening to me right now.

I kissed Ashley harder, deeper, grabbing his face and pulling him to me. His hands slid up to my breasts and squeezed, his hot body pressing against mine, his long, hard dick digging into my stomach. I was moaning, groaning uncontrollably into his mouth as Dylan lapped my clit. He gripped my ass harder, his fingers digging into me, and sucked on my pussy until I was dripping wet, even as Ashley plundered my mouth.

I was in the middle of the most erotic experience I'd ever had—maybe ever would have—and my head was reeling. The whole room seemed to be spinning.

I clung to Ashley, certain I would fall over if I didn't. There seemed to be no blood in my legs. My knees felt wobbly and I was breathing in shuddering, shaking breaths, gasping for oxygen in-between kisses... and I never, ever wanted it to end.

But then it did end.

Dylan kissed his way up my butt cheek with warm, sucking kisses, then drifted his tongue up my spine as he stood. He brushed my hair off the back of my neck with his knuckles, sending tingles straight to my clit, and started kissing my neck. Then he placed his hands on my waist and pressed himself up against my backside. I felt his balls, firm and heavy, pressed right up against the base of my spine, and his long, hard cock...

He was bare.

He'd lost his underwear and was now naked, pushed up against me. I groaned into Ashley's kisses. Dylan's tongue did some crazy thing to the base of my neck, right where it met my shoulder, and I shuddered as he licked me, my body overflowing with want. I was so hot, pressed between them, I was sweating. My hands shook as I dug them into Ashley's hair... as his hand ran down my body and in-between my legs.

He drifted his fingertip over my clit, drawing a couple of tight, teasing circles, then slid his finger deeper... and right up inside me.

I was sopping wet, and he growled into my mouth as he started fucking me with his finger.

Then he slid a second finger inside me, and a third. I gasped as he stretched me, clawing at his shoulders to keep from collapsing as I broke our kiss. I threw my head back, against Dylan's chest, and he pressed his lips to my temple. He was holding me up now; he'd slipped one arm around my waist and held me as Ashley screwed me with his fingers.

And *holy shit*... was that his pinky? Where the hell was that going—?

"Oh, *God*..." I pushed up onto my toes as Ashley shoved a fourth finger inside me. He fucked me with his whole hand except his thumb, which was massaging my clit, as I twisted and writhed in Dylan's arms.

"Dylan's big," Ashley breathed in my ear—and my brain blew apart. I couldn't scrape my thoughts off the insides of my skull to pull together any kind of coherent reaction, except... *Holy. Fucking. Hell.*

Dylan was going to fuck me.

And Ashley was getting me ready for it.

Because apparently, Dylan had a huge cock—bigger, even, than I'd thought?—and my head was gonna explode.

I felt Dylan shift behind me, drawing me towards the bed as Ashley's fingers suddenly slid away. I didn't remember walking there, or my feet hitting the ground. I somehow remained upright, but the two of them took me there, laying me out in the middle of the bed. I was dimly aware that Dylan was rolling on a condom as Ashley kissed his way down my body. Then Dylan was moving in, prowling in like the leopard he was, the muscles in his shoulders working as he crawled up over me, and Ashley shifted aside.

I glanced down. I saw Dylan's cock, hard and ready. And yes, he was huge, but I couldn't even process that. All I could think about was pulling him to me so I could feel all his gorgeous, smooth skin against mine. I wanted to be smothered by his heat, his smell...

Then Ashley drifted his fingers lightly down my arm—and I closed my eyes, suddenly overwhelmed. I wrapped my legs around Dylan's hips as he lowered himself over me. Ashley's hand continued down and then he lifted my hand, drawing it toward him. He lay my hand on his cock. I felt his hard shaft, steely and silky and hot under my palm.

"Open your eyes, Amber."

I heard Dylan's voice, so close above me, felt his breath on my face, but it took me a moment to process his words. When my eyes drifted open, he was there, his green-gold eyes locked on mine.

And I almost couldn't take it.

I drew a shaky breath.

I glanced down at my hand in Ashley's lap. He was stretched out beside us, tilted a bit on his hip to face us and settled back against the pillows. Watching.

I wrapped my hand around his cock, feeling how hard he was as he pulsed in my grip... as Dylan ran the head of his cock down between my legs and pleasure rushed through me. Dylan's cock felt slippery against my pussy from my own wetness, and he groaned a little in the back of his throat. I shifted beneath him, undulating my hips, unable to keep still. Fucking dying for him to fuck me—and put an end to this overwhelming want.

I looked at his face, at the tension written all over his beautiful features. The lust he felt, as desperately as I did. His eyelids lowered slightly, his pupils wide and dark. His lips parted as he shifted his hips... and he thrust into me with a low groan.

My head rocked back as the feeling smashed through me. As he filled me, deep. As he pulled back out and then thrust in again. He rocked into me a few more times, finding room for himself. He was long and thick and I felt it to the tips of my fingernails. My toes tingled. My nipples ached as his chest brushed mine.

When he was fully inside me, he paused. I met his eyes again as he lowered his body carefully over me. His arms seemed to be shaking a bit. Maybe he was holding himself back.

He kissed my face, my neck, as he fucked me in a slow, hot rhythm that set my body aflame, one delicious spark at a time. His groin pounded against my clit, the head of his cock seeming to batter my womb, sending shivers of hot-cold through me. My whole body was going haywire, struggling to just keep up, to register everything I was feeling.

I squeezed Ashley's cock every time a new sensation hit me, or the pleasure rushed through me, so intense... as Dylan fucked me closer and closer to orgasm. I tried not to forget Ashley was here as Dylan took over my body. I stroked him up and down, squeezing the head of his cock and running my thumb over his piercing, listening to his harsh breaths.

"You want to come, Amber?" Dylan choked out in a rough, lust-drunk voice, "or do you want to save that for Ash...?"

Oh, God. I hadn't even thought about that. Who I was gonna come with, or when or how.

Did I have to make decisions like that right now?

"Make her come."

No. I didn't have to make decisions like that. Because Ashley answered for me.

And Dylan didn't ask again.

He kissed me, his tongue filling my mouth, his taste flooding my senses, his smell and his warmth and his weight overwhelming me again... the rhythm of his cock invading me, his body thrusting against my clit as he possessed me. I kissed him back, my head spinning, my toes tingling, and every part of me dazzlingly, frantically alive... as I rode the wave of pleasure that he just kept driving higher and higher and higher... until it finally smashed apart.

I cried out into his mouth and he tore himself away, letting me breathe. I gasped and clung to him as the pleasure ripped through me... distantly aware that Ashley had put his hand over mine on his cock; slowing me down. Maybe I was about to make him come.

Or maybe *we* were.

I heard him hiss out a breath between his teeth.

Dylan kept fucking me, slow and rough, rocking my body as the orgasm pulsed through me. I felt him breathing with me. I felt his body tense, saw the change in his face when I looked up at him. I heard the groan catch in the back of his throat, shifting into a growl as his hips rammed against me and he came.

I squeezed him closer with my thighs, brushing kisses all over his face as he sank against me. Kisses on his full lips as he breathed raggedly. On his cheeks and his chin and his strong, stubbled jaw. He pressed into me a few more times as his cock jerked, and I felt him inside me like I'd never felt another man.

I'd never had a man this size inside of me.

And maybe... maybe I'd just never wanted a man inside of me as much as I wanted him, right now. Even *after* we'd just come.

We stared at each other. His eyes were hazed with pleasure, looking down into mine as he caught his breath. Then he kissed me, soft and sweet and lingering as my heart pumped life through my body and the sweetest air filled my lungs.

It'd *never* felt so sweet to breathe as it did breathing the same air as Dylan Cope, wrapped naked in his arms.

It was pretty much at the split second he stopped moving that Ashley took my hand again and pulled me toward him. Only then, I realized he'd let go of me at some point and lifted my hand off his cock, so he could put on a condom.

Dylan shifted off of me, and Ashley drew me over him. I went where he pulled me, and Dylan helped lift me. My legs felt like jelly, but I managed to straddle Ashley's hips. He settled me over himself, lining up his cock so that when he sat me down in his lap, he filled me in one deep thrust.

The pleasure rose again, fast; I'd never really come back down. And I rode him with abandon, too aroused to do anything but chase my next orgasm. His hands squeezed my ass, my pussy squeezed his cock, and he dropped his head back against the headboard. He looked at me from under his heavy eyelids, his blue eyes dark.

And it was unbelievably erotic, that Dylan was watching this.

That Dylan *wanted* this.

He lay next to us, and his hand roamed over my body. His fingers caught my sensitive nipple and squeezed. Twisted a little. Tugged until my mouth dropped open and my eyes met his.

He watched me intently, his eyes on mine as I fucked Ashley.

I didn't stop until I felt Ashley surge up beneath me. I felt his orgasm hit as he lifted his hips off the bed, as his cock flexed inside me. Dylan rolled my nipple between his fingers, his eyes darkening as he watched—and all of it set me off. I came with a soft, ragged scream, my hips jerking against Ashley's... and finally collapsed against his chest.

As I came down, gradually, my entire body shaking and damp with sweat, someone ran his hand gently down my back.

I couldn't even figure out who it was.

In the moment, it hardly seemed to matter anymore.

CHAPTER EIGHTEEN

Ash

FUCK ME.

When I woke up in my bed, kind of squished up on the edge of the mattress with this soft, warm body curled against my back, I tried to get a grip as the memories of last night pummeled me. I wasn't drunk. I wasn't hungover. I was painfully sober and aware of every single fucking thing that had happened in this bed.

And as I looked over at Amber and Dylan in the morning light... yeah, I was *fucked*.

I rubbed my eyes and peered over at them. *Jesus Christ*. We were triple-spooning, the three of us all lined up in a row, facing the same direction. Dylan had his arm over Amber's waist and she was nuzzled up into the back of my neck, her tits pressed against my back.

I extracted myself as quietly as I could. I pulled on my jeans, T-shirt and Vans and stumbled out the door.

By the time I got back from the coffee shop down the block, they were both awake. And they were still in my bed.

Actually, they were cuddling.

They were being cute together, fucking laughing about something, and looking sexy as fuck all snuggled up together, naked, under my blankets.

"Fuck, it's cold out there," I grumbled, putting a coffee for Dylan and one of those hippie teas Amber liked on the table by the bed for them.

"It's October," Dylan pointed out. "You might wanna think about putting on a little more than a T-shirt."

Yeah. Probably would've thought of that if I'd had my head on straight. If I hadn't woken up next to Amber and Dylan after the hottest night of my life and kind of lost my shit for a minute there. Because last night, I'd fucked Amber twice and watched Dylan fuck her three times.

It had all started out slow and kinda tender, and by the end, it was the kind of frantic, animalistic fucking that probably woke up the neighbors.

Not to mention that I'd experienced another one of Amber's brain-melting blowjobs *while* Dylan fucked her.

And now I wanted to do it all again.

A lot.

"Oh, look," Amber teased, "he's pouting."

"He does that a lot," Dylan said. "You get used to it."

"I'm cold," I muttered, sitting down on the bed and sipping my hot coffee.

"Then come back to bed," Amber said.

But I just sat where I was. Watching Dylan's thumb stroke up and down her bare arm. They had a blanket pulled up around their chests, and I couldn't see his other hand. Who knew where that was?

I dug for my stash in the bedside table and lit up a joint. One drag, then two, and I already felt better, the tightness in my chest loosening. But my heart was still beating too fast.

I told myself it was from the jog to the coffee shop in the cold. But I was a fucking liar.

I held the joint out, offering it to them. Dylan declined, but to my surprise, Amber sat up and took it, sucking back a couple of experienced little puffs. She hugged her knees to her chest, still covered with a blanket.

"So, I've always wanted to ask you..." Her gaze drifted down my arms as she blew out the sweet-smelling grass smoke. "About your tattoos. *Get Money* is pretty clear. But is that *Fuck Bitches* as in 'have sex with bitches' or *Fuck Bitches* as in 'to hell with bitches'?"

I sipped my coffee, just looking at her. Her eyes were softer than usual. And she still had the same small, pleased-as-fuck-with-herself smile that she'd been wearing since I returned and found her lazing in bed with Dylan. Though that was pretty much how most women looked after getting in Dylan Cope's pants. The dude was not only gorgeous; he was hung like a fucking horse.

And I'd been told, by more than one woman, that he fucked like a stallion.

When I didn't answer her question, Dylan ventured, "Pretty sure it's both."

Amber giggled as she took another toke, the pot going to her head. "Just a tip, though," she told me, "women don't love it when you call them bitches. In case you were unclear on that."

"I'm pretty clear. But thanks."

She raised an eyebrow, passing the joint back to me. "So then you're *trying* to offend people when you get tattoos like that?"

"I'm not really thinking about 'people' when I get tattoos. It's my body."

"Oh?" Her gaze slid down my side, and drifted over to my dick, like she could see right through my clothes. "So then you *didn't* get that sexy-as-fuck tattoo of all the flames and the bird-dragon taking a nose-dive into your pants so that 'people' want into them?"

"Wow." Dylan chuckled. "I gotta say. I'm loving how she sees right through your bullshit, Ash."

"It's a phoenix," I informed her. "You know, rebirth from the flames? Not a 'bird-dragon.'"

She shrugged. "Either way. Sexy."

I stared at her as she lay back against Dylan.

"Who's Danny?" she asked, all innocence as she blinked her green eyes at me.

Great.

She'd seen the fucking flower tattoo. The one way the hell up between my legs. The one that said *Danny 4Ever*.

"He doesn't know," Dylan answered for me, biting back a laugh. The story of how I'd gotten that tattoo always made him lose it.

When I threw him a murderous look, he crammed his fist into his mouth to shut himself up.

"He *what*?" Amber asked.

"Get him to tell you the story," he whispered. "It's fucking hilarious."

Amber studied my face. Then she relaxed farther into Dylan's arms and said, "It's okay. He doesn't want to tell me."

"Doesn't matter," I said, taking a pull off the joint, then handing it back to her. "Ancient history."

"Forgotten history," Dylan said, grinning.

I ignored him.

It was definitely weird, though, seeing a woman lounging in his arms. The guy gave out hugs left and right, and I'd seen him cuddle with a chick before, but not often. I'd definitely never seen him this at ease with a woman in bed, *after* sex.

Usually, Dylan was the first one to get up and hit the shower and get on with his day. I was more down to loiter in bed, for obvious reasons. And the girls, sometimes they stayed for the same reasons: to gawk at Dylan Cope and make themselves available in case he felt like another round. Though sometimes, they bounced as quickly as he did.

But this morning, he wasn't going anywhere, and neither was she. I could see it in their body language.

Dylan looked more than comfortable sprawled out in my bed, with Amber in his arms smoking my joint. Busting my balls with her, and drinking the coffee I'd bought him.

And I *liked* it.

I just wasn't sure *why* I liked it so much.

I'd been in love with a woman before. With Summer, for sure. If I was being honest, I was well on my way there with Elle. But I'd never felt that strongly about any of the women Dylan and I brought into bed with us. In part, because a lot of them, for me, were little more than an excuse to get in bed with Dylan. That was the truth; one I'd never admit to anyone, even Dylan.

And in part, because those women just didn't mean that much to me. The chemistry just wasn't there. Not to sustain more than a night or two, or at most, a few weeks or months of fun times.

It had definitely never felt like *this* with a woman in bed between us.

So much more than skin-deep.

I hit up the shower mainly so I could be alone to think. Get my head around things. Dylan and Amber were still cuddling and goofing around in my bed. It was as if having sex had shot them both up with fairy dust and, overnight, they were both totally gone over each other.

I could very fucking easily have fallen back into bed and seen if they were up for another round.

But that was probably inadvisable, until I got my shit together.

Until I figured out how I was gonna handle this. So far, I wasn't handling it so fucking well.

Amber had accused me of being nicer to her, and she wasn't wrong.

Something had changed between us the night of Zane's party.

Maybe it was seeing her and Dylan out of the house together, and all dressed up, looking like the perfect couple.

Maybe it was feeling like a third wheel.

Maybe it was seeing her hanging out with Katie and Maggie and looking like she fit right into Dylan's world.

Maybe it was when she got drunk and let her guard down, forgot about the stick up her butt and started being nice to *me*. When she leaned up against me in Zane's kitchen in the middle of the night, and all I wanted to do was put my arm around her, take care of her, because she was Dylan's. I knew she was Dylan's.

I'd known it from moment one, that she was made for him.

And maybe I wanted a piece of that.

But then she'd touched *me*. She put her hand on my stomach and slid her fingers gently down toward my crotch, and my dick fucking leapt to attention. And the way she looked up at me, her green eyes all needy and soft, with heat building behind them...

In that moment, I knew she wanted me.

And I fucking wanted *her*.

I wanted to bend her over Zane's kitchen counter and give it to her. But I wasn't gonna do that. She was pretty wasted, for one, and she was there with Dylan, too. It wasn't the right time.

So I'd stopped her, because I had to. Because if she put her hand on my dick with that look in her eyes, I didn't want to be responsible for what I might do. Truth was, I was kinda drunk, too. And it had been long enough since I'd sank my dick into a warm, wet pussy... I didn't trust myself.

The next day, I suggested she take photos of Dylan on his back deck because I knew that would put her directly in his naked path. I *needed* to stoke the fire between them. Make it combust. Because as of that moment in Zane's kitchen, when I realized I could have her... I also realized I'd been missing out on an opportunity.

An opportunity to have a piece of something that might actually have a chance at holding Dylan's attention. To get my hooks into this girl, who also had a chance of hooking Dylan.

Maybe Amber Paige Malone would be the fucking sexy glue between us.

Stupid, maybe. Desperate thoughts. But what could I say? Since Dylan and I had started taking chicks to bed together, I'd never met one with the potential to keep a good thing going. Someone who could potentially deepen the fucking tenuous intimate connection between Dylan and me.

When I saw the opportunity to fuck Amber in my dining room, when she was drooling over the photos she'd taken of Dylan, hell yeah, I took it. At that point, I was probably scared as shit that he was gonna fuck her first, and I'd be fucked right out of the equation. I suddenly needed to know, like *now*, if I could really have her.

If she really wanted me, even half as much as she wanted him.

And when I slid my hand up her skirt and felt her heat, her dampness through her panties... I knew. I fucked her to make sure that as much as she might be Dylan's, she'd also be mine.

Then the girl surprised the shit out of me.

Minutes after I'd made her come, she went down on me like a fucking Hoover.

She did it again in my bed in the night.

And then the next morning, she ran the fuck away.

And it bothered me. A fucking lot.

I knew Dylan had to step in or we might lose her. The girl was skittish as a deer at a hunting convention.

I'd told him what happened, that I'd fucked her. And as soon as he heard those words, I could see it in his eyes. He wasn't jealous. Dylan never got jealous. But it was like he now had permission to go after her himself—hard.

Just like I'd suspected, he'd been waiting, holding back. He really was gonna let me have her.

At least, have her *first*.

But now that I'd made the first move, I'd had my chance with her... all fucking bets were off.

He'd dropped me off at my place so fast my head kinda spun. Then he went to collect her from Liv's.

For a couple of hours, I feared I'd made a huge fucking mistake.

Then his text came in.

Meet us at the Back Door.

I'd never walked those ten blocks into Gastown so fucking fast— with my fists jammed into the pockets of my jeans the whole fucking way, because I had the hard-on from hell. And when I got to the bar, I just tried not to blow it by getting drunk while I waited for them.

When Dylan walked in, hand-in-hand with Amber, carrying her backpack for her, and she was wearing those skin-tight jeans with the fuzzy little pink sweater that hugged her perky tits, and they walked right over to my table... I was as relieved to see her as I was to see Dylan.

I liked her.

I liked the way she and Dylan liked each other.

I wanted her to like me.

So it was official, then.

This girl was doing something to my head. Sparking ideas of the three of us, together.

Which, of course, was dangerous.

And yet I was drawn to it like a dumbass moth to a motherfucking flame. And yes, I knew there was a very real chance I'd get burned here.

As I got out of the shower, I knew what I had to do to handle this.

I just had to set some hard limits.

Beginning with reminding myself that I was not falling in love.

Regularly and repeatedly.

Second, we were gonna have to get Amber's head around the fact that she was *ours* now, Dylan's and mine, and she wasn't fucking around with anyone else. Dylan had told me how she'd flipped out when he asked her to be exclusive with us. I might've had my own issues with monogamy, in the past, but that was definitely a hard limit—a woman fucking around on me. I was a greedy bastard and I didn't share. Not with anyone, ever. Except Dylan.

Dylan was different.

Dylan was my exception for almost every-fucking-thing.

Every limit I'd ever had, I'd pushed for Dylan Cope. For him, I'd already bent, broken and abused my limits until they were so fucking muddled I'd almost forgotten what they were.

The thing was, when I walked back into the bedroom and saw Amber in my bed, kneeling over Dylan with her camera in her hands... I knew I'd press my limits for her, too. To see that look on her face, right now. And the look on Dylan's as she took a photo of him, lying back on my bed.

I tossed my towel aside and joined them.

It was just sex, right?

Fucking *great* sex...

As Amber leaned down over Dylan to kiss him and I ran my hands over her tight curves, I told myself I could be careful with the rest of it. Mind the limits. Push aside any inconvenient stirrings of deeper feelings I might mistakenly develop for her, tuck them back out of the way where they wouldn't fuck with things.

Same thing I did with my feelings for Dylan.

At least, I tried to.

Everyone was allowed to have secrets, right?

Secret thoughts. Secret desires. Secret feelings.

It didn't actually change anything between us, because it didn't fucking matter anyway. Out in the open or hidden away, my feelings for Dylan would never change a thing.

I'd told myself long ago that I'd take whatever I could get with him. That it would have to be enough.

But the fact was... as I watched him pull Amber onto his lap... as she straddled him and took his thick cock up her pussy and started to ride him, her waves of caramel hair dusting her shoulders as she tipped her head back... and she reached her hand out to me... The way I was already feeling about being with both of them... It was already starting to fuck with my head. It was already starting to feel *too* good.

So I couldn't really fucking help it, could I?

Maybe this time, I'd just have to get burned.

Maybe for once, it would be worth it.

"You're gonna fall for her," I told him.

Of that, I was totally fucking sure.

Whether I was gonna fall for her or not, I really didn't know. I didn't *want* to fall for her.

But Dylan? He had no fucking choice.

I knew it.

I just wondered if he knew.

If he was afraid of getting burned, like I was.

Amber was standing in the back of the Dirty Deed and I was on the dock, finishing a smoke. Dylan was untying the boat. He looked up at me, his reddish hair blowing around, and squinted in the morning light.

"What?"

I flicked my chin at Amber in the boat. She wasn't listening. I was pretty sure she couldn't hear us. She was busy taking photos of the mountain view across the water.

"Her," I said, looking him dead in the eye. "You're gonna fall for her."

And what did Dylan say?

Nothing.

He just fucking laughed.

CHAPTER NINETEEN

Amber

I STOOD in the middle of Katie's art studio, holding my camera and turning in a slow circle, just taking it all in. Her art show was in full swing, and I was surrounded by people.

She'd let me in early so I could scope out the space and check out the studio's lighting, with its partial loft and high ceiling and the skylight windows above. I'd taken some photos while the paintings for the show were hung. Then I'd left for a dinner break, and gotten changed at Ashley's condo downtown—into the new cocktail dress that Dylan had bought for me yesterday.

It was A-line, turquoise, and came with turquoise stone earrings. It looked gorgeous on me and fit perfectly, because he'd taken me to get fitted the day before.

I wasn't totally sure how I felt about accepting such a gift, but I accepted. Mainly because the fact was that I owned only one party dress, and his friends had already seen me in it. I kinda doubted they were all gonna show up to Katie's big art show in the exact same outfit they wore to Zane's housewarming/birthday party a week ago.

I was right.

I'd returned for the art show wearing my new dress, with Dylan and Ashley on my arms, like the world's sexiest pair of accessories. Which raised more than a few eyebrows. I felt it when we walked in, when the guys greeted their friends and introduced me around, again. I'd met many of these people at Zane's party, but there were a lot more people here tonight.

And this time, I was getting the feeling that we weren't just getting looks because they'd *both* brought me.

It was because they'd both brought me *again*.

It definitely didn't seem like anyone was shocked about Dylan and Ashley sharing a woman, per se. More like they didn't usually keep the ones they shared around for this long. Or maybe they just didn't bring them out in public this much?

I didn't know whether to be flattered about that or horrified on behalf of those other women.

But I quickly distanced myself from both of them, using my camera as a convenient excuse. I was here to photograph the event for Katie, not to serve as the entertainment.

As it turned out, there was plenty going on here to upstage the spectacle of our little threesome. Like Katie's giant, stunning portraits of gorgeous rock stars. Which was a relief, because I felt kind of self-conscious about the fact that I'd spent the last three days pretty much in bed with two of those rock stars.

Other than when Dylan had headed into the city today to work, rehearsing for Dirty's new album, the three of us had been pretty much inseparable. Ashley, apparently, didn't work all that much, because he spent whatever time he wasn't in bed working on his Camaro in Dylan's garage, working out in Dylan's gym, riding his mountain bike around the trails on the island, or making food for us.

I hadn't even met his band yet. They weren't at the art show.

All of Dirty was, but despite all the famous people in attendance, it was still Dylan and Ashley who made me most nervous.

In bed together, it was strangely comfortable. Here, it was intimidating.

Maybe it was sharing them with all these other people—especially all the women fluttering around them. Unfortunately, it made me feel grossly insecure. Not that I saw either of them overtly flirting with any of those women, but what if they decided to take someone else home tonight?

I could be pissed about it, I could be jealous, I could be hurt, but I couldn't exactly stop them.

I didn't own Dylan or Ashley. Despite the proposal that Dylan had made to me that first night, at the restaurant, asking me to be exclusive with them until they went on tour, we hadn't talked about it again. We'd never actually promised exclusivity to one another.

I hadn't asked them if they were still sleeping with other women.

And they hadn't yet asked me if I was with any other men.

Though maybe it was assumed.

When and how would I fit another man into my repertoire anyway? The idea was ridiculous, when I already had *two* such hot and willing men taking up all my free time. Between the two of them, I was getting laid on a stunningly frequent basis.

The way I saw it, it would be insulting to both of them, not to mention downright comical, if I actually tried to hook up with another man.

But as for the two of them... The more I thought about it, the more I had to wonder. They were more than satisfying me. But could one woman really satisfy two men like Dylan Cope and Ashley Player?

Could I?

And in the end, did it even matter? In the end, was I just going to take all I could get from this and run, before they took off on me?

I realized, as these questions ran through my mind, that I was still trying to treat whatever this was between Dylan and Ashley and I the way I would if I were traveling. As a stopover. A temporary diversion on my way to somewhere else.

The problem was, right now, I wasn't going anywhere.

I still hadn't booked my ticket to Thailand.

And I really didn't know what to do with this sudden shift in my focus—it was so entirely new to me. This was the first time—since I'd briefly pushed the pause button on my travels for my incredibly-brief marriage—that I wasn't planning for my next trip, looking forward toward my next destination. Years of being on the move hadn't prepared me for this: staying still, just being where I was. And being so wrapped up in what I was doing and who I was doing it with, that I wasn't thinking about tomorrow—about the pursuit of the next great photograph.

There was only this moment, here at Katie's art show, right now.

With Dylan and Ashley.

I kept looking at them across the room. Checking them out. Taking photos of them. And getting tinglies every time one of them looked over at me and made eye contact. Feeling my entire body flush hot whenever I caught one of them checking me out.

And getting jealous as fuck when I couldn't catch their attention because some other bitch was hogging it.

Like when Summer, the gorgeous DJ, put her hand on Ashley's arm and left it there the entire time they were talking.

Like when some blonde I didn't even know gave Dylan an overly-familiar hug and then kept hanging around, even when he was talking to other people, putting her hand on his back and laughing at his jokes.

I told myself it didn't matter.

I told myself I was here to do a job, the one Katie had hired me to do, first and foremost. The fact that Dylan and Ashley had been already planning to attend the same event before I was hired was inconsequential. It was a mere convenience of transportation that I'd come with them. They had a boat. I needed a way here from the island.

End of story.

It mattered so little that the blonde was now following Dylan around, in fact, that I made a point of walking right over to them and taking a photo of them together. She was pretty, after all, and she'd worn a fantastic dress. She cuddled right up to Dylan with the world's most massive smile on her face, thrilled to be photographed with him, while he just stood there, narrowing his eyes at me slightly. I shot him a dirty look after I took the photo, and he raised his eyebrows at me.

I turned away and got busy elsewhere.

Because *fuck*.

What the hell was I doing?

And who did I think I was kidding here, exactly? Myself?

I was coming down with a serious case of the feels for these guys —*and* the green-eyed crazies.

I did not want the feels. The feels were total bullshit.

Apparently, crazy-hot rock star sex made you weak.

Crazy-hot sex with *two* rock stars? It was dangerous to a girl's sanity.

I already knew love made you weak, vulnerable, and in some cases just plain stupid. Like me with Johnny O. I did not want to go falling for Dylan or Ashley—or worse yet, *both* of them—just because they'd opened the door and I'd tripped, camera-first and unintentionally, into their world.

I did not want to get hurt.

Doing what I was doing, right now, was just plain dangerous. When I took a step back and looked at it, why I would even want to take the risk of falling in love with either of these men made no sense to me at all.

I could not understand why I'd want to risk my heart like this.

So I tried to just forget about both of them *and* their adoring fans, and absorb myself in what I was here to do. Photography. The art show. These I could handle, even with all the famous people, the wealthy people, the beautiful people drifting through the room with champagne in hand, buying up Katie's twenty-thousand-dollar paintings like they were picking out a new shade of lipstick.

And Katie herself, with her sweet, unassuming smile, her little champagne-colored dress, and no airs about herself whatsoever? Katie, I could totally handle. I could probably even stumble through a conversation with her husband. If he was married to her, he had to be cool, right? Despite his million-megawatt smile and perfect hair, his chiseled-handsome face and leather pants, there had to be a regular dude in there somewhere.

But the rest of it?

I should probably run screaming from the rest of it. If I had any sense at all.

"So what's your big dream?" Katie asked me. "Like, if there were no limits and no fears involved, what would you do with your photography?"

It was late, maybe two a.m., and there were maybe a dozen people left in her studio. She and I had been sitting by the little kitchen area drinking wine for the last half hour, talking about everything under the sun.

Everything except my weird-ass three-way… whatever-it-was.

"Honestly," I told her, "I'd do shows like this. Put together exhibits of my work and do gallery tours and see if I could get a book published."

"That sounds amazing."

"That would be a start. I actually think I want to teach, in the future. I had this amazing lecturer in university. She taught the history of photography and it was all kinds of interesting. I think it's an important subject for young artists, especially in the age of iPhone cameras. To look back and see where photography came from and why. It's such a new art form in the scope of art history. And I think with all my experiences traveling, I'd make a kickass professor. I'd have to go back for another degree and work my way up there, but I wouldn't mind. I actually love education. Next to traveling, academics is my happy place."

"Then you should do it."

"Yeah. I probably should. It's expensive though, and right now I'm too restless to settle into that routine. I needed a break from it for a while, you know? See the world. Photograph the people of the world. Find myself and all that crap."

She grinned. "Any luck finding yourself yet?"

"Nope. Pretty sure Amber Paige Malone is still drifting around out there somewhere, lost as fuck."

Katie eyed me knowingly, which was impressive since she was kinda drunk. "She's probably a lot closer than you think."

I sipped my wine and rolled my eyes. "Please. Don't get all wise on me now. I saw you doing all those shots with your husband after the place cleared out, and I've got the photos to prove it. You may look like you have it all together, Katie Mayes, but I know you were nervous tonight, and I'm really trying to hold onto this opinion I have of you that you're just a normal girl underneath it all, like me."

"Oh, I'm normal as shit," she said ultra-seriously.

That made me giggle. I liked Katie. I wanted us to be friends. And I realized: maybe this was what had me so torn in two tonight. So nervous and so compelled. I was drawn to this world—Katie's world. It had little to do with Dylan and Ashley. I just wanted a taste of what Katie had—such success with her art, on her own terms. Her own studio. Her work selling.

And I was uncomfortably aware that to have these things, she had to stay still, at least some of the time.

"It's amazing, what you're doing here, you know," I told her. "You're so young, and you're selling your work for so much money."

"Oh, I don't kid myself that it's about my talent," she said easily. "It's got at least as much to do with the famous people in the paintings as it does my ability to paint them. I don't even *try* to ask for as much money for the ones of the non-famous people."

"Okay. But trust me. Just because someone scribbles out a painting of your husband doesn't mean it's worth anything, Katie. Your work is breathtaking-gorgeous. More than that, it evokes emotion. That painting of Seth's face almost made me cry. There's just something in his eyes that you rendered with paint, that had me... I don't know, heartbroken. The one of Dylan is just... *damn*, I don't even have words. Like, I know he's beautiful and an underwear god and all, but you made him otherworldly and somehow intensely real, flesh and blood, all at once. And all the ones of Jesse... anyone could tell you're head-over-heels in love with the man, the way you paint him."

"Thank you." I watched the blush on her already rosy cheeks deepen.

"You two make a great team," I mused.

"Yeah. He provides the beautiful face, I provide the paint." She grinned like a fool in love. "Seriously, I couldn't do this without him."

"I bet he'd say the same about you. You know, he looks at you so much, it's pretty nauseating." I wondered if she actually knew how much he looked at her.

She laughed. "Trust me, he's not *always* this attentive. He gets pretty sucked up into his music sometimes. But I don't mind. I get pretty obsessive about my work too. It balances out."

"You understand each other. That's good."

"How about you?" She raised an eyebrow at me, studying me, and I squirmed a bit. I couldn't imagine being cross-examined by this girl; she'd probably just throw kittens at you until you surrendered to the sweetness. "You still sticking to that story that there's nothing going on between you and Dylan... and Ashley?"

I sipped my wine, stalling. "Maybe?"

"You sure you wanna lie to me like that?" She blinked her big blue-green eyes at me, and I felt instantly shitty. It was like lying to Bambi. Or a Care Bear.

"I guess I'd hate to lie to you..."

She laughed, triumphant. "So tell me, then. Is it Dylan? Or Ashley? Or...?"

"It's both."

"Ah. So the rumors are true."

"What rumors...?"

"The ones about Dylan and Ashley liking to... well... hook up with the same girl," she said, rather diplomatically. "I kind of wondered if it was bullshit. Or maybe like it happened one time and the guys just won't let it drop?"

"It's not bullshit."

"So what are they like?" She blushed again, immediately. "I mean, not in bed. Just in general."

"They're great," I said awkwardly, because I was kinda shitty at opening up about personal stuff. Even with someone as nice as Katie. "And they're *ridiculous* in bed." I took one look at her sweet, slightly embarrassed but definitely non-judgmental expression, and decided to go on. "Like... have you ever been with a guy who was just miles and miles of solid, thick muscle and silky skin and he'd hold you down and say the dirtiest shit to you you'd ever heard and have his way with you until you couldn't walk, and all you wanted was more?"

A slow smirk spread across Katie's face, and she threw a glance at her husband.

"Right," I said. "So... multiply that. You know, by two."

"*Wow*. How *do* you walk?"

I shrugged, grinning. "Not sure, actually. I have been feeling a little wobbly..."

"No doubt." Katie sipped her wine, considering. Her expression grew pensive, serious, as she narrowed her eyes at me. Then she told me, "I'm gonna ask you something a very wise woman asked me when I was falling in love."

Oh, God. "Okay..."

"Are they good to you?"

"Yeah," I said, without having to think about it. "They are."

Huh. I hadn't really asked myself that question, though. Which was fucked up, right?

But, yes. They *were* good to me.

So far.

"Look, I don't know you very well. Yet." Katie smiled at me. "And I don't know where you're headed with these guys or how long you plan to stick around. But either way, I want you to know you're always welcome here."

"Thanks, Katie."

"Jesse gave me this studio, but I'm gradually paying for it. It may take me a *lot* of shows, but I'll get it paid off. I want to pay my own way. It's important to me."

"I totally respect that."

"But I also believe sometimes you need to take help when it's offered," she added meaningfully. "I'm making my own way now, the art is selling, but I never would've been able to get this far, this fast, without Jesse's help and support. Or Dirty's. So. Anytime you want, you can have a show here, and I'll help you get a crowd in."

"Um..." I studied her; her soft, kind eyes. "Look, no offense, okay? But is this just sweet drunk talk? Because if it is—"

"It's not drunk talk. Yes, I'm kinda drunk. But it's not drunk talk. Brody hooked me up with this art promoter and I've made some contacts of my own, too, in the gallery circuit. Plus, the guys know a lot of people with money. And there's no shame in accepting the help. I can help you set up and work with the promoter and fill the room with buyers. You can give me a cut of sales just like any gallery so you won't feel like it's a handout, except my cut will be lower than anywhere else in town." She beamed, looking pleased with the idea. "So it's good for both of us."

"How is that good for you? I mean, trust me, my photos won't be going for twenty grand at my first show."

Katie cocked her head a bit, like I'd said something silly, and blinked at me. "Because I'd be helping a friend," she said simply.

"Oh."

"Yeah," she said, laughing a bit. "Deal?"

She held out her hand to me.

I told her I would think about it—seriously—and I shook her hand. I promised her that if or when I was ever ready to do a show of my own, I'd be in touch with her. I meant it. And I thanked her, profusely, for the offer. It was a lot to process, but I was pretty sure I would take her up on it, someday.

I was also pretty sure I'd check in with her tomorrow, to make sure it really wasn't just drunk talk.

Then Dylan collected me, and once we'd said all our goodbyes, I left with him and Ashley. It was late, near three in the morning, and the guys had already decided we weren't boating home. Instead, we drove to Ashley's condo.

They were both pretty quiet as Ashley pulled me into his

bedroom. Dylan followed, and for some reason, I was afraid to speak first.

Maybe because I wasn't sure where we were all at. From moment to moment, our three-way "situation" (I was refusing to call it a relationship, even in my own mind) had me ill at ease. Or elated. Or any number of other emotions.

Scared. Excited. Nervous.

Scared again.

Excited again...

And the guys hadn't really said much to me the entire way home.

My head was still kinda spinning from Katie's offer, and also, if I was being honest, from all the mental imagery of Dylan and Ashley schmoozing with all those other women tonight.

I hoped maybe they were just being quiet because they were tired, and not because Dylan was pissed at me for giving him the world's dirtiest look at the art show, as if he'd had his hand right up that blonde woman's dress instead of, you know, just standing there beside her. But when I glimpsed the look on his face—the way he was undressing me with eyes... that clearly had nothing to do with it.

Ashley stood me in front of the bed and started taking off my new dress, while Dylan turned on a lamp and stripped off his clothes. He pulled back the covers and lay down naked on the bed. He stretched out on his side, his cock just barely covered by the sheet, watching as Ashley stripped me down to my lace panties. They were new, too, a gift from Ashley to go with the dress. Skimpy, sexy and black.

Ashley stood behind me, kissing my neck, running his hands teasingly over my body, making me warm. I stirred, anxious for more, as Dylan's gaze moved slowly over me. It drove me fucking insane when Dylan looked at me like that—like he wanted to lick every last inch of my body like an ice cream cone with his long, adept tongue. Slowly.

Except he wasn't making a move to do that.

Ashley pressed a soft kiss beneath my ear and I reached back, pressing my hands to his thighs, gripping him through his jeans. "Come here," I said to Dylan. My voice was breathy, anxious. Hungry. "Please."

But Dylan just shook his head at me, once, and said, "We want an answer to our proposal, Amber."

"What...?"

"We want a commitment," Ashley murmured against my neck.

"You haven't given us one yet," Dylan added, still watching us from the bed. He looked incredibly comfortable lying there, naked, in front of both of us. His gaze, though, was intense, restless, as he watched me in Ashley's arms.

I actually had to struggle to follow what they were saying as Ashley's hands drifted over my curves.

"Um... did you just use the word 'commitment'?" I asked, as Ashley kissed his way down my neck. "I thought men, in general, were allergic to that word."

"Who said we were 'men in general'?" Ashley retorted as he grabbed my breasts and squeezed. "And I don't wanna have to worry, every party we take you to, about any of those other assholes getting their hands on you."

"Oh—"

"We would all agree to commit," Dylan said. "And since you're on the pill, we'd all get tested, so we could lose the condoms."

"We wanna go bareback with you," Ashley added, his breath warming my ear, his fingers plucking at my nipples now, making me shiver. He felt it and pinched harder.

Oh...

"That means no other partners," Dylan said. "For any of us."

Oh, God. My panties were getting wet. Soaked. It was what they were saying, what Ashley was doing—what Dylan's eyes were doing —and their voices, husky and low, borderline commanding, as they laid out what they wanted.

"We wanna be clear about our expectations," Ashley said. "And yours. Everything out in the open, for all of us."

"Everything," Dylan agreed. "And in case you're wondering if we're serious about this, we are. We had a similar arrangement with another woman, briefly, last year. Before Ash hooked up with Elle."

"What woman?" I asked, before I thought better of it. I was instantly dreading that it might've been Summer. For some reason, that particular woman made me all kinds of envious. Maybe it was the rapport she seemed to have with Ashley. She wasn't even the most beautiful woman at that party tonight, but there was just something about her. She was sexy as hell. Like if I were a guy, I'd totally want to hit that.

"You don't know her," Dylan said. "Her name is Kitty."

Kitty?

Seriously?

Now I had a head full of a very feline-looking babe in some kinky Catwoman outfit. Maybe Summer would've been preferable.

"We weren't with her long," Ashley said. "We're hoping this time will work out better. With you."

"Until when?" I blurted. Because as much as I'd tried to get my head and my heart around what Dylan had laid out for me on our first date, I still did not relish the idea of being dumped and forgotten the minute they went on tour.

No matter how serious things got between the three of us—or didn't—I still wasn't comfortable with that forecast to the end of our arrangement.

"Whenever," Ashley said, and his hands fell away from me as he started getting undressed. He stripped off his shirt, and I crossed my arms loosely over my chest, feeling weirdly exposed.

"That's pretty vague. I thought we were being clear here."

"Forever." Ashley shrugged as he shucked off his jeans, like it was no big deal, like he hadn't just tossed out the word *forever*. "Or tomorrow. As long as we all want to be here."

I looked at Dylan. He just lay there, a slight, crooked grin on his lips, as Ashley tossed a strip of condoms at him. He caught it and tore one off, his lust-hooded eyes never leaving mine.

I did not know what to say. Because I did want to be here,

despite my fears. And I did not particularly want an expiry date on this.

But *forever*? In a ménage à trois? I wasn't exactly the world's most conventional girl, but I wasn't sure I was that freaky either.

Now, I really didn't know if I preferred *Forever* or *Until we go on tour*.

So I defaulted to my usual non-response. "Can I think about it?"

"Yes." Dylan reached for me, yanking me into bed. I lay down beside him, and I felt Ashley slide in behind me. They were both naked as they pressed in around me, hot and strong. "We don't want to pressure you, Amber, if this isn't what you want..." As Dylan spoke, he ran a heavy hand down my curves, possessively, like he *knew* I wanted.

Oh, I want...

"We just want to make things clear," Ashley repeated, his breath hot on my neck, "for all of us."

"This way, we build trust," Dylan explained, and ripped the condom packet open with his teeth. "You don't have to worry about us hooking up with someone else behind your back."

"Why would I worry about that?"

Wow. That was so nonchalant, I almost bought it.

"Babe." Dylan rolled the condom onto his hard length, then caught my chin and lifted, steering my gaze up to meet his, which was raw with lust. "Saw you looking at Ash and Summer tonight."

"There's nothing going on between me and Summer," Ashley said. He hooked a finger in the back of my panties and tugged. Then he slipped his other hand inside.

"Okay," I said, my breath catching as Ashley's fingers slid right on down and under, slipping against my wet opening. I bucked my hips back to meet his touch.

"And this way," he said, "we don't have to worry about you hopping on a plane and jetting off to the other side of the globe without telling us."

"Hngh..." I couldn't quite formulate a sensible response, with his fingers teasing my pussy and Dylan peeling my panties down my thighs. Dylan slid his hand over my clit and massaged me with his palm, making me arch my hips toward him now, hungry for more... just as Ashley pushed a finger up inside me.

I gripped Dylan's shoulder and held on, because *fuck*. As usual, the sensations of them both touching me... it was too much to register, too much to anticipate, too much to process. The feelings just took over and melted my thoughts to incoherent mush.

"So we're clear?" Dylan's voice was all husky as his gaze slid down to my mouth. He pushed my panties all the way down my legs, sliding them off my feet with his foot. "Anyone wants to hook up with someone else, they tell the other two first. Anyone wants to jet off to Thailand, they tell the other two first."

"Okay," I breathed, unsure how they'd gotten me to agree when I was supposed to be thinking about this. But right now, *fuck thinking*. "Deal..." Then his mouth slid over mine, and we were done talking.

Other than when Ashley whispered some filthy, filthy words into my ear while Dylan hiked up my thigh and rammed his cock into me... we didn't speak another world.

CHAPTER TWENTY

Dylan

"JEALOUS?"

I punched Ash lightly on the shoulder. His only response was to glare at me. Then his eyes locked on Amber's ass as she disappeared into my boat.

I could *feel* his jealousy when I'd asked her to come into the city with me so I could bring her to rehearsal, then take her to dinner.

But fuck it.

I wanted to show her more of my world.

And I wanted some time with her, on my terms, when she didn't have one pretty toe out the fucking door.

Since Katie's art show a few nights ago, when we'd asked Amber to be exclusive with us, she'd still been acting flighty. But that hadn't dampened my desire to lock her down. If anything, the hard-to-get thing was kinda driving me nuts.

I hated chasing women, but for some reason, it was getting me hot trying to cage this one in.

Way hot.

Every time she looked at me and her green eyes softened a little more, it got me hard.

Every time she fucked me, it felt like a small victory.

But she was still too wild, too unpredictable, too fucking skittish.

She still kept dropping comments about "When I'm in Thailand..." and "When I head overseas..." Bullshit like that. And I wasn't having it. Not if there was anything I could do about it.

I wanted the girl here, in my fucking time zone. In my house. In my bed.

I just plain wanted her around.

Didn't feel like I had to explain that to Ash or ask his permission.

Besides, Ash was just being fucking greedy. He got to have her to himself pretty much all day lately, every day, since Dirty had been in daily rehearsals at the church.

Today, she was mine.

So we headed out in the Dirty Deed, leaving Ash on the dock feeling sorry for himself. But not before Amber kissed him goodbye, and he'd grabbed her ass and locked her into a several-minute make out while I got the boat ready. Then I'd grabbed her hand and propelled her up into the boat while he grinned and adjusted his wood, winking at me like a prick.

I knew he envied the fact that I got to take her to work with me. But more than that, he was jealous that I got to go play with my band at all.

I wondered if he'd take Amber into the studio with the Pushers once they got together to record their new album. They hadn't met in a while, and I was pretty sure Ash was jonesing to play. It had been too long since we'd all been on tour, and I could understand he was getting antsy. I was, too.

Lucky for us, we had Amber to entertain us until then.

If we could just get her to forget all about her little plan to disappear to fucking Thailand.

Amber and I were almost the last ones to arrive at the church, but not quite. We weren't late. I made sure of that.

I knew I had a reputation for holding things up, deservedly; there was something about keeping to a schedule that I was just naturally allergic to. But I definitely wasn't gonna give anyone the opportunity to even try to suggest I was late because I had my head up Amber's skirt. Fuck that.

I strolled through the door with my arm around her at exactly eleven-fifty-eight. Dirty had an official start time of noon; if you showed up earlier, you jammed with whoever else was around, but at noon rehearsals got underway.

Zane threw me an impatient look anyway. He was wandering around the stage in a ripped T-shirt, jeans and bare feet, a backwards ball cap keeping his blond hair out of his face, mic in hand and clearly itching to get going.

I took my time anyway, introducing Amber around again. Making sure she knew everyone, and everyone knew her. Making sure they remembered her name and no one was gonna get her mixed up with some other chick they'd seen me with in the past—Zane's specialty.

Today, like most rehearsal days, it was a small crew at the church. The band, and usually one of our technical crew, which today was Jimmy. Management was usually around in the form of Brody or Maggie or both. Today, Brody was here, but he'd probably only stay for a bit. Maggie would stay the whole day. She'd bring in food for us and would probably do coffee runs and take notes for whoever felt like making her their personal bitch—another of Zane's specialties.

Jude was also hanging out. When he pulled a full day at the church, he usually let Elle's bodyguard, Flynn, and Zane's bodyguard, Shady, take off, so they were already gone. The church was pretty remote and secure, smack between a bunch of farmers' fields and some industrial lots, and so far we'd been lucky keeping the location a closely-guarded Dirty secret.

It was pretty much an unwritten rule that no media of any kind was allowed at the church. We'd made a one-time exception for Liv and her crew while filming the documentary series, and that had come with a shit-ton of rules about what she could and couldn't show on-camera. Revealing Dirty's rehearsal space to the world was not allowed.

"We weren't expecting a photographer," Brody said when he greeted us, eying Amber and the camera in her hand. I'd already told her she could shoot the band while we played and hung out; insisted on it, really.

"It's just Amber," I told him. "You won't even notice her."

"Yeah?" He looked at her. "And what does she plan to do with the images?"

Amber glanced from me to him, probably thinking I was a real asshole for putting them both on the spot. But she was a professional; I knew she could handle Brody.

"Well, if you let me take photos here today," she said diplomatically, "I might want to sell some to magazines. With the band's permission. And I'll probably want to consider including any exceptional ones in an art exhibit one day. Or in a book or something."

I looked at her and she glanced at me. She'd never mentioned that before, wanting to put her work in galleries or books. At least, not to me.

"There'll be exceptional ones," I said. I had no doubt about that. Not only had I seen a bunch of her work online by now, I'd seen her photos of my house and some of the shots she'd taken at Katie's art show. The girl was modest about her work, but she had talent.

I'd once been to an exhibit of Linda McCartney's photography. The room was filled with intimate portraits of rock stars, celebrities. But there was one photo of B.B. King, just an open-mouthed blur coming out of the black as he wailed on his guitar; I'd had to stand in front of it and stare at it for a long while. I couldn't stop looking at it. *Rapture.* That was the only word that came to mind, to express the feeling she'd conveyed with that photograph.

It was fucking transcendent.

And there was something about Amber's photographs that gave me that same feeling. She had a way of capturing something in people that could be felt as strongly as it could be seen; this incredible, raw intimacy that she managed to convey with her camera.

Brody, however, looked unconvinced. And a little annoyed with me that I'd sprung this on him without warning.

"You've got a release for me?" he asked her.

"Of course." Amber pulled a wad of crumpled papers from her backpack and Brody raised an eyebrow at me. "Dylan already explained the need to keep the church's location private. I won't include anything identifiable, like the stained glass window. Or any evidence that we're even in a church."

I knew Brody would like that, but he still didn't look happy as he perused the release she'd given him. "Maggie, fire this off to Nolan's office." He handed the release off to Maggie as she approached; Nolan was one of our lawyers. "Tell him we need a quick turn-around. Amber here wants to photograph Dirty today."

"For fuck's sake, Dylan," Elle complained. She threw me a dirty look from where she stood onstage, holding her bass. "You could've warned me you were bringing a photographer. I'm so fucking bloated right now..."

I looked her over; she looked totally fucking fine. Sexy, actually. Pregnancy had definitely amped up her cleavage.

"You look beautiful, babe," Seth said. He was kneeling beside her, twiddling on his guitar.

"You can take as many photos of me as you want, sweetheart," Zane offered into his mic. He winked at me, and I flipped him a subtle middle finger, out of Amber's sight.

"You can have copies of all the photos I take, if you want," she was telling Brody. "And do whatever you want with them. Well... except sell them." She smiled, tentatively.

Brody just kinda glowered at her, crossing his arms over his chest. *Damn.* He wasn't making this easy for her. Probably wondering if she was just some opportunist, hanging out with me to get access to Dirty.

"She's really good, Brody," I informed him. Kind of an under-statement, but I didn't want to oversell it.

Amber frowned at me. "You haven't even seen much of my work."

"You think I haven't searched you?"

"Like online?"

"Yup."

"Oh."

"So you shoot bands?" Brody asked.

"Not specifically, but—"

"What about that epic shot you took of Johnny O at Lollapalooza a few years back?" I put in.

The shot *was* epic. Kinda made me epically jealous when I saw it, knowing she'd married the guy. Dude was hot. Not that I'd ever really noticed or cared before, but that photo made it pretty hard to miss.

Amber looked at me, her eyes widening a bit. "Yeah... He let me hang out while he did his set and I took a few photos. We'd just started... um... dating." She shot a nervous glance at Brody, probably wondering what he'd make of that.

His eyes narrowed as he considered that, letting her sweat.

"Don't be such a bear," Maggie said, poking Brody's shoulder. "She's Dylan's friend." There was a definite insinuation on the word *friend*, as she gave Amber a little girl-to-girl look.

I draped my arm around Amber's shoulders. "She's staying. We'll make the release work. And Elle can veto any pictures that make her look fat."

"I heard that," Elle said. "And yes, I can."

Brody looked less-than-thrilled, but finally relented when he realized no one was standing in Amber's way but him.

Everyone was still waiting for Jesse to arrive (fine by me; let him be the late one now). So while the rest of the band got warmed up, I showed Amber around the church. I brought her up to speed on what was going on in the life of my band. It was refreshing to me that she knew virtually nothing about Dirty, and frankly, didn't seem to care, other than for the fact that it was important to me.

Over the years, I'd kinda waffled back and forth between dating groupies and dating women who had nothing to do with my rock star life. Adulation was enjoyable, to a point, especially in the early years, but more and more I'd found myself attracted to women who had their own thing going on, something else to talk about besides my band... and who didn't go all fangirl over my bandmates.

Especially Zane. The guy would never touch a girl I was into; we'd been friends long enough I knew that for a fact. But he'd definitely eat that shit up.

Despite the fact that Amber hadn't shown any interest in him, he was still keeping an eye on her now; probably wondering what she was made of.

Honestly, if he brought a woman to rehearsal, I'd be doing the same thing.

I explained to Amber that Dirty had spent the better part of the last year writing songs for the new album, our tenth anniversary album, and at this point we were pretty much just putting the finishing touches on the songs. Taking things as far as we could, creatively, before going into the studio to start recording the album.

She could probably tell I was pretty fucking excited about it, and grinned at me as she listened.

At the beginning of this year, we'd had a song deficit, only a few new songs that were worthy of the album. But since bringing Jesse's sister, Jessa, back into the fold as a songwriter, and now Seth, we'd ended up with a surplus. We'd only recently managed to figure out which songs were making the cut. As it turned out, about a third of them were written by Jesse and Zane, another third by Jesse, Zane and Jessa, and the rest were written either by Seth or by a combination of Seth, Elle, and the others.

Elle had always contributed to the bass line as the songs came together, elaborating on Jesse's suggestions, but she and Seth had really clicked creatively, and for the first time, she was co-contributing lyrics and entire melodies. I would always come up with the drum parts on the songs, or embellish the basic beats that Jesse or Zane or whoever laid down. And DJ Summer was even collaborating on a few songs this time. She'd joined Dirty onstage for some special concerts over the past few years, here or there, but this was the first time she'd be playing on a Dirty album.

Everyone was swept up in the new music, and all the plans for the album were finally clicking into place.

"We're calling the album *To Hell & Back*, after this killer song Seth wrote. But that's top secret," I told Amber with a wink. "Hasn't been announced yet."

"Your secrets are safe with me," she said, lifting her camera to her face and snapping a photo of me and my dumbass grin.

"The documentary series we filmed with Liv when we were searching for a rhythm guitarist will start airing in December, I think, and we're going into the studio to start recording in thirteen days."

"Sounds like you're counting down the seconds."

"Believe me, I am. Once we're done that, the album promo will get going, heavy and hard, so we'll be pretty busy. The tour is coming together, too. So next year should be a great year. We've all been itching to get this album out, get back out on the road..."

Well, *shit*.

Amber clouded right over at the mention of the tour, and the smile kinda fell off my face. She tried to hide it by lifting her camera again and taking some photos of the band onstage; Zane, Seth and Elle were up there, getting antsy, waiting on Jesse and me.

So maybe it was better not to mention the tour.

I wasn't sure how to backpedal the hell out of what I'd told Amber on our first date, about our relationship ending when Ash and I went on the road. I was already realizing that proposal was a major fuck up for many reasons, not the least of which was that I was rapidly losing interest in the idea of leaving Amber behind. Just picking up and leaving her in the dust in two-and-a-half months made no fucking sense. Not if things continued on the way they were now.

But I also didn't want to scare her off, send her running to the opposite end of the globe by laying out a different plan—one where she stayed ours, and only pulled out her passport when she was hopping on a plane with *us*.

Before I could figure out something less douchy to say, though,

Jesse strolled in. While Zane gave him shit about being late, I gave Amber a kiss on the forehead and left her to do her thing, hopping up onstage.

We worked through a few of the new songs, and I made sure we played the best ones destined for the album, for Amber to hear. "Blackout." "She Makes It Easy." "To Hell & Back."

When we took a break from playing, Amber sat in on a band meeting. We still had all sorts of dumbass minutiae to get through for the album. Like were we officially changing "To Hell and Back" to "To Hell & Back"?

"I vote for the ampersand," Elle said.

"Ampersand," Jesse agreed.

"Katie likes the way it will look with her design for the album cover," Brody said, "and I think we should go with the ampersand."

It was unanimous. The ampersand took it.

Amber grinned at me. I could tell she was getting a kick out of this. A bunch of rock stars fussing over punctuation.

I gave her a little eye roll, but I liked the feeling of having her here.

She stayed out of the way, taking photos when we were onstage and when we were goofing around, but not when we were in our meeting. Her instincts were good, and everyone seemed to be comfortable with her here, which spoke volumes. If she'd pissed anyone off, they would've made it known and she would've been kicked out on her ass—whether she was my "friend" or not.

Didn't happen.

But her presence did raise a few eyebrows. Especially when she sat on my lap to show me some of the images she'd taken of me at the drums.

I ignored those eyebrows.

The fact was, this was all new territory for me. And for everyone else, too. I'd never brought women to shows or into the studio with me, much less to rehearsals.

Never. No one.

So of course, they wanted to know what the deal was with this particular woman.

Only wished I knew what to tell them.

I cut out of rehearsal early so I could take Amber to dinner. Which just raised more eyebrows.

But oh fucking well.

I didn't want to miss this dinner, or my chance to bring Amber to it.

When we pulled up at my mom's place in the burbs, I could tell Amber was confused. Probably thought I was gonna take her to another upscale restaurant downtown, like I'd done on our first dinner date. Probably the last thing she expected was for me to pull into the driveway of a rambling old two-story house with a tire swing on a tree out front and a literal white picket fence.

There were cars all jammed in the driveway, and as we got out of the truck and she smelled the barbecue, and heard all the voices and the screams of kids at play flowing out of the house, she figured it out.

"Oh my God." She gawked at me. "You didn't."

"Didn't what?" I sauntered over and put my arm around her shoulders.

"You brought me to a family barbecue?"

"Pretty much."

Exactly much.

I didn't tell her ahead of time, because I had a feeling it might freak her out, or maybe she'd even make some excuse for why she couldn't make it. But even so, I was surprised by how freaked out she looked.

"Dylan—"

"Dylan, baby! Is that you?" my mom called out from a window somewhere.

"Hey, Mom," I called back.

"*Fuck me*. Your mom's here?"

"She is." I steered Amber toward the house, getting her moving. She suddenly weighed like a ton of bricks. "This is her house."

"Oh, *shit*," she muttered, as people started spilling from the backyard, heading around to the door on the side of the kitchen. My sisters, Jocelyn and Julie, carrying plates of grilled meat and trailed by a bunch of kids.

"Dylan's here!" Julie called out when she saw us.

"You're late," Jocelyn informed me. "Go help Stan on the grill."

Then they disappeared into the house with the kids.

"Who was that?" Amber asked, sounding mildly panicked, and probably assuming correctly that the two red-haired women were related to me.

"My sisters. The tall, bossy one is Jocelyn. She's the oldest. The one with the glasses is Julie." As we rounded the side of the house and the backyard came into view, I pointed out another redhead supervising the rugrats playing on the patio. "The ridiculously-freckled one is Sam. And that's Lydia." I pointed her out; my youngest sister was looking sullen, as usual, her pale, strawberry-blonde hair hanging over her face as she sipped a wine cooler by the barbecue, where my uncle Stan was grilling.

"You have *four* sisters?" The panic was now edging on terror. I instinctively pulled her closer, wanting to ward off her fears.

"Yup."

"Um. Any brothers I should know about?"

"Nope. Brothers-in-law, though. That's Jocelyn's husband, Clay, and Julie's boyfriend, Brad." I pointed out the guys drinking beers in the garage, checking out Brad's latest work-in-progress, a 1970 Chevelle. "Don't worry, I'll introduce you. My cousins are probably in the house, and my nephews and nieces are around here somewhere, too..."

"Holy fucking shit." Amber grabbed my arm, stopping me just as I started steering her into the yard. "Dylan. I am not gonna remember all these names."

I laughed. "I wouldn't expect you to. Just come drink some booze and eat some food. They don't bite."

"You don't understand. I'm *terrible* with people." She clung to my arm, and I could feel her hand getting sweaty in mine. "Families make me twitchy. I'm *especially* terrible with families."

"Why?"

"Because they make me nervous. I don't have a normal family, Dylan. We didn't have family barbecues. We don't even like each other that much. I'll feel all awkward and stuff..."

"Don't." I took hold of her pretty face, tilting her mouth to mine for a kiss. I brushed my lips over hers, lightly, and felt her soften a bit. "You're beautiful, Amber Malone. And smart and charming—"

"Charming?" She scoffed.

"Hey. You charmed me." I ran my thumb over her freckled cheek.

"You're just easy to charm," she grumbled.

"Hardly."

"Dylan!" Clay called out from the garage. "Introduce us to your friend." When I looked over, he was wearing a shit-eating grin as he checked out Amber, a little too slowly.

"See?" I said, pulling her closer and draping my arm around her shoulders again as I steered her over to the garage. "Charming my family already."

"Oh, God. What's that one's name again?"

"Clay."

"Do we like Clay?"

"Yup. As long as he doesn't keep eye-fondling you like that."

"Right," she said under her breath. And as we stepped into the garage, she extended her hand, put on one of her sweet-ass smiles, and said, "Hi. I'm Amber."

Four hours and many, many rounds of my mom's food later, Amber and I said our goodbyes and climbed into my truck.

"Take care of that one," Clay said, nodding his approval toward Amber as he shut my door and rapped his knuckles lightly on the side of the truck. On the other side, Jocelyn was saying goodbye to Amber.

Clay was thirteen years older than me; he'd been around since I was nine, so he was pretty much the closest thing I'd ever had to a big brother. Maybe, in a way, he was kind of also like a father now that Dad was gone. So it meant something, his approval.

"I will," I said.

He and Jocelyn and their sons waved goodbye as we pulled out. Julie and my cousins with the younger kids had already headed home to tuck all the little ankle biters into bed.

When I glanced over at Amber, she was waving at my little sister, Lydia; she was sitting alone on the front porch and waved back.

I grinned to myself.

Amber had handled herself pretty fucking well, considering she was "terrible with people" and there were almost forty people she'd never met before crammed into my mom's house, many of them under the age of five and about as hyper as the Tasmanian Devil. Plus, my family was so enraptured with the fact that I'd actually brought a woman to a family dinner, they were all over her.

Amber had spent more time talking to Lydia, though, than anyone else—even though she had no way of knowing how that would hit me in the heart.

Lydia had always been kind of a misfit. She wasn't "gifted" with music or math like me and my other sisters, and she looked different than the rest of us. The reality was I knew she'd never felt as pretty, and she'd always been more socially awkward. She'd been diagnosed with a learning disability from a young age and had struggled through school. She was sweet, though, hilarious when you got her to open up, and if anyone held a gun to my head and forced me to pick a favorite, it would be Lydia.

Julie and I were closest; closest in age, and we'd been through school together, shared a bedroom for many years, and we were the most alike. Jocelyn was a lot older and had always looked out for me. And Sammy was a sweetheart. But Lydia had my heart in a way that I'd told her, in secret, the others never would, just because she was Lydie.

She was a woman now, but she'd always be little Lydie to me.

And Lydie never had to do anything to impress me. She didn't have to be anything different than what she was. She was just special, from the very first moment I met her, the day she was born; when I was six years old and I got to hold her, and she looked up into my eyes.

"You got along with Lydia well," I said.

Amber smiled. "You sound surprised."

"Not exactly. Just... there was a lot going on in there. Cope family functions are a little... loud."

She laughed. "Understatement."

"Yeah. And sometimes a person like Lydie goes unnoticed."

She looked over at me. "Really?"

"Yeah. I think she's always felt kind of invisible. Jocelyn's fucking brilliant, went through school on scholarships and now she's a professor. My dad was so fucking proud of her, maybe because he barely made it through school himself. Never went to college or anything. And Julie's always been the bubbly one who pulls everyone together, likes to bake and hand-make everyone's Christmas presents, and she's always been so bonded to Mom that way. And Sammy's so cute. She's always been popular, and she sings in a vocal group and plays guitar and dances..."

"And then there's you," Amber said, her tone slightly accusatory.

"Yeah." I laughed. "There's that."

"Big brother the rock-star-underwear-model. I could see how a girl could feel like she might disappear."

I grinned, but then got serious. "Thank you for taking an interest in her."

Amber looked genuinely surprised. "She's interesting. And besides... she reminds me of you, actually."

"Really?"

"Yeah. Not the emo part. But there's this thoughtfulness in her eyes. This deep, kind quality. She has your eyes."

"Does she?"

"Yes." A silence fell, and I could feel her eyes on me as I drove. "So why didn't you tell me you were taking me there?"

"Honestly?" I glanced at her. "Thought you might've been scared off if I told you."

"Uh, yeah." She smiled, but then she looked away, the smile fading. "Guess you're starting to figure me out then, huh?"

I was.

I was figuring out how she used her camera to distance herself from people. How she used it to protect herself, avoid getting close.

How she often felt like she didn't quite fit in.

She was a lot like Ash that way.

Ash used his rock star image, his player persona, his cocky attitude and crude tattoos to keep people out. And he'd always lived on the edge, keeping himself on the outside of things, not even wanting to fit in.

But maybe that just helped to explain why I liked Amber so much. Because I'd been drawn to Ash from the first day I met him, too.

Maybe I'd just always preferred the misfits.

When I took Amber home to bed at the end of our date, and Ash was waiting up for us... and he joined us in my bedroom... It hit me that it felt kind of *off*. For the first time ever, I was so focused on *her*, on wanting her... it felt uncomfortable having him here, in my bed, while I was with a woman.

I didn't like the feeling.

So I tried to ignore it.

Amber had pulled out her camera when we were coming back on the boat, and she didn't put it away when we got home. Her, taking photos of me, had become foreplay that we all enjoyed. She kneeled above me on the bed, taking photos of me laid out beneath her, as I slid my hands up her thighs, under her dress. And Ash started feeling her up.

Clearly, he'd missed her, and I watched his hands roaming over her body, undressing her, until she couldn't hold the camera steady anymore... caught between the arousal of watching him make her feel good, and that odd discomfort.

I watched him remove the camera from her hand, pull her down to the bed, and fuck her. It was the only time, so far, that he'd fucked her in my presence *before* I did.

And it turned me on.

As always, I was transfixed by the pleasure I saw him giving her. But more than that...

I was fascinated by *her*.

And yes, I could feel myself starting to want her in ways I wasn't used to wanting a woman.

I wasn't a caveman, but women, in my life, had always been for fucking and fun. Relationships were serious things. I wasn't a serious guy. So for me, hanging with women was casual, or I didn't bother with it.

Sure, I'd been in love. Kinda-sorta, and briefly.

But I'd never *really* been in love.

I'd never really cared to be.

I'd accused Ash of being jealous. But I was feeling it now, whenever he touched Amber: a twinge of serious jealousy like nothing I'd ever felt before.

By the time he came, then rolled off of her, panting, and Amber reached for me, pulling me to her... it had me so worked up... so hungry for her and so fucking *confused*. I got so totally lost in fucking her... I almost forgot he was in the room.

When she cried out my name as she came, it made me come... and for a moment there, I actually did forget.

It was the hottest sex I'd had with Amber yet.

CHAPTER TWENTY-ONE

Ash

I WAS JEALOUS. I could admit that to myself. Seeing Dylan and Amber coming back from their date last night, all aglow. They looked so fucking perfect together, and I could see how wrapped up in each other they were getting.

Kinda blew me away that they still wanted me around, actually.

After the three of us ate breakfast together, Amber walked Dylan down to the dock and kissed him goodbye before he got into his boat. It was a long, lingering kiss, and his hands were on her ass. She stood up on her tiptoes to give it to him, her body pressed up against his, arms wrapped around his neck.

I watched it from his bedroom window, which was the only place the dock could be seen from either house. And yes, I'd gone straight up there when they left, so I could watch them.

Then I watched Dylan take off in the Dirty Deed. I knew he'd be gone most of the day, rehearsing with Dirty at the church.

When Amber came back into the house, I was already in the kitchen, pouring myself a coffee. "Any plans for today?" I asked her as she slid onto a stool at the island.

She started making herself a pot of tea with the water I'd just boiled for her. "Not sure. I was thinking about going to see my mom later, maybe. I should really do that soon…" She didn't sound enthusiastic about it. She leaned her chin on her hand and gazed at me. "And I still have some of the images from Katie's art show to get through. I told her I'd have them to her by the end of the week."

"Or, you could hang out with me."

She smiled at me.

I really wasn't sure at what point she'd started doing that, but she had. Regularly.

I also wasn't sure at what point I'd started longing for those smiles, but every time she did it, it hit me straight in the gut. Gave me this weird bubbly feeling in my chest that I really couldn't remember feeling since I'd been with Summer. I'd totally forgotten about that feeling, actually. Or maybe I'd convinced myself it had never been real.

But now here it was.

Every time Amber Paige Malone smiled in my direction.

About half an hour later, as I slowed my boat down in a secluded little tree-lined bay around the far side of the island, Amber, in the co-pilot seat, looked over at me. When I cut the engine and dropped the anchor, she gave me one of her bright smiles again.

"So what are we doing here?" she asked, gazing around. It was dead quiet, other than the rhythmic lap of the water against the boat, and the odd bird. The coastline that swept around us was dense with trees, not a house or other boat in sight.

"Absolutely nothing," I said. I grabbed each of us a beer out of the cooler, cracked them open, and handed one to her.

"Don't you have work to do?" she asked me as she took the beer and reclined in her seat.

"Nope."

I stripped off my long-sleeved Ramones shirt and stretched out on the floor, which was covered with clean but rough boat carpet. I lay my shirt down, then lay down on top of it. There was a cold breeze off the water, but down here, the wind was blocked. And the sun was out; it already felt warm on my chest.

Amber sipped her beer, cozy in my hoodie, which was giant on her, with the hood flipped up over her hair, and I enjoyed how her pretty eyes moved slowly over my bare chest. "Like, don't you have a band or something?"

I frowned. "A band?"

"Yeah. That's what I heard, anyway."

"Hmm." I pretended to search the recesses of my brain, shaking my head. "Nope. Doesn't ring a bell."

"Really? I could've sworn you guys were called the Penny Pushers or something? Or maybe it was the Party Poopers. The Pickle Pumpers?"

I laughed. "Shit. I'm calling the boys. We are definitely changing our name to the Pickle Pumpers, stat." I dug my phone out of my pants and pretended to text that to someone.

Amber grinned. "Seriously. Don't you ever work? Or are you that ballin' that you don't even have to? On the rock star early retirement plan?"

"I wish." I stashed my phone away. "I've been writing. Got a new album in the pipeline. We'll be getting together in the studio soon."

"Cool. Guess I should actually listen to some of your stuff." She bit the side of her lip, looking adorably bashful. "I know some of Dirty's music. But I don't think I've heard yours."

"Don't bother," I said. "It's shit."

She laughed. "What?"

"Old news. You can wait 'til the new album comes out."

She shook her head at me, still smiling. "Okay?"

I shrugged. "Maybe you can do a photo for the album cover or something."

She sat up, looking excited, though I wasn't sure if it was an act or what. "For the Pickle Pumpers' new album? I'd love to!"

I grinned. "Perfect. So that's one item down." I pulled my phone back out and this time I did write a text, reading it aloud to her as I typed. "Just... hired... kickass... sexy... photographer... to... do... new... album... cover... SEND."

"You didn't."

"Just sent it to the band and our management company."

She laughed again. "Nice. You've got a concept in mind?"

"I was kinda hoping you'd come up with that. I'm on the early retirement plan here." I stretched in the sun, getting comfy again.

"Hmm." She sipped her beer, thinking. "Okay. Think I've got something here. Remember when the Red Hot Chili Peppers did that thing where they played shows wearing nothing but a sock on their penises?"

"Sure. 'Socks on Cocks.'"

She giggled. "Right. And they wore them on the cover of an album, too, I think..."

"Yeah, *The Abbey Road E.P.*."

"Right. So I'm thinking something in that direction."

"I like it."

"BUT with pickles. Obviously."

"Obviously."

She snickered, sipping her beer. "We should really collaborate more often."

"Yup." I threw my arm behind my head like a pillow, watching her. "So tell me. How was it working with Dirty yesterday?"

"Good. I mean, I just photographed them a bit while they rehearsed. They were really nice about it, though, especially considering they had zero warning I was coming."

"Sounds like a classic Dylan move."

"He really operates on his own wavelength, huh?"

"You know it. But I've never met a drummer who doesn't. They're always strange animals."

"Always?"

"Always. And trust me, his band was nice to you because no one was gonna say anything to him in front of you. But they're gonna bust Dylan's balls today."

"About what?"

"About you, sweetheart."

Her smile faded. "What? Why?"

"Because the number of times Dylan Cope has ever brought a woman with him to any sort of band anything is exactly zero."

She blinked at me. "Really?"

"Really," I said, now wondering if I should've told her that. If it freaked her out, Dylan was definitely gonna be pissed at me for saying it. "I mean, he brought you there as a photographer, right? That's probably what they'll think."

That wasn't what they'd think. But if she knew that, Amber didn't say anything.

"And how was the barbecue?" I asked, looking to change the subject.

"Oh. It was great."

"Let me guess," I said, reading between the lines of that response. "He didn't tell you where he was taking you?"

"Not so much."

"Damn." I laughed a little. "Was it that bad?"

"Not at all, actually. Dylan's family is... Hang on. I'm searching for the right word."

"Intense?"

"No." She smiled. "Not exactly. I was thinking more along the lines of *exuberant*, in a good way. They're so loving. Honestly, it kind of freaked me out at first."

"I know what you mean. First time I met his parents, they hugged me and called me 'son.' Don't think anyone's ever called me son."

"You're close with his family?"

"Pretty close. They come out here a lot. Hang out. His brother-in-law, Brad, works on my Camaro with me. We have 'exuberant' barbecues with ginger kids running all over the place." She grinned at my use of her word. "Miss his dad, though. He was awesome."

"Tell me about him."

I shrugged. "Just a textbook awesome dad. Was always there for his kids, all five of them. Worked hard. Was totally involved in family life. Proud as fuck of his only son. He died pretty suddenly, about three years ago. Brain tumor. Just started acting strange overnight, like he wasn't himself. Had headaches, stuff like that. It took him out fast, so at least he didn't suffer too long. But it was hard. On everyone."

"Wow." Amber processed that, shaking her head, her light-green eyes soft with sympathy. "And I get bummed sometimes because my dad can be kind of a jerk. I don't know how Dylan stays so positive when he's been through a loss like that. I think I'd still be grieving."

"That's just Dylan. Not his nature to dwell. He doesn't really do depressed." I sat up and took a swig of my beer. "But trust me, he was heartbroken when his dad died."

Amber was silent a moment, looking at me. "You're different that way," she said. "I mean, you strike me as more of a dweller."

"You, too."

Her mouth twitched in a hint of a smile. "I guess that's why he likes us?"

"Huh?"

"Because we're kind of alike, you and me."

"We are?" I said, but by now, I kinda knew she was right.

"I think you know we are," she challenged. "And for some reason, he likes whatever it is about us that's different from him, maybe."

"Maybe."

"His mom told me a bit about your family," she said, carefully. Maybe she wasn't sure how I'd take that. "Your Aunt Ginny. The one on your fridge, right? She really likes her. Said she's met her a few times."

"Yeah. Ginny's kinda my angel."

Amber smiled at that.

"She's my dad's sister. She's been like a long-distance mom for me, all my life. She's super Christian, really involved in her church, and family is important to her. She just always liked me, for whatever reason, looked out for me. She lives in Colorado, so I go visit her there whenever I can. Her and Uncle Joe and their little guy, Aidan.

They're pretty much my only family, so I try not to forget about them whenever shit with the band gets crazy and takes over."

Amber's eyes had softened even more as she listened, and she said, "That's nice, Ashley."

"Yeah. My dad raised me, technically, as in he provided me with a home and occasional meals, but he was kind of a deadbeat, and Ginny knew that. She's his younger sister. I don't know... somehow he didn't inherit the same genes for giving a fuck. Until I started to become successful, anyway. Once I had a song on the charts and my picture in *Rolling Stone*, he took an interest."

"Where is he now?"

"Out east. He has a little shack out near Chilliwack, where he grew up. With his degenerate dad."

At that, Amber raised an eyebrow.

"Trust me," I said, "he's a degenerate. But I like to think the Calegari men improve slightly with each generation."

Amber cocked her head a little but kinda smiled at me, sympathetically. "Slightly?"

I shrugged.

"Calegari? You're Italian?"

"The degenerate is. I'm a Player."

She just kept smiling and shook her head. "Right."

I wasn't sure why her looking at me like that made me want to squirm, but it did. Maybe it was just that I wasn't used to talking so much about my fucked-up family.

"Do you ever see them?" she asked.

"I send them money sometimes," I said, "but I don't visit much. They pretty much only come around when they want something."

"And what about your mom?"

Blank. I went kinda blank at the mention of her.

What the fuck could I say? Usually I didn't say shit about my mom to anyone, because the truth was there wasn't anything to say. At least, nothing nice to say.

"She left when I was thirteen."

"Left?"

"Yeah. As in she said she was going to pick up eggs and never came back. I remember that specifically because it was Father's Day, and I was gonna make breakfast for my dad. Try to impress him, I guess."

I looked away. I couldn't handle any more of the sympathy in her eyes.

"Do you know what happened to her?" she asked.

"Nothing happened. She sent a letter about three years later saying she was sorry for leaving, but no return address. No phone number. She had no family left and the friends we asked said they didn't know where she was. My dad was pretty bitter. I wanted to pay someone to find her for a while, but he wouldn't, and I couldn't afford to on my own as a kid. And by the time I was an adult, I guess I'd grown bitter, too."

"You didn't look for her?"

"She didn't look for me."

Amber went silent. When I glanced at her, she was staring at me.

"Hey, it's not like I'd be hard to find. I'm pretty hard to miss, right?" I indicated my bare upper body, all the tattoos.

"You don't have to make jokes, Ashley," she said, gently. "I get it. At least your dad comes around when he wants something, right?"

Wow. Nailed it.

The truth was, I'd always been pissed at my mom because she didn't want anything from me—even my money. At least my dad pretended to give a shit. Made an effort at remembering I existed, when it served him.

How did this girl get me so damn well?

Maybe she was right. Maybe we were alike.

"Tell me about your parents," I said, needing out of this line of conversation before I ended up saying too much sad, stupid shit.

Amber shrugged and sipped her beer. "Nothing much to tell."

I stared at her for a long moment, waiting for more. But she just drank her beer and stared back at me.

I pulled my knees up, resting my forearms on them. I took a swig of my beer and considered how hard to push her on this.

"I seem to remember a conversation we had recently," I told her. "Everything out in the open, right?"

She blinked at me. "Everything?"

"Everything."

She licked her lips and looked off for a moment. Then she took a deep breath, her nostrils flaring a bit, and looked into my eyes. "Can I ask you something first, then, Ashley?"

"Sure."

"There's really nothing going on between you and Dylan?" she asked, holding my gaze. "Other than sharing women?"

"No," I said, my heart suddenly beating too hard. "There's nothing going on."

It was true.

It was also a lie.

The *whole* truth was that there was a whole shit-ton going on—in my mind. But I lied, looking her right in the eyes. The same way I'd done to Dylan, a thousand times.

She nodded, seeming to believe me. Then she sighed.

"Okay, then... My parents. My mom still lives here. Liv sees her more than I do, because I'm away traveling so much, but also because she handles her better. Mom's become pretty... eccentric over the years. Living alone. Living with her delusions."

"Delusions about...?"

"About the way things are. Between her and our dad." She sighed again and glanced around, kinda like she was looking for a way out. No chance, unless she wanted to dive overboard and swim for shore. Instead, she went on. "He left her, long ago. Liv and I were still kids. We still saw him after the divorce, sometimes, even after he moved to Toronto, but they never got back together like my mom always seemed to think they would." She picked at the label on her beer bottle. "They were in love. Like really in love. And their relationship was crazy. It was explosive and unstable. Bordering on violent."

"He hit her?"

"I don't think so. They pushed each other around when they fought, though. They screamed and threw stuff. She hit him a few times. It was bullshit. It was better that he left. But my mom never saw it that way."

Well... *that* gave me a picture of why Amber was so defensive, careful, when it came to getting involved with Dylan and me. If that was her early example of people "in love."

Hearing it made me want to push past her doubts even more than I already did.

Make her want to stay.

It wasn't lost on me that I'd started to care about her. To want to keep her around for more reasons than just because she was an intimate connection to Dylan.

I wanted to show her that she was safe here, with me, with what she'd just shared with me. Safe to open up to me.

"Far be it for me to give advice," I said, "but if I were to give advice, I'd say you should talk to your mom. Try to repair that relationship. While you can. If I had a chance to do that with my mom, I would."

"Why don't you try to find her?" she asked. "You could afford to pay someone to do it now, right?"

"I did. About six years ago." I looked at her pretty face, then away. "Turned out she'd died about a year before that."

"Ashley. I'm sorry."

Amber reached out and slid her hand over mine, and I turned my hand to grip hers. I looked up into her green eyes again. "Are you really gonna stay with us like we asked you to?"

It came out before I knew I was gonna ask. Maybe. Or maybe I just didn't want to pussy out and stop myself, so I blurted it before I could think it through.

Amber squeezed my hand and said, "Yes."

That night, Dylan got home late and found Amber in my bed. She'd fallen asleep after we had sex, but I was still awake. He got undressed as he made his way to the bed in the near-dark. He didn't say anything. I didn't even know if he knew I was awake.

He just peeled back the covers and slid in next to Amber, and started kissing her. He started at her clit, and by the time he reached her mouth she was wide awake and whimpering that sexy, desperate sound of hers; that sound I'd noticed she only made for him.

He climbed on top of her and they started going at it, and by the time he buried his dick in her, they were both panting hard, wound up on the feel of each other, groping skin-to-skin in the dark.

He rode her with a single-minded intensity that left no doubt in my mind that he'd missed her, that he'd been thinking about her while he was away today. That he'd been thinking about *this* the entire way home.

Amber reached out in the dark and gripped me with her hand. Her fingers dug into my arm. And I just watched. Seeing them together like this... it blew my fucking mind. It was like I was sitting on the edge of goddamn heaven, gazing in.

I was rock-hard.

I watched him make her come. Felt her fingernails digging into my muscles as she cried out and gasped.

I watched him come, his hips rolling between her spread thighs, his muscular ass clenching as he shot off, as he buried his face in her neck and groaned.

Amber's mouth was free, so I leaned in and kissed her. She kissed me back, hungry and soft... breathless kisses.

As Dylan pulled out and shifted off of her, I rolled right over and took his place. Amber was all limp and warm, sleepy and spent, but she took me. She spread her legs for me.

We'd already tossed the condoms, and I slipped into her tight, wet warmth, bare. I wasn't even gonna pretend it didn't turn me on like hell to be fucking her with Dylan's come still coating her. Coating me.

Dylan lay back and watched me fuck her. Even though I barely looked at him, I could practically feel his eyes on me. They were on us, on Amber for sure... but I could almost pretend he was enjoying watching me pump into her, and it pushed me over the edge. I felt the rush and I didn't even try to hold it back.

I slammed into Amber and let loose, filling her, ridiculously mind-fucked over the fact that I was coming where he'd just come. I groaned and kissed her soft mouth as I relaxed, letting her tight pussy squeeze me as the aftershocks twitched through me. She ran her fingertips gently up and down my spine and breathed softly against me.

It was almost perfect...

But something was nagging at the back of my mind. The knowledge that this was all gonna fall apart on me. Because it always did, right?

Whenever I let myself care... care so much that there was so much to lose... I ended up losing.

But I shoved aside those bullshit thoughts. I didn't want to listen to them anymore.

I wanted this.

I pulled out and shifted down, sealing my mouth over Amber's pussy. She gasped and squirmed, but I pressed her thighs apart and went to town. I worshipped her with my tongue, rolling the smooth steel ball of my piercing around her clit until she came with a helpless little scream, clawing at my hair.

When I came up for air, they were making out. Dylan was kissing the fuck out of her, and his dick was hard, thick and heavy against his thigh, inches from my face.

I rolled away.

Rationally, I knew as I looked at them entwined in my bed, kissing in the aftermath of what we'd all just done, looking perfect as fuck, that I'd never be able to keep them both.

No matter whatever happened between me and Dylan that one time... I'd never be able to *have* them both.

No matter how much I wanted them.

We'd promised Amber: everything out in the open. We'd all promised each other. *Everything*.

Everything except my secret love for my best friend.

Late in the night, Dylan woke up. I was already awake. I was sitting on the edge of the bed, by the window, smoking a joint, looking out at the water through the trees. I could feel him stirring, knew he wasn't sleeping. I knew the sound of his breathing, awake or asleep. Usually the dude slept like the dead, especially after he'd been laid.

I looked over at him in the dark. He looked back at me, met my gaze briefly, but I already saw what he was doing.

He was watching Amber sleep.

"You're gonna fall for her," I said quietly. Just like I'd told him before. But it was worse than that; he was already falling.

And just like he did before, he laughed. But he didn't look me in the eye when he did it.

CHAPTER TWENTY-TWO

Amber

IT WAS A BEAUTIFUL DAY. Cool, but nice enough that we could hunker down behind the windshield in our jackets, with the cover off the ~~Falcon~~ Silver Sparrow, as Ashley drove me into the city. The skies were a brilliant blue without a trace of cloud, a rare sapphire-clear day in autumn as we sped toward Vancouver.

True to my word, I was staying. It had been a week ago that I'd promised Ashley, in this boat, that I would stick around. And I'd officially put my travel plans on hold, at least temporarily.

No more hitting up Google to research Thailand. No more watching airline ticket prices in case there was a price drop.

I put out feelers around Vancouver again, in case any work came up. And I'd picked up a couple of gigs this week, as assistant to an old friend from college on some shoots she was doing. Not exactly high pay or high prestige, but at least it kept me working. My pay for the Underlayer shoot had come through, too. Plus, Katie had given my number to that art promoter she'd told me about, and he'd called; said he had some events coming up that I might be able to shoot, and that he wanted to see my work. So I was planning to follow up on that.

Meanwhile, I'd insisted that I start paying at least some token rent. I wasn't about to take a free ride from anyone, even from two guys I happened to be fucking.

The guys didn't like it, but they'd finally agreed when they could tell I wasn't going to budge.

I was still living at Ashley's house, technically, in his guest room, but I spent pretty much every night in Dylan's bed—with Dylan *and* Ashley.

When I didn't spend the night in Dylan's bed, it was because we'd all spent the night in Ashley's bed instead or, occasionally, in Ashley's bed in the city.

We'd also headed over to the big island—Vancouver Island—for a couple of days, and driven up to the very end of the highway at Tofino to rent a cabin and surf. According to Dylan, Ashley got twitchy when he went too long without surfing.

It wasn't exactly California, but the waves were pretty good, just coming off of a storm. It was cold as shit, and we had to wear wetsuits. Ashley had his own, and Dylan and I rented from a shop in the little town. I'd learned to surf while I was in Australia a few years ago, which meant that I could actually get up on the board, but that only lasted about three seconds. After I'd bailed and swallowed cold saltwater for the third time, I called it a day and headed back up to the cabin to lounge by the fire.

Dylan didn't last much longer; he'd come to find me and took me for a walk on the beach, and we'd sat on the rocks watching Ashley do his thing. Even in a wetsuit, with not a slice of skin showing, he looked sexy on that board.

I'd taken some photos, and afterwards, we'd spent the night in front of the fire, having sex. Slow, passionate sex that somehow had me feeling like I was in this incredible dream I never wanted to wake up from.

How did my life suddenly become this good?

Not that it was so bad before, but seriously.

All three of us had already gotten the results from our blood tests back, and passed with flying colors. The guys had insisted to me that they were safe; that they always wore condoms, except with

Kitty, whom they'd also been tested with. So that was good, I supposed.

Great, actually, because it meant I could fuck them both without condoms. Which felt so good it was kinda scary.

It went without saying that this was the best sex I'd ever had.

With anyone.

It still blew my mind, whenever I paused to think about it, that I was having sex with *two* men. And I didn't feel weird about it. Maybe because they didn't make me feel weird about it. They treated it like it was so *normal* that it put me at ease. Made me feel wanted, and safe with them.

Too safe.

In the back of my mind, I just kept wondering if I was gonna discover something about either one of them—or both—that would turn me off enough to send me packing. Unfortunately, the image of Johnny in that hot tub with all those naked chicks had burned itself permanently into my brain, and that feeling of utter shock and betrayal? It had left a little crack in the foundation of my trust that might never fully heal.

But so far, nothing scandalous had been revealed. No giant skeletons had come tumbling out of the closet. No naked chicks had suddenly appeared in the symbolic hot tub with my men.

So I just kept dating both of them—together.

And sometimes, separately.

It all just seemed to be working out a little too well.

How was dating two men, even if they were okay with it, ever going to work longterm? Just seemed like it was against the laws of nature somehow. Like things were *bound* to go wrong.

Stupid or not, I felt kinda greedy. There was more than enough hotness here to go around, and around. Many, many women could be enjoying Dylan Cope and Ashley Player—and definitely had, before I came along—and yet here I was, hogging them all to myself.

But they'd asked me to be exclusive, right?

Truth was, I'd just never been this lucky. And most of the time I didn't know how to get my head around it and just plain enjoy it.

I really wasn't sure what I was doing, at all. I was just kind of going along with what they'd asked me to do.

But officially, I was definitely smack in the middle of a ménage à trois. And the whole thing was starting to get under my skin. Starting to get to me.

Starting to *mean* something to me.

I hadn't even told my sister all of what was going on. I'd told Liv it was just about the sex. Partly so she'd stop asking questions, because I knew she wouldn't want more details on that.

But whenever I looked at Dylan or Ashley—like I was doing now, catching Ashley's eye as he drove his boat, the wind whipping his dark hair back as he smiled at me… I knew it was about a lot more than just sex.

And maybe *that* was the only real problem.

Somehow, I'd ended up in a relationship.

And I really wasn't sure how I was getting out of it with my heart intact.

My mom's little old house was the same as it ever was. Every single thing in the exact same place.

Literally.

It had been this way for over twenty years. Since before my dad walked out.

I could understand, if you lost a child—like if your child *died*—how you might not be able to bear changing anything. How you might want to keep the child's bedroom intact for years afterward; decades, even. That, I could understand.

But keeping your home a shrine to your ex-husband, who'd walked out on you two decades ago—complete with his recliner in the same spot and his ashtray next to it, even though you'd never smoked? That, I could not understand.

And it wasn't like Liv and I hadn't taken Mom to see doctors.

Repeatedly. They all said there was nothing wrong with her, medically.

Her sanity was intact.

Of course, they'd never been inside her home.

"How've you been?" I asked her, after a brief hug, as she shuffled us into the kitchen. I watched her putter around, preparing to make tea. She was overweight, too much bulk on her previously thin frame, weighting down her delicate bone structure, and she seemed listless, tired. But she'd been this way for years. Combination of a poor diet, comfort eating and a sedentary lifestyle.

And too much time spent living in the past.

I used to tell her if she took better care of herself, she might attract a new man.

I was a teenager. I didn't know that was the wrong thing to say, for so many reasons.

I didn't say shit like that anymore.

"Oh, I'm good," she told me as she put the kettle on to boil. "Do you still like chamomile tea?"

I'd never really liked chamomile tea. Tasted like soap to me. For some reason, she could never remember that.

"Sure," I said.

"Your father prefers Earl Grey," she said. Because that, she remembered perfectly.

It made my skin fucking crawl the way she said *prefers*. In the present tense. Like he came over for tea every Sunday or something, when in truth, he hadn't spoken to her in years. I didn't even want to look in the cupboard when she pulled out the tea, afraid she might have Earl Grey stocked up for him, just in case.

Who was I kidding? Of course she did.

"Have you been getting out?" I asked her, gently. She never got out as much as I wanted her to, but I always hoped. Then maybe she'd make a new friend at the park, or join a yoga class, or something. Take up knitting. Bake something for a community bake sale. Whatever it took to get her more of a *life*.

But I wasn't going to push. Ever since Ashley had told me I

should go see her, try to make amends with her, salvage whatever relationship we might still have, it had been weighing heavily on me.

I did not want to wake up one day, days or years from now, to find out I'd missed my chance. That she was gone, and I'd never tried.

"I've been doing walks, every Saturday," she informed me, sounding proud of herself. "I drive up to Queen Elizabeth Park and walk all the way around."

"That's great, Mom." It was great. However, a walk once a week was hardly enough. "How's work?"

"I'm still doing three shifts a week at the greenhouse," she said. "It keeps me busy."

Right. *Busy*.

We both knew she spent many more hours a week obsessing over her lost love than anything else.

"Could you pick up a few more shifts? They seem to like you there."

"Oh, they do. They always ask. But three is enough for me."

I left it at that.

"Enough about me," she said. "Tell me about your trip." She poured the boiling water into the pot and set the tea to steep, and joined me at the table. "Did you have a good time?"

"Yes. Brazil was amazing. I got a ton of photos. I don't even know what I'll do with them all. You know, I always shoot way too much, but it was so gorgeous. And so moving... I think I'll have to go back one day. I still haven't fully processed it all. But I managed to sell some images, and even picked up a few assignments along the away."

"That's wonderful, Amber." My mom's hazel eyes softened as she gazed at me, and she laid her hand on mine, giving it a squeeze. Her hand was soft and doughy, and she had long, beautiful fingernails that she'd painted a meticulous pink. That had never changed.

She'd always been proud of me; that had never changed, either.

"And where are you off to next?"

"Thailand, I think. I've been wanting to go back there for a while and stay longer than the first time. I have some friends there now, a couple I met while I was in France. I can stay with them a while, and travel around, too."

"That sounds lovely."

"Yeah. Will you worry about me this time?" The last time I went to Thailand, she'd read some news article about a tourist being kidnapped there, and worried about me. She told me I was crazy for going there. But that was a long time ago, one of my first trips to a foreign country.

"Amber, dear." She squeezed my hand again. "I'd worry about you if you *stopped* doing these crazy things."

That made me smile. Because sometimes my mom just understood me, even when I couldn't understand her.

"I met someone," I told her, before I could second-guess it.

"Oh?"

It was always dicey to bring up the subject of men with my mom. But I decided to take the risk, given that I was here to try to foster more of a bond with her. Couldn't exactly do that if I locked her out of my personal life, right?

I decided not to mention that I'd met *two* someones, though.

"I've been thinking, about what it would be like to be with someone longterm. Be in love. Maybe get married someday." She was the only person I'd said that to, and somehow, I felt safe saying it here, to her. "I haven't thought about that a lot since, you know, Johnny. But... I think maybe it's important to me. To get married one day. Have a husband. Be a wife." She listened as she poured us both a tea, a slightly dreamy look on her face. "I don't think I really knew it was so important to me until I started feeling something for someone again. I don't know." I shrugged. "Maybe even have kids someday... Does that surprise you?"

"Amber," she said, her gentle gaze holding mine. "I wouldn't be surprised if it was the *most* important thing."

Wow.

I'd never talked about this with my mom. I'd never talked about wanting to get married or have kids. I'd only ever talked to her about my travel plans and my photography dreams. I'd always been scared to talk about marriage with her.

But she was taking it better than I'd expected.

"It was the most important thing to *me*," she added. "The day I married your father was the happiest day of my life..."

And then off she went.

She started spouting off the same old crap about my dad that she'd been saying for the past twenty years. About their life together. About their undying love. Talking about him like they were *still* together, when he'd left her two decades ago and never looked back.

He'd *remarried*, for Christ's sake. Fourteen years ago.

It was so fucking *sad*. Listening to her go on and on...

And it made me angry.

I barely got another word in, but what would I say? Reminding her he was gone never helped. Telling her he wasn't coming back could only do damage, sending her into one of her downward tailspins, where she stopped answering her phone and lost her job and gained more weight.

I managed to excuse myself about half an hour later, leaving her house just in time for the hot tears to spill down my face. Tears of anger and frustration and disillusionment.

I just did not know how to have a relationship with my mom when it was so tainted with her fucking delusions.

I walked up the road and sat on the curb. I texted Ashley that I was ready to leave. It was earlier than he probably expected. I didn't know how long he'd be, so I just sat here. At least I stopped crying as the anger overtook the sadness. And then the surrender kicked in. I gave in.

I gave up.

I tried to feel sympathy for my mom, but I just couldn't. Not really. Not a lot. Maybe I'd burned it all out in the first ten years or so after Dad left, as I grew up.

We'd taken her to the doctors again and again, and they'd all said the same thing. She wasn't medically depressed. She didn't actually believe Dad was still married to her, or that he'd just gone out for groceries or something and was coming right back. She *wanted* to live in her memories. She *chose* to shut us out, to shut everything out, when she heard what she didn't want to hear. She still ate, still bathed, still went about the motions of a normal-ish life.

She'd been through counseling, but without any diagnosis of depression or anything else, she refused to take any kind of medication, and I wouldn't exactly want her to.

When I'd suggested pot, to maybe mellow her out and possibly open her mind to see things differently, she'd flatly refused.

Your father never smoked pot. Why would I start now?

As a grown woman, it became harder and harder for me to feel for her. To feel anything but resentment for the situation she just kept creating for herself, for Liv and me.

Our mom, the nutcase.

A woman who couldn't see that her divorce was the best thing that ever could've happened for her children.

I knew she'd loved my dad something fierce. I knew she was wildly attracted to him. I would hear their loud crazy arguments, their loud crazy makeup sex. I'd see them grab and shove each other, and apologize, and act like they'd die without each other. And as a kid all I could do was sit there and watch. I couldn't make them stop.

They were infatuated with each other. They tore each other apart.

My sister would blaze right into the middle of it and raise hell, screaming at them both.

Not me. It scared me, that kind of love. That kind of passion.

It scared me more when Dad left her; when he left us all and broke our hearts.

I didn't want any part of that.

It was better to be free. I wanted my freedom. I needed it. I never wanted to depend on anyone or anything.

I was a free agent, right?

Fuck me.

This was always how I felt after I left my mom's place.

Fucking terrible.

Years ago, it had sent me running. Running all over the fucking globe trying to get away from it.

And my mom? She never seemed to have a clue how much it hurt us all when she carried on like this.

The worst part, for me, was that I knew I'd always been kind of like her.

Liv was more like Dad. I was like Mom. Overly-sensitive inside and prone to shutting people out. But unlike my mom, I was kind of a smartass on the outside. It was a defense mechanism, and I knew that. Just like her, I sometimes lacked a filter and said stupid shit. The difference was I regretted that shit, while my mom seemed utterly unaware.

I was stronger than her, maybe. And at least slightly more self-aware. But ultimately, I was scared. I was afraid of ending up like her. Broken and alone, waiting for someone who was never coming back. Someone who didn't love me enough to stay.

I craved my independence. I always had, maybe because of how I'd grown up.

But the truth was, I craved other things *more*.

I looked down at the scripted initials, tattooed inside my left wrist. *MCOA*. I pressed my right thumb over them and held on tight. Sometimes, like right now, it was hard to even look at those letters. To remember what they represented to me.

Marriage. Family. Children. All those things I secretly craved most. All those things my upbringing had given me an aversion to.

I totally fucking craved belonging and affection.

I craved *love*.

For all her faults and weaknesses, Mom was right; deep down, it really was the most important thing.

When Ashley picked me up in his truck, I went silent. After a few abrupt and very forced responses of, "It was okay," and "Everything's fine," to answer his questions, I went dark.

As we headed back into the city from my mom's place in New Westminster, my mind kept wandering away, down each side road we passed, until I finally blurted, "Pull over."

Ashley pulled over. He pulled off the busy street and down a side road, then down another, quieter road off of that one, and parked. There was nothing around. We were in some suburb. Just some houses farther down the street, nothing close to us but trees.

Ashley took one glance at me and turned off the truck.

Then he waited.

Maybe he thought I was going to burst into tears. Maybe he thought I was going to start screaming and bitching, venting about my mom.

Instead, I unbuckled my seatbelt and threw myself on him.

The result of that was fast, hot, greedy, bitey, scratching, passionate comfort sex. Sex that I needed right now, so fucking bad, and he gave it to me.

He reclined his seat back as far as it would go and I rode him in a frenzy as all my emotions—fear, longing, anxiety, frustration, desire—crashed through me. And he drove up into me just as hard. Just as needy.

I didn't even wait for him. The orgasm hit me frantic and fast, splitting me open. I whimpered and moaned, and he gripped my hips, holding me still as he pumped up into me and let go. He was breathing hard as he came, kissing and sucking on my throat, and I realized I hadn't even kissed him.

I'd raked my fingernails through his hair and gripped his neck and pushed him down against the seat, but I hadn't kissed him.

I kissed him now, shuddering and softening as I relaxed. I kissed him slowly, tasting him, breathing with him as he came down.

I looked into his blue, blue eyes, and he looked up at me.

And, okay.

Maybe it had taken me a while to admit the depth of my feelings for him, but I did care about Ashley. A lot.

And it bothered me.

Maybe because something else was bothering me, too.

It was the way I'd seen him look at Dylan; that exact same way he just looked at me when he came. Enraptured. Lost. Fucking helpless.

And the way Dylan pretended not to notice.

It was confusing and fascinating and painful to watch.

I was growing more certain by the second that whatever was going on between them was bound to self-destruct; like a powder keg, it would blow—and very possibly, take out everything around it.

How could it not?

I climbed off of Ashley and righted my clothes.

I'd entered into this whole thing terrified of getting myself hurt. But the fact was that as the days passed, I was getting more and more scared of one—or both—of them getting hurt, too. And the thought of either Dylan or Ashley getting hurt didn't sit well with me. At all.

I glanced over at Ashley, and he shook his head at me a little as he zipped up his jeans. That look said, *You're fucking crazy, and I like it.*

And I tried to smile. But it was getting hard to do when I just didn't know how we were all getting out of this damage-free. It's not like the three of us were gonna ride off into the sunset together in some kinky three-way marriage or something.

I knew that.

Someone was bound to get hurt here.

And whoever it was... I knew we were all going to suffer for it.

Because I cared about them both. They cared about each other. And by now, I knew they both cared about me, too.

Maybe... just maybe... we were even falling in love.

CHAPTER TWENTY-THREE

Amber

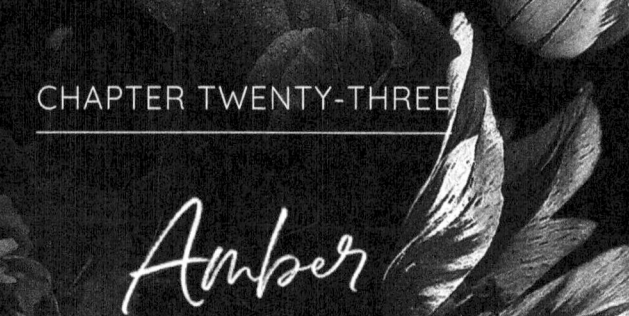

THE NEXT EVENING, we arrived in L.A. just in time for an Underlayer party that Dylan had to be at.

He'd decided he couldn't go without us, so he flew us all down with him—me, Ashley and Con. I kinda got the feeling he also wanted to give me a little taste of travel, because maybe he worried that asking me to stay with him and Ashley was kinda clipping my wings. I didn't mention it, but I appreciated the gesture and the impromptu mini-adventure.

The party was at a club in Hollywood, and we went straight there from the airport, not even swinging by Dylan's house in Santa Monica first, though I would've liked to see it. We pulled up to the red carpet in a limo and as it turned out, the party was star-studded.

Honestly, I was kinda bummed I hadn't brought my camera. Though when I'd started getting interested in photographing celebrities—photographing Dylan naked by his pool?—I wasn't sure. But hey, a girl could evolve. Anyway, it wasn't like I could just start snapping photos even if I had it with me. I wasn't gonna be a tool about it when I was here with Dylan.

So I just tried to look pretty and composed on his arm, in the little yellow Betsey Johnson dress I'd borrowed from Katie—better than letting Dylan buy me another new, crazy-expensive one—then hung back with Ashley while he worked the room a bit.

I knew we should talk about the elephant in the room—about whatever wasn't being said between Dylan and Ashley, despite Ashley assuring me that nothing was going on between them. Clear the air. Address the fact that maybe this arrangement of ours just wasn't going to work for any length of time.

Bail the hell out before we all went down with the ship?

But it was incredibly hard to do that when I just kept getting swept up in their world. When they were both so into me... and so good to me.

When Ashley held my hand the entire time we were at the Underlayer party, while Dylan did his thing, so I wouldn't have to be alone.

And when Dylan got us out of there so damn fast, because clearly he'd rather spend the night with us than with a ton of other people fawning over him. Despite the fact that we'd flown here so he could make an appearance, he didn't seem particularly interested in that party. Instead, he said he wanted to check in at the club.

"The club?" I asked.

"Dylan's club," Ashley said.

I looked up at Dylan. I was curled up between them, sipping champagne in the back of the limo. "You own a club?"

"Yup."

"Let me guess," I teased. "Strip club?"

"Nope."

"It used to be a gay bar, actually," Ashley told me. "Dance club. Then it was a rock bar for a while. Then Dylan took over. It's a dance club again, most of the time. Pushers played there last year, though."

"Cool. So... if you own the club, why do we need Con?" I grinned at Con, who was sitting across from us. "No offense, Con."

"None taken."

"We've been all over Vancouver without security," I pointed out. "Why do you need it here?"

"Because this is L.A.," Ashley answered for Dylan. "People don't bother Dylan in Vancouver as much."

Bother? Interesting word. Dylan never seemed bothered by much, so I was kinda curious to see how this night would play out.

When we rolled into Dylan's club, they seemed to know he was coming. The staff were all over us, whisking us to a private area in the back corner, lavishing us with the VIP treatment. Drinks, and a lot of them, were immediately served up.

And if I thought Vancouver parties were intimidating, I was really thrown into the fire here.

As in, women were all over my men.

And yes, I'd definitely come to think of them as *my men*.

Objectively, if I took my knee-jerk jealousy out of the equation, nothing was actually going on. Dylan and Ashley gave out hugs and cheek kisses where expected, but they weren't exactly frolicking in a hot tub with anyone in front of me.

By the time we finished doing the rounds at Dylan's club and headed out to another one to do it all over again, I was kind of getting used to it. Mostly because either Dylan or Ashley would always hold my hand in-between the hugs and cheek kisses, and if they couldn't, Con would be by my side, so I was never left alone.

In the next club, the guys seemed to know some of the staff, and we were whisked off to a VIP area where we settled into a booth. A few people hung around, friends of Dylan's and Ashley's, and our table was loaded with drinks. I'd been pacing myself so far with the booze; it was still kinda early and I didn't want to be wasted by midnight, what with all the free liquor flowing. But I decided to let myself go a little when Ashley handed a gorgeous martini my way. It was just the way I liked them—extra olives—so I dove in while the guys goofed around and laughed and got caught up with their friends.

There wasn't exactly a lack of stuff to keep me entertained here. The cocktail waitresses were little more than naked and the place was packed, the dance floor already off the hook, the whole place grinding to Dua Lipa's "Blow Your Mind."

Actually… upon closer inspection, the sexy waitresses were all incredibly tall and… broad-shouldered.

Because they were *men*.

Or more specifically… drag queens?

I glanced over at the two men I'd come with. Ashley met my gaze and lifted his pierced eyebrow, maybe trying to read the look on my face. Dylan winked at me.

I shook my head and sipped my martini, kinda giggling to myself.

Who are these guys?

I was still trying to process everything as the details came into focus… but that was definitely a dude dancing over there in the raised cage—in a sparkly miniskirt and platform heels. And *damn*, could he/she dance.

I was still watching him dance when a woman strode over to our table, with purpose. The way the crowd parted for her, I half-expected her to be carrying a tray of drinks, but she wasn't.

She also wasn't half-naked. She wore a tucked-in blouse and pencil skirt, and would've looked too classy for this place if not for the heavy makeup.

I looked, incredibly carefully, as Ashley rose to greet her… but I was pretty sure she was a woman. No male could get curves like that, no matter how many drugs he took or surgeries he underwent.

After she'd gotten—and given—her cheek kiss, then leaned in to exchange one with Dylan, her heavily-lashed eyes landed on me.

"Amber, this is Kitty," Dylan said, sliding over to sit closer to me. "Kitty, this is Amber."

I stared at her. She was curvy as hell, with long, dark hair. And a lot older than I might've expected. She looked close to forty.

She was literally nothing like me, other than the fact that we were both female. But this had to be their previous "arrangement"— the woman Dylan and Ashley had a three-way commitment with, briefly, last year. How many women were named Kitty?

"Hi," I said, offering my hand. "Nice to meet you." It was. I was fucking intrigued.

"Likewise." She shook my hand and smirked a bit as Ashley slid in close on my other side. I was wedged in-between him and Dylan, and Kitty didn't miss it. She raised her chin, eying my half-empty glass. "What can I get you, Amber?"

"You work here?"

"This is my club," she said, placing a hand on her cocked hip. Everything about her, like this club in general, screamed *sex*.

"Oh. Um, another martini would be great."

"How about you two?" That small smirk played on her lips as she looked the guys over.

"We're good," Ashley said.

Kitty nodded. "Be right back." Then she walked away, hips swaying in her tight skirt.

I looked at Ashley. Then Dylan.

"Um, you guys could've given me a heads up." I aimed that mainly at Dylan, who now had a history of blindsiding me. Then I gave Ashley a pointed look, because he *knew* Dylan had a history of blindsiding me. He could've filled me in, at least.

"Didn't know she'd be here," Ashley said.

"It's her bar," I replied, doubtful. "And please tell me she's a woman, or I may need a lot more than two martinis to get my head around this."

"One-hundred-percent female," Ashley assured me with a tiny smirk. "From birth."

Dylan leaned in close to my ear, his breath on my neck. He put his big hand lightly on my throat, drifted his thumb over my bottom lip and said, "I so wanna fuck you right now."

"Why?" It fell out of my mouth before I could think about it, and Dylan chuckled, his hand dropping to my thigh.

"Because you're extra-fucking-cute when you're jealous," Ashley said.

"And, you look like you'd enjoy my cock inside you right now," Dylan added in my ear, giving my thigh a squeeze.

Well, I would.

"Later," I said, still too fascinated by everything that was going on around me—and a little annoyed that they hadn't told me we were coming here. To Kitty's club...

I gazed around. The crowd seemed to be about one-quarter female, one-quarter straight male, and half gay men. And people of *all* orientations were definitely staring at my men.

Ashley grinned and squeezed my bare knee under the table. His hand slipped up my thigh, under Katie's cute dress. The dress was short and sexy, and felt oddly demure in this place, for such a small amount of fabric.

Both of them still had a hand on my leg when Kitty returned with my drink. I noticed Dylan's other arm was now on the back of the seat, behind me, and his thumb was drifting over my shoulder.

I kinda hoped they were marking their territory. I didn't mind if they wrote their names all over me in magic marker right about now.

Kitty placed the martini in front of me on a cocktail napkin.

"Thank you."

"My pleasure." Kitty sat right down on Ashley's other side. "So." She looked Ashley over with eyes that left no doubt that she'd seen him naked, often, and wanted to again. "Where've you been all my life?" Then she looked at me again, so I answered.

"Everywhere?"

"Sounds about right. Where are you from, Amber?"

"Vancouver."

"Washington? Or north of there?"

"North."

"Ah. Canadian girl." Her gaze swept down over my chest, as if there was something remarkable about Canadian boobs that she had to see for herself. "Pretty," she remarked, almost to herself. "These guys showing you a good time tonight?"

"Very."

She smiled and leaned into Ashley a bit. "She's adorable. You bringing her back to my place after?"

Ashley's eyes met mine. "We're keeping this one to ourselves."

Kitty didn't look happy about it, but she was quick to hide it with a smile. "Typical." She stood up and aimed her eyes at me. "They like to share, but they don't like to *share*, you know?"

I just smiled, unsure of what to say.

"Have a lovely night. Drinks are on the house." She winked at me, leaned in to kiss Dylan on the cheek, gave Ashley a lingering hungry look, then sashayed away.

"*That's* your ex?" I asked in her wake.

"I guess you could say that," Ashley said.

"How long were you... committed to her?"

"Maybe three months?" Ashley glanced at Dylan, like he wasn't even sure.

Dylan sipped his beer. He was studying me, and I noticed he hadn't said much since Kitty showed up. Other than the thing about wanting to fuck me.

I reached under the table and put my hand on his dick. He was hard.

"She seems to have a thing for you, Ashley," I said, trying not to sound bothered by it.

"She does," Dylan said.

"You're wondering why we're not with her anymore," Ashley said.

"Something like that."

I glanced at Dylan; his eyelids lowered as he looked at my mouth, in that way he did when he wanted to kiss me. I squeezed his dick and he shifted his hips, spreading his thighs a bit.

"Can't stay with someone you don't love," he said simply.

When I looked at Ashley again to see what he thought of that, he leaned in and kissed me.

After Kitty's club, I fucked Dylan in the back of the limo while Ashley went with Con to "get smokes." Or maybe that was just code for *I'll give you a few minutes to fuck Amber in the back of the limo.* But Dylan and I made use of that time. Or, I did.

I pounced on him and rode him like a wild woman. The booze was hitting me, but more than that, it was the high of seeing all those women—and various other people—wanting him, and him wanting *me*.

I wasn't even going to pretend to be above it. It was a massive turn on.

I fucked him, hard, until I made him come, and holy *hell*, was that a turn on. Watching him lose it, feeling him lose it, his cock pulsing and his breaths cutting off and his mouth dropping open, his entire big, muscular body tensing beneath me as I fucked him right over the edge. I came when he did, but it wasn't enough.

By the time Ashley opened the door and pulled me out of there, I was all wound up.

Lucky for me, Ashley took me back into Kitty's club and down some back hall, into a bathroom. It was maybe a staff bathroom or something, because no one was around and the music was so far away I could barely hear it thumping through the walls. He pressed me up against the wall, wrapped my legs around his waist, and fucked me.

Having sex in a dirty bar bathroom shouldn't have been a turn on, but right now, it was. I'd just come with Dylan's cock inside me. He'd barely gotten his pants back on when Ashley had dragged me out of the limo. And I couldn't get enough. My pussy was still swollen, so sensitive, and I went off fast, shuddering in Ashley's arms and crying out as he pounded me. Twice.

Then he came with a groan and buried himself in me.

I was glad we were in a bathroom, actually; by now, I really needed to clean up.

I didn't say a thing about it, but it wasn't lost on me how much Ashley liked to fuck me right after Dylan did.

I was becoming accustomed to the pattern, even as it frightened me.

CHAPTER TWENTY-FOUR

Amber

SUFFICE IT TO SAY, Dylan Cope and Ashley Player knew how to party.

I'd never barhopped so much in my life. I kinda lost track of the different bars we slipped in and out of over the course of the night. The last bar we hit was the most rock 'n' roll of the lot; some band the guys knew had just come offstage and Highly Suspect's "Fuck Me Up" was playing, loud, as we walked in.

We met up there with Pepper, the drummer from Ashley's band, and I was so excited to finally meet a member of the Penny Pushers. Maybe I felt like it would be a window into getting to know Ashley better or something. Maybe I was just drunk and feeling friendly. But apparently Pepper was an enthusiastic dancer, and the two of us hit the dance floor for a while.

Then Pepper bought me a drink and I got chatting with him by one of the bars. Mostly about the Penny Pushers, because I wanted to know more about Ashley's band. But then I realized, maybe belatedly—thanks to the alcohol—that Pepper seemed to be flirting with me.

Which was weird, since I'd come here with Ashley and Dylan, and I would've thought he realized that. But maybe not?

Either way, it was even weirder because I knew he was married;

Ashley had mentioned it. But then he dropped some not-quite-casual comment about his wife not being here. Which was all kinds of gross.

I didn't get the overt feeling that Ashley's drummer was trying to fuck me, like now. But I got the sense he was definitely trying to stir up trouble. Why? I couldn't guess. I'd just met the man. He actually seemed like a nice dude. Funny and kind of hyper-friendly but just way too drunk. He seemed like he was maybe in some *My-marriage-is-in-trouble-and-I'm-stumbling-around-looking-for-ways-to-make-it-worse* phase... or something. Whatever it was, I definitely didn't want a part in it.

So I decided to steer clear of him for the rest of the night.

In fact, I managed to steer myself all the way to the other side of the crowded bar, completely losing him, Ashley and Dylan... and running into someone from my past.

"Amber!" Stacy squealed when she saw me and leaned in for an air hug and not-quite-touching cheek kiss, both sides. I hadn't seen her in a long time, yet she looked exactly the same. Aged more than the four years it had been, maybe, but the same. Still blonde, still flashy, still trashy.

She had a smile pasted on her face but her eyes picked over me like a vulture sniffing out rot. Probably hoping to discover that something horrible had happened to me since we last saw each other.

Finding me intact, the smile got bigger and faker. "How the hell are you?"

"Great. You?" I asked, because it seemed like the quickest way to get this run-in over with. I was instantaneously regretful that I didn't have my two hot men hanging off of me at the moment, and yet grateful that Dylan and Ashley were nowhere in sight. Stacy the Slut would be on them like white on rice. Or like a groupie on... well, a rock star.

I definitely wasn't the one who'd come up with her cruel nickname. The first time I heard it, I was horrified. However, when the nickname fit...

"I'm *epic*," she said, wobbling a little, at which point I registered how wasted she was. "You know... Johnny's here."

I felt my face freeze up in the fake half-smile I was wearing. And hers spread across her face as she realized that no, I did not know that my ex-husband was here.

"Haven't seen him in a while myself," she said. Then she leaned in and added, "I think he's even hotter now than he was... back then." She dropped her voice like we were sharing a special secret. You know, because we *both* knew how hot he was *back then*.

As in, back when she fucked him while he was married to me.

But she probably didn't think I actually knew about that. Stacy had always seemed to think I was way dumber, and she was way smarter, than was actually the case. I refused to let it bother me, though. Any of it.

Water under the bridge, right?

"Where is he?" I asked sweetly, like I actually cared. All I cared about was not running into him.

"Oh, right over there." She waved her hand in the direction I was headed, where the crowd buzzed and swirled in a fangirl vortex, the way it had around Dylan and Ashley everywhere we went tonight, and it was pretty clear there was a VIP sitting over there.

Fuck.

I pushed past Stacy, not even bothering with a *Nice to see you* or a *Hope you get herpes*. I put my head down and tunneled through the crowd, aiming well around the rock star vortex—when a giant wall of a dude blocked my path. Incongruously, he had a girly-looking glass of pinkish bubbly in his hand.

"From Johnny O," he said when I looked up. He put the drink in my hand as I just stood here, caught off-guard. "This way."

Then he threw up a meaty arm and parted the sea of people—and there was Johnny O'Reilly. My ex-husband, seated in a booth with a bunch of people, mostly hot chicks, on either side of him.

When the crowd shifted, he looked up and saw me. And he got the most smarmy, self-satisfied smirk of a look on his gorgeous face—

even as his gaze traveled down my body and back up, checking me out.

I drifted toward him, because I wasn't about to let him see me run away. It was like we were in a tunnel; him at one end and me at the other, and there was nowhere else to go. He stood to greet me as I got close, the smarmy look fading—maybe I'd imagined it?—and his face kinda lighting up a bit. But he was definitely checking me out.

My tiny yellow dress, which had felt so damn demure in Kitty's club, now had me feeling pretty naked.

"Amber," he said, in a low, sexy voice, reaching across the table to gently grasp my elbow and pull me in. He gave me a quick kiss on the cheek as I stood here, not knowing what to say. I really had nothing to say to him at all.

Yet here I was.

"Hi, Johnny," I managed.

He gestured to the empty chair next to me, across the table from him. I put the drink he'd sent me on the table. I didn't plan to drink it. I didn't want a thing from him.

But I sat down, and he did the same.

"How the hell have you been?" he asked me, his gaze crawling all over me.

It was a stupid question. He hadn't seen me or talked to me in four years. There was no way to answer a question like that succinctly and even approach honesty. No way to fit four years of my life into one simple sentence.

So I went with a one-word answer, not really saying anything at all. "Good. You?"

"Always," he said, as if that said anything at all. "You look great."

"Thank you." I didn't bother saying a thing about how he looked, obviously. He looked fucking hot, and he knew it. If the half-dozen scantily-clad young chicks with the midriff-baring shirts and big boobs, lined up on either side of him, didn't already tell him so, the way I was looking at him probably filled him in.

Johnny was Irish-Italian and naturally dark-haired, but he highlighted his hair blond and it looked killer on him, that contrast of dark and light. His eyebrows were dark, his skin deeply tanned, his teeth as white as his T-shirt, and his jewelry gleamed. His eyes were an aquamarine-blue that I'd thought had to be colored contacts the first time I met him. They weren't. And his body was seriously ripped, but not in any kind of practical way. Ashley was ripped because he worked hard and played hard—in the gym, on a surf board, on his mountain bike. Dylan worked out like crazy but he also got a workout on the drums daily.

As far as I could ever discern, Johnny just lifted weights so he could admire himself while he fucked a girl.

I wasn't gonna pretend the result wasn't excellent, but right now, his perfection just kinda irritated me. He was too fucking pretty, and too fucking pleased with himself.

How did I ever fall for this guy?

"How's Liv?" he asked, still checking me out. Like he gave a shit about my family.

The girl sitting on his left was leaning on him, and before I could answer, she turned and purred something in his ear. She didn't seem to like him paying attention to me, and gave me a nasty, pleased-with-herself look as he pulled her onto his lap. She then sat there with her boobs in his face, sipping her drink and chatting with her girlfriend as he waited for me to answer his question.

I resisted the urge to roll my eyes. Honestly, Liv thought Johnny was a piece of shit, which was probably why he asked. It probably irritated the fuck out of him that a woman was actually immune to his charms, even if she was gay.

"She's good."

What the hell was I doing here? Was I really chatting with my ex-husband about my sister while some chick sat in his lap? She was talking in his ear again, and he held his finger up toward me as if to say, *One sec, while I snuggle with this babe.*

I glanced around, looking for Con. I wasn't exactly in danger, but I didn't want to back out of here alone, with my tail between my legs. I knew I could count on Con to get me out of this. He'd promised me he'd always be in my sight, and he'd given me a signal to use if I needed out of a jam.

And there he was, as promised.

He was leaning on the raised bar against the far wall, surveying the room. I could see his head up above most of the others, and he was looking around, probably trying to keep tabs on Dylan and me at the same time.

I looked around; I couldn't see Dylan or Ashley in the crowd. So I gave Con our signal. It involved me running my fingertip over my bottom lip. It was sexy, as far as signals went, and I was pretty sure, as I did it, that Con had chosen it to amuse himself.

Unfortunately, he wasn't looking at me.

I did it again, and realized Johnny was staring at me. I smiled a bit, dropping my hand.

"So, tell me what you've been up to," he said, his piercing aquamarine eyes intent on me, even though the chick was still in his lap.

"Um..." I glanced up again, and Con caught my eye. I gave him the signal... and he started heading over.

Fucking *finally*.

"I've been busy. You know, photography."

"Yeah? How's that going?"

I jumped up to meet Con as he arrived, holding up a finger toward Johnny as if to say, *One sec, while I snuggle with this babe.* Then I turned to Con, leaned up against him and said in his ear, "Pull me onto your lap."

He stood there looking down at me, and his eyebrow slowly rose. My hands were pressed to his hard chest, and I was glad he looked so hot tonight; he wasn't wearing his biker vest, but a soft Henley shirt that hugged all his muscles.

"You drunk?"

"Just pull me onto your lap. Please."

"Jesus," he said, shaking his head a little and eying my tiny dress. "You are gonna get me in trouble, Amber Paige Malone..."

"I'm not."

"No?" His gaze flickered past me. "Why you wanna make Johnny O jealous?"

Right. So he knew who Johnny was. And my motive was pretty transparent, at least, to him. Which was probably a good thing. Last thing I needed here was Con thinking I was actually coming on to him.

"Because," I said, "he's my ex-husband and he's a douche and he fucked like five hundred other women behind my back when we were together."

Con stared at me. He glanced at Johnny over my shoulder again.

Then he moved to sit in my vacated seat and drew me onto his lap. I glanced around as I draped my arms around his broad shoulders, but I still couldn't see Dylan or Ashley anywhere. The place was pretty packed, so hopefully they couldn't see me either.

"Connor, this is Johnny," I told Con, like Con was more important—and like he didn't already know who Johnny was.

"Connor," Con said, extending a hand. Johnny shook briefly, sizing Con up, then dismissed him just as quick.

"So, you were telling me how you've been," he said to me. "Still traveling the world? Been back to Miami lately?" He took a sip of his drink and kind of smirked at me.

Clever. He was referring to a particularly intense night of lovemaking that we'd enjoyed in the early days of our relationship—*before* I found out what a lying slut he was.

"No," I said flatly. "Always found that place pretty obnoxious." I pretended to be trying to recall some distant, unimportant memory. "Were we there together?"

He smirked again, appearing undaunted—until Con cut in. "Maybe we'll go there soon, babe." He put his hand on my waist and pulled me closer.

"Oh! That would be *amazing*." I put my hand lightly on his neck and laid the batting eyelashes on pretty thick.

And so it went.

Every time Johnny tried to talk to me, Con cut in. I flirted—with

Con. Johnny got increasingly pissed off that he could barely get a word in. I was pretty sure it had little to do with me. If I hadn't parked myself on Con's lap right in front of him, he might've already tired of talking to me. But Johnny O'Reilly did not like being one-upped, by any man. Least of all some big, handsome biker dude with a white-toothed smile that rivaled his own for blinding brightness.

He got pretty agro about it, actually, his jaw hardening and his focus shifting from me to Con, completely. "The fuck is your problem?" he suddenly snapped, about the fourth time Con cut him off.

"No problem," Con said cooly.

"I'm talking to Amber."

"Not anymore."

At that, Johnny set his drink down, lifted the girl off his lap and set her aside.

Then Con set me aside.

Uh-oh.

Johnny stood up. Con stood up. They were about the same height, but Johnny was easily fifty pounds lighter and I'd never actually seen him in a fight. Con, however, very possibly had a weapon on him, and his fists looked like anvils as they clenched at his sides.

"How about you back the fuck away from my table," Johnny suggested, as I scrambled to my feet. Then that beefy dude who'd given me the bubbly suddenly loomed, giving Con some serious stinkeye. Johnny's muscle, obviously.

Great.

I grabbed Con's arm and tried to pull him away, but it was about as effective as a gnat landing on a bull. I didn't even think he felt me. He and Johnny were trading expletives, only some of which I heard over the music and my rising panic.

Then Johnny's security guy shoved at Con, kind of knocking him into me. I stumbled back. Con shoved back, pushing the guy away from me. Johnny tried to grab me. I was pretty sure he was trying to yank me out of the way, but I pulled away from him—total instinct. I bumped up against Ashley, who'd suddenly appeared. He intervened, stepping between me and Johnny. I couldn't even hear what was said as I got bounced around. Everyone was kind of shoving around us now.

And then, out of nowhere, Dylan clocked Johnny.

I didn't even see Dylan coming. He was just suddenly there, and his fist was cutting through the air, and... *damn*.

Johnny went down, hard, smashing into the table. Girls screamed and fluttered everywhere like birds taking flight, and the last thing I saw was a pile of bouncers descending on the scene before Ashley pulled me into his chest and took me away.

Back at Dylan's house in Santa Monica, I tended to the damage on his face. He had a bruise over his left eyebrow, with a nasty-looking but shallow scrape, probably from a ring. Apparently, Johnny's bodyguard had managed to get one in before Con and the bouncers stopped him.

The house felt empty around us. It had just gone up for sale; Dylan said he wasn't keeping it, that the house on Isabella Island was his permanent home now and he didn't need two. Which meant that this house had been pretty much cleared of his personal belongings and staged to sell.

I peeked in the freezer in hopes of finding a bag of frozen peas or some ice to put on his bruise, but the best I could find was a half-full bag of freezer-burnt strawberries, probably left behind from some party where margaritas were to be had.

I wrapped the bag of strawberries in a dish towel and sat myself on Dylan's lap. He was sitting at the dining room table looking kinda tired and wired at the same time. Probably the adrenaline dump from getting in a fist fight less than an hour ago.

Ashley lay on the couch in the adjoining living room, his feet up on the arm, smoking a joint. He watched as I carefully cleaned Dylan's wound with a damp tissue. Dylan winced a little as I dabbed at the raw scrape; I wanted to make sure there was no dirt in it, but it looked okay.

Johnny had really gotten the worst of it. I'd seen him briefly at the front door of the bar before we left. He was pretty pissed that Dylan had given him a black eye; apparently, he was playing a show tomorrow night.

"I've never seen you like that before, man," Ashley said, grinning just a little. "I've never seen you cold-cock a guy."

"Because I never have." Dylan hissed a bit as I pressed the cloth with the bag of frozen strawberries to the swollen bruise over his eye. "And I didn't actually knock him out."

"Dude. You had him reeling. There were definitely a few seconds there where Johnny O was trippin' the light fantastic in outer fucking space."

I cringed, recalling it. I'd definitely seen Johnny's head kinda bounce off the table. And as much as I'd almost convinced myself, once upon a time, that I hated the guy, I didn't actually want to see harm come to him.

"Well, thank you for coming to my rescue," I said, with only slight sarcasm.

"He grabbed at you," Dylan said. "Didn't like that."

"I think he was trying to get me out of the way of the two giant bodyguards going at it."

"Hard to know, from where I was standing." Dylan's green eyes met mine, his warm hand settling gently on my bare thigh. "You had him pretty riled up. Sitting in Con's lap like that."

Oops. "You saw that?"

"Yup," Ashley said.

"That was just for Johnny," I explained, in my defense. "He was being a douche. I don't care if we were only married for sixteen days. It's poor form to have another woman in your lap while you're having a conversation with your ex-wife."

"Yup," Dylan agreed.

"Don't worry, babe," Ashley said. "I'm pretty sure Johnny O had it coming."

"Still." I lifted Dylan's hand and kind of winced at the sight of his knuckles; raw and slightly swollen. He'd need ice on those, too.

Maybe we'd have to send Ashley out to get some. "I'm sorry you hurt your hand," I said, kissing Dylan's unbruised cheek. "And your face."

"It's okay." He looked at me under lowered eyelids; despite whatever pain he might've been in, he was clearly thinking about other things. "Long as you're here to kiss it better..."

So I kissed him, tilting his head back and going in deep and slow, kinda loving that he was in a vulnerable state and I could take care of him a bit. Actually, it was turning me on; my pussy was starting to throb...

"Hmm. Always thought of myself as a pacifist..." I murmured, nibbling at his full bottom lip as I wriggled a bit in his lap. "Who knew violence could be so... exciting?"

Dylan chuckled.

"Jesus," Ashley said. "Get a room."

"Have one," Dylan murmured in-between kisses. I could feel his dick getting hard under my ass. "Upstairs. You might have to help me out, though..."

I did help.

I led him upstairs and since his right hand was sore, I helped him out of his clothes. Then I laid him back on the bed. And since he said his head was pounding too much to fuck, but his dick didn't seem to agree with that, I went down on him.

While I did that, Ashley helped himself to shoving up my little yellow dress and fucking me from behind.

He also asked Dylan if he was okay—a couple of times—in a soft, concerned voice, while he fucked me. Dylan said yes, and groaned as I cranked up the intensity of the blow job, sucking him harder, faster, rolling my mouth over his swollen head and tonging his slit... kind of weirded out that they were talking to each other while I was doing this.

I kept trying not to ask myself the questions that were now nagging at the back of my mind every time the three of us ended up in bed together. The fact was, I was pretty busy down here, what with Dylan's giant dick in my mouth, so I had no idea if they were looking at each other while they enjoyed me.

And either way, I'd probably never know what they were really thinking.

Out of nowhere, I thought of that dumb joke some of my guy friends in high school used to say to crack each other up. *It's not gay unless there's eye contact.*

When Dylan came in the back of my throat, and Ashley came deep in my pussy, only seconds later, I didn't even want to know where they were both looking.

As Ashley slipped himself out of me and I kissed Dylan's hip before rolling away, I just told myself to keep playing along, playing within whatever carefully-laid boundaries they'd arranged between themselves.

Who was I to complain about what I was getting here?

As I relaxed back on the pillows next to Dylan, he took my hand, lacing his fingers through mine—and Ashley went down on me. And a pleasured sigh escaped me.

Who was I to ruin *this*?

Dylan rolled toward me and his wounded hand drifted to my breast, his fingers teasing my nipple as Ashley spread my thighs wider and delved his tongue deeper. Dylan leaned in and flickered his tongue over my nipple, and I arched my back. Then he raised his head and kissed me, and I melted as both of them worked me with their mouths.

And I just tried to shut off my brain and enjoy this for all it was worth.

I tried, and I failed.

I was afraid that if I brought up the whole question of how they really felt about each other—or more specifically, how Ashley really felt about Dylan—all of *this* might just fall apart.

Even as I came, I couldn't help wondering about it—about something happening between the two of them. A touch. A kiss.

More?

I wondered about it, and it didn't turn me off. But it scared me, even as the orgasm ripped through me. I wrapped my hand around Dylan's neck, holding him to me as we kissed. My other hand was buried in Ashley's hair. I was holding on with everything I had, even as the world spun out from under me.

I didn't like the feeling as I came down—the sensation of free-falling, of not being sure of how to land, of where I really fit in.

I was in-between them right now... but what if that changed?

CHAPTER TWENTY-FIVE

Dylan

WHEN WE GOT HOME to the island, it was raining out. I got pretty drenched tying up the boat, while Amber and Ash jetted up to the house. I didn't mind. I found them in the pool, with the heat cranked up, and quickly joined them.

It was Saturday, I had no rehearsal to go to, and we spent the rest of the day cozy inside my house while the rain pelted down outside, lashing the windows.

Amber chose the music—Van Morrison—because she said Ash always got to. Which was fair enough; Ash usually did commandeer the music selection. I usually let him, since he also cooked for me.

Ash made dinner, which was beef nachos, vegetarian for Amber. She helped him dice veggies on the island, while I sat on one of the built-in bench seats in front of the wall of windows, just watching.

It was pretty damn perfect.

Amber was wearing a long, black sweatshirt she'd found in my closet, with the Eagles' *Hotel California* album cover on it, which I didn't even remember owning. I kept offering to take her shopping since she hardly had any clothes, but she kept refusing. Instead, she'd started hanging out around the house in mine. I didn't mind. The shirt hung almost to her knees and her legs were bare underneath, the sleeves rolled up. Her soft hair was tied up in a loose ponytail, chunks of it falling out around her face. And she kept looking at me.

Ever since I'd knocked out Johnny O last night, she'd been looking at me like that. Soft and tender.

It was making me melt.

"What?" she asked me, a smile twitching at her mouth.

I got up, passing her on my way to the fridge. "You look pretty," I told her as I put my hand on her ass and leaned in to kiss her neck, slowly, inhaling her soft scent. She sighed and stirred, closing her eyes. I gave her tight ass a lingering squeeze, then went to the fridge.

"Why are you so damn perfect?" she asked me, gazing at me as I poured her a glass of wine. "Like, you're annoying me right now. Can you please just tell me a couple of things girls hate about you? There has to be something."

I laughed. "Yeah. There's probably a few."

"Few dozen," Ash put in helpfully.

"Like what?" Amber pressed.

"Like you haven't seen him after he plays a show," Ash said. "He sweats a few hundred gallons onstage and his feet smell fucking terrible."

"That can be remedied with a shower," Amber said, unimpressed. "Tell me something gnarly."

"It's pretty gnarly, believe me," he said.

"Besides," she added, eying me up and down, "he'd be wearing a kilt, right? So I'm thinking the hotness of that would probably overshadow the stinky feet. By a long shot."

"You might think," Ash said.

"How come Ash doesn't have to give you a list of his shittiest characteristics?" I inquired.

"Because A," she said, "they were obvious from day one—"

"Thank you," Ash said. "I try to be transparent with people. It's kinda my new thing."

He shot me a sidelong look and I smiled. He was definitely

opening up, or something. Amber had brought out a whole lot of good shit in him.

"You're welcome," Amber said. "And good for you. Transparency takes courage. I'm rather opaque myself, I know."

"You are not," I said, sounding a little more sarcastic than I meant to.

"Sarcasm." She narrowed her eyes at me. "The ladies *love* that."

"What can I say?" I joked. "I'm perfect." I leaned in and kissed her until she gave in, kissing me back until I was pretty sure she almost forgot what we were talking about. But then I felt her pulling away.

"And B," she said, "Ash already gave me a list. He confessed to me about all his bullshit. Including his lack of commitment to recycling."

I snickered. "Recycling? I thought you wanted gnarly shit."

"Polluting the planet is plenty gnarly to me."

"How about that carbon-coughing gas-guzzler of a Camaro of his? He tell you about that?"

"Didn't have to," she said. "I smelled it from the driveway."

"He also throws out his clothes when he gets tired of them," I said as I dropped back onto the window seat with a beer. "I've told him about a thousand times to donate them to charity."

"How did this turn into a 'shitty things about Ash' conversation?" Ash asked.

"Come to think of it," Amber teased, "most conversations we've had since I met you have been a 'shitty things about Ash' conversation."

"Huh," Ash said. Then he set down his spatula. He'd been making salsa in my food processor, but prowled over to where Amber was chopping at the island. She screamed when he grabbed her by the waist and spun her around so fast she almost dropped the knife.

Ash pressed her wrist gently to the countertop and she let the knife drop. Then he walked her over to the bench by the window, not two feet from me, laid her down, and crawled over her.

"I must've missed that conversation last night..." he said, snaking his hand up her bare thigh and under her shirt—my shirt. "And this morning. You know... while my tongue was up your sweet cunt and you were speaking in tongues." He dragged her panties down her thighs and then peeled them right off.

"Did you just use the C-word on me...?"

"Yup. Spread your legs."

She spread her legs as his hand slid up her thigh again, gasping when his fingers struck gold. "I... um... object to that word being used by you... to describe my... sex parts... ."

"Sure you do," he said as he went down on her and her eyes rolled back in her head.

"*Fuck*... that feels good..." she gasped. "Your piercing... oh my God."

"I know," Ash mumbled. "Why do you think I have it?"

"Huh?"

"It's for the ladies, Amber," he informed her as he kissed her pussy. "Feels good on the clit."

He'd shoved the sweatshirt up to expose her, and her tidy little landing strip of caramel-colored hair beckoned to me. I knew how soft it was, how she smelled. How she tasted.

I wanted to shove Ash aside and taste her, right now.

I didn't.

"I... uh... noticed." She fought her way up onto her elbows to watch as he shifted lower between her legs, tonging her, deep. "You, um, really got your tongue pierced for the ladies?"

"Uh-huh. Definitely not for my singing career..."

"What do you mean?"

"I have to remove it," he said, coming up for air, "when we go into the studio. And when we're playing shows a lot, I take it out. It fucks up my singing."

"Ohh," Amber sighed, kinda struggling for breath as he flickered his tongue over her clit again, teasing her. "So... it's just for me?"

"Yeah, sweetheart," he said. "For you and your pussy."

"Oh..."

He paused, glancing up at her. "I mean, it feels good on a guy's cock, too. When you rub it against the underside of his—"

"Uh, I don't have one of those," Amber said. "So let's just go back to the pussy thing..."

"No problem," he said, and went down on her again. And this time, he didn't stop to make conversation. Amber mewled and whimpered and started falling apart right next to me, and I just sat here, frozen.

Fuck me.

This was all starting to get... complicated.

As I watched them, listened to them, I didn't even know what the fuck to do. My dick knew what to do. I had a raging fucking hard-on, but my head was all over the fucking place.

The thing was, I didn't do complicated. I didn't know *how* to do complicated. It made me uncomfortable, and I didn't like uncomfortable.

Last night in L.A., I'd had moments of such sheer fucking happiness... and such total discomfort, I didn't know what to do with it all. Except fuck Amber. Repeatedly.

I knew this was all my fault, in a way. My doing.

I'd wanted Amber around, at first, to help Ash. To yank him out of his funk. To make him happy again.

Yes, I was curious about her from day one, and that curiosity quickly progressed to interest, then genuine affection, then a sense of attachment that I'd rarely felt toward a woman.

But we'd surpassed that place long ago.

Now, I was feeling twinges of possessiveness that I'd honestly never felt toward a woman in my life. There was a part of me that wanted Amber to *myself*. In a big way.

Which meant that watching what was happening right now was hitting me in a really weird way.

It wasn't as if I'd never seen Ash eat a chick out before.

But I'd definitely never felt like this about it before. All twisted up.

It was fucking with my head.

I almost got up to leave, wanted to, but I was somehow rooted to the spot, transfixed, even as my heart sledgehammered in my chest. Then Amber's head fell back as she moaned, and when her eyes drifted open, they looked into mine, upside-down.

"You never told me your gnarly shit," she said, gazing up, dreamily, into my face.

No. I didn't.

"I wanna know… your gnarly shit…" she said, her voice growing raspier as Ash drove her closer to ecstasy.

I'm falling in love with you, I wanted to say. *Is that gnarly enough for you?*

But I had no idea if she wanted me to say that or not.

So I didn't say a thing.

Sometime later, the three of us were in my bed. I was on my back and Amber was riding me, facing away from me. I was running my hands all over her round little ass, squeezing her, enjoying the fuck out of the view, and Ashley was on his knees in front of her, making out with her. Kissing her, his hands in her hair.

At one point, she looked at me over her shoulder and said, "Come, baby," as her hips bobbed up and down.

When I came, I heard her gasp my name.

But she never stopped making out with Ash.

Then Ash turned her around, pushing her over me on her hands and knees. She kissed me, and I closed my eyes. I knew when Ash started fucking her from behind. And I kept kissing her, wouldn't let her go. Even when Ash came and fell limp against her, panting, I was kissing her.

"Shit," he said suddenly, startling us both. "Did I leave the nachos in the oven?" His eyes met mine, wide and still sex-dazed. "*Shit.*"

Then he ran out of the room, naked, to deal with what I hoped was not a fire in my kitchen. There was definitely a faint burning smell drifting up the stairs...

Amber lay down on top of me with a sigh. "Should we be helping him...?"

"Nah. He'll yell if the house is on fire."

She giggled. Then she kissed my throat.

Her hand was on my chest and I picked it up, turning her wrist out to see the scripted lettering of her tattoo, as she lay her head on my shoulder. I kissed her tattooed wrist, then asked her, "What does *MCOA* mean?"

Amber's smile faded a bit. "It means Michael, Cathy, Olivia, Amber. My parents, my sister and me." She stared at the initials a moment, as I drifted my thumb over them. "We used to be together, the four of us, always. Now... we're so distant most of the time. But I got the tattoo to remind myself that we started out so close." Her voice got pretty sad at the end of that statement, and I wondered if I should've asked.

But I wanted to know. And I was glad she'd told me.

She'd never really said anything to me about her family before. Even when I took her to my family dinner and my mom asked, Amber had very little to say about her parents. She had little to say about anything personal. She was still guarded around me at the best of times.

"It's funny," she mused. "Liv never let us call her Olivia. I never understood, because I always thought Olivia was such a pretty name."

"You love her." I didn't have to ask if that was true. It was obvious by the tone of her voice when she talked about Liv. It was like the way I talked about my sister Julie; like someone who'd always just felt like a part of me.

It was the same way I probably talked about Ash.

"Of course I do. She's my sister." She smirked and added, "If I ever have a daughter, though, I'll probably name her Olivia, just to piss her off." Her green eyes met mine and I couldn't help smiling.

The girl was melting me like a hunk of chocolate left out in the sun.

I could understand why she'd want to name her daughter after her sister, and pissing her off probably had little to actually do with it. Amber just liked to act a lot tougher than she really was.

Kind of like Ash.

She gazed at me and said, "You still never told me your gnarly shit."

Right. That.

"I sucker-punched your ex-husband last night," I offered.

"Yeah. But that's just a point in your favor."

"You looked scared," I told her, in all seriousness.

She blinked at me. "I guess I was, a little. But, hey, I've seen worse." She rested her chin on my chest as she gazed at me. "You know my old jeans with the Venezuelan flag patch on them? I saw a guy get stabbed in the street, like two feet in front of me."

"Shit. Someone you knew?"

"No. Just wrong place, wrong time. I held his hand and I got his blood on my jeans. He didn't die or anything, but it was plenty scary."

"Shit," I said again.

She shrugged. "What can I say. I'm a woman of the world, Dylan Cope. I've seen much worse than a bunch of drunk rock stars getting into a jealous brawl."

I knew she was making jokes to deflect from the point. Fact was, she was scared when the shit hit the fan and the fists started flying. She was right in the middle of it, and she could've gotten hurt. But I was pretty sure she was more scared about one of us, Con or Ash or me, or maybe even Johnny, getting hurt.

"Seriously," I told her, "I don't want you to think I'm that guy. Other than some random drunken bar fights where I jumped in to pull guys apart, I've actually never been in a fight. I've never hit someone in the face like that."

"So why did you do it this time?"

"Because I was pissed." I laid my hand on her cheek. "I saw

Johnny grab at you and you pulled away from him, and I just saw red. I swear to you, though, I don't usually lose my temper like that. I mean, look, Amber... I—"

"True story," Ash said, walking back in. "You've got his Underlayers all tied up in knots, Amber Paige."

Amber had turned to look at him, and slid off of me a bit. Now, she just stared at me.

And *damn*, I wanted her alone.

I wasn't even sure where that conversation was going, but I really wanted to have it.

I glanced at him. "Nachos?"

"Burnt to a crisp."

He flopped onto the bed next to Amber, and for whatever reason, I wanted out. So I got up and started pulling on my jeans.

"I put them in to crisp up a bit before putting the toppings on," Ash was saying, "then forgot when Amber got all sexy." He smacked her bare ass and she grinned. "But we've got more."

I pulled on my shirt, and when I looked at them again, he'd started kissing her. "You get to come, baby?" he asked her.

"Yeah," she said softly. "You made me come."

"I meant after that. Dylan take care of you?"

"Um..." She glanced at me. I didn't make her come, but fuck, when he left, I just wanted to talk to her.

Now I felt like an asshole.

Ash pushed her over onto her back. "Can I get a little help here?" he asked me, his eyes on Amber as he shifted over her and started kissing his way down her body.

And yeah, normally I'd be all over that. I'd already lost track of the times we'd made Amber come together, one of us between her legs, one of us sucking on her tits... My dick throbbed at the thought, but I still didn't make a move toward the bed.

What the hell is wrong with me?

"I'll take care of the nachos," I said. "You guys just..."

I didn't even bother finishing that sentence. Amber looked at me, but then her eyes rolled closed as Ash went down on her. "Stay..." she breathed, reaching out a limp hand for me.

"I'll be back," I said.

I took a lingering look at her lying there, getting off on Ash's face between her legs.

Then I went to the kitchen to make dinner, for the first time in pretty much as long as I could remember.

CHAPTER TWENTY-SIX

Ash

THE NEXT NIGHT, we hit up a party at Summer's place. It was the Sunday before Halloween, which meant it was a Halloween party, and she'd gone all out. Decorations, dry-ice fog rolling through the house, the works.

I hadn't been to one of Summer's parties in a few weeks, and if I didn't show my face at one of them soon, she was probably gonna start worrying about me. She'd already been blowing up my phone, wondering where the fuck I'd been. It wasn't exactly like me to ditch on her parties when I was home from tour.

And Summer's parties were always epic. Great music 'til all hours of the night. Beautiful people. Easy sex.

Both Dylan and Amber came with me, and while Amber seemed to be having a good time, something was going on with Dylan. He'd been acting weird since last night, when he'd walked out on us to make nachos. Like dinner had ever been more important than eating Amber's pussy?

He'd been distant and kinda distracted all day, which was not normal for him. Seemed like something was bothering him, but he didn't want to talk about it.

I'd tried, a few times, to ask, but he just shut it down. Said he was just preoccupied, thinking about Dirty going into the studio.

Which was bullshit.

Dylan never got stressed about making an album. But he was stressed right now.

I watched him most of the night, making the rounds, talking with people, laughing. His arm was slung around Amber pretty much the whole time. Him in his zombie Khal Drogo costume with the black wig and beard braid and war paint, her as zombie Daenerys, with the blonde wig and the toy baby dragons clipped to her shoulders—both of them with their melting, rotten, zombified skin.

I was zombie Jon Snow, no wig needed, but I kinda dug the big faux fur cloak and badass sword. (Amber had insisted on the fur being fake.) I'd suggested the *Game of Thrones* theme, since we were now in the middle of making Amber (who'd never seen it—WTF?) binge watch the entire series with us. Dylan was the wiseass who'd suggested the Khal Drogo/Daenerys Targaryen/Jon Snow threesome costume. And Amber was the one who'd insisted it had to be creepy, since it was Halloween, which meant we'd spent hours layering on latex and painting each other, then glopping on the fake blood and puss. Really, we'd done a commendable job. If the rock star thing really didn't work out for me, maybe I could get a gig as an FX makeup artist in Hollywood? Because from where I was standing, watching them and smoking my joint, Dylan and Amber were the best dressed at the party.

Summer had even awarded us a prize for "best threesome costume"—three bottles of booze.

But since then, it was like Dylan had forgotten that we'd all come together.

He didn't seem to give one fuck about sharing Amber with me tonight. But I just let him have her. It wasn't like him to hog a girl we were both involved with, especially at a party, but I let it slide.

Whatever was bothering him was maybe just making him forget his fucking manners.

I considered—very, very briefly—forgetting mine too, when Summer came by to check on me, wearing sinfully low-slung white leather pants and a wisp of an excuse for a white shirt, with a red cross on it. And a little nurse's cap. Summer had amazing tits, and a beautiful body that I knew all too well. Never mind that I used to be in love with her.

I wasn't now.

But yes, I was fucking jealous about Dylan and Amber cozying up without me. And when Summer hugged me in her skimpy costume, and I touched the small of her bare back... I almost let my hand slide down over her tight ass.

Almost.

Luckily, I didn't. Because as much as I might've been tempted to get petty on account of the jealousy, groping Summer was not gonna go over well with Amber or Dylan. We'd made a promise to one another. A commitment.

It probably wouldn't go over well with Summer, either. Because she and I had agreed, years ago, that "we" were done. I knew neither of us wanted to blur the line by screwing around.

Usually, that wasn't a problem. My bed was rarely empty; I had plenty of lovers to keep me from groping my ex in a moment of weakness.

So did Summer.

So I kissed her on the cheek and released her, and when she asked me why I was smoking alone in the corner, I told her, "Just admiring you from afar."

She was accustomed to me flirting with her, so she just smiled and rolled her hips a little as she walked away, winking at me over her shoulder.

Then I gathered up Dylan and Amber and got us the fuck out of that party before I did something stupid. Like get drunk and stick my tongue down my ex-girlfriend's leather pants.

Because when I thought about it... I wasn't actually one-hundred-percent sure that Summer would turn me down if I tried, which would've made a move like that extra stupid, and extra risky.

With Dylan and Amber... I just wasn't willing to take those kinds of risks.

By the time we got home, Dylan was all over Amber. Barely even got her to his bedroom by the time he had her naked.

I moved in behind her, smoothing my hands up her sides, her slender curves, freaked the fuck out that they were gonna forget I was even here. But Amber moaned and tipped her head as I kissed the back of her neck, where she didn't have any latex or makeup and I could taste her sweet, flowers-and-candy-smelling skin... and relief swept through me. Clearly, she wanted me here.

I turned her toward me as Dylan started taking off his costume. Amber undressed me as we kissed, awkwardly, trying not to eat the zombie crap off each other's faces.

Then the three of us ended up in the bathroom, fucking laughing as we peeled latex and goop off of each other, then showered.

Afterwards, when we were finally clean—it took a while—I took Amber to the bed first, before Dylan could get his hands on her again and she forgot about me.

I needed her tonight. Fuck Dylan being greedy.

I sat back against the headboard and took her with me, pulling her onto my lap. She straddled me, grabbing my dick and easing me up inside her pussy, warm and eager.

Dylan slid into bed beside us and I closed my eyes, letting the sensations sweep through me... Amber's tight pussy, devouring my cock.

As she rode me, I looked up at her. Dylan put his hand on her neck and pulled her over to him, so he could kiss her. When they pulled apart, I tracked her hand, smoothing over his cock and starting to stroke him. I didn't want to stare at him, but what she was doing was kinda giving me permission.

So I fucking stared.

I stared at Dylan's cock in her slender hand. Fucking huge. Thick. Swollen. The head bright-red as she squeezed and pulled, and he melted onto the bed with a groan of pleasure.

I started to feel my own rush building; watching what was happening right next to me was getting me there, fucking fast.

"Yeah. Come, Ashley…" Amber whispered, as her pussy squeezed me, and I realized I was giving her all the signs that I was about to blow. My hands gripping her hips, fingers digging into her ass. My breathing heavy, erratic, my chest heaving. The low, guttural groans.

My dick, hard as fucking granite as she rode me, up and down.

I looked at her pretty face, her soft lips parted, her hair tumbling over her cheeks. Her hard little nipples as her tits bounced in front of me.

And I looked at her hand on Dylan's cock.

I heard her soft panting and his low moans, and I fucking blew.

My hips lifted up off the bed and I ground my teeth together, stifling the growl.

My mind shattered into a million fucking pieces as I collapsed, shuddering.

When I'd scraped my shit together again, I rolled and threw Amber down, in-between us.

I crawled over her, kissing her soft skin. Sucking and biting at her nipples. Lapping her clit with my pierced tongue.

Dylan joined in, sucking on her tits while I was down south. When I moved up and kissed her sweet mouth, he ate her out with a fucking passion.

He ate her out, when I'd just come inside her.

Amber's soft cries filled the room. She had one hand in my hair and one in Dylan's, and it made me feel intensely connected to him. Working in tune with him, working her body with him… It made me feel connected to them both. Like I was a part of something so fucking incredible, I couldn't even fathom how I'd gotten here or how I'd ever deserved it, or what the fuck I was gonna do to keep it.

When I looked in Amber's eyes, I could see a flash of that same vulnerable, scared-as-fuck feeling in her.

Then Dylan lifted himself over her, spreading her legs, and drove into her. The sounds they made together had the blood raging to my dick all over again. I slipped my hand over her thigh, wanting to touch her, wanting to touch *them*, wanting to keep that connection.

Then I shifted closer to them and slid my hand up.

I couldn't even say why I did it, exactly. I knew I shouldn't have. But as my hand slid from Amber's thigh and up over Dylan's, then up over the curve of his ass, all I wanted to do was touch him.

I really, really shouldn't have.

I knew there was an implied trust when we were together with a girl, a trust that went into effect, every time, without need of words. We'd never talked about it outright, but we didn't need to. I knew Dylan wasn't into dudes. He didn't want some guy's hand on his ass while he fucked a girl. Even mine.

But I did it anyway.

My heart was fucking slamming in my chest at the feel of his smooth skin under my hand, his muscles tensing.

Somehow, I just knew that he wasn't gonna stop in the middle of fucking Amber to deal with me and my hand, especially when he was so close to making her come.

And he didn't.

He went right on fucking her like my hand wasn't there. He drove her there, and Amber came with a scream and a shudder. Her nails dug into his back; there was no mistaking where both of her hands were on his body, no matter how caught up he was.

Then he came, with a low groan that made my dick harden, his muscles flexing beneath my hand.

I closed my eyes, and I could *feel* what he was feeling as he blew into her.

Then I pulled my hand away, before he could come down.

I rolled away and got out of bed, before either of them could say anything. I went into the bathroom to get a moment alone.

I breathed deep and slow and threw some cold water on my face, and willed my dick to snap out of it.

Then I looked at my face in the mirror, at my eyes, my pupils blown wide.

And I thought about what happened between us, that one time.

That one time when Dylan came... in my face.

By accident.

For a while, it had become a bit of a running joke between us. Because fucking seriously. He *came*. In my *face*.

It happened when we were in bed with Kitty. It was dark, Dylan had explained afterward, and he got "confused."

It *was* dark. We were all drunk.

Maybe it was inevitable, in a way. We'd been in bed together, with a woman, so many times, we were bound to cross some kind of line, at some point. Even accidentally.

Maybe the only strange thing about it was that it never happened sooner.

I knew it didn't mean anything.

But it had always left those nagging questions in my heart.

Was it really that dark? Was he really confused?

So we'd made a joke about it, kinda feeling each other out. Me, trying to figure out if it meant something more. Dylan, trying to figure out if I wanted it to mean more. Both of us feigning total innocence in the matter.

Him: *It was dark. I got confused.*

Me: *I was drunk. I barely noticed.*

Right. Like a dude blowing his load on your face was no big event. Who would notice that?

Then the joke, somewhere along the line, had died, and it became just one of those things that got filed away under the category of my sexual attraction to men, and we never talked about it again.

Of course, to me, it was never a fucking joke.

And just like then, I was allowing myself to wonder, right now, if what just happened might mean more than it actually did.

For just a minute, I wanted to let myself live in a world where that could be a possibility.

But then reality hit, like it always did.

I walked back into the bedroom to find Dylan up and getting

dressed, saying something about needing some air. He often went out on the back deck at night to look at the water and soak up the fresh air and just be alone for a while, but still. He didn't look at me. He was looking at Amber, and as soon as she darted into the bathroom to clean up, I went on the offensive.

Maybe so he couldn't bring up the fact that I'd just violated him first.

"I told you. I knew you were gonna do this."

He looked at me. "Do what?"

"Fall for her." I yanked my jeans on.

He didn't respond to that right away, but he had guilt written all over his face. "How did you know that?"

"How did I know? Let's see. From day one? Because she's exactly your type."

"My type?" He looked at me kinda blankly.

"You know, the *au naturel* girl-next-door hippie type who happens to be gorgeous, with a head full of dreams and ideals. You've got a type, man."

He raised an eyebrow. "I do?"

Christ. Seriously?

"You're kidding me, right? Remember Vickie? Remember Lolabella, or whatever the fuck that chick's name was from Coachella? Fucking Annie?"

"Shit. I do have a type." I couldn't even tell if this was news to him or if he was putting me on. Fucker just pulled on his shirt, unfazed.

"Yeah. Well, unfortunately for those girls, they either turned out to be too much drama, or too much dumb."

"Dumb?"

"Hello. Annie?"

"Annie wasn't dumb. She was just—"

"She was dumb as fuck. You can say it. She's not here." I took a step away from the bathroom, but I could hear the water running. I was pretty sure Amber couldn't hear us. "The thing is, Amber's amazing. And she just gets better the more you know her. Peeling all those layers back... She's real. She's complex and smart and sensitive and strong and sexy as fuck, and she's everything you ever wanted in a girl."

Dylan scoffed a bit. "Don't think I even knew everything I wanted in a girl."

"Yeah. Well, I did."

He stared at me. "What are you so pissed off about?"

"You're falling in love with her."

Silence. He just stood there, staring at me, so fucking calm as I inwardly raged, my chest heaving.

Then: "So?"

"*So?*" I grabbed my shirt and yanked it on. "You're gonna fucking leave me."

"What the hell are you talking about?" he said. "Leave you? I'm not going anywhere. However I feel about Amber doesn't change anything."

"If you really believe that," I said, "you're fucking kidding yourself."

Then I stormed out before he could bring up the whole my-hand-on-his-ass thing, wanting to punch something, like some fucking drama queen. But I really couldn't help it. I was fucking *pissed*.

Mostly at myself.

CHAPTER TWENTY-SEVEN

Amber

I SPENT the morning in Dylan's house, alone, looking through some unsorted photos from my South America trip. The guys had gone into the city, on separate boats, Ashley to do whatever Ashley did when he went into the city—which would likely include getting groceries, to feed the bottomless pit that was Dylan's stomach—and Dylan to attend a morning meeting with Dirty at a recording studio.

Dirty was going to start recording their new album tomorrow, and Dylan was clearly excited about it.

I was excited that when he got back from his meeting, I was going to have him all to myself; Ashley said he'd be gone for most of the day.

And I was kind of freaking out.

I was planning to drag Dylan to bed as soon as he got home, obviously, which would mean that—other than that fast, frantic limo fuck in L.A.—we'd be having sex alone, just the two of us, for the first time. Which meant I was also kinda nervous.

And I was worried.

I figured I should ask him about what happened last night. Ashley touching him, while the three of us were in bed. I'd seen Ashley put his hand on Dylan's ass while he was fucking me. Because I had Dylan on top of me at the time, his cock inside me, and I was about to come, it had been kind of exciting. Arousing, if you asked my lady parts.

But in the dim recesses of my rational mind, it was also kind of alarming.

I didn't know what to do with it. What to think.

But I knew I should ask.

It wasn't that I felt threatened, exactly. Though maybe that was part of it? But I just really needed to know what it meant. To Dylan.

I was pretty sure I already knew what it meant to Ashley.

Even if you were right there on the bed, watching your buddy fuck a girl, then come with that girl, you didn't *accidentally* reach out and put your hand on his bare ass and leave it there.

As for Dylan's non-reaction, I really couldn't figure out what that meant.

In a way, maybe I just plain understood Ashley. Clearly, he was hot for Dylan. Well, so was I.

I could hardly fault him for it.

But Dylan? The man was still a bit of an exotic mystery to me.

As I turned it over in my head, my thoughts turned to Johnny and what he'd said to me at the bar in L.A., as we were saying goodbye.

He'd asked me if I was with Dylan Cope.

You really have no right to ask me that, I'd informed him.

I know I don't, he admitted. Then he'd offered, grudgingly, *Dylan's alright*. Which, coming from Johnny, with his huge ego and his eye swelling up from the blow of Dylan's fist, was pretty high praise.

You like Dylan? I'd asked him, surprised.

You could do worse, he'd said.

Then he made a point of kissing me on the cheek before he left, while throwing Dylan a look that said something like *Eat shit and die*.

I smiled a little at that memory. Because really, only Dylan Cope could punch a guy in the face and still have his respect moments later. Johnny hadn't pressed charges against him, and the media hadn't even attacked. The incident was on the web, thanks to about a million cell phones capturing the chaos of the brief brawl, but Dylan's involvement in it had been so out of character, no one had seemed to want to dwell on it or make him the bad guy.

So far, I hadn't met anyone who'd had an unkind word to say about Dylan. I was no longer under any illusion that he was perfect. Ashley had warned me about his stinky feet after concerts; I was pretty fucking sure that confirmed his humanity.

But maybe he was just perfect *for me*.

A nice guy. No drama. No bullshit.

A nice guy who had so much going for him, was so effortlessly charming and sexy and desirable, it kinda scared the shit out of me.

Made me wonder what he saw in *me*.

Really, my self-esteem wasn't *that* low. I knew my good qualities as well as I knew my not-so-good ones. But *still*.

Me and Dylan Cope... alone?

It was almost too exciting for me to handle.

I'd just finished eating lunch when I heard the Dirty Deed pulling in, and my chest got all fluttery. My breaths got short. My palms started sweating. My pulse throbbed between my legs, and I felt myself getting wet.

I was about to have Dylan all to myself.

All.

To.

Myself.

When he walked into the house and found me lying on a couch in the living room, he ditched his jacket and headed straight over, his eyes running up and down the length of my body.

I'd worn one of my long, soft, figure-hugging dresses—with absolutely nothing underneath. This one was a soft ivory color, and I usually wore a bikini beneath it on hot days, because it was pretty see-through.

"Are you hungry?" I asked him. "I just had lunch."

"Already ate," he said, his gaze settling on my pussy. "But I could eat." His lips quirked in that slight, crooked smile that made my lady parts ache. "What are you up to, Amber Paige?"

"Just waiting for you," I said, honestly. "I'm catching the six o'clock into town. I asked Liv to meet me for dinner." I'd asked her to dinner *before* I knew I'd have Dylan all to myself this afternoon. Which meant I was now kinda regretting it. But I wasn't gonna bail on a date with my sister, even for Dylan Cope.

"I'll drive you," he said, immediately.

"Okay." I'd learned by now not to bother trying to fight when he insisted on giving me a ride into the city. "But until then, I was thinking... I mean, if you don't have other plans..." I sat up and picked up my camera, which was sitting on the coffee table, and told him, "You should get undressed." Then I got to my feet, standing in front of him with the camera, turning it on.

By now, I knew how to seduce Dylan Cope. The see-through dress didn't hurt, but I knew how hard it got him when I took my camera out.

I glanced down now and I could see the firm bulge of his cock, pressing against his jeans. He was already getting hard.

He liked my attention focused on him, through my lens. Liked me taking photos of him. It was foreplay.

Maybe it was also a tease. That the camera was between us and he couldn't quite see me, couldn't quite get to me. Couldn't quite have me, fully, while it was between us.

I fully expected him to start stripping, immediately.

But instead, he reached out and took the camera from my hands, setting it back down on the table.

"I'll get undressed," he said, without making any move to do so, and instead, he cocked one of his incredibly sexy eyebrows at me. "But ladies first."

Okay. Now I was *really* nervous.

Sure, I'd been naked in front of him. A lot. But there was usually so much going on, between the two hot men who were naked with me, and all the touching and mind-melting arousal that I didn't have much mental ability to feel self-conscious. Anytime I'd been standing in front of Dylan while my clothes came off, it was because Ashley was taking them off—while doing other things to me that kinda distracted me from the fact.

Now, we were standing in Dylan's living room, alone, in broad daylight. He was staring at me, and there was nothing at all to distract from the fact that he was about to see me, buck-naked.

"Are you sure?" I asked, stalling. "Having sex with the clothes on can be pretty sexy."

His eyes, hooded with lust, drifted down my body, slowly and deliberately.

"I want to look at you," he said, his voice all rough, as he met my eyes again. "I want to see your eyes and your tits and your bare pussy. I want you to show it to me."

Well okay, then.

Truth was, I really didn't want him leaving his clothes on, either. So fair was fair.

I gathered my dress in my hands, lifting the soft skirt up my legs... up my thighs... his gaze following all the way. Then I took a breath and in one quick motion peeled it up and over my head. I tossed it on the floor and shook out my hair as his eyes drank me in.

He drifted closer, stopping right in front of me. He put his hand lightly on my cheek, his fingertips just cupping me, his thumb drifting over my mouth.

"Fuck, you're pretty, Amber," he murmured.

Then he started kissing me. He leaned in and put his mouth on my neck, and my knees quivered. He kissed his way down my throat, and down between my breasts. Then he skimmed a thumb over one nipple, which was already achingly hard, and teased it with his tongue. Just a soft flutter, and I arched my back, giving it to him, strung taught like a bow.

He closed his mouth over my nipple and sucked, lowering himself to his knees. He teased my nipples with his soft kisses, with gentle flicks of his thumbs, as I gasped and shifted, restless on my feet, my fingers digging into his soft, wild hair. Needing more... but he was going so fucking slow.

Then he moved me back, inch by inch, until the backs of my knees hit the couch, and he pushed me back onto it. He started kissing his way down my stomach... slowly.

"Aren't you getting undressed...?" I asked, my voice a shuddery whisper as he went down on me.

Slowly.

He ate me out like he'd never seen me naked before, like I was new to him. Like he'd been dreaming about eating me out all his fucking life.

He held me down with his big, warm hands pressing my thighs apart. And he took his time. Exploring. Kissing and sucking. Flickering teasingly with his tongue as his jaw stubble scraped softly against my thighs. Latching onto my clit with his warm lips until I almost had to push him away.

"I don't want to come yet," I gasped, sitting up. "Please... take off your clothes."

At that, he grinned at me. He sat up, pulled his shirt up over his head and dropped it on the floor. I watched how he moved, so fucking beautiful, his muscled shoulders working as he stripped off his jeans. His briefs went next, and when he was naked, he kneeled before me again and slipped his arms around my back. He gathered me in, yanking me toward him so my ass was on the very edge of the couch.

He held me there, pressing his hips between my thighs... but his cock was just out of reach.

And I was overwhelmed. By him.

I was always overwhelmed by him.

In a really fucking good way...

The strength of his arms around me. The heat off his skin. His amazing smell, like citrus and man-soap... and naked flesh.

The gentle insistence of his fingers as they slid down to play with my clit.

The softness of his hair as he lowered his head to suck my nipple into his mouth. He rolled it in his teeth until my head fell back and I cried out.

"*Please.* You have to fuck me right now. I *need* to feel you inside me when I come..."

I didn't have to tell him twice. He released my nipple and pulled me toward him, sealing his mouth over mine, delving his tongue in, deep... At the same time, he lined up the head of his cock with my pussy and shoved into me with a groan.

And *fuck*, he was big.

Not just long, but broad. He stretched me to my limits and maybe a bit beyond as he sank into me, as he pressed in as far as he could get. It wasn't exactly painful. That full, stretched feeling, as long as I was slippery-wet—which I always was when Dylan fucked me—was mind-blowing. I couldn't think. I could only feel.

Could only feel *him* as he started to move.

"I'm gonna fuck you slow, Amber..." he told me, leaving hungry, sucking kisses on my throat. "Until you come. And then I'm gonna do it again..."

Oh, God... It really wasn't gonna take long.

It never did.

Usually, Ashley could fuck me longer. But Dylan usually fucked me first. I had no idea if it was an arrangement they'd made beforehand, or if it was just how they both preferred it. But it was almost always Dylan's cock that filled me first, drove me to orgasm first.

And it was different than when Ashley fucked me.

Dylan had more mass. He had more muscle bulk on his body, and he felt different between my legs as he pounded into me.

It also felt different in other ways.

The truth was, Dylan just turned my head on in ways that had me primed for orgasm before he'd even touched me.

Dylan turned my *heart* on.

Ashley didn't do that to me.

Ashley was harder. He fucked harder, in general, but his body also felt harder between my legs. And sometimes I could feel his piercing, hitting me in unexpected ways, in ways a man's cock had never done before.

If I'd never had Dylan, sex with Ashley would easily have been the hottest sex I'd ever had.

But I *did* have Dylan.

I had him right now.

Alone.

And I wanted to enjoy it—like all fucking day.

But every time I opened my eyes and actually looked at him, at his beautiful face, tensed with lust... or let my hands drift over his skin, the heavily-muscled curves of him... or let myself actually focus on what he was doing, his strong body drilling between my legs, his big cock filling me as he kissed me everywhere he could find skin to kiss... as he pushed me back and held me down against the couch, his hands on my wrists... I knew I was going to come—too soon.

Fuck...

He rolled his hips and started stroking in and out a little harder, teasing me as he skimmed his lips over my breast, his breath tickling me... and I totally lost control.

My pussy squeezed around him, my thighs tightening on his hips, and the explosion gripped me... a current of pleasure radiating out from my pussy and up my spine, hitting me in the head with a smack of bliss.

Then I actually *came.*

My pussy convulsed and I screamed. My body spasmed beneath him.

I saw his face above me, dimly, his eyes on mine, and heard his groan of pleasure. "*Fuck*... so sexy..." he murmured, as he watched me roll in bliss. My head rolled around on the couch cushion. My pussy fluttered around him as he kept fucking me.

I was *lost* in bliss.

All I knew was Dylan fucking me... and I never wanted it to stop.

Eventually, he slowed, than stopped his thrusts. But he was still hard, still buried inside me. He was looking down at me, one hand drifting down over my throat, smoothing away the hair that had stuck to my sweat.

When I could speak again, I panted, "That was... the *longest* orgasm... I've ever had..."

And his eyes sparked with golden flame. "Let's give you another one," he said.

I was limp, destroyed, but his body was still tense between my legs; he hadn't come yet, and he started fucking me again, merciless, driving me back up toward that delicious peak, despite my feeble—and quickly abandoned—protests.

"Come, Amber," he commanded me softly, still watching me. "Yeah... like that..."

And this time, when I came, he sped up his thrusts and drove into me hard, over and again, as I screamed. He groaned and buried his face in my neck, and I felt his cock stiffen, jerking inside me as he joined me, flooding me with his warmth.

I heard him say my name as he dragged his teeth lightly over my skin.

Amber...

He stayed like that, buried inside me, for a long time, as we both lay here, shuddering and panting, gradually floating back down to Earth.

And I felt it.

I felt *it*.

I wondered, was he feeling it, too?

He was the one who'd removed the camera. Made me come out from behind the lens. He'd had sex with me, alone, without Ashley. Without even mentioning Ashley. And for the first time, I lay here in the aftermath feeling naked and exposed, confronted with my feelings for Dylan Cope.

The feelings I'd been so afraid to face.

I'd had sex with Ashley alone. More than once.

It never felt like *this*.

Maybe I'd been afraid that whatever was between the two of us —Dylan and I—wasn't actually real or of any substance. That it was just a kink. Just sex. That he *needed* Ashley in the room with us.

But when we were alone, without Ashley... it was very, very real.

Scary real.

If I thought sex with both of them was hot... sex alone with Dylan was off the charts. Not just because he was beautiful and sexy and had a huge cock. Not just because he knew how to fuck. Not just because he knew what to do with his strong hands and his gorgeous mouth and his green-gold eyes to make me melt in bliss.

Because my heart was all wrapped up in him.

I had big, beautiful feelings for this man.

Scary feelings.

And scariest of all... I felt like I could actually depend on him. *Trust* him. Like when he pushed himself up on shaky arms and looked down at me with those gorgeous eyes of his, I could ask Dylan Cope to do pretty much anything... and he might just do it for me.

Like I might actually be able to count on him to do something that was an incredibly foreign concept in my mind...

Stay.

"Isn't this civilized," Liv remarked as she sat down across from me at the vegetarian restaurant where I'd asked her to meet me for dinner.

"I know. Family meals. When have we ever had these?"

"We would. If you were ever in town."

"Here I am."

Liv just raised an eyebrow and picked up her menu. She perused it, or pretended to, then asked, "So when do you leave?"

"What?"

A waiter appeared at the table, and my sister said, "I'll have the butternut squash ravioli, a cup of soup and a martini, Bombay if you have it." Then she looked at me. "And she'll have..."

"A house salad."

"And a martini for her, too," Liv said. "And get an entree," she prodded me. "I'm paying."

I stifled the urge to roll my eyes. "I want the salad. They have a kickass dressing."

Liv frowned and handed off our menus to the waiter, who gave me a sympathetic smile. Maybe he had an annoying big sister, too.

"And extra olives in the martini, please," I added, just before he vanished.

"So," Liv said, "I'm assuming we're here so you can announce your latest airline ticket purchase and globetrotting plans."

I just looked at my sister for a long moment, searching her hazel eyes. Then I asked her, "Why don't you like it when I go away? It's not like we hang out all the time when I'm here."

"I never said I didn't like it."

"The disapproval is dripping off of you. But I'm happy when I travel. I love traveling, and I love the work I do while I'm traveling."

"I know you do."

"So?"

"So..." She hesitated, then sighed. "Every time you come back, you're just a little less of the Amber I used to know." Her voice had softened, and I glimpsed something in her eyes. Sadness?

It kind of stunned me.

"What?"

"You change, Amber. Every time you go out there on your own, you come back more... *alone*. You get more prickly and jaded and more stuck in your ways. And that chip on your shoulder just gets bigger."

"It does?"

"And I get more and more worried about you."

I blinked at her. "You're worried about me?"

"*Yes*. I'm worried that you're giving up on the idea of ever not being alone."

I didn't know what to say to that.

Was she right?

After an uncomfortable silence, the waiter returned with our drinks. Liv raised her martini in reluctant toast, sighing again. "Wherever you go this time, I just hope you have fun."

I touched my glass to hers and sipped. "Me too." It was tough to swallow around the lump forming in my throat. I was trying to work up the nerve to ask her what I wanted to ask her. And it had nothing to do with leaving.

"You're twenty-seven," she went on, "and you should be partying and falling in love, not wandering from hostel to hostel, alone."

I set my drink down. My heart was beating too hard and my palms were starting to sweat; I was afraid I'd drop the glass. "I'm not going anywhere."

She stared at me, like what I'd said didn't compute *at all*. "Say that again?"

"I'm not going anywhere. That's not why I asked you to meet me today. I just thought we should have dinner. You know, we're sisters. And I'm here right now." I looked away, unable to take that shocked look on her face anymore. "Did you know that Dylan has regular family dinners at his mom's place? Like all the time, when he's home from the road. And sometimes, his family even goes to visit him on tour..."

When I glanced at Liv, her eyes had narrowed at me.

"Dylan?" she asked. "As in Dylan Cope?"

As if there were any other Dylan in our lives.

"I went to see Mom," I told her. "A few days ago."

Liv's back straightened; she seemed annoyed by the topic change, but she let it slide. Barely. Her eyes narrowed even more and she asked, "And how did she seem?" like she already knew the answer. Because of course, she did.

"She seemed exactly the same. It's like a fucking time warp over there. Nothing ever changes."

"She's too old to change, maybe."

"No one's too old to change, Liv. Growth is always possible, as long as we're alive."

She sipped her martini, eying me the entire time, then set the drink down on the table. "What are we talking about here? I'm lost."

"I think I need some big sister guidance."

If I thought she looked shocked before, that was nothing. "You do?"

"Yeah."

I searched for the right words. I knew Liv would understand my fears without me having to explain them to her. She grew up in the same house I did, and she'd always tried to protect me from the things I'd had to see there. But I didn't want to talk about my fears. For the first time, I wanted to talk to her about getting past them.

So I asked her, "How do I stay in one place for a while and just trust that it's going to be okay no matter what happens? Like how did you do that with Laura, when there was such a risk?"

"A risk of what?"

"Well... she was straight, before you. You took a risk with her, that she'd stay."

"She wasn't straight, Amber. It's not like she magically transformed into a lesbian because she hooked up with me. More like she figured out who and what she really was. And if you're seriously considering staying in one place for a while to see how a relationship with someone you care about might pan out, maybe you'll figure that out, too."

"Maybe."

"'Growth is always possible, as long as we're alive,' right?" she said, quoting me.

"Right."

"Isn't that what you're looking for when you're out there, anyway? With your camera? Who and what you really are...?"

"Maybe I'm avoiding looking for it."

Liv sat back in her chair and stared at me some more. "Well, damn, Amber Paige. You are figuring some shit out, aren't you?"

I fucking hope so.

On that note, I went for it.

"Do you think... Is it possible to like cock and pussy in equal amounts?"

Liv stared at me. Then one eyebrow slowly raised above her glasses.

A male throat cleared and the waiter, who was very obviously gay, leaned in to place Liv's soup in front of her. Before he withdrew, he told me, "I'm thinking the answer to that is a no. Kind of an apples-and-oranges situation, hon."

I smiled awkwardly and waited for him to depart. My stomach had kinda fallen at his words, but he was a stranger. I needed to hear from my big sister on this.

When he was gone, I looked at Liv. She wasn't touching her soup; she was still staring at me.

"Jesus," she muttered. "Those two are doing a fucking number on you, aren't they."

"It's just... it's Ashley," I confessed. "You can't say anything to anyone, okay? This is private stuff. But I think he's in love with Dylan."

"Uh-huh." If Liv was surprised by that, she didn't show it. She didn't show a thing; no judgment, none of her trademark dry humor. "And the only reason that would bother you is if you're in love with Ashley. Is that it?"

"Not Ashley," I said. And I watched how her face changed.

I watched as she started to get it. To realize what it would mean if I was in love with either Ashley or Dylan—and not the other. How many hearts stood to break here.

Mine included, very possibly.

"You're in love with Dylan Cope," she said, sounding kinda defeated about it. Like she already knew this was a battle she couldn't possibly win, so she was laying down her sword in advance. "The man you swore, just a few weeks ago, you didn't even have a crush on."

"I mean, at what point do you know you're in love?"

"You *know*."

I picked at the olives in my drink, stabbing them with the little toothpick they'd come on, unable to look her in the eye. "I know," I agreed. "I'm falling for him. I know I am. I *want* to love him. I don't even care if I get hurt anymore."

"*I do*," my sister said.

And the tears hit me; I sniffed and held them back as my throat constricted and my chest started to tighten.

"Have you forgotten about Johnny?" Liv asked, like she couldn't resist making one quick jab, just to make sure I hadn't totally lost my ever-loving mind.

"You're the one who told me that Dylan is nothing like Johnny," I reminded her calmly, still not looking at her.

She sighed, and I decided not to be mad at her for giving me a hard time. I knew she loved me. She really didn't want me to be hurt.

"And what about Ash?" she asked. "You're sure you're not in love with him, too?"

I shook my head. "I don't know."

The truth was, I didn't even want to fathom it. Because I cared about Ashley, a lot. That much I knew, for sure.

"No, Amber," my sister said. She put her hand on my wrist and squeezed, until I looked up into her eyes. "You *know*."

CHAPTER TWENTY-EIGHT

Dylan

I ARRIVED at the studio feeling all kinds of distracted.

We were recording the new Dirty album at Left Coast Studios, and today was our second day. Yesterday had gone well. We'd recorded the title track, "To Hell & Back," in a matter of hours, by candlelight, and it felt surreal and powerful and fucking amazing being in a room together again, just Zane, Jesse, Elle, Seth and me. Playing our music together.

Woo, our longtime producer, was producing the album, and Jesse was co-producing. If you asked me, it was shaping up to be our best album since our debut, *Love Struck*. I'd voiced that opinion to the rest of the band, and while they wouldn't all admit that they were as sure about that as I was, I knew we all felt it.

We had a kind of magic going on in the room that we hadn't felt, on that level, in years—now that we had Seth back, and Jessa's input on the songs again.

I was as sure as I'd ever been that the album was gonna be killer.

What I wasn't so sure about was what was going on at home.

When I walked into the studio and saw my band there, my drums, I relaxed a little. This was my second family. My second home. Other than being on the road, onstage, the studio was my favorite place to be with my band.

Of course, my band life had its limitations. Because the two people I cared about most weren't here. They weren't a part of this, and for the first time in my life that felt off—that someone I was intimately involved with wasn't a part of *this*.

I'd been able to tour with Ash quite a bit, so he was often part of the picture. Sometimes I even brought him to gigs or events with me, even if the Pushers weren't involved. He'd been my plus one more often than a woman ever had been. The Pushers were coming on the next tour with us, too; at least, part of it.

But what about Amber?

I had a shitty feeling about what was gonna happen with her once things ramped up with the band and promo got crazy and we took off on tour.

And she went to fucking Thailand or wherever without me.

When I met her, I didn't even want a girlfriend. Now, I definitely didn't want a long-distance one.

I wanted her.

But I definitely didn't want to hurt *him*.

I was kinda dreading heading home at the end of the day, facing those two people I cared about so much. Knowing that one of them might get hurt by what I was gonna have to do, if things continued like they were.

The problem was, I wanted Amber to myself in a way I hadn't wanted a woman since Ash and I started doing the threesome thing.

Maybe I'd never really wanted a woman this way.

Getting serious about a woman had always seemed to get in the way of the other things I wanted.

But not Amber. She just fit, in every way.

And then there was Ash…

Putting his hand on me the other night.

Fuck.

What the fuck was I gonna do?

I flopped onto a couch, barely listening as the band talked about the song we were planning to record today, "Blackout." It was one of my favorites, but I really wasn't tuned in. There was some breakfast stuff laid out on a table, but I didn't touch it. Didn't put in a coffee order when Maggie asked what we wanted.

I just tried to look like I was here, when in reality, my head was gone.

I never realized until now how much I could want this. A woman who understood me. Who gelled with me like Ash did, but challenged me, too. Kept things interesting. Held my attention.

I'd never had a woman in my life who just *fit* the way Ash did. Someone who I just had that easy, effortless chemistry with.

I knew Amber had chemistry with Ash, too.

But the fact was, I couldn't be with Ash in the way I was starting to suspect he really wanted me to. It was never about that, for me.

"You okay, man?" Zane asked, tossing a bagel at me. I caught it and nodded.

"I'm good," I said. "Let's get going on this song." I wanted to play so I couldn't think about this anymore.

"Still waiting on Jesse," Woo said.

Right. I glanced around... I hadn't even noticed he wasn't here yet.

Elle frowned at me and patted my leg. She was sitting next to me, and I hadn't even noticed that either.

"Rough night?" she asked. She was with me last night, here at the studio, so I could only assume she meant whatever happened to me after that.

"Just tired," I said, and I got up to go tinker with my drums. I tossed the bagel back in the box and grabbed an apple, stuffing it in my mouth. Figured maybe if my mouth was full, no one would try to get me to talk.

Why did I let it go that far?

Let Ash touch me like that?

Because you want him to be happy.

I knew that much was true, in my own defense. Stupid, maybe, but true.

And the way I felt about Amber... I *knew* I couldn't share her with Ash forever.

When did this shit get so fucking complicated?

I sat down behind my drums in the drum room, and tried to shut out all the noise. The noise in the studio. The noise in my head. But I couldn't quite tune it out. It was consuming me, in a really fucking bad way.

When Amber walked into my life, I really didn't see this coming. I really wasn't looking for a relationship. Now, I didn't know what to do about it—or what I'd do without her.

I'd just seriously never been in this position before.

Kinky threesomes were one thing. Even committed with Kitty between us, it was all about sex.

With Amber, it was about so much more.

It was about *everything*.

She fit into my life in every way a woman could... so much so, that now it was starting to feel like Ash was the one who didn't fit the same way he used to.

The worst part about that? I was pretty fucking sure that Ash was starting to feel it. That's why he was pushing it. Why he accused me of falling for her, of planning to leave him.

Why he touched me like that, while I was fucking her.

Just... *fuck*.

Everything was changing.

And the most fucked up part was... I didn't even want to stop it.

That night, I got back to the house before Ash did. Amber said he'd gone into the city mid-day, but I didn't ask for details. I just swept her up in my arms, carried her upstairs, dumped her on my bed and stripped her naked. There was an urgency building in me, this need to be inside her, to fuck her before Ashley came home.

So I wouldn't have to share her.

"You're home... um, early," she said, kinda breathless as I went down on her.

I had her crying out, begging for cock, within minutes, and then I gave it to her. Hard and fast and for a long fucking time. I couldn't get enough of her. The idea of making her mine was making me fucking crazy.

I'd never lost my shit like this over a girl.

Ever.

I had her on her back on the bed, her legs spread around my waist, her hands pinned beneath mine, and I fucked her like that until she came. I didn't touch her clit with my fingers. I *had* to make her come with nothing but my dick driving into her, my body slamming against hers.

She gasped and half-screamed and fucking shivered, and I watched her face. The way her mouth dropped open and drifted closed. The way she licked her soft lip. The way her eyes softened as she melted, her body going limp beneath me, and she looked at me the way she did.

Gone.

I was totally fucking gone for this girl.

Had been, for a while now.

No way was I giving her up, or sharing her with fucking anyone.

"So good..." she murmured in her soft, sexy voice.

My balls tightened and I felt the pressure building, creeping down my spine. Rushing toward her...

"Amber... *fuck*, I'm gonna come."

"Yeah... baby..." she breathed, her hands smoothing down over my ass and squeezing. Her whole body tightened around me as I rammed into her, deep.

And the most intense orgasm I'd ever had tore through me.

It was all I could feel, every-fucking-where, as I shot into her.

I groaned as the pressure released, as I fucking melted over her. My brain swirled. I saw black.

I drew a ragged breath and collapsed against her, just trying not to crush her in the process. My whole body had turned to jelly. "*Holy fuck.*"

"Yeah," she sighed and kinda giggled, her hands drifting lightly up my back, then into my hair.

We lay like that for a long while, breathing hard. I couldn't think. My brain had finally shut down.

Thank fuck.

Eventually, Amber slithered out from beneath me to take a quick shower. "I'm all covered in come," she said, kissing my cheek. I smacked her ass as she went, and watched her dash into the bathroom, naked.

While she was gone, I tried not to start brooding and fucking sulking again. It was pretty much all I'd done today. We didn't even finish recording "Blackout" because the drums needed to be laid down again. I kept fucking it up, and I never fucked up. I had the song nailed in rehearsal, could play this whole album backwards and forwards, but today, I'd fucked up.

Woo had finally called it and sent me home early.

And everyone had definitely seemed a little concerned and confused by my performance.

Why so tense? Elle had asked me gently as I left.

He just needs Ash and their girl to polish his knob, Zane had cut in. *He'll be good as new tomorrow.*

I didn't even bother responding to that. Zane had been making juvenile jokes about Ash polishing my knob for the last five years. Was probably just jealous we'd never invited him in for a gang bang.

When Amber came back to bed, she collapsed against me, all soft and warm and smelling of my shower gel, and I put my arm around her. She lay her head on my chest. I could've fallen asleep, I was that comfortable, even though it was barely seven p.m..

I laid my hand on her bare hip and ran my thumb up and down the curve of her hipbone.

"I've been thinking," I told her. "You asked me to tell you about my gnarly stuff. My worst qualities. And I realized I never really answered you on that. So I guess that's one of my worst qualities."

"What is?"

"I just tend to avoid confrontations and drama and, I dunno, upsetting people."

"That doesn't sound like a bad quality to me," she said.

"I can be pretty laid-back."

"I noticed."

"Some people find it aggravating."

She peered up at me. "Why?"

"I dunno. Maybe you get mad about something, get worked up, and I don't. Instead, I check out. That can infuriate some people."

Her lips twitched in amusement. "Bet it infuriates the shit out of Ashley."

"Sometimes."

"So why don't things upset you?"

"They do. I just don't dwell on them. Or I avoid them. I disappear." Even as I said it, I knew I wasn't being fully honest. I'd be upset as hell if she walked out of my life right now, got on that plane to Thailand or wherever.

"So what does upset you?" she asked me.

"People I care about being upset, I guess."

She shook her head, rolling it back and forth on my chest a little.

"What?"

"No one's that perfect, Dylan. You have to have some shitty qualities. Everyone does." She gazed up at the ceiling. "Like me, for example."

"You?"

"Me. I'm impatient, flighty, sarcastic, and I can be overly judgmental. Hard on people as a way of driving them away. Pretending I don't care as much as I do." She looked at me. "That's pretty shitty."

I just stared at her. I heard what she was saying, and I'd definitely seen evidence of all those traits in her. But if I told her they honestly didn't bother me, would she believe me? How did I make her see that, without her thinking I was just trying to be "perfect" or something?

"Well," I said carefully, "you're strong. You're independent.

You're so passionate about your photography. I respect all of that. You have ideals and you stand up for them, and for yourself. You're also beautiful and sexy and intriguing as fuck. When I'm not with you, I think about you way too fucking much, and when I'm with you, I don't want to be anywhere else."

"Really?" she said, kinda trying not to smile, but her eyes were sparkling.

"Really. And... this thing happens, when you smile at me. I feel it, deep. I feel you, even when you're not around. Does that sound lame?"

"It's not lame, Dylan," she said softly.

"I want more of it," I told her honestly. "Even if I just had you, I want more. That's some intense chemistry, Amber."

She just gazed at me.

"And you're brave. You were willing to take a chance on Ash and me."

"Okay... have you seen the two of you?" Her lips quirked. "I wouldn't be the only woman to take that chance, you know."

"But you were scared. And Ash was a dick to you at first. And you still took the chance."

"Because you're that hot."

I shook my head, smoothing a thick lock of her hair off her cheek and admiring her. Her delicate cheekbones and her freckles. And that blend of sass and fear in her eyes. "Man. You are so like him, you know?"

"What?"

"That self-protective thing. Making jokes. Saying stupid shit to avoid admitting how you feel."

She kinda rolled her eyes. "It's not stupid to point out how hot you are. It's factual. And don't think I haven't noticed how you keep avoiding shit, too."

"What shit am I avoiding?"

"I don't know. But you just told me that's what you do. So, you tell me. What exactly are you avoiding telling me right now?"

I didn't answer that. I honestly didn't know how to say it.

I'd never said those three words to a woman before. I was all nervous and worked up about it, like some virgin—afraid I was gonna blow it by rushing it too hard and too fast.

What if I scared her right onto that plane?

"I mean, if you don't want to tell me," she said, her tone taunting, "I could always ask Ashley. See if he knows what's up. Surely he knows your most annoying qualities, if anyone does..." She sat up, swiping her phone from the bedside table.

I didn't stop her, even though my heart was pounding, wondering what Ash would tell her. She texted something, presumably to him. I couldn't read it from where I lay.

When her phone pinged with an incoming message, she read it, but she didn't turn it to show me. She looked at me, though, her green eyes wide.

I took the phone from her hand and read the conversation on the screen.

Amber: What's the most annoying thing Dylan's done lately?

Ashley: Fell in love with you.

By the time I looked up, Amber was getting out of bed. I watched her slip on her little lace panties with the flowers on them. She was so fucking sexy, even when she was running scared.

"Where're you going?"

"Just getting dressed," she said, too brightly.

"Why?"

"Because we're done here. Right?" I watched her put on her bra, getting the straps tangled up. She swore, tore it off and started over again, trying to pretend like she wasn't totally flustered. "I'm gonna throw together a salad and make some balsamic dressing. Ashley said he'd do steaks for you guys when he gets back—"

"We should talk, Amber."

"Yeah. Should," she said, pulling on her jeans. "But you know, I'm an avoider, and you're an avoider, so for now, let's just go have dinner." She slipped on her blouse and fluffed her hair. "Ashley will be home in a few, and we'll have some beers." When I didn't move, she tugged the sheet off of me. "Come on! It'll be fun."

Then she gave me one of those smiles of hers that hit me right in the heart—with just a glint of terror in her eyes—and bolted out of the room.

CHAPTER TWENTY-NINE

Ash

I ROLLED OVER IN BED, stretching, and found myself pressed up against Amber's naked body. I was naked too, so I rubbed up against her a bit, enjoying the feel of her warm, soft skin. I slipped my arm over her. Then I glanced across the bed.

"Where's Dylan?"

"Gone," she said, sleepily. "He got up early and went to do some stuff, then head to the studio."

Fine with me. I would've liked him to be here, but hell, I was glad to have Amber alone.

Lately, I was growing more and more afraid of losing her completely to Dylan... and losing Dylan in the process. I didn't even want to admit to myself how much that fucking terrified me. But it was starting to creep in through the cracks in the walls I'd put up to shield myself from it all.

Any day now, it was all gonna come crumbling apart around me.

I knew that. And all I knew how to do to prevent it from happening was hold on tighter.

So I pulled Amber close now.

"You kiss him goodbye for both of us?" I asked her.

"Of course."

I let my hand drift over the soft curves of her body, over her tits.

She stirred and kind of whimpered. It seemed to me that she'd been getting softer with me all along the way, opening to me, letting me in, the way she'd done with Dylan in bed from the start.

In the beginning, when I'd first fucked her, I'd definitely seen her as a way to get closer to Dylan. Maybe I'd used her, just a bit. I was always afraid that he was gonna fall for her. And now, I knew that he had.

But along the way, I'd definitely started falling for her too.

Which just complicated the fuck out of things. But how was I to know? The girl annoyed the shit out of me. Or so I'd thought. I really didn't think I'd end up liking her so damn much.

Truth was, I really didn't think I'd *let* myself like her so much.

So fucking much for that.

As I slipped my hand down between her legs and she started rubbing herself against my fingers, at the same time that she grasped my cock and started jacking me off, I knew I had to man up and face the fucking music. Because I could feel it when we were alone. When Dylan's vibe wasn't screwing with my head and he wasn't here to see us… There was something real, right here, between me and Amber.

And we both felt it. I knew it when I looked into her green eyes.

I knew it, because she looked as scared as I felt.

"Hey," I said, suddenly wanting to cheer her up. "You wanna watch it again?"

"Watch what?"

"The commercial."

A slow smile spread across her pretty face, lighting her up. "Okay."

I found my phone on the bedside table and pulled it up. We'd watched it together last night, the three of us. Liv had sent it over—the finished Underlayer commercial. As I played it back now on my phone, Amber and I watched it together.

"Shit, he looks beautiful," she said. "It turned out so good…" She sounded regretful about that, but not disappointed. Liv had done gorgeous work, as usual. I knew Amber was proud of her; proud of her and Dylan both.

The commercial was hot, slick, and gave you everything the world knew and loved about Dylan Cope. How fucking gorgeous he was. His killer bod. And how he fucking rocked on the drums.

Toward the end, there was a single shot of him wearing his kilt, as he delivered his line to camera: *It's what's under the kilt that counts.* And because he was Dylan, he managed to do it without sounding like a douche. He looked fucking hot in the kilt, but in a way that made you love him rather than hate him.

Dylan was the boy next door who grew up into a god.

He was everything you wanted to be, or wanted to have.

And Liv understood who Dylan was; both sides of him. The rock god *and* the boy next door. It was Liv who'd pushed for that scene. She'd pushed for the kilt, because let's face it: everyone loved Dylan Cope in a kilt.

But the things *I* loved about him went far beyond some piece of clothing he was famous for wearing onstage.

And I knew by now that Amber was falling in love with much more than that, too. She'd never really even seen that part of him. She'd never been to one of his concerts. She'd never even asked to see him in his trademark sexy kilt. She wasn't a fangirl.

She was *the* girl.

"God. I was such an asshole at that shoot," she said.

"Yeah. You were."

She threw me a dirty look. "As were you."

"I was." As the commercial ended, I tossed the phone aside and rolled toward her. "Thought that's what you liked about me..."

"No. I like your pierced dick. And these eyebrows." She put her hand on my face and smoothed her thumb over my eyebrow.

"Eyebrows?"

"All twisty and angsty... Your eyebrows say it all, Ashley Player."

"Yeah? Are they telling you how much I wanna kiss you right now?"

"As a matter of fact," she said, her green eyes softening, "they are."

So I kissed her.

We rolled around in Dylan's bed for a while, with the smell of him still on the sheets, groping, making out. Then we got down to business and fucked like animals.

While we fucked, we kept talking about Dylan.

"What would you do... if he was here right now?" she whispered.

"I'd eat your clit while he fucked you," I told her, sucking on her neck for emphasis—and the girl fucking went off. She went nuts, riding me from beneath, jerking her hips to meet my thrusts as she cried out and clawed at my ass and her pussy pulsed with her climax.

Jesus...

She was the perfect fucking woman.

I made her suck me off after she came, licking her sweet juices off my dick and taking me deep in her throat.

"You take Dylan's cock that deep, baby?" I asked her as I slowly fucked her mouth. Of course, I knew she did. I'd seen her do it. "That horse cock of his, you take it that deep?"

She moaned in response and seemed to be trying to laugh, but I was already gone, coming down the back of her throat.

"Jesus... *fuck, yeah...* suck me deep, baby..." I kept the dirty talk going, because I figured with her mouth full, it was only polite that I carry the conversation.

Then I ran out of fucking words as my brain overloaded with pleasure.

Afterwards, I collapsed face-down on the bed. She was definitely laughing, and smacked me on the ass.

"Horse cock?"

"Have you seen it? Is there a better way to describe it?"

"Maybe a sexier way. I'm not really into bestiality."

"With that horse cock up inside you all the time, you sure as fuck are."

"Don't." She laughed again and smacked my ass, harder this time.

I just lay here, fucking spent, in the afterglow. Nothing could've made this moment better, other than Dylan being here with us.

And sure, I didn't *have* to tell her how happy I was. I could've downplayed it, gotten up and gone on with my day. As usual. But maybe I'd learned from my fuck up with Elle.

Took a fucking while, but I'd learned.

So I was gonna tell Amber how I felt about her.

I wanted to tell her, *had* to tell her, upfront—fucking *now*—instead of pretending like everything was cool. I'd done that before and been crushed.

So I spit it out.

"All jokes aside," I said, "I'm starting to fall for you, Amber Paige Malone."

She was lying beside me, her head on the same pillow, her face close to mine. She was still smiling, but that smile started to fade, maybe when she realized I really wasn't joking. That there was no punchline coming.

She didn't say a fucking thing, so I pushed myself up on my elbows and looked down at her, and kept going.

"I'm telling you that because honestly, I don't want to fall for you if you're just gonna jet."

Her mouth opened long before any words actually came out. Then she said, "Oh. I mean... I just thought..."

I sat up all the way, pulling my knees up in front me. "You thought what?"

"I thought... we were just kind of, you know... sharing a kink." She blinked at me. "You and me."

"What *kink*?"

"Dylan," she said.

I stared at her.

"I mean... I thought to *you* he was a kink." She swallowed, her eyes getting wider the more she spoke. "Or maybe, I just hoped..."

She trailed off. But the look in her eyes as she stared back at me told me she *knew*.

Sure, she hoped. But she fucking *knew* Dylan was more to me than just some kink.

But to her, that's all this was? Some fucking *kink*?

That's what she thought we were doing here?

"Please tell me you're fucking kidding me," I said, way too quietly.

She sat up. And the fucking pity on her face as she looked at me was too much for me to take. I pulled away as she reached for me. "Ashley, I—"

I flew out of bed, grabbing my clothes along the way, and walked out of the room before I could hear another word.

CHAPTER THIRTY

Amber

I FOUND Ashley on the back deck, above the point, overlooking the water.

He'd hopped out of bed so fast after what I'd said—that stupid comment about us sharing a kink—that I was afraid I'd really hurt him, when I definitely didn't mean to.

He stood with his back to me, leaning on the railing in his black T-shirt and jeans, feet bare. His hair was mussed from the sex we'd just had, from my hands clawing through it. He looked vulnerable and sweet, and angry.

As I neared him, I could both see and smell it: he was smoking.

"How's quitting going for you?" I ventured, standing next to him.

He didn't answer me. He didn't even look at me.

I wrapped my cardigan around myself; I hadn't bothered to pull on anything but panties underneath and it was pretty chilly out here. I leaned in closer to Ashley so I could feel his warmth; I was on his right side, the *Fuck Bitches* tattoo on his bicep in my face.

I touched my finger to the tattoo, lightly tracing the *F* with my fingertip.

He tensed a little at my touch, but still wouldn't look at me.

"You don't have to be like this with me," I told him.

He took a drag of his cigarette. "Like what?"

I dropped my hand and leaned on the railing to look up at his face. "Like... the guy who gets offensive tattoos and drinks too much when he's angry and lies to his lovers."

"That's who I am."

"Yes. But there are many other parts of you, too. And by now, I think I've met them all." I leaned in closer, until my shoulder pressed against his arm. "I like them all."

He didn't say anything. He just stared out over the water, not really looking at anything at all. But his blue eyes gleamed a bit, wet.

"I know how you feel about him, Ashley," I said quietly. But my words felt loud between us.

He looked at me, finally, his blue eyes crashing into mine.

"And now, I know how you feel about me," I added, softly. "But did it ever occur to you that maybe you're falling for me because you think he's falling for me, too? And maybe you want me to be the thing that keeps him connected to you. You know... sexually."

The thought had occurred to me, long ago, and I couldn't exactly pretend it wasn't true anymore.

"That's not true," he said, his voice thick with emotion.

"Isn't it?"

He looked away again.

"If I wasn't in bed between the two of you, he wouldn't be there, right?"

He said nothing, but he shook his head a little. I couldn't tell if he was agreeing with me or disagreeing.

"At least, you don't think he would be," I ventured.

Ashley still said nothing.

"So... why don't you find out? Just tell him how you feel."

He laughed a little and flicked his cigarette in the water. Then he pulled out a fresh one, shaking his head. "You think it's that easy?"

"It doesn't have to be easy. Lots of things in life that are worth doing aren't easy."

He lit his smoke, falling silent again.

"Don't you think he's worth the truth?" I pressed. "Don't you think he deserves to know? Don't you think he'd *want* to know?"

"Maybe he doesn't."

"Then too bad for him. Tell him anyway."

I watched him smoke, ignoring me. The gleam in his eyes had dried, but he didn't look happy.

"Come on." I elbowed him lightly. "Don't be a coward, Ashley."

I meant it as a bit of a joke, since I'd never really thought of Ashley as a coward, but it came out all wrong.

Like stupid tough talk.

Really tough talk, given that I hadn't found the courage to tell Dylan how *I* felt about him.

I'd been trying to convince myself for a while now that Ashley telling Dylan his feelings was the right thing to do—for Ashley and for Dylan. And that was true, as far as I could see. But I also *needed* Ashley to tell Dylan how he felt, because I needed to find out if Dylan's heart, in any way, belonged to Ashley.

Because I wanted Dylan for myself.

I didn't even have the courage to admit that to Ashley, right now. I didn't want to confuse things for him. I didn't want to make this any harder for him than it already was. But I was also afraid he'd reject my advice if he thought I was telling him for selfish reasons.

I was, and I wasn't.

I wanted Dylan, but only if he wanted me, too. I couldn't be the runner-up, the consolation prize, if what Dylan *really* wanted was Ashley—and the two of them weren't together only because they'd never found the courage to take the chance.

I couldn't let myself fall for Dylan Cope any harder than I already had if his heart—or even half of it—belonged to someone else.

"It's not about cowardice," Ashley said, finally. "It's about accepting the truth, Amber. Dylan isn't in love with me. I've accepted that. I've accepted having him in my life the only way I can have him."

"With a woman between you."

He said nothing.

"How do you know that's the only way? I saw you touch him, when we were having sex. You put your hand on him. He let you, Ashley."

"It doesn't mean anything."

"What if it does?" I challenged. "What if he's open to being touched by you again, and more? Don't you want to know?" I knew I did. As much as it might crush me, I had to know.

"I already know."

"Know what?"

"He's never judged me," he admitted. "But he's not into guys like I am. It's there, but we don't really talk about it."

"Which part?"

"Any of it. About me and the guys I sleep with."

"You're afraid what he'll think?"

He didn't answer that.

"He'll think you like dick," I said, enunciating every word carefully.

Ashley glanced at me. He cocked his pierced eyebrow, so at least I was managing to amuse him somewhat.

"*Big. Deal*," I said. "He already knows. So why do you care?"

He shook his head at me. "It's not just about dick, sweetheart. I wish it was that simple."

I took a breath and sighed. "It doesn't have to be easy *or* simple. It just has to be the truth."

He considered that.

"Okay," he said. "The truth is, I'm not gay. People say I'm bi, but that doesn't feel right to me either. It's not a half-and-half, fifty-fifty situation. If we're talking percentages, I'd say I'm a solid sixty-six-point-six percent straight."

"Uh-huh," I said. "Interesting math." But watching him squirm while he tried to explain it to me? I'd never seen him squirm like that before.

"I'm like, one-third into dudes at best," he concluded, raking a hand through his hair. He took a drag on his cigarette, then tossed it in the water.

"Right." I stared at him, and my skepticism must've been written all over my face. "And what percentage of your heart belongs to Dylan Cope?"

That hit home. I knew it did.

He stared at me, his blue eyes blown. "Where did you come from?" he asked me, his voice kinda choked and rough.

"Well... Brazil." I shrugged. "But you know I was born here. I—" I didn't get to finish that sentence because he kissed me. It was a soft, devout kiss, and as his body pressed in close to mine and I felt his warmth, his heartbeat, his fingers digging into my arms as he held me to him, I could feel how much he really did care about me.

Maybe Ashley's feelings for me weren't *only* based on a misguided desire to keep Dylan intimately attached to him. If Dylan wasn't even in the picture, maybe Ashley really would fall for me?

But Dylan *was* in the picture.

And I wondered, like I had many times now, was it even possible to love two people at once? Equally? Or would there always be an imbalance, one who owned your heart more than the other, and always would?

And what if *you* were the one who didn't get equal real estate in the equation? Would it be worth it to stay, or better to break loose and find something that was one-hundred-percent your own?

These questions reeled in my head as I allowed myself to cling to Ashley, selfishly, for a lingering moment on Dylan's deck.

When we broke apart, I told him, "I've never seen two guys closer than you two."

"Amber..."

"Unless, you know, maybe if they were married or something."

Ashley drew away until we weren't touching anymore. "Well," he said, clearing his throat, "there was that one time he came in my face."

I froze. "He... *what?*"

His eyes found mine. "He came—"

"Oh," I said. *Oh.*

Shit.

I did not need that visual. Weeks ago, maybe it would've piqued my curiosity or turned me on. Now it only scared me.

"He loves you, Ashley," I choked out. But I couldn't help it; jealousy burned behind my words, making my throat tight. I swallowed with difficulty.

Ashley went silent.

I didn't know how or when or if he was going to talk to Dylan about any of this, but I knew, either way, I had to take a step back. Bow out of the equation and let them work this out—whatever it was between them—first. No matter how long it took.

They were best friends long before I ever met them, and Ashley was probably in love with Dylan long before I ever was, too. They were sharing women and complicating things between the two of them long before I got all twisted up in it, and I had no business in the middle of it, complicating things any worse than they already were.

Especially when I didn't even *want* to be in the middle of it anymore.

I knew right now, hearing those words, that I didn't.

He came in my face...

And somehow, I *wasn't* in the middle anymore. It felt like Dylan and I had somehow switched positions and now everything was out of balance.

Or maybe I was never in the middle at all.

I hugged my cardigan tighter around my waist and looked away. "It's cold out here. I should get dressed. Can you still take me into the city today?"

"Yeah," he said. "Of course."

I nodded and started toward the house, but Ashley's voice stopped me.

"What if I tell him," he asked me, "and it doesn't work out?"

I turned to face him. "What if it does? What if it's the best thing you ever had?" These were questions I'd been asking myself a lot lately—about Dylan and myself. "Isn't that what's really got you so scared?"

CHAPTER THIRTY-ONE

Amber

AFTER LUNCH, Ashley gave me a ride into the city in his boat. Then he drove me to Jessa Mayes' baby shower in his truck. And I barely knew what to say to him.

I tried not to insult us both by making small talk. Ashley wasn't a small talk type of person, and neither was I. We'd shared comfortable silences before, but this time I couldn't get comfortable at all.

I kept silently berating myself for my advice to him. Objectively, honesty was decent advice. But it was advice I really should've been taking *myself*.

Where did I get off telling Ashley he should bare his soul to Dylan when I didn't even have the courage to do it myself?

Just like Ashley, I was afraid to tell Dylan how I felt about him. What I hoped to have with him. Somehow, the fact that the guy was so damn laid-back about everything only made it seem harder.

Before I met Dylan Cope, I might've thought it would be easier to pour my guts out to a person like that. Not so. Ashley was incredibly easier to open up to. I could predict his responses, and I knew he'd pull no punches with exactly what he thought. At least I would know where I stood with him the second the words were out of my mouth; sooner, even.

But Dylan?

The man had very possibly spent *years* pretending he didn't notice his best friend was in love with him, and politely tolerating his affections, out of some misguided desire to spare him pain.

I cringed just thinking about it.

What if he'd been tolerating my affections for the same reason? Because he was just too damn polite to brush me off or tell me that the end was coming?

What if Ashley was wrong, when he'd texted me that Dylan was in love with me? Dylan had said we should talk about it. But we still hadn't done that. Thanks to me avoiding the subject.

But then again, he'd avoided it, too.

Worse, what if his reaction to me opening my heart to him was the same as my reaction to Ashley? What if I was just an enjoyable kink to Dylan, but not much more?

Oh, Jesus.

Poor Ashley.

By the time we pulled into the driveway of the old heritage house in Dunbar, I was pretty wound up about it. But what could I do? I'd just have to get in line, *behind* Ashley, and wait my turn. If it turned out what Dylan wanted was Ashley, I'd have to deal with it. If not... I'd just have to woman-up and tell Dylan how I felt about him... and *hope* he felt the same.

"You want to pop in?" I asked Ashley, trying to sound cheerful as he put the truck in park, but as usual, I was shit at cheerful. "Say hi to the girls?"

"No, thanks. Baby showers aren't really my bag."

"Right." I unclipped the seatbelt and leaned over, without thinking about it, and kissed him on the cheek. My hand was on his shoulder and I squeezed him lightly. He very purposefully didn't turn to kiss me. I'd hurt him; I knew that. Or disappointed him. Or pissed him off. Probably all of the above. "I'll probably just crash with the girls tonight, okay? You know, give you and Dylan some time..." My words trailed off and his blue eyes caught mine.

"Sure."

"Thank you for the ride." I slid out my door, dragging my purse, my camera, and the gender-neutral gift bag with me. Since no one yet knew the gender of Jessa and Brody's baby, the bag contained an adorable selection of organic cotton baby onesies with elephants, owls and guitars on them, in yellow, green and taupe. "See you tomorrow?"

"Yeah." He attempted something akin to a smile, but he was shit at cheerful, too.

"Take care, Ashley." I cringed at how fucking casual that sounded.

I knew I could've handled this whole thing better, if I actually knew how to. But I'd done my best. I'd said what I felt I should say. I was *trying* to be brave here, and let the chips fall where they may.

What else could I do?

But somehow, as I watched Ashley drive away, it felt like my efforts had fallen way short of the mark.

I took a few deep breaths and put on my *So happy for you and your baby* game face, then rang the bell. It kind of felt like my heart had just been torn out and splattered all over the driveway. I couldn't really stand Ashley in pain.

Maybe I did love him, in a way.

But just not the way I loved Dylan.

When I walked into the house, Jessa's baby shower was in full swing. The house belonged to Dolly; I was told she was Zane's grandma, and that she'd taken Jessa in as a teenager when her mom died. Zane had bought the house for Dolly, which was beautiful, but way too large for one little old lady. It was lovingly decorated, as well as clean and tidy—much like Dolly herself—which told me he probably also had someone here to help her take care of it, and possibly take care of her, too.

Dolly was super sweet and sat smiling in her rocking chair while the younger women whirled around her, drinking and chatting and fawning over Jessa's belly, and Elle's too. Elle was barely showing, but everyone seemed excited about both babies joining the extended family.

Maggie and Katie had thrown the shower, and it was smallish, ten women in total. Besides the two of them, Jessa, and Dolly, there was Jessa's friend Roni, Katie's sister Becca and her friend Devi, Elle, and Summer, who was apparently tight with Elle. I was honestly kind of surprised I'd made the cut. Though knowing Katie, as I now kinda did, she already saw me as part of the family. Or at least, she really wanted me to be.

I felt honored. It was a pretty cool family.

Plus, after pretty much living with two men, it felt good to be surrounded by women and do girlie stuff. And to try to forget, for a little while, that look on Ashley's face when I told him what we had was just a kink.

God, I was such an idiot sometimes.

The caterers served up afternoon tea with dainties and those tiny sandwiches with the crusts cut off. We drank mimosas, while Jessa and Elle drank sparkling apple juice. Meanwhile, I took photos of everything; the shower photos would be my other gift to Jessa.

We'd all been told to email Maggie a baby photo of ourselves beforehand, and we played that game where we had to guess which baby photo matched which woman. Some people were easy to guess, as they looked exactly like their baby picture; others were impossible. As far as baby shower games went, it was actually pretty fun; I got stitches from laughing so hard.

Dolly's was the easiest to figure out because of the old-school photo style; it was a black-and-white photo that had been painted with color, the way they used to do it, her little lips and cheeks colored pink.

Mine was ridiculous, given the weird little suit I was dressed in, with the short pants and polka-dot bow tie. The bow tie was pink, but still. I'd tried to find a better photo—one where I wasn't dressed like a boy—but no such luck.

"So who's the boy?" Summer asked when the photo came up on

Dolly's TV screen, where Maggie was projecting the images. "Shit, is someone in this room trans and I didn't sniff it out?"

"It's Amber," Maggie said. "Did anyone guess Amber?"

Everyone consulted their little pieces of paper where we'd written down our guesses earlier. I was kinda flattered that no one had pegged me for the kid in the suit.

"I wasn't born a boy," I said, feeling myself blush as everyone looked at me. "But my older sister was kind of... butch. So, you know. Hand-me-downs." Unfortunately, baby Liv had preferred wearing boy clothes, and I'd inherited all her used clothing. You know, because my parents couldn't be bothered to get me my own clothes, so that in the future, I wouldn't have to endure moments such as this.

"You make an adorable butch baby," Katie said, putting her arm around me.

"Thanks."

In the end, Jessa won a giant gift pack of teas, chocolates, bath salts and other indulgences, for making the most correct guesses. And Maggie won a bottle of wine, provided by Katie, for being voted the absolute cutest baby, with her big gray eyes and honey-colored skin and her little round face. She was wearing a lace dress and her hair was in a bow in the photo.

"Sweetie," Roni told her, "I don't say this to women, believe me. But you *need* to procreate. Don't waste those adorable genes."

The rest of us agreed.

Maggie left that alone, pouring herself another mimosa.

Jessa opened her gifts, the most impressive of which was a whole collection of beautiful baby clothes knit by Dolly. Second to that was the all-terrain stroller wired with its own sound system, from Zane; the girls who knew him best seemed the most surprised by his thoughtfulness. Elle actually texted him to tell him what a good job he'd done, but Katie brought us up to speed. "He just paid the bill," she said. "Maggie picked it out."

Again, Maggie just drank her mimosa and shrugged.

Afterwards, the girls wanted to keep the party going, and since I wasn't really in any hurry to head back to Dylan's and walk into whatever conversation he and Ashley might've been having, I went along.

We all went for dinner downtown. Then we sent Dolly home in a cab, and the rest of us went back to Jessa's place in North Vancouver. We weren't done celebrating; in fact, we were just getting going as the post-dinner drinks kicked in. But Jessa was so very pregnant, she needed to get off her feet and, as she put it, "put on stretchier pants."

When we arrived at Jessa's house, Maggie took us straight into the giant "party room" downstairs, where Summer did her DJ thing. She threw on a remix of Halsey's "Bad at Love" and I glanced over at her; she wasn't looking at me, at all, so she definitely didn't mean to call me out with the song. But I felt pretty exposed. How had this become the theme song of my life?

Fortunately, no one seemed to realize it.

Katie poured the wine, and more sparkling apple juice for Jessa and Elle. Dimly, I wondered where I was going to sleep tonight and how I was going to get there, but the thought vanished with my first sip and never returned.

There was dancing, drinking and of course, girl talk. Brody wasn't home; apparently, he'd gone on an ice fishing trip way up north with Jude, to give Jessa girl time. And without any men around, the conversation definitely took a different turn than it would have. Eventually, maybe inevitably, it landed on men.

Specifically, it landed on *me* and men. As in, the two men I was currently involved with.

Everyone seemed incredibly curious about my relationship with Dylan and Ashley, and I couldn't blame them. But I really didn't feel like voicing my feelings—*at all*—or even acknowledging them right now.

I knew I was falling for Dylan. Head-over-heels and hard. Scary enough on its own, if you were as bad at love as I was, but on top of that, I knew I didn't feel the same way about Ashley. Which was natural, probably, but also fucking sucked.

I couldn't even bear to fully face it myself, or relive the painful conversation with Ashley from today, so I definitely wasn't going to open up about it here.

Instead, I gave the girls a vague response and a smile, and just let them assume whatever kinky shit they wanted to assume about the three of us. Then I helped myself to another glass of wine, passed the bottle off to Katie, and turned the conversation over to Jessa's girlfriend, Roni. She seemed pretty game to talk about her love life. In vivid detail.

As it turned out, Roni had been seeing some hot biker guy who liked to fuck her on his Harley. And a few of the girls, including me, were pretty curious about the, um, physical logistics involved in that. Which Roni was more than happy to divulge.

Eventually, Maggie left the party with some flimsy excuse about having to be up early, even though the girls all *boo*'d her as she left. Roni ended up rubbing Jessa's feet for her—grudgingly—on the couch. Summer and Elle were spinning music and chatting across the room, while me, Katie, her sister, Becca, and her best friend, Devi, ended up in a pile of cushions on the floor, talking.

Devi asked Katie how she was doing, which I discovered was partly because Katie and Elle, her husband's ex, weren't exactly close; they were civil and seemed to share a mutual respect, but they weren't exactly friends. Also, it was because we were at a baby shower for Jessa, Elle was pregnant too, and apparently, Katie wanted to be.

"We're trying," Katie explained to me. "But it's not happening."

"You're so young, though," I told her, "and so healthy."

"You have tons of time," her sister agreed.

"If you want it, it'll happen for you," I said. I fully meant it when I said it, but really, what the fuck did I know about it?

It seemed to make Katie feel good, though. She gave me one of her sweet smiles and said, "Thank you, Amber." And I just hoped I'd done my duty as a friend. The way Devi gave me a nod and clinked her glass to mine, I figured I'd said the right thing.

"Fucking right, it'll happen," Devi said. "Don't stress about it, babe."

"Besides," I added, deciding to go that extra mile, "you and Jesse are gonna have like the world's most adorable baby—"

"Uh... nobody panic..."

I stopped mid-sentence as Jessa shuffled into the room. I hadn't even noticed her leave. Everyone looked over at her and went really still; she had a hand on her belly and looked kinda pale.

Katie and Roni got to their feet, and Summer turned the music down so we could all hear Jessa when she said, "... but my water just broke."

I soon discovered that a pregnant woman's water breaking was not at all like it was in the movies. At least, it wasn't in Jessa's case.

There was no giant gush of liquid on the floor. There was no mad dash for the hospital. Jessa just calmly went to call Brody, though I wasn't sure what he was supposed to do about it since he was over a thousand miles away.

"Okay, ladies, I think that's our cue to clear out," Katie said, starting to clean. We all pitched in and had the party room tidied up in minutes, then beelined for the front door. Jessa reappeared as we were putting on our jackets, phone in hand, looking slightly less calm and more pale.

"Brody's flying back?" Katie asked, which made the tiny crease between Jessa's eyebrows deepen.

"Tomorrow," she said. "That's as soon as he can fly out. They don't exactly have an international airport in Mosquito Lake, Saskatchewan."

Frowns rippled over the faces of the gathered women. I'd never heard of Mosquito Lake, Saskatchewan, but it definitely didn't sound like much of a travel hub.

"Who the hell goes fishing in a place called Mosquito Lake?" Devi remarked, and Katie elbowed her.

"Brody and Jude," Elle offered dryly.

"They're *ice* fishing," Roni muttered, clearly unimpressed with the whole idea. "Which is even more ridiculous."

"I think it's just a name." Jessa rubbed her belly in soothing circles. "It looks lovely there. Brody showed me pictures..."

"Not much of a name, tourism-wise," Summer pointed out.

"I *told* him not to leave," Roni said. "It's too close to your due date. Now he's sitting in some shack on the ice drinking beers when he should be here, with you."

"It's okay." Jessa laughed a little, but she sounded kinda scared. "The baby isn't due for two weeks. Who knew this would happen?"

Katie rubbed her back soothingly. "Sweetie, I'll stay with you until he gets home. Jesse can come over, too."

"No. It's okay," Jessa said, sounding less-than-thrilled at the prospect of her brother coming over. "Maggie's my on-call Brody-fill-in. She'll come. And actually..." She looked at me. "I was going to ask Amber to stay."

Now everyone looked at me.

"Oh..." I said. "What?" I glanced at Katie and I knew my eyes were wide. Why did Jessa want *me* here instead of her sister-in-law?

"To take pictures," Jessa explained. "I've been meaning to ask you. To surprise Brody. He's been saying he wants to take photos, even video, of this whole process. I think he overestimates the free time he's gonna have on his hands while this happens, and also, I really don't want video of this. But some nice photos, I could live with that." She smiled hopefully at me. "What do you think? I know it's not exactly a glamor gig—"

"I would love to," I told her, touched that she'd ask me.

"And I know it's a lot to ask. We'll pay you, of course. But if you already have plans over the next, well, twenty-four hours or so, I understand."

"No. Seriously." I reached out and squeezed her hand. "I would love to."

The smile spread across her face, almost wiping out the worry in her eyes.

"Are you sure?" Katie seemed hesitant to leave, though not offended. "I can stay with you until Maggie comes."

"Really," Jessa assured her, "it's not a big deal. I already spoke with my midwife and she said the best thing to do now is sleep, so I can save my energy for when labor really starts."

"It hasn't even *started* yet?" Devi said, and Katie elbowed her again.

"Shit. This is not like in the movies," Summer muttered, voicing my own thoughts.

"Nope." Jessa sighed. "This is just the beginning of the beginning. Unless contractions start. And I'd really like as few people here as possible when they do. I'm nervous enough."

"Okay. Well…" Katie hugged Jessa and held her, carefully but tight. "*Please* let me know if you need anything. I'm just a text away."

"Thank you." Jessa hugged her back, and they held on a while. "Next time you see me, though, I'll be handing you your niece or nephew. Save the help for that. I'm gonna need it."

I saw the smile spread across Katie's face, over Jessa's shoulder. There were tears in her eyes when she said, "I can't wait," but she whisked them away before she pulled away, before Jessa could see them.

Then the girls rallied out the door in a flurry of hugs and whispers of *I love you* and *Call me.*

"Call me," Katie made *me* promise as she left. "Jessa won't ask for help."

"I will."

"Like if Maggie needs a break, or if contractions start before Maggie gets here—"

"Believe me," I assured her, "I'll call you," horrified at the thought: me, struggling to figure out what the hell to do if a baby started coming out of Jessa.

I closed up after the girls and when I turned back to Jessa, she held her phone out to me. "Could you try Maggie again? I haven't been able to reach her yet."

"Oh. Of course."

"Thanks." She grimaced. "I have to go take care of some more water breakage..."

I wrinkled my nose a little, though I tried not to.

Yeah. I'd make a terrible midwife.

Jessa headed upstairs. I found Maggie's contact open on the screen and called her, but she didn't answer. I left a voicemail, striving to sound urgent-but-calm, then started unpacking my camera and getting it ready, popping the backup battery on the charger, making sure I had a fresh memory card in—just in case there were any sudden photo ops. I wasn't sure what to expect, how quickly things would progress.

Or wouldn't.

After a few minutes, I wandered upstairs and in through the open door of the master bedroom. Jessa was nowhere to be seen, but the door to the en suite bathroom was closed.

I rapped a knuckle softly on the door. "You okay in there?" I called gently, not wanting to startle the baby right out of her.

"I'm good," she said, sounding faraway and pretty tired. "Did you reach Maggie?"

"No, but I left her a message, and I'll keep trying. I'm sure she'll call back soon."

"Okay. Can you call Zane?"

"Zane?" I repeated, unsure if I'd heard her correctly.

"Zane Traynor. He's in my contacts."

"Um. Zane's your backup Brody-fill-in?" *What about Katie?*

"Zane??" Jessa sounded mildly horrified. "God, no. But he might know where Maggie is."

"Oh. Okay..."

I dutifully searched her contacts for Zane's number, though I was curious... It was close to midnight. Why would Dirty's cocky lead singer, of all people, know where Maggie was?

Unless...

Oh. My.

I took a breath and dialed his number. I barely knew the guy, and I felt kinda like a stalker calling his personal phone number in the middle of the night, even though Jessa asked me to.

"Jessa?" he answered after a few rings, sounding kinda sleepy but not exactly like I'd woken him up.

"Um, no. It's Amber." I introduced myself, awkwardly, not exactly expecting him to remember me, considering how many women he'd probably met in his life. I started to describe myself as *Dylan's friend, the photographer*, but that was so incredibly lame, I went with *Liv Malone's sister* instead—rather than the more straightforward and no doubt memorable *The girl who got wasted at your birthday party and went home with two of your friends*.

"Uh-huh," he said. "Where's Jessa?"

"She's here, at home. Her water just broke," I explained, "and she wants Maggie to come over. She asked me to call you to see if you know where she is."

After a slight pause, Zane said, "I'll send her over," in his smoky-sexy-sleepy voice.

Then he hung up.

Exactly seven minutes later, Maggie was at the front door.

Which was incredibly interesting, if you knew that Maggie—who'd professed to be "completely single" at the shower, when the girls were dishing on their love lives—lived about half an hour away, on the opposite side of downtown, near Granville Island. Zane's new house in West Vancouver, however, was easily a seven minute drive from here at this time of night.

"I didn't know you were seeing Zane," I said, quietly—since maybe it was some kind of secret?—as she hurried into the house, looking flustered.

"What? I'm not seeing Zane," she said, her clear gray eyes fixing on me. I could've almost thought she was joking, but there was no trace of amusement on her face.

Oops.

She either wasn't seeing Zane, possibly, or more likely, given the vibe I was getting off of her, she wanted me to shut the fuck up about it.

Message received.

"Okay. I—"

"Where is she?" She tossed her purse on a table and headed across the foyer.

"Upstairs. Cleaning up..."

I followed Maggie up the stairs, filling her in. I didn't want to seem rude or anything, but I was deeply relieved that she was here, so that the pressure was off me. I really didn't know Jessa very well, I knew next to nothing about giving birth, and I wasn't exactly sure how I could be helpful other than taking photos and maybe calling 9-1-1.

Now that Maggie was here, it was kind of exciting, actually. I'd never experienced a birth before.

When we walked into the master bedroom, Jessa was standing there, looking a little lost. She'd ditched her pretty but comfortable party clothes and changed into loose-fit yoga pants and what looked like a man's white T-shirt, stretched over her belly. I felt bad for her when I saw the look on her face, somewhere between fear and *I-wish-it-was-tomorrow-already*.

Luckily, Maggie knew what to do. She swept right in and took charge.

First order of business: giving Jessa a hug. Then she stuffed a few last-minute items into the hospital bag Jessa had prepped. She steeped peppermint tea. And she calmed Jessa down when she started babbling anxiously about Brody not being here and what if she went into active labor and what if he missed it and how could she do this alone.

"You're not alone," Maggie said firmly. "You've got some of the best medical care on the planet. Brody will be back. You're going to be fine. Now fill me in on what the midwife said."

So Jessa filled Maggie in, and they got to planning out the next twenty-four hours.

First, sleep.

Then breakfast, then a morning walk.

Acupuncture at a clinic that specialized in treating pregnant women, which could, apparently, sometimes help to induce labor.

Then a disgusting smoothie made of castor oil, frozen fruit and almond butter, which was also supposed to help induce labor. "The almond butter's to help disguise the taste a bit," Maggie explained to me, "because apparently it tastes like shit and makes you sick."

All of this, assuming the contractions hadn't started on their own.

If they did, we timed them, then headed to the hospital when they were a few minutes apart and intense—*intense* defined as Jessa being unable to speak through a sentence while she was having one.

If the contractions didn't start, tomorrow at midnight, Jessa had to check into the hospital anyway. "Basically, we have twenty-four hours from the time the water broke," Maggie filled me in, "to try to induce the labor naturally. After that, the hospital takes over and induces medically. With drugs. And Jessa's hoping to avoid that. She wants to do this whole thing drug-free, which I told her is insane, but hey, I'm not the one with a baby about to come out of me." She gave Jessa a look, and Jessa gave her a look back.

"Why twenty-four hours?"

"Because when the water breaks," Jessa said, "that means the amniotic sac has ruptured and now bacteria can get in there and cause infection."

"For whatever reason," Maggie said, "they put a twenty-four hour time limit on that."

"What about sex? Can't that induce labor?" I'd heard somewhere that orgasm could bring on contractions, but maybe that was just another movie fact? And Brody wasn't here anyway...

"Not now that the sac has ruptured," Maggie said. "Bacteria."

"Oh. Right."

Maggie asked me to help her strip the bed so we could put on the waterproof sheet. We got Jessa's bed all cozy for her, and I took a few photos of the girls talking as we worked.

Jessa ordered Maggie, "Don't judge me," then asked her to put one of Brody's T-shirts on a pillow like a pillowcase. "I need to smell him right now. It's an animal thing."

"Jesus," Maggie said, but she snuck a smile at me as she did as requested. "You want to crawl off into a cave somewhere and have this baby there? Maybe Brody can clean the baby off with his tongue and chew through the umbilical cord after it comes out of you."

"Ew," Jessa said, but she laughed, and the anxiety that had been weighing on her seemed to crack.

I could see why she'd chosen Maggie to be here. It wasn't just Maggie's managerial efficiency. The two of them had an easy, loving friendship underlaid with deep trust, and Maggie had put a smile on Jessa's face for the first time in an hour.

I took a photo of them standing there in the glow of the bedside lamp, Jessa looking beautiful, tired and very pregnant as Maggie handed her a pillow wearing a man's blue T-shirt.

"He looks so good in blue," Jessa said softly, her voice kind of far away. "His blue eyes..." Maggie steered her onto the bed and as she helped her get comfortable, Jessa asked, "Do you think the baby will have blue eyes?"

"I don't know," Maggie said. "Yours are brown. Isn't that a dominant gene?"

Jessa looked mildly alarmed, though still sleepy, as she tried to make sense of this. "Really? Is that how it works? I always thought the baby would have his eyes..."

"Well, maybe it will." Maggie caught my eye and muttered, "What the hell do I know about babies?"

"Now what?" I asked, handing Maggie a cup of tea as she perched on the edge of the bed.

"Now," she answered with a shrug, "we keep Jessa entertained and comfortable until she falls asleep."

"Well, mission accomplished."

Maggie looked over her shoulder, to find Jessa curled up in fetal position, asleep. Before we slipped out of the room, I took a photo of her like that, hugging her Brody pillow to her chest.

I barely even knew Brody, but I knew he was gonna love that photo.

CHAPTER THIRTY-TWO

Dylan

"THANK YOU FOR CALLING," I told Amber. "But get your ass back in there before you miss all the action."

It was about two in the morning. Amber had been with Jessa for over twenty-four hours now, and I missed her.

Jessa had finally gone into labor a few hours ago, without need of any drugs, which was apparently what she'd wanted; Amber had been keeping me updated by text all day and night. But this was the first time she'd actually called.

I liked to think it was because she'd finally hit the point where she couldn't stand not hearing my voice.

"I will," she said, and I could hear the softness in her voice over the line. She was tired. Emotionally wrung out, but still exhilarated. I could tell the girl was on fire, doing what she loved, no matter how tired she was. "It's fucking crazy in there. I've never experienced anything so..."

"Raw?" I filled in for her, making my best guess of how it would feel to experience something like a baby coming out of my friend's body.

"Yeah." She laughed a little, blowing off some nerves. "It's that. It's unlike anything I've ever felt. I can only imagine how it feels for Brody. For Jessa." She sniffed a little, and I wondered if she was crying. "I'm gonna go get some more images. Hopefully I don't get kicked out. Everything's going pretty smoothly, but if any shit hits the fan, apparently me and the midwife get bounced and the obstetrician takes over. I should get some more shots while I can, just in case. Brody's on the edge. I think he's gonna cry soon. I don't want to miss it." She laughed again. "That sounds awful."

"Naw. It's what they hired you for. Go do your thing."

"Okay." There was a small pause and a sharp intake of breath. "I... I miss you."

Those soft, hesitant words of hers rocked right through me. I squeezed my eyes shut, savoring the feeling. "I miss you, too."

"I'll call you again when I can, give you the update."

"Good. Amber?"

"Yeah?"

I looked out at the water in the dark; I was standing on my back deck in the cold. "I'm proud of you."

She sniffed loudly. "Don't do that. I can't shoot if I can't see." She sobbed a little and added, "I'm hanging up now, for real."

"I love you." The words spilled out before I could think about it. There were tears in my eyes; the girl was fucking slaying me.

Amber Malone had such a capacity for compassion, she just didn't even have a clue... the girl was all heart.

There was so much to her I knew she hadn't even let me get near yet. I wanted to keep peeling back all the layers of her and expose it all, kiss her and keep her and make her feel safe to be naked like that with me.

Shit... I'd never felt so mushy-romantic with a woman. It was kinda nice.

With her, actually, it was becoming addictive.

"Goodbye, Dylan."

She hung up. I knew she'd heard what I said.

But she hung up.

I looked out at the water. I blinked back the tears in my eyes and got my shit together, grounding myself with that serene, unchangeable view. It was here a long fucking time before I came along.

Wasn't in the least moved by my tears. It was steady. Permanent. Filled with a kind of wordless promise.

The way I wanted to be.

For her.

When I made my way back into the house, I found Ash waiting in the kitchen. He'd made a late dinner of wings and dirty rice for us after I came back from the studio, then we'd hung out, tinkered in the workshop, listened to some music.

He'd been kind of off, tense, ever since Amber went into town for the baby shower. I figured he was missing her, too.

And his growing attachment to her was worrying me.

Maybe I kept hoping he'd lose interest, like he so often did. Realize he wasn't as compatible with her as I was and let me have her.

Something selfish like that.

But it just didn't seem to be happening.

And I was getting more and more scared, every time he looked at me with that anxious look in his eyes, that he was gearing up to confess something to me I did not want to hear—like the fact that he was falling for her, too.

I'd thought he'd gone to bed a while ago. But here he was, staring at me, and I felt myself tensing up. He glanced at the phone in my hand as I stashed it in my pocket.

"Hospital?" he asked.

"Yeah."

"Heavy?"

"Yeah."

"How is she?"

"Good, I think. I mean... she's in the middle of having a baby, so maybe... not good?" I swiped a bottle of water from the fridge. Would've rather had a beer, but I was planning to hop in the boat in a while, and I was never gonna be that guy—driving after I'd been drinking. Not with Amber around, counting on me to be decent. "She's having it any minute now." I shook my head, my mind kinda blown. "Sounds like Brody's gonna be a dad before the sun's up."

"Cool," Ash said, but then he shook his head, too. "Fucking crazy, actually."

"Yeah."

"But I meant... how's Amber?" He met my eyes, and there it was. That fucking anxiety, his eyebrows pulled together with a deep crease between them.

"Happy, I think." I settled in, leaning on the island. "You know, taking photos, that's her happy place."

Ash said nothing. He grabbed a beer from the fridge and joined me at the island. He leaned beside me as we drank.

After a moment, he opened his mouth to speak. I could feel him trying to work up the nerve.

Fucking shit.

Here it comes.

"I told her... I'm falling in love with her," he said, finally.

"You did?" I looked into his eyes, and I saw all the vulnerability there. He was serious, and whatever had come of it, it wasn't good.

"Day before yesterday. While you were at the studio." He turned to look directly in my face, his brow all creased, studying my reaction to this. Like he was worried what I'd think.

"And...?"

"And..." He sucked back a hard breath. "And she doesn't love me." He took a pull off his beer, but he was still watching me.

"She said that?"

"She didn't have to. She, uh, tried to let me down easy."

I watched him swig his beer, not even sure what to say.

"So... am I supposed to get the gun now?" I offered, attempting a joke.

He stared at me.

"You said if you fell in love again, that I was supposed to—"

"Amber's a special girl," he said quietly. "You know that, right?"

I knew. But I didn't know what to do with his pain anymore. I didn't have a clue what to say about what he'd just told me; that Amber didn't love him.

I had so many mixed feelings over hearing that it wasn't funny.

Relief that Amber wasn't in love with Ash. Sympathy for Ash that she wasn't in love with Ash. Hope that maybe she wasn't in love with Ash because she was in love with me.

Guilt that maybe she wasn't in love with Ash because she was in love with me.

"Actually," he said, his voice rough, "she told me I'm in love with you."

He looked away and guzzled more of his beer.

I said nothing as he rubbed a hand through his hair. But a deep, dark chasm was opening up inside my guts, making my stomach drop out the bottom.

"Actually," he said, "she told me to *tell* you I'm in love with you."

"Ash—"

He turned and hit me with a kiss before I knew what was coming. I didn't push him off. I fucking froze as his lips pressed to mine. He breathed against my face, a hungry sound, in-between a sigh and a groan. He pushed up against me and his hands gripped my face, like he never wanted to let me go.

The feel of him, his nearness, the smell of him... all of it was familiar. It didn't repel me.

But it didn't turn me on.

And he felt it; that this wasn't gonna end well. I felt it, with a shocking kind of nakedness I'd never felt before.

This wasn't about Amber.

It was about Ash.

It was about *me*.

Which meant I needed to be straight with him—no fucking pun intended.

I had to let him go. Because including him in my intimate life, sharing a bed with him in any way, was only hurting him.

I knew that now. It was obvious to me, grossly obvious in a way that hit me with a wave of shame, because I'd never even realized it before.

I should have.

I just didn't.

He broke away. We stared at each other for a long, intense minute. He was still gripping my face in his hands. He was breathing hard.

I wasn't. I could barely breathe at all.

"Ash..." I pretty much whispered. "I've gotta tell you something..."

And for sure, he knew.

I knew he could feel it when he looked at me with that fucking wounded look in his eyes, when his hands dropped from my face like I'd burned him.

He knew he wasn't gonna like what I had to say.

But I had to say it anyway. I *had* to. I knew it with every fucking part of me.

It was beyond time.

CHAPTER THIRTY-THREE

Ash

"I'M SORRY," Dylan said, like that was the most important thing. Like he had to lead with that, no matter whatever shit came after.

That he was fucking *sorry* about whatever he had to say to me—right on the heels of me admitting I fucking loved him.

That I was *in love* with him.

"Don't tell me you're fucking sorry," I said. "Just tell me the truth."

"Okay." He swallowed. He looked fucking scared. I'd never seen Dylan look so fucking scared, and it was pissing me the fuck off. "I just... I can't..."

"Can't what?"

"Be with you." He swallowed again. "Like that."

"Like *what*?"

"I can't kiss you back, Ash." His voice was pained and too fucking quiet.

"Like fuck you can't." I stared him down. "It's not hard. I know you know how to suck face, Cope." I wanted to challenge him. I wasn't making this shit easy for him. If all he was was scared to love me, I was not fucking letting him off the hook.

"Not with you," he said quietly.

And it tore my fucking guts out.

"Yeah? What about what happened with Kitty?" I accused.

"What happened?" he asked, as if he didn't know. Looking all fucking kinds of guilty.

But I wasn't gonna mince words anymore. I wasn't beating around the motherfucking bush anymore.

My life and my feelings for him were not some fucking joke.

"You came in my fucking face," I said, throwing it at him the way I'd always wanted to.

"By accident," he said.

"*Fuck you* it was an accident." I was all up in his face, and I'd never wanted to hit the guy so fucking badly. I wanted to beat the ever-loving shit out of him.

But he was totally calm when he said, "I got carried away."

"Carried away?" I spat right back in his face. "*Carried away?* An impulse buy at the fucking checkout aisle is getting carried away. Drinking 'til you throw up is getting carried away. *You came in my face.*"

"You were both there," he said, still calm. "She was sucking my cock and the two of you were making out and she had her hands on me and I lost control. So fucking sue me."

I took a deep breath and ground my fucking teeth.

I did not wanna unleash on him all the hateful fucking angry shit I wanted to say right now.

"Let me guess," I said instead. "Next you're gonna drop the world's worst fucking cliche in my face and tell me you were *curious*. Like some sorority girl on spring break feeling up another chick's tits."

He said nothing, but his jaw worked a bit.

Good.

I wanted to piss him off. I wanted him to say something mean and give me an excuse to punch his motherfucking lights out. Drag him to the floor and fucking pound him with everything I had.

"I thought we were just messing around," he said, still calm. "We were drinking a lot. We were fucking women together. I didn't know you felt…"

"Fuck you, you didn't know," I snarled.

"Ash..." he said, his voice and his eyes going soft, and totally fucking sad. "I love you, but..."

And I drew back. My head snapped back, like he'd motherfucking sucker-punched me.

Those words, coming out of his mouth, were pretty much my worst fucking fear come to life. Me, Dylan, and the *I love you, but...* conversation.

I didn't want him to go on. I didn't need him to.

I could fill in the blank myself. I could imagine a whole shitload of ways that sentence could finish, and none of them were anything I wanted to hear.

I love you, but I don't love men that way.

I love you, but I don't love you that way.

And the worst, the most important of all, the most fucking true of all...

I love you, but I'll always love Amber more.

"I'm gonna ask Amber to come on tour," he said.

I nodded, stiffly, even as my chest cracked.

"I want her to move in with me."

It actually felt like someone had hit my breast plate with the claw end of a hammer, and split me right the fuck open. Everything inside me was gushing out, making me vulnerable and raw and fucking fragile.

Helpless.

Because there was nothing I could do to stop it.

I cleared my throat and finished my beer, but my hand was fucking shaking. "You're choosing her," I choked out. "But that's perfect, right? 'Cause she's choosing you, too."

"It's not like that," he said. "You're coming on the tour, too."

"Yeah? How's that gonna work? You two are the hot new couple and I'm the boy toy on the side?"

"You know that's not how—"

"The Pushers aren't coming on the tour."

Dylan kinda froze, staring at me. "I just talked to Brody like two days ago. He didn't mention anything."

"Brody doesn't know. The new album isn't gonna be ready in time. There's just no way."

"What do you mean, not ready?"

"I mean, why do you think I'm always hanging here instead of working?" I tossed my beer bottle into the trash, thinking how that would irritate the shit out of Amber. "The Pushers are on fucking hiatus."

"What?"

"Truth is, we haven't even started on the new album. We're supposed to be writing. We aren't writing shit."

"You're writing all the time, man. I hear the stuff you're working on."

"Yeah. Me. While Pepper's off in L.A. dealing with his marriage falling the fuck apart."

"I didn't know that."

"And Janner blew his royalties on another fucking binge in sin city. He's a bona fide addict now. And Coop's off fuck-knows-where. He can't even stand to hang with Janner anymore."

"Well... what the fuck are you gonna do? You can't just let the album and the tour slip away."

"Yeah, and I can't hold the band the fuck together by my goddamn self, either. They don't wanna be here, I'm not forcing anyone."

Dylan stared at me, absorbing those words. "I want to be here," he said, his green eyes holding mine, unflinching.

"It's your fucking house," I said, helping myself to another beer; those were mine, at least.

"That's not what I meant."

"Yeah." I sucked some beer back. "Well. I wish you well, man. You got a great band and a great woman."

He sighed a little, hissing through his teeth. "Ashley—"

"I mean it." I looked away. It was getting harder by the second to look at him anymore. Especially when he called me fucking Ashley.

I was gonna have to walk away soon, but in a way that made it look like I was totally fucking fine, so he didn't come after me.

How the fuck was I gonna pull that off?

All I really had to do was come to fucking terms with the fact that Dylan wasn't—and would never be—falling in love with me.

Super fucking easy, right?

Simple.

But I hadn't come to terms with it. I'd lied to Amber; I'd never accepted that Dylan wasn't in love with me.

Maybe I never, ever would.

"You're really taking her on tour?" I asked, trying not to sound bitter about it. Apathetic; I sounded fucking apathetic. But it fucking grated me.

Dylan had never taken a woman on tour with him before.

"Yeah," he said. "At least, I'm gonna ask her to come."

I tipped my beer at him. "I hope she says yes." I took another swig, and tried like hell not to look so goddamn devastated. Destroyed.

But *fuck*...

Did I just lose Amber *and* Dylan, in like a two-day span?

"Seriously," I said. "She's the perfect girl. I thought she was the perfect girl for me. For us. I was wrong." I shrugged, downing the rest of my beer. "I've been wrong before." I slammed the bottle down on the counter. "She's the perfect girl for *you*."

Dylan didn't even say anything. What could he say?

For once, I was right.

CHAPTER THIRTY-FOUR

Amber

WOW.

I'd just witnessed pure love in action.

That was the only way to describe it.

All I could feel was awe and gratitude with every part of me. I'd actually had to remove myself from Jessa's delivery room, twice, to burst into tears in the bathroom, before scraping my shit together and going back in.

Some professional.

I definitely didn't see a future for myself in birth photography. If this experience was any indicator, it would wreck me.

These two people, people I barely knew—well, barely knew until last night—had welcomed me into this intimacy in their lives, and shared their love with me. Now, I felt like I knew both Jessa and Brody in an incredibly intimate, personal way.

The whole experience was beautiful, moving, and totally life-altering.

When I wandered out of the recovery room for the last time, in a total daze, I did not feel like the same woman who'd walked into the hospital the night before.

And it was all because of my camera. My camera had gotten me here.

And it really hit me... That *this* was what my photography was ultimately all about: bringing people together.

I was still trying to wrap my head around the profound majesty of it all. But I'd always been drawn to photography, and maybe now I knew why.

When I'd taken that class about the history of photography in university, I'd definitely fallen in love. It had introduced me to the fascinating fact that there was a time, not so long ago, when human beings had such a limited view of the world. We hadn't been into space yet. We'd never seen the Earth from the air. We'd never seen the world from the top of a mountain, and most of us had never even seen it from the top of a tall building.

The earliest explorers got to see the world in a whole new way; a way that most people would never even dream of. But it was photography that gradually brought those views to the masses. Because of photographs, an ordinary person could see places and things and people that they would otherwise never get to see in their lives.

Photography totally opened up our view of the world, and I believed that it still had the power to do that. To make us see each other in ways we never would've had a chance to before.

The power of photography had invited me into the delivery room, where Jessa and Brody's baby boy had entered the world. I'd been one of the very first people to see him as he squirmed and cried and gazed up into his daddy's eyes for the first time, as he latched onto his mother's breast, as Brody cried and Jessa laughed in delirious ecstasy.

My camera had captured it all, so they could share those moments with their loved ones. So that years from now, they could see themselves in those tender moments, the way I'd seen them.

My work was never about keeping myself at a distance. It wasn't about keeping some imaginary safe barrier between myself and my subjects. It was about making contact. Breaking barriers down.

It was about *connection*.

So why was I so fucking afraid of that in my own life?

Why was I so afraid to let Dylan pull me out from behind the lens, where he could really see *me*?

As I pushed outside, through the door from the hospital, I actually felt kind of reborn myself. It was the surreal, floaty feeling from the lack of sleep, from being inside the hospital too long, so focused through my camera, and the adrenaline, the early-morning sun shining in my eyes; I knew that. But it was something else, too.

It took me a long minute, as I blinked, my eyes adjusting to the light, to see the man standing there, looking at me, his auburn hair flaming in the morning sun.

"Hi," I said, unable to keep the surprise from my voice.

"Hi."

I drifted toward him. "Um… I don't think they're allowed visitors right now. I just got kicked out so they could sleep. You might have to come back later in the day."

"I'll come back," Dylan said, taking a step toward me. "But I'm not here to see them right now. I'm here for you."

I blinked up at him. I was seriously sleep-deprived. "Me?"

"I didn't want you to have to go home alone."

"Oh. Well… thank you. I could use the ride. In all the excitement, I left some things back at Jessa's house, and—"

"Amber. I'm not talking about Jessa's place. I'm talking about *home*." He reached out and pulled me closer. "We'll go get your stuff. Then you're coming home with me."

He kissed me, and I sank into his arms. I was so fucking tired. And so glad to be held—by him.

"Okay," I whispered, giving in… unable to fight this anymore.

Maybe I was tired of fighting the love I felt for him.

Maybe, in a way, I'd just finally learned what love was.

As we walked into the silence of Dylan's house, I asked, "Ashley's sleeping?"

"He's gone," Dylan said.

"Next door?"

"To the city."

I turned to him. I was processing too slowly, probably, but again, lack of sleep. "He didn't come back with us...?"

"No." Dylan stood in front of me, his green eyes on mine. "We had a talk."

"Oh." I got the feeling I knew what that talk was about, more or less, from the look on his face. "So... he told you...?"

"That you told him to tell me he's in love with me? Yes."

"Oh."

"Yeah."

"And... how did that go?"

"Not so good."

Shit.

I followed him into the living room, where he dropped onto the couch, looking exhausted himself. I wondered if he'd slept at all.

I sank down next to him and put my hand on his thigh. I was kind of afraid to touch him any more than that. Was he mad at me? I didn't know. I'd rarely seen Dylan mad. Well, other than the time he straight-up punched my ex-husband in the face, I'd *never* seen him mad.

I wasn't even sure what an angry Dylan Cope looked like.

"I can understand..." I said, treading carefully. "I mean, why he was afraid to tell you for so long. Sometimes... it feels easier to just avoid things than face them head-on. You know that."

Dylan had told me he tended to avoid drama. But I wasn't talking about him. I was talking about myself now as much as I was talking about Ashley. There was so much in Ashley that I recognized in myself.

His fears.

That self-protective chip on his shoulder.

"You know something about that, too," Dylan said, and it wasn't exactly a question. Of course, he'd told me over the phone that he loved me. And I'd said exactly nothing in response. He was probably wondering what the fuck, right about now.

"I might know something about that."

"Yeah? You want to tell me about it?" He raised an eyebrow at me expectantly, like he was too emotionally tapped out to ask me twice.

Which meant I should really give him an answer.

And as he patiently waited for me to speak, it occurred to me that I'd only told Ashley. Ashley was the one I'd talked to about my parents. About the things that scared me and scarred me most. It had just seemed easier to talk to him about it.

At the time, I thought it was a sign that our relationship was deepening. I was growing to trust him. And maybe that was partly true.

But it was also because talking to Ashley was like talking to some guy I'd meet on my travels. Someone I could share an intimacy with, without truly becoming intimate, because as soon as I moved on it wouldn't matter.

Because it didn't matter to me, truly and deeply, what he thought of anything I might tell him.

That was the painful truth of it.

But I cared, truly and deeply, what Dylan thought.

"I do want to tell you," I said. "It just kind of stuns me how hard it is."

"Why? You can tell me anything, Amber. I'm hardly gonna be shocked by anything you have to say. You've met my friends, right? You really think anything you tell me will come as much of a surprise to me, after everything I've been through with people like Ash and Zane in my life?"

I smiled a bit. "Maybe not. But that doesn't mean it's easy. It doesn't mean I don't feel... I don't know, embarrassed, trying to tell you about my parents."

"What about your parents?"

"How they used to fight, in front of us. In front of Liv and me."

He laid his hand over mine, on his thigh, and squeezed. "Lots of parents fight, Amber."

I shook my head. *Not like mine.*

"Look..." I sighed heavily, weary, but knowing we needed to have this conversation. After the courage it took for Ashley to say what he said to Dylan, I could do this, right? "I'm not gonna sit here and blame my parents for my problems. I'm a grown woman. But they used to yell at each other, Dylan, a lot. And I can't even pretend it didn't fuck me up." I had a hard time meeting the compassion in his eyes as I spoke, so I stared at his broad chest instead. "They screamed and smashed things. I mean, *screamed*. They'd keep us up at night like a couple of lunatics. They'd storm out. They'd walk out on each other. On us. Be gone for hours, or days. When whoever had walked out came back, they'd scream again. They'd grab and push. And afterwards, they'd make up. They'd cry and kiss and be all over each other." I shook my head again, as the memories came back. The awful feelings of instability and uncertainty, of being in that house. "They were so in love." I could feel the tears welling in my eyes, as I allowed myself to go back to that place in my mind where I always felt so damn unstable. Like the ground could fall out from beneath me at any given moment.

My mom or my dad could *leave*. Or they could erupt in a rage. They never directed their rage at me, but that wasn't what scared me.

I managed to look up into Dylan's eyes. He looked back at me, steadfast.

"They were crazy about each other, literally. Passionate. Their love was so... volatile. It was violent. And as a little girl all I could do was sit there and watch. I couldn't do anything about it. Liv, though, she was different. A different personality, and she was five years older than me. She would storm right into the middle of it and scream at them, tell them to stop, try to drag them apart. But nothing would stop them. It never stopped, until the day my dad walked out, and he didn't come back. He broke Mom's heart." My voice broke, and tears started streaming down my face. My heart broke, for her, all over again as I said the words to Dylan. It broke for *us*, Liv and me.

Dylan took my other hand in his, as I sat here trembling with emotion.

"Mom never recovered from it. He broke all our hearts, but she never recovered. She still talks about him like he walked out yesterday. She *knows* he's gone, but she talks about him like he's coming back, like he never really left. I mean, she talks about him like he's still *with* her. Like they're still in love. It's sickening. And... it scares the shit out of me."

"I can see that," Dylan said, his hands tightening gently on mine. "I can imagine... that the whole idea of loving someone would be fucking scary. If that's how you grew up."

"That's what I thought love was," I said. But, no. It was *worse*. "I thought that's *all* love was. I thought that was the only kind of love there could be between a man and a woman, if they were really in love. If there was passion. I thought that was what passion looked like. That was what passion *felt* like. Painful and heartrending, fucking scary and unstable. Traumatic. That it was something you never recovered from." I pulled my hand from his to swipe the tears from my cheeks. "I know that's why I've kept the bar so damn low with men. Why I've let them treat me so shitty. Why I've let them use me up and dump me. Because I couldn't bear to hope for more and find out I couldn't have it. Or worse, that it didn't even exist." I sniffed, looking at his perfect face. "And then... I met you."

Dylan reached up to smooth his knuckles along my jaw. He brushed my hair back and laid his hand gently on the side of my neck. "There are all kinds of passion, Amber," he said, looking in my eyes. "Not all of them painful."

"Yeah. I'm learning that now." I sniffled and dabbed the tears from my eyes. "It's strange, you know, how differently my sister and I came out of that situation. It affected us both so powerfully. But Liv takes no shit. I just kind of avoid the shit."

"Well... what if it's not shit?" His mouth did that cute quirk, that crooked smile of his that totally slayed me. "What if it's really fucking good?"

"Yeah." I shrugged uncomfortably. "I guess I never really... um... asked myself that before. Until you came along."

He laughed. He fucking *laughed* at me.

"And I thought *I* was bad at relationships," he teased.

"Please. I'm fucking terrible at love."

"Terrible?"

"I've been dumped by every guy I've ever dated," I admitted.

Might as well just lay it all out there.

Dylan raised *both* eyebrows at me. "Every guy?"

"Every guy."

"Even Johnny O?"

"Even Johnny O."

"You didn't dump his ass? I thought he cheated on you."

"He did. And then he sat me down and suggested we'd rushed into things. Really, he let me down easy, considering how many vaginas he'd been up inside behind my back."

Dylan's eyes flashed with something that I was pretty sure was anger, on my behalf. "Amber—"

"Don't feel too bad for me. We really weren't together all that long. And we did rush into it. You know, me and my low bar."

He considered that, his green-gold eyes thoughtful. "Have you ever been with anyone longterm?"

"Not really." I tried to smile. "What, are you telling me you've had a serious relationship with anyone? And Ashley doesn't count."

"Why doesn't Ash count?"

"Because you were never in love with Ashley." I swallowed, staring into his eyes. "Were you...?"

"No," he said, growing serious. "No. Ash doesn't count. But I've had a couple of girlfriends. I've never dated anyone exclusively for more than a few months, though, so you've got me on the relationship thing. Guess I'm kind of a virgin when it comes to making those work."

That perked me up, actually. "Well, then... maybe we can be virgins together."

"Yeah," he agreed, pulling me toward him, his eyelids instantly lowering. "So let's go pop our cherries together."

I grinned and he kissed me. The heat between us ignited so fast, I lost my breath and fell against him, panting, moaning into his mouth.

"Shit," he said, pulling back. "I almost forgot... You got me all distracted with those cute teeth of yours, smiling at me."

"Cute teeth?" I panted.

"These little fangs." He nudged my upper lip up and pressed his thumb to one of my eyeteeth. "Cute as hell."

"Yeah? You like the fangs?" I smiled, showing them off, as I slid my leg over his lap to straddle him, cozying into his crotch. I wrapped my hands around the back of his neck. "If I was a vampire, would you let me drink your blood so I could stay alive forever?"

"Totally." He drifted his thumb over my cheek. "As long as I get to look at these freckles for eternity. Kinda lose my mind over these..."

He kissed me again and nibbled on my bottom lip, and I moaned softly, kinda dazed and floored by his words. ... *for eternity...?*

"Jesus." He pulled back. "You did it again."

"Did what?"

"Distracted me. I was trying to ask you to come on tour with me."

"What?" I pulled back to look into his eyes.

"Tour," he said. "After the album comes out. We're leaving in January. Bunch of dates in Australia, South America, the US, Europe... Whole bunch of places."

"Um. You want me to go travel the world with you?" My heart was suddenly pumping a billion beats per minute.

"Yeah. Is that cool?"

Holy shit.

"Have you met me? I fucking love traveling. But, wait... Do I have to ride in a car behind the bus with the other bitches? Because that's not happening."

He laughed. "What?"

"I saw *Rock Star*, with Marky Mark. Jennifer Aniston had to ride in a car behind the tour bus with the other girlfriends and wives, while the guys in the band took groupies on the tour bus with them."

"Not happening," he said, smoothing his thumb over my bottom lip. "No fucking way. You get to eject any idiot who tries to take your place at my side. Or I'll get Jude to do it."

I shook my head, trying to consider all the angles of what he was offering. "I dunno, though." I wrapped my arms loosely around his neck, playing with his hair. "Sounds kinda gross, Dylan. I don't want to be your convenience pussy, warming your bed while you're working on the road and too busy to see me except to fuck. We'll hate each other by mid-tour and break up and I'll leave you in some random country and we'll never see each other again."

"That sucks."

"Yeah."

"Hmm." He gripped my hips and pulled me closer against him. Probably trying to distract me with his massive hard-on, which was now jammed against my pussy.

I narrowed my eyes at him.

He smirked.

"Hear me out, though," he said. "I've been thinking about this, and I think what it comes down to is ownership."

"Ownership?"

"Yeah. You've gotta have ownership in something to really feel a part of it. To know we're on equal footing. We learned that lesson with Seth."

"Seth?" I asked, confused.

"We never gave him rights to the songs, in the beginning."

"Oh..."

"Yeah. Even though he was one of our primary songwriters," he explained, "he didn't get the songwriting credit, and that meant he didn't make the same money as the rest of us. He didn't get what they call publishing royalties. Even though Jesse and Zane have always written most of Dirty's music, me and Elle have always shared the songwriting credit, so that the band splits the publishing royalties equally, four ways. Lot of bands do that, to keep things equal, avoid conflict. Jessa was also credited as songwriter on the first Dirty album and gets the publishing royalties for those songs." He paused and sighed a little, shaking his head like he now couldn't fathom what they'd done. "In the beginning, leaving Seth out of the publishing rights seemed to make sense, because we hired him on almost like a laborer or something, like a crew member. We didn't originally hire him to write songs. He got paid a cut for the shows, for the album he played on, and a lump sum for the songs he'd co-written, but that was it. No ongoing publishing royalties. It sounds shitty now and pretty crooked, but we did it because when it came down to it, we didn't really trust him. Brody didn't trust him, for good reason. Seth was already pretty heavy into drugs, hard drugs, and we all knew it. So Brody and our lawyers advised us to structure his deal that way."

"It was probably for the best, then," I offered.

"I don't know. I think the band figured that at some point in the near future Seth would prove to us all that he was one-hundred-percent in, and we'd bring him in closer, give him an equal cut. But that just never happened. By the end of the first world tour, he'd already spiraled out of control, and we let him go."

"That's so... sad," I said. "It's hard to imagine some out-of-control drug addict when you meet Seth. He seems to have his shit so together."

"He does. Now that he's back, things are so different. And we all sat down and had a conversation about it, realized that in order for this thing to work, we need to bring him in tight, give him a real stake, and treat him like an equal part of this. So, with his new contract, Seth gets the shared songwriting credit and now he'll be paid an equal share of royalties on the new songs, just like Jessa and the rest of us, so we're all on equal footing. We even gave him a generous signing bonus when he came back, to start things off on the right foot. Show him we're serious about the band's future with him."

"That sounds like the right thing to do," I said, still wondering what this had to do with me. "Smart."

"Yeah. So, what if you were hired as Dirty's tour photographer?"

I stared at him. "Tour photographer...?"

"Then you get paid. And you get to take photos all the time, and if you get sick of me you can go take photos, and if I piss you off, you can go take photos, and you can just generally get paid to take photos of everything until you forgive me for being annoying and you come back to my bed."

"Um—"

"And you get regular checks issued to you by band management."

"Well—"

"So then you have a bunch of money when you leave me in some foreign country never to be seen again. But most importantly, you'd own the rights to your photos, so you'd always have that. And you could do your gallery tour, or your coffee table book, or whatever the hell you want to do down the road... no matter what happens between us."

"Hmm. That does sound like a better plan..." I was playing it cool, maybe, but tingles of excitement were rising in me; the whole idea was giving me goosebumps.

Dylan ran his hands up my arms, pulling me closer. "But then, maybe you're so happy because you get to do all your favorite things that you don't leave me. And we live happily ever after."

"My favorite things...?"

"Yeah. Taking photos. Making money taking photos so you can support yourself. Traveling the world. And fucking me."

"Are those in order from most to least favorite?" I teased.

"You tell me." He leaned in and kissed me, slowly.

"Mmm..." I broke away, before I hit the melting point and totally dropped the ball on this conversation. "No. Fucking you goes above everything on that list, except making money to support myself. That's gotta be in first place, right alongside fucking you, because if I can't support myself, I can't respect myself. And if I can't respect myself, trust me, I'm gonna be a lousy, grumpy lay."

"I dunno, Amber. You're kinda sexy when you're grumpy."

I frowned, doubtful.

"See?" He kissed my pouting lips. "Duck face."

"What?" I laughed.

"Ash calls that your duck face. I believe the exact term was 'fucking adorable duck face.'"

My face fell. "Ashley Player thinks I'm adorable when I'm grumpy?"

The happiness faded from Dylan's face a bit. I could see it in his eyes, how the mention of Ashley bothered him.

Ashley taking off didn't sit well with either of us.

"Of course he does," he said.

"Oh." I felt my eyes fill with tears again, but I quickly blinked them back.

"He cares about you," Dylan said, his voice low and husky. "He would've loved you. If you..."

"If I let him," I finished, my voice soft and parched. And I knew he was right. "But... I just can't, Dylan. If that's what you want... believe me, I understand." I was trying to, at least. "You knew him long before you met me. You guys have tons of history, memories. You have this amazing, beautiful bond. If you want him in your life that way... with a woman, and the two of you... I understand. It just can't be me." The tears had run over again, and I swiped them from my cheeks. God, it had been such an emotional night. "That's not an ultimatum. I'm just telling you... That's how I feel. I just... I can't love Ashley. Not the way I would have to, to live like that. It's hard enough, the whole idea of..." I stopped short before saying it.

"The idea of loving me," he finished for me.

"I'm sorry. This is all new for me. I know I'm bad at love. But... I know how I feel. I know how I feel about you, and about him. I care about him. A lot. I think he's an amazing person. I really do. He's complicated but so loyal to you, and he has a big heart beneath all the angry, rough edges. But I just don't love him like that. It kinda kills me that I don't. But I don't. And if you need a woman who does, who can make room for him that way..."

"I need *you*," Dylan said, pulling me against him, his green eyes delving deep into mine. "I need you, Amber."

I sighed with relief, but I did it quietly. I didn't want to be so happy for myself when it meant it was hurting someone I cared about. "What about Ashley?"

"You know I love Ash," he said. "But I'm never gonna love him the way he wanted me to. There's nothing I can do about that."

It hurt; I knew that. I could hear it in his voice.

"That must be so fucking hard." I cupped his beautiful face in my hands. "To know that he's hurt and there's nothing you can do about it."

"Yeah. I hate it. But keeping him around, doing what we were doing, that's only gonna hurt him more. I was hurting him all along, Amber. I just didn't realize it until last night." He shrugged. "I guess I was a little slow on that."

"You really didn't know he was in love with you until last night?"

"No."

"Wow." I tried to smile a bit. "You are slow."

He looked like he felt really fucking bad about it, and I wrapped myself tighter around him.

"Sorry. Too early to make jokes?"

"I'm always good for jokes, Amber," he said. "I just can't laugh about this."

"Okay. How about we make each other a promise, then?" I gazed at him, so full of hope, and brushed my fingers over his full lips. "To help each other through this relationship thing. I'm not even asking for forever, and I'm not promising it. I just know I want to see you onstage rocking out in your kilt and I want to wake up next to you every morning and I want to see the world with you. And I promise to give you all the space you need in your friendship with Ashley. You'll give me the space I need to do my photography. I'll try like hell not to scratch out all your groupies' eyes on the road.

And you'll keep me happy by doing that thing where you screw me with your big dick until my eyes roll back in my head and I forget my name. Deal?"

"Deal," he said, his eyes darkening as his hands slid over my ass. He gripped me tight and ground me against his stiff cock. "But do you think you can be satisfied with one man, now that you've had two?"

He was teasing me, taunting as he pressed his hard-on against me... his incredibly *large* hard-on... But I knew there was a touch of fear behind the words.

"If that man is you," I said, "totally fucking yes."

Then I kissed him, with all the love I already felt for him... and all the potential of the love that I knew we could share.

Maybe I wasn't asking for or promising forever, but I so fucking wanted it.

With *him*.

"Besides," I told him, "you're so freakin' tall, you've got incredible reach. You can hit all the important places at the same time, and I can just close my eyes and imagine there are like three of you. So... we're totally covered."

"That's good," he murmured against my lips. "I wouldn't want to miss any important places."

"You know, there's this one place you've never quite hit, at the base of my spine..."

"You serious?" He gripped my hips and spun me around, immediately, dumping me on the couch. Then he dropped to his knees and flipped me onto my stomach.

"Um... yeah..."

He pushed up my dress and tongued the base of my spine. "Here...?"

"Yeah." *Oh, fuck...* "And... um... a little to the left... or the right..."

His tongue traveled to the left... to that little indent at the top of my butt cheek.

"Oh, *God*, yeah... *there*..."

He licked across to the matching little indent on the right side and tongued it thoroughly.

I groaned helplessly.

"You're telling me there are *three* sweet spots back here I totally fucking missed?"

"Yeah. 'Fraid so..." I moaned as he flickered his tongue back across to the one on the left, then flickered it around at the base of my spine—where it felt like a billion nerve endings were having micro-orgasms. "*Ahh, fuck...* I'm sure we could probably find a few more, if you wanna get exploratory... Like the backs of my knees are pretty fucking sensitive..."

"*Jesus.* What kind of shitty lay am I, I missed all this shit...?" He grabbed my hips again, flipping me over onto my back.

"You're not a shitty lay, Dylan..." I managed as he crawled over me. "You're the best lay I've ev—" He silenced me by smashing his mouth to mine. Then he ripped down my panties and I felt him fumbling with his jeans.

Then his hard, bare cock pressed against me, wanting in.

"Do you realize," I whispered between his kisses, "you haven't even let me see you in your kilt yet, either? Or let me fuck you while you're wearing it.... Or blow you..."

"*Fuck.* We are totally gonna have to remedy that..."

Then I shifted my hips to take him before he got any ideas about getting up. Yes, I wanted to see him in his kilt, but more than that, I wanted him in me, *now*.

Just as he started to push into me, though, I took a breath and asked him, "Do you miss him, here?"

He stopped. "I don't need him here, Amber." He took my hand and placed it on his hard dick, as if to prove that to me.

"Are you sure?" I asked, even as I started stroking him. "I don't want you to regret it in a week or a month or a year from now. I don't want you to miss screwing women with him and resent me."

Dylan's eyes softened as he looked down at me. "I'm not gonna resent you, Amber. This is what I want." He leaned down and kissed my neck. "You." He kissed my jaw. "Me." He kissed my lips, softly. "Guess I'm just a selfish man... I want you all to myself."

"Good," I breathed as he finally pushed all the way into me. "Be selfish," I whispered. "Please..."

Lucky for me, though, Dylan was never *that* selfish.

He fucked me deep, swirling his hips to rub the thick base of his cock against my clit, over and over until I was ready to combust. When he got me there, he slowed right down, drawing out my pleasure until I couldn't stand it, until I was shaking, until he'd almost stopped... and the slightest teasing thrust of his cock set me off.

As I came, I uttered those three beautiful words I hadn't said to any man in a long, long time... and never really *felt* like I did right now. In the tips of my fingernails. In the marrow of my bones. In the deepest, most damaged depths of my heart.

"I love you..."

"*Amber*," he whispered, as he kept fucking me. As my pussy squeezed and fluttered around him and the bliss rolled through my body.

Helpless. I felt totally fucking helpless.

If there was any feeling more vulnerable than this, I couldn't imagine it.

My heart and my body were in Dylan Cope's hands.

And I wanted more of it. I wanted to be his.

I wanted to be helpless and vulnerable and raw, and feel everything I could feel with him.

"I love *you*," he breathed, as his body tensed and his hips ground into me. "I can't fucking believe you're mine..."

Then he came, with my name on his lips.

CHAPTER THIRTY-FIVE

Dylan

I PULLED into the lot at Left Coast Studios mid-morning and parked my truck. Dirty was deep into recording the new album, and it was going so well, I was fucking bursting to play it live. I couldn't fucking wait for January.

Maybe we'd even convince Brody to book us a few gigs, just for some fucking fun, before the official tour.

I could see that everyone was already here. Shady and Flynn were outside having a smoke, which meant Zane and Elle were in the studio. If Elle was here, Seth was probably here, too. And Jesse and Katie were just climbing out of his Ferrari across the parking lot.

Katie waved over at Amber, before Jesse took her hand and pulled her into the studio.

I'd brought Amber along today, because she and Katie were gonna spend the day together while the band was in the studio. Now that Amber was staying put, she'd decided she needed some clothes and things of her own, so Katie was going shopping with her.

I was totally on board with that plan.

I'd told Amber she could turn one of the entire guest bedrooms into a dressing room for herself, one of those giant walk-in closets that chicks liked, if she wanted to. We had the space for it.

Maybe I figured the more stuff she had in the house, the more comfortable and settled she'd feel—and the more likely she'd really stay.

But she'd just looked at me like I was crazy and said, *Half of your closet will be fine. I want to bump into you while we're getting dressed in the morning.*

God, I loved this girl.

When I looked over at her she was smiling, and it made me smile. Seeing her getting comfortable, making friends. Fitting in. Dirty was my family, and anyone I was gonna get serious about *had* to fit in.

I already knew I was beyond serious about Amber Paige Malone.

And I knew that meant I'd have to dig deep to make this relationship thing work. To be selfless and flexible and respect her needs. All of them.

To never give her a reason to ditch my ass.

She smiled over at me, and I asked her the question I knew I had to ask. The one I'd been more than a little scared to ask. "Are you sure?"

"Sure about what?"

"About Ash," I said.

We hadn't talked about it again, but I wasn't sure the conversation was over. I wasn't sure it ever would be.

"Oh." Her smile slipped. "I'm sure," she said, but she seemed kinda surprised that I was asking.

I hadn't even seen Ash since he took off several days ago. We'd talked over the phone a couple of times. I knew Amber had talked to him, too. I knew he was hiding out, doing his thing, pulling away. Protecting himself. Doing what he felt he needed to do right now.

But it wasn't like he was never coming around again.

"Okay," I said. "But... if you change your mind... if you want to reopen that door... I never want to tell you that you can't, Amber. I honestly don't know how I'll feel about it if it ever happens. It's impossible for me to know that right now. I can't tell you I'll like it. But I'm not gonna tell you that you can't, if you want him back."

She stared at me, her green eyes wide.

"I told myself I wouldn't share you anymore, with anyone," I told her. "But Ash is different. He's just always been different. I'm never gonna be in love with him and I'm never gonna fuck him. But I'm officially leaving that door open, okay? For you."

Amber blinked, just kinda shaking her head as she stared at me. Then she leaned over to me. "You're *incredible*." She kissed me, sweet and slow.

I let her drive the kiss, just enjoying all her sweet and soft and warm, and hoping, selfishly, that it was all gonna be for me—always.

"I love you, Dylan Cope." She pulled back a bit and peered up into my eyes. "And I'm telling you, right now, there's no one else for me."

While the band got set up and comfortable—which involved Seth arranging pillows for Elle where she sat on the couch, Zane one-way flirting with Maggie, and Jesse fussing over which guitar to play—Amber and Katie headed across the street to pick up coffee for those who wanted it.

Brody had stopped by, but he wasn't staying. Usually he spent more time checking in on us when we were recording, hanging out, but this was the first time he'd been into the studio since his son was born.

I pulled him aside when I sensed he was trying to slip out.

"I'm bringing Amber on tour," I told him.

He stared at me. "Okay." If he was surprised, he didn't show it. He also didn't exactly look thrilled, because bringing another body on tour meant a hike in expenses—which would come straight out of my paycheck—but he knew he could hardly say no to me. Jesse was already bringing Katie, and just because they were married didn't give them special privileges.

"And I want her to be our tour photographer."

At that, Brody sighed, like he knew from the look in my eyes this conversation wasn't gonna end the way he wanted it to.

"We already have a tour photographer," he said. "One who's got a ton of experience shooting bands, including Dirty."

"Then he'll have other bands to shoot," I said, fucking firmly. I wasn't backing down on this. "He doesn't need this. Amber needs this. *I* need this."

Brody just stared at me some more, taking that in. I knew it was unheard of for me to make this kind of request. I also knew about the requests the other guys in the band made, on a regular basis, in pursuit of pleasing a woman.

Jesse with his cherry-vanilla lattes for Katie. Zane with his jelly-beans for Maggie, purple, orange and red only. Seth with his special chairs with all the cushions for Elle; since they'd announced she was pregnant, he was stuffing pillows behind her back every fucking place they went.

Not to mention that we'd already hired Katie as an artist; Brody could hardly cry nepotism on this. The ship had sailed on that.

So I returned his look, steady. "When have I ever asked for anything for a woman, on tour with me, in the studio, backstage, anywhere?"

We both knew the answer to that: never.

"How about Ash?" Brody challenged. "You bring him along everywhere, like he's your wife."

I'd expected to get some digs like that, now that Amber and I were a couple. Because everyone would want to know how it had played out. And where Ash now stood.

Why he wasn't around as much anymore.

But really, family or not, it was none of their fucking business.

Ash deserved the respect of privacy, and anyway, I was never gonna tell anyone besides Amber what really went down between us.

"Yeah," I said. "Well. Now I'm bringing Amber."

In the end, Brody let me have my way. He had more important shit to deal with right now anyway, what with a brand new baby at home. He looked like he hadn't slept much, and he wasn't gonna battle me over our tour photographer, when all it would take was one phone call to let the other guy down and make me happy.

I walked him out to his truck and told him not to worry.

"She'd better be good," he said, his tone insinuating that I'd be hearing about it if she wasn't.

"She take good photos of you and your woman and your newborn son?" I asked, knowing full well she had—she'd showed them to me.

And he shut right up.

"Give my love to Jessa," I said, trying to soften my demand by kissing up a bit. "We'll swing by on the weekend with food."

"Good," Brody said. "Bring me beer."

I pulled him into a quick hug. "Get some fucking sleep. You look like shit."

As he drove away, Jesse joined me outside. Amber and Katie were just returning from the cafe across the street, and Katie handed off the tray of coffees to Jesse. "Have fun," she said brightly.

Jesse scowled. "Where're you going so fast?"

Katie threw her arm around Amber's shoulders. "We're going on our date."

"Brunch," Amber clarified, smiling at me. "And then I'll be back for your truck."

I pulled out my keys and tossed them to her. Then the two of them turned and started back across the parking lot. Amber flashed a smile at me over her shoulder and gave me a cute finger wave.

Jesse stood there, looking a little put out as we watched them walk away. Maybe he'd been hoping for a quickie before we got to work. Not a bad idea.

I was admiring Amber's hair, the pretty caramel color and the thick waves of it that just licked her shoulders—thinking about how I'd buried my hands in it last night while she sucked me off—when Jesse said, "I'm not Ash," and threw me a look.

"What?"

"My wife and I aren't coming to bed with you and Amber, so you can put that out of your mind."

"Wasn't in my mind," I said. He really thought I was looking at Katie that way?

I wasn't looking at Katie at all.

"She's cute," he admitted, visibly relaxing now that he'd gotten that clear.

I grinned. It was kinda nice he was so protective of his wife. But I really didn't mind him looking at Amber. As long as he knew he was never touching her, either. "Yup."

"She's a keeper?"

"She's a keeper."

"Huh," he said. "Never would've thought."

"Thought what?"

"You. And a woman. For the long haul. Kinda thought you were closet in love with Ash."

I took my coffee from the tray. "Can't imagine why."

He didn't touch that.

We both watched as the girls headed away down the sidewalk, tossing their hair as they laughed, their cute butts moving in their tight jeans.

"Think maybe we can find one of those for Zane?" Jesse said.

"Nope." I sipped my coffee. "Zane's not into keepers."

"We'll all be crawling in grandchildren and he'll still be playing the field?"

"Looks that way."

"The guy's really missing out."

"Yup. Try telling him that."

"I have."

The door swung open behind us.

"Hey, assholes." Zane sauntered outside. "Get your asses back into the studio so we can record this fucking song."

I shoved my coffee at him. "In a minute."

Then I took off in a jog.

I caught up to the girls just as they were reaching the end of the block. I was pretty sure Jesse and Zane were watching; they weren't exactly used to seeing me run after a girl.

Then I did something they definitely weren't used to, maybe just to fuck with them a bit.

No matter what an attention-whore and an exhibitionist I might've been accused of being, I'd never been one to indulge in PDAs with a woman in broad daylight, in the middle of a work day. Mainly because it might've given that woman, and my friends, the wrong idea about where she stood in my life.

But I walked right up to Amber and Katie, reached between them, grabbed Amber and pulled her into my arms. Katie had been talking, but trailed off. Amber's eyes got wide. I pulled her close against me, her face tipped way back to meet mine. And I laid a kiss on her. Deep. Thorough.

Fucking slow.

She melted in my arms.

I kissed her like that until I was sure Katie had blushed and turned away, and the guys finished whistling and making crude comments, quit staring at my girl and fucked off back into the studio.

And then when I'd well and truly made my point, I kissed Amber some more. Just because I could.

Maybe she didn't ask for forever... but if it was up to me, forever was what she was gonna get.

EPILOGUE

Roni

"WHAT THE *FUCK*, TAZE."

I stormed over to my boyfriend, just as he took off his helmet and ruffled a hand through his blond hair. We were in the street, in front of Jessa and Brody's house; the driveway was already full of cars and Taze had just pulled in behind my car as I parked at the curb—on his fucking motorcycle.

The motorcycle I'd told him not to bring.

At least he wasn't wearing his Sinners cut, just a generic leather vest over his long-sleeved Jack Daniels shirt.

"What?" he said.

"I told you not to bring the Harley."

I looked all up and down the street, and there was no sign of Jude's Harley, but still. That didn't mean he wouldn't be here.

I was pretty damn sure he definitely would be.

Taze just gave me a look, the same look he gave me whenever I told him to do anything. He swung his leg over the bike, getting off, and sauntered over to me. "It's cool, babe," he said, as if that meant anything.

Everything was always "cool" with Taze—until it wasn't. The man never thought two seconds into the future. It was a fucking wonder he'd survived this long as a member of such a badass motorcycle club. The fact that he was able to dress himself in the morning, much less remain breathing and out of jail, sometimes stunned me.

My latest boyfriend was twenty-three going on thirteen. I liked younger men; they were exuberant as fuck in bed. But I didn't appreciate having to babysit this one.

He slung his arm around my shoulders, and I shrugged him off.

"What's wrong with you?" he griped.

"What's wrong with *me*?"

"Yeah. You need to get laid," he concluded, his gaze dragging down to my chest and groping my boobs.

I clenched my teeth and stuffed down my irritation. I was *not* getting into a fight with him in the street in front of Jessa's house on a Sunday afternoon. Her neighbors were out, walking their dogs and puttering in their gardens. And besides that, we'd been getting into too many fights lately. And not good fights. These weren't *You-annoy-me-so-much-I-just-want-to-fuck-the-shit-out-of-you* fights. More like *We-aren't-compatible-and-this-isn't-going-to-work-out* fights.

Still, I'd invited Taze to this little party, and it wasn't his fault I was all tense and surly about it. He didn't know I'd only asked him to meet me here because I didn't want to show up alone.

I sighed and shoved the tray of samosas I'd brought from my favorite Indian restaurant into his stomach. "Just carry this, okay?"

By the time we made our way into the house and started doing the rounds, I was feeling a little less surly, though a lot more tense. I didn't exactly want to be here today. I told myself I didn't have to stay long. It was a meet-the-baby party, and even though I'd already met the baby, Jessa had always been a great friend to me. So maybe I didn't have to stay long, but I wasn't going to completely miss this.

Even if Jude might be here.

He wasn't. And it's not like I was disappointed about it.

I definitely didn't keep looking around, gazing at the doors, waiting for a glimpse of him.

Fuck. When did I become so fucking pathetic?

I needed to get the power back.

Since when did I let Jude Grayson have so damn much of it over me?

I grabbed myself a glass of bubbly from the tray on the bar and went to find Jessa. Thankfully, I'd already managed to lose Taze at Brody's Donkey Kong machine.

I found Jessa on a couch with Katie on the other side of the party room and settled in next to her, half-listening as they talked about baby stuff. I held out my finger to the baby in Jessa's arms. He was half-dosing, but he wrapped his teeny, tiny little fingers around my fingertip.

I watched Taze across the room, playing arcade games with Zane and Dylan, and sighed.

After we left this party, I was definitely gonna have to break up with my boyfriend. I'd have to do it in a way that made him feel like it was his doing, though. Shouldn't be too hard to orchestrate; Taze wasn't exactly the sharpest knife in the drawer. However. I knew, from experience, that breaking up with a biker wasn't always the world's easiest task.

Especially if he didn't want to break up with you.

It was the entitled, bossy, alpha male thing. No matter how smart they weren't, they still felt like they owned you. Saw you as their property. I didn't always mind—in bed.

But sitting here in a house full of Jude's friends with Taze thinking I was all his? It suddenly rubbed me wrong.

Or maybe it wasn't so suddenly.

Jesus. When did I start selling myself so damn short?

The moment Jude Grayson decided I wasn't worthy of him?

I only realized Katie had departed the couch when Jessa started filling me in on the trials of breastfeeding as a new mom, in detail. Something about a blister? Sounded horrendous, but I really wasn't listening all that well. I was thinking about men, while one of the best friends I'd ever had was unloading on me. She'd just had a baby, for Christ's sake. Probably the single biggest event in her life. This was a definite sisters-before-misters situation, and I was shitting the friendship bed.

So I took the baby from her arms and said something I hoped was compassionate and comforting, but shit, I knew next to nothing about breastfeeding or babies.

Jessa sighed and smiled at me gratefully. "Thank you. Sorry to vent. I'm exhausted. Never thought I'd meet someone who wanted my boobs in his mouth more often than his daddy does, but damn, he feeds for like forty-five minutes at a time. Every hour. It's draining. Literally." She looked at her newborn son's scrunched, sleepy little face and her eyes turned into two giant pupils, like some anime unicorn. "God, I love him so much." She cooed over him a minute, then collapsed back on the couch and gazed around the room. "Let's talk about something else. How's Taze?"

"Taze... is Taze."

"Oh." She studied him for a minute. "He's hot," she offered, probably trying to be supportive. Looking at the brightest side.

"Trust me, he's hottest when he keeps his mouth shut."

Jessa smirked. "Sounds like love."

"It's not." I was eying Dylan and his new girl, Amber, across the room. She was leaning into him while he played Ms. Pac-Man. "Speaking of which," I muttered, "I give them a month."

"What? Why?"

"Because they hooked up in a kinky threesome situation with Ash. Those never work out." I'd been in enough threesomes of my own that I felt like I could speak with some authority on the subject.

Or maybe I was just jealous of what they had.

Maybe I was just feeling a little bitter that my latest relationship—which had also started out in a threesome situation—wasn't going as well as I'd let on.

Anyway, Jessa didn't seem to agree with me as she gazed over at Dylan and Amber. "Maybe this one will."

Maybe.

Maybe I was just regretting that I didn't hook up with Dylan Cope myself when I'd had the chance—the night of Jesse and Katie's wedding. Because surely Dylan Cope was a better catch than Tyler "Taze" Murphy.

Maybe I was regretting that instead of hooking up with Dylan, I'd hooked up with Jude that night instead.

Except I didn't regret hooking up with Jude.

Not exactly.

Who could regret sex like that, with a man like that?

My only regret was what a giant douchebag he'd turned into since then.

The baby wriggled in my arms, and I rocked him a bit, trying to settle him. "*Shh*, baby Nick. Promise me, when you grow up, you won't be a douchebag to the ladies, okay?"

They'd named him Nicholas, after Jessa's dad. Middle name Jesse, after Jessa's brother, and last name Mason—Brody's last name. As for Jessa taking Brody's last name herself, she just kept saying, *We'll get to that.* Brody hadn't proposed yet, formally, but he'd definitely put the feeler out; it was Jessa who'd been adamant she wasn't going to be pregnant in a wedding dress.

I'd never say it out loud, because it was pathetic as fuck, but I was kinda *hoping* they'd get married—so I'd get to be a bridesmaid. I figured I was next in line, behind Maggie and Katie, for such an honor, and Jude was definitely in line to be one of Brody's groomsmen. I didn't give a crap about weddings, in general, but I definitely harbored a bullshit secret fantasy of being in a wedding party with Jude so maybe we could repeat our little wedding night hookup.

So pathetic.

"Oh, shit. I think we've got a diaper situation." I passed little Nicholas carefully back to his mommy. "I mean, I guess I could change him for you, if you want..." It was the most half-assed offer ever, but for Jessa, I'd do it.

"No, no. I'll do it." Jessa took him from me, rubbing the tip of her nose against his and kissing his little cheeks.

Thank fuck. I didn't really want to get baby poop on my new sweater. It was cashmere, soft and clingy, a kind of muted green that made my eyes pop. Plus, it did epic things to my boobs.

And Jude hadn't even seen me in it yet.

Yeah. *Pathetic.*

Jessa took the baby into the downstairs washroom, to change him on the change table. While she did that, I said hi to Brody, then wandered upstairs to the baby's room, alone.

They'd converted one of the guest bedrooms into a nursery, and it was adorable. Sweet and soft, with cream and yellow walls and furniture, a little cloud city with animals floating in the clouds on one wall—baby giraffes and lions and elephants.

I pulled the little stuffed monkey from my pocket. It was small, just a couple of inches and kinda flat. Purple. Old. I'd cleaned it, but it had been well-loved. It was the only memento I had from when I was a baby, and since I didn't exactly see myself reproducing anytime soon, I figured little Nicholas should enjoy it.

He really didn't need it. He didn't need anything. Jessa and Brody's kid was getting a pretty epic start in life. Better than I'd had. Better than a lot of us had. And I was happy for him. I was happy for Jessa, really. She deserved everything she had, and more. Jessa made good money on her own, but the fact was Brody was wealthy, he loved her like crazy, and their kid would never want for anything, stuffed toys or otherwise.

But it felt important to me that I give him my little monkey.

I placed it in the crib, because I really didn't need anyone to know who it was from. I just needed baby Nicholas to have it.

Then I turned to look around again. I breathed in the new-baby scent. Clean baby clothes and diaper cream and fresh air. There was just something about being in a baby's room. Everything so hopeful and new, and bright...

Until someone darkened the door.

I turned to find Jude looming.

His broad shoulders pretty much filled the doorway, and he was staring me down. He wore a fitted black V-neck T-shirt that showed off every single curve of his sculpted upper body, not to mention his nipples. And dark gray jeans molded to his sculpted lower bod. Dark tats all down his bare arms. Dark hair, dark eyes, dark expression on his face. Just dark.

"Hey," I said, swallowing. My voice came out a weak little croak, and I wanted to kick my own ass for it.

"Hey." His voice was low and pissed off. "You here with that fuckin' Taze kid?"

I drew my shoulders back, found my backbone and crossed my arms. Didn't hurt that doing so shoved up my boobs in my new sweater. Didn't hurt that he noticed it, either.

His gaze dropped, briefly, to my cleavage, before returning to meet my eyes, a little darker and more pissed off than before.

From his tone and the word "kid" I was gonna assume he didn't approve—of Taze, or of him being here. I wasn't fucking dense. I knew Taze's motorcycle club, the Sinners, were rivals of Jude's club, the Kings. And as Dirty's head of security, not to mention their lifelong friend, anything—or anyone—connected to Dirty, including the home of their manager, Brody, and their songwriter, Jessa, was Jude's territory. Which meant it was the Kings' territory. That's just how things worked, in the MC world.

Which meant that, in Jude's eyes, Taze wasn't welcome here.

I understood the MC world about as well as any woman could, and I wasn't about to disrespect the Kings on purpose. Which was why I'd made Taze leave his Sinners cut at home.

Why I'd told him to leave his damn motorcycle at home and bring his truck.

"He's not a kid," I said evenly. "And yes, he's here with me."

"He's a Sinner," Jude replied, as if I needed reminding. "Next time you plan on bringing one to a Dirty affair, you run it by me."

My eyebrows raised at his tone. I did not appreciate being told what to do. By anyone.

Least of all by a man who had no claim whatsoever over me.

Who *wanted* no claim over me.

"Next time I plan on bringing Taze to a Dirty affair," I retorted, "I'll bring him."

Jude's chest rose as he drew a silent breath. His nostrils flared and his jaw ticked.

"He's here for me, Jude. Not to cause shit. He left his colors at home. For *me*."

Jude looked around, without really looking at anything, and seemed to consider that. Then he took a step into the room. His dark eyes landed on mine again, heavily. "You're lucky I haven't kicked his ass out yet."

"You're lucky you didn't try."

Now his eyebrows rose, and a surprised chuckle rumbled out of him. "You think I'm afraid of some kid? Some *Sinner*? You think I couldn't have half my club here in ten minutes to back me up, he wants to cause trouble?"

I placed my hands on my hips. "I didn't mean you're lucky because he'd raise shit if you tried to throw him out. I meant you're lucky because *I'd* raise shit."

Now he laughed. The dimples flickered in and out of his cheeks —and my pussy took notice. Of course, my pussy took notice the second he'd appeared, but now I felt my core clench with want.

I took a breath and said nothing, which I hoped just relayed how little I cared about any of this.

He shook his dark head and said, "I forgot for a fuckin' second." His gaze drifted south of my face again as he added, "You always were more dangerous than a pack of angry assholes, Roni."

I tried not to smirk, but I kinda relished that compliment.

He moved in on me, suddenly, which I didn't expect, and I had to back up to avoid touching him. I ended up against the crib, with Jude looming over me. His eyes searched my face. For what, I had no clue.

"How've you been doing?" he asked me.

I gathered from his tone that he was totally fucking serious.

"What, you mean since you last saw me?" I asked dryly.

"Yeah," he said, his dark gaze snagging on my lips. "Since then."

Well, *shit*.

Were we talking about this?

I'd been stealthily avoiding Jude since the night of Jesse and Katie's wedding like ten months ago. The night we'd secretly fucked.

I was pretty sure he'd been avoiding me, too. Though probably for different reasons.

The only time I'd seen him since, I was in the middle of a threesome at a Sinner's party, with Taze and one of his friends. I'd brought Jessa to that party, and Brody, Jude and Jude's brother, Piper, had come to take her home. Which was fine. Their prerogative.

What wasn't fine was Jude sticking around afterwards to be a douchebag.

"You mean," I said, unflinching, "since you strolled right on into my private affairs?"

"Door was open," he said, equally unflinching. "Didn't think I had to knock."

He didn't knock. He'd walked right in and stood there, staring at me until I'd pushed both guys off, grabbed my clothes and stalked out.

"And you figured interrupting the sex we were having was totally cool."

"Didn't mean to interrupt," he said, deadpan. Then his molten-dark, hellfire eyes, which had been locked on my lips, met mine.

"Right." I kept my response short. I was starting to come unhinged by his closeness. By his sexy alpha male smell. I was millimeters from telling him to go fuck himself, actually, but I really didn't want to play my hand. I didn't want him to know how much he could get to me, and how fucking fast.

How much he'd gotten under my skin.

Then. Now.

Always.

"The Sinners are bad dudes, V," he said, and his voice was almost... soft.

"Mm-hmm. Wouldn't they say the same about you?"

He blinked, slowly, and kept staring at me. "You saying I'm a bad dude?"

"I'm saying whomever I screw is none of your concern." Those felt like decent parting words, a thinly veiled *Fuck you*, so I started to step around him to leave. But then I stopped.

Because sometimes I just couldn't resist playing with fire.

Jude's fire.

"Why would you even care if I'm dating a bad dude?" I asked him.

He was still staring at me, that same impassive expression on his face, but his eyes were smoldering like fucking brimstone. "I wouldn't want to see anything bad happen to you, Roni."

I leaned in close to him, really fucking close, and said, "Then don't look."

When I drew back, his dark gaze left my face and trailed down my body, slowly and deliberately, drinking in every curve. Then he said, "Hard not to."

I turned on my heel and headed for the door.

Fuck. Him.

Jude Grayson did not get to look at me like that, when he had no intention of following up that look with *anything*. When he had no intention of being with me, of being mine, of wasting his precious time on me.

Because apparently, I was beneath him.

And yet he still felt the right to butt into my personal business and try to make me feel like a fucking whore.

As if he had any right to judge who I fucked.

The man wasn't exactly a virgin himself.

I went straight downstairs and found Taze in the party room, where I sat myself on his lap. He spread his hand on my upper thigh, possessively, as he drank his beer and talked with Seth about guitars or something. And I wrapped my arm around him.

Taze *was* hot.

And maybe he wasn't so expendable.

Maybe I wasn't done with him just yet...

Years ago, I'd fucked Jude's friends to try to get his attention. But I was young then.

Now, I was older, a little wiser, and I was no longer interested in fucking Jude's friends. Instead, I was fucking his enemies—to try to forget about him.

To remind myself I didn't belong to him.

To try to erase the feeling of his naked body ramming against mine. Of his hands on my skin. Of his hips between my legs.

... Among other things.

The problem was, it wasn't working.

At. All.

Because every time I thought about Jude, every time I heard his name, it all came right back to me. All the feelings stirred up by that night. Not just the feelings of being fucked by him—the thrill of screwing him on that couch in the lodge in the middle of the night, and the Earth-shattering orgasm that resulted—but the feelings for him that I thought I'd put to bed.

The feelings stirred up when he'd *kissed* me.

The feelings I still felt for him... would maybe always feel for him, because for some reason I was just totally fucking cursed like that. Because Jude Grayson, a man who didn't want me, just plain did it for me.

I was hooked on him.

And the worst part? As he stepped into the party room and his dark eyes met mine across the room... I was pretty sure he knew it.

THANK YOU FOR READING!

Turn to the end of this book to read an excerpt from
Jude and Roni's story, the next book in the Dirty series...

Dirty Like Jude

He was the one that got away. She was the one he never got over.

And if you're hungry for Ash's story,
don't miss *Hot Mess*, book one in the spinoff Players series!

ACKNOWLEDGMENTS

Thank you to the amazing bloggers and readers who continue to support me by writing and sharing such glowing, passionate reviews of my books. To my incredible and ever-growing ARC Team, I'm thrilled to have you along for the ride. THANK YOU.

To my friends and family who continue to support and encourage me and just generally buzz with excitement every time you hear I have yet another new book coming out—thank you for being so proud of me and what I do.

Thank you to all the wonderful girlfriends in my life. My book club girls. My sister-from-another-mister, Brittany. Guin. Lauren. Chris. Marjorie. Thank you for your messages of support, for making me laugh, for reading, for cheerleading, for being a part of this.

Mr. Diamond. How far we've come. How incredibly far we have yet to go—together. Thank you for absolutely everything. Thank you for making us a dinner reservation at that incredible Italian place we've heard about so we can celebrate this book after it comes out, and plan out all the other ones to come. How I cherish our dates-slash-business-meetings. These books wouldn't be what they are without you. XO

To my readers: THANK YOU for reading this book! Without your feedback, enthusiasm and support, none of this would matter. I'm honored and grateful to have such an amazing and feisty cheering section in my corner! I'm so honored that you chose to read this love story; my intent as a romance author is to spread love. If you've enjoyed Dylan, Amber and Ash's story, please consider posting a review and telling your friends about this book; your support means the world to me.

With love and gratitude,
Jaine

PLAYLIST

Find links to the full playlist on Spotify and Apple Music here:
http://jainediamond.com/dirty-like-dylan

Train Song — Benjamin Gibbard & Feist
Young Lust — Pink Floyd
Finer Feelings — Spoon
"F.B.G.M." (feat. Young M.A.) — T. Pain
This Is What You Came For (feat. Rihanna) — Calvin Harris
The Way It Is — The Sheepdogs
Should I Stay or Should I Go — The Clash
The Boys In the Bright White Sportscar — Trooper
I'm a Lady (feat. Trouble Andrew) — Santigold
Girl — The Beatles
Kiss — Allan Rayman
Fever — The Black Keys
My Moon My Man — Feist
Forget to Forget — Shy Martin
Something Perfect — ISLAND
I've Got a Hole Where My Heart Should Be — The Sheepdogs
I'm On a Boat (feat. T-Pain) — The Lonely Island
Back in Black — AC/DC

Is You Is Or Is You Ain't My Baby? (Remix) — Dinah Washington
Hey Baby — No Doubt
Girls and Boys — Blur
Hey Ya! — Olivia Noelle
What Lovers Do (feat. SZA) — Maroon 5
Let's Fall In Love — Mother Mother
(Fuck a) Silver Lining — Panic! At the Disco
Suck My Kiss — Red Hot Chili Peppers
Lovegame — Lady Gaga
Lonely Alone — Chelsea Cutler & Jeremy Zucker
She's Always a Woman — Billy Joel
Water Under the Bridge — Adele
Something Just Like This — The Chainsmokers & Coldplay
Back in the Saddle — Aerosmith
Anything Goes — Guns N' Roses
All the Time (feat. Lil Wayne & Natasha Mosley) — Jeremih
Counting Stars — OneRepublic
No You Girls — Franz Ferdinand
One Kiss — Calvin Harris, Dua Lipa
Feeling Good — The Sheepdogs
Green Eyes — Coldplay
Make a Start — Plested
These Days — The Black Keys
Bad Habits — Delaney Jane
The Fire — Bishop Briggs
Up All Night — Beck
Blow Your Mind (Mwah) — Dua Lipa
Fuck Me Up — Highly Suspect
One Track Mind (feat. A$AP Rocky) — Thirty Seconds to Mars
Crazy Love — Van Morrison
Laid Back — The Sheepdogs
Medicinal — Miles Hardt
Unsteady — X Ambassadors
1950 — King Princess
Drumming Song — Florence + The Machine

We Never Change — Coldplay
The Scientist — Coldplay
Head over Heels — Allan Rayman
You've Got to Hide Your Love Away — The Beatles
You Know I'm No Good — Amy Winehouse
Bad at Love — Halsey
Mushaboom (Mocky Mix) — Feist
You're The One — The Black Keys
Writing on the Wall — Bob Moses
Pretend — Goody Grace
We Found Love (feat. Calvin Harris) — Rihanna
I Got You — Jack Johnson
Woman — John Lennon

EXCERPT: DIRTY LIKE JUDE

Dirty Like Jude

*A second chance, enemies-to-lovers romance,
featuring a badass, strong and silent hero,
and the wild-hearted heroine who brings him to his knees.*

CHAPTER ONE

Roni

I felt his weight settle over me, the warmth of his naked body. His morning wood, hard and eager between my legs.

I was just barely waking up. My eyes weren't even open yet and he was already pinning me down to the bed. The head of his cock nudged into me as he nuzzled into my neck and kissed my throat… gently. He was already starting to fuck me, and even though I didn't usually let him get so damn snuggly while he did it, I let him.

He knew if he snuck up on me while I was half-asleep, I'd let him.

He filled me, deep, with a low, pleasured groan as he kissed my neck. I wrapped my legs lazily around his waist as his toned body slid against mine. His hips started pumping between my thighs, slowly.

I didn't even bother opening my eyes.

Generally, my boyfriend knew what I liked in bed, and he usually tried to give it to me. Sometimes he tried to change things up, get a little more... gentle. To lukewarm reviews. But despite his best efforts, no matter how he came at it, I wasn't totally thinking about my boyfriend when we were in bed anyway.

Actually, I wasn't thinking about Taze at all. Other than to vaguely register the fact, somewhere in the back of my mind, that I wasn't thinking about him.

Taze was blond, and I was definitely picturing someone a lot... darker.

Darker skin. Darker eyes. Darker hair.

Darker general fucking aura, by miles.

Unfortunately it had come to the point where, if I didn't close my eyes during sex, my boyfriend's sandy-blond hair was, frankly, a total and utter distraction. It jarred me from my fantasies.

Taze was also leaner than the man in my head, but he was strong and muscular enough that if my eyes were closed—or if it was at least very, very dark—I could maintain the illusion enough to reach orgasm. Quickly.

I'd never wanted to just get there so quickly as when I started totally disassociating myself from the person I was actually getting there with.

Minor problem with that: Taze liked to do it *forever*.

With the lights on.

Therefore, eyes closed.

He also liked to do it in the morning, like right now, when there weren't any lights on but the sun was starting to pour in the windows. I didn't love the morning sex. Daylight stripped the illusion away, made it harder, even with my eyes closed, to lose myself in my head.

Plus, there was the guilt. I felt guilty for always closing my eyes. Especially when he asked me to open them, which he sometimes did.

Hoping he wouldn't, I made a sleepy, pleasured sound and bit his throat as I buried my face in his neck. He was pretty busy groaning filthy shit into my ear anyway... which was another problem with sex with Taze. I loved dirty talk. *Loved*. But with Taze, I actually had to mentally drown out his voice, because it sounded nothing like the one in my head.

His voice.

Thinking—obsessively, single-mindedly—about another man was pretty much what my sex life had been reduced to lately. Or for about the last ten months.

Basically, my entire relationship with Taze.

Maybe because right around the time I'd first hooked up with Taze, a certain dark horse from my past had reared its wicked head. And fucked me.

Literally and figuratively.

God, that fucking night... I was still having flashbacks of it.

All. The. Time.

Even when I was just in bed by myself.

Or when I was buying fucking groceries.

And one thing I was definitely not gonna do was lie to myself about it.

I'd lie to Taze. I knew for a fact that he lied to me. That there was a ton of shit about his life I'd never know.

That was the way it usually went with bikers—outlaw bikers—a breed of which I'd dated a few. And yes, they'd all lied to me. Or lied by omission. And I'd accepted those lies. I'd accepted those men as they were, and I'd accepted Taze just the same.

For now.

But what I wouldn't do was lie to myself about how I felt.

Running into my own personal dark horse—which was exactly how I'd come to think of him now—at Jesse Mayes' rock star wedding, ten months ago, had quite honestly stirred up all kinds of feelings in me.

And not just feelings. Memories. Regrets.

Longings.

All that crap.

Running into him *again* at Jessa Mayes' meet-the-baby party six days ago didn't exactly help matters.

Especially when he cornered me, alone, in the baby's room and virtually incinerated my clothing with that *look* in his hellfire eyes.

Seeing him up close, those molten, panty-melting eyes of his, the thick muscles bulging from his black T-shirt... Hearing his voice, *fuck*, that deep, rough voice of his... Fucking *smelling* him, that intoxicating alpha male smell of his... It all just reminded me of how he'd *felt*—naked, with me.

How fucking amazing his skin felt...

So smooth... silk poured over hard muscle, sliding against mine...

Yeah. I was *almost* there...

Then Taze's phone started buzzing on my bedside table and simultaneously blaring AC/DC, "Dirty Deeds Done Dirt Cheap"—and fucking shattered my fantasy.

Not unusual. Unfortunately.

Taze picked it up, also not unusual. Right when I was *that* close.

I groaned and slapped his shoulder.

I knew it was one of his MC brothers because they all had that same fucking ringtone. There was definitely too much of a good thing, and that ringtone was it.

Especially when I was so *close*.

Taze knew I was close, so he didn't stop fucking me, though his efforts were far less than half-assed as he carried on a stilted, brief conversation—mostly *Uh-huh* and *Yeah, brother* on his end—*while* he fucked me. He'd slid half-off of me, his upper body twisted to the side so he could lean on his elbow next to me as his hips kept grinding. But the angle was no good for me.

No good at all.

I groaned in frustration again as he hung up. He looked at me, his hazel-brown eyes half-lidded with sleep and sex, and blew out a breath. "I've gotta go," he said, his morning voice all raspy with pre-orgasmic tension.

I said the only thing a woman could say in this situation.

"Fuck. Off. Are you serious?"

He dropped the phone and shifted over me, pumping into me a few more times—you know, just to make things worse. At least he looked regretful, especially when I pressed up against him, panting, seeking friction. Then he swore under his breath.

"I gotta pull out, babe."

Then he did pull out. Before I could come.

I went limp in defeat as I watched him ease off the condom and pull on his jeans. "I can't believe you're fucking serious."

"Club business. You know I've gotta go."

He leaned in to kiss me, a quick, sloppy kiss, then left me there, naked on the bed. His gaze dragged over me one last time as he yanked on his ratty T-shirt and scrubbed a hand through his shaggy blond hair. He shrugged on his black leather Sinners cut and grabbed his phone. "Later, 'kay?" Then he left the room, still fighting his erection into his jeans as he went.

I flipped my middle finger at the patch on the back of his cut, the big one underneath the one that said SINNERS MC: the silhouette of a naked woman straddling a motorcycle, backwards, back arched and boobs thrust out. That bitch had fucked with my sex life more times than I cared to count.

I heard Taze leave my place and I sighed. Really, what good was a boyfriend when the one thing this particular one was good at, he wasn't available for?

I considered finishing myself off, obviously, but the mood was kinda ruined. Instead I checked my own phone, which had also buzzed while we were fucking. Yes, I'd been thinking about another man, fetishistically, while we'd fucked, but at least I didn't check my phone while Taze's dick was inside me.

I'd missed a call from Jessa.

I got up and headed into the bathroom to start the shower,

dialing her back. I put the phone on the counter on speaker and stepped in under the water while it rang. And rang.

While I waited for Jessa to answer, I ducked my head under the hot water and let it lash down on me, waking me up. Washing away Taze's touch and smell.

Wishing it was someone else's touch, someone else's smell that lingered on my skin.

Jesus. *My life.*

Sex with Taze—my entire relationship with Taze, for that matter—was *supposed* to help me forget about my dark horse. Yet somehow every time I was with Taze, all I could think about was Jude Grayson.

"Roni." Jessa finally picked up. "How are you?"

"Fantastic," I said, really heaping on the sarcasm. She would know it was sarcasm. Ever since we were teenagers, Jessa and I had answered one another's *How are you?* with pretty much the opposite of how we were actually feeling. "You?"

"Stupendous. Do you have time to swing by this morning?"

Yeah. I had a little time. For Jessa, I'd make time. Especially since she'd just had a baby—two weeks ago—and had way less time for me in general.

As long as Jude wasn't gonna be there.

One unnerving, lust-charged confrontation with him while pressed up against baby Nick's crib was enough for me.

"What's up over there?"

"Just hanging with Nicky. Brody's gone to work."

Perfect. If Brody wasn't home, the likelihood of running into Jude at Jessa's place was pretty damn nil.

"I really need to talk to you," she added. "As soon as possible."

Which gave me pause. Jessa never "needed" to talk to me.

"I'll be over as soon as I can," I told her. "With coffee."

ABOUT THE AUTHOR

Jaine Diamond is a Top 5 international bestselling author. She writes contemporary romance featuring badass, swoon-worthy heroes endowed with massive hearts, strong heroines armed with sweetness and sass, and explosive, page-turning chemistry.

She lives on the beautiful west coast of Canada with her real-life romantic hero and daughter, where she reads, writes and makes extensive playlists for her books while binge drinking tea.

For the most up-to-date list of Jaine's published books and reading order please go to: jainediamond.com/books

Get the Diamond Club Newsletter at jainediamond.com for new release info, insider updates, giveaways and bonus content.

Join the private readers' group to connect with Jaine and other readers: facebook.com/groups/jainediamondsVIPs

goodreads.com/jainediamond
bookbub.com/authors/jaine-diamond
instagram.com/jainediamond
tiktok.com/@jainediamond
facebook.com/JaineDiamond

Printed in Dunstable, United Kingdom